THE GHALIAN CODE

SPACE ASSASSINS 3

SCOTT BARON

"Some Warriors look fierce, but are mild. Some seem timid, but are vicious. Look beyond appearances; position yourself for the advantage."

— Deng Ming Dao

CHAPTER ONE

Ornate boots crunched loudly, their steps echoing in the silent halls as they ground deep into the debris littering the formerly opulent estate's tower. Delicate sculptures lay in ruin, smashed to shards, and artwork and decorative wall hangings depicting brighter times rested on the ground where they'd fallen in the chaos.

Blood was everywhere. Red blood, green blood, even some blue blood. All manner of men and women had fought and died here, some by magic, but most by far more primitive means.

Blades and cudgels had cut a brutal swath through the poor house staff who happened to be caught outside of the defensive lines on the ground floor. They had been slain with no discrimination, and with no mercy. The attack had obviously been swift and had taken them unaware, despite their state of general readiness.

Smears of green blood on the floor where the attackers' bodies had fallen were sticky testament to the efforts of the estate's security teams. They had fought well, the man thought of the slain staff at his feet. Only his guards lay there, however.

The enemy had taken their dead and wounded with them,

leaving neither overt signs of who had led the attack, nor whom they worked for. But he knew. Who else would dare to do such a thing? And in his own home, no less. A show of force in a visla's estate while he was away on business.

It was a ballsy thing to do, and against Visla Dinarius Jinnik, it was particularly so. The man had *power*. More than any visla for at least thirty systems. Someone had made a calculated choice in this attack.

Visla Jinnik kept moving, stepping over the cold bodies of his men. The magical lift discs to the upper floors seemed to still be functional, but he cast a protective spell around himself as he boarded, just in case the intruders had left behind any little surprises for him in the way of wards or traps.

He went straight to the top of the tower. The level containing his personal quarters. A place staffed by his most trusted men and women and protected by his most skilled guards. Just as was the case down below, the scene was one of carnage.

Here, however, the fighting had apparently been far more intense. The walls, he noted, were greatly damaged by some dangerous magic gone astray. It was one of the reasons magic was almost never used in close-quarter fighting.

While spells could be greatly effective against an approaching enemy, once you were in the thick of combat, those same spells could just as easily take out your own men by accident as well as your intended target.

And while that was bad on land, it could be even worse in space, blasting a hole in the side of a ship and venting attackers and defenders alike into the frigid void.

So, no one used spells in this kind of fighting except as a last resort. Which, judging by the stray damage, it had been.

That little quirk of magic was what led to the development of enchanted blades. While they were somewhat limited by their wielder's reach, the magical weapons could slice through armor and flesh alike.

All of Visla Jinnik's personal guard carried them and were well trained. And their proficiency with the weapons was apparent by the corpses and limbs strewn about the place.

The fighting had obviously been fierce, as a few of the Tslavar mercenaries sent to invade his home still lay dead on the floor, their comrades unable to retrieve their bodies in the heat of battle.

Despite the horrible loss of life, Jinnik smiled, though it was pained, not one of joy. Merely one of appreciation. His men had served him well, and their surviving families would be well taken care of for it.

He looked at the uniform on one of the few mercenary bodies left behind. No markings. Nothing to tie the man to any one cause or organization, as he had expected. They were an anonymous fighting force, and if seen or even captured, their true loyalty would be easy enough to deny.

On he continued, crossing the wide foyer by the lift discs and heading into his personal chambers. Furniture was scattered and smashed, and the signs of fighting were even more intense in the narrower confines of the corridor.

Something caught his eye. Something horrible. A servant's head had been severed and placed carefully on the leg of an upturned table. The visla paused and stared at this new horror, his boots now slick with gore.

"Poor Sidisa. You did not deserve such an end," he said to no one in particular. Not for lack of ears around him, but because all of them were dead.

He felt his already bubbling rage grow even stronger. Even in the heaviest of combat, this was just not done. There was no tactical purpose for such a thing. Except one.

Someone was making a point.

He carefully scanned the area, taking in every detail he could. Then, with a heavy heart, he walked to the doorway of the room adjacent to his own suites. Four of his most trusted guards lay dead at the threshold, fallen where they had made their last stand.

He took a deep breath, then stepped over their bodies into the room.

The damage inside was minimal. Barely noticeable, in fact. All of the violence had taken place leading up to this place. The crux of it all. The true reason for the assault on so fortified an estate.

There were bloody bootprints marking the floor, but only one body in the room. Her name was Willa, and she had been with the family a long, long time. A gentle soul, and a wise teacher. And now she was as dead as the others, long cold where she lay on the floor.

Visla Jinnik bent down and picked up a doll. It was the likeness of a man called Suvius the Mighty. A great gladiator warrior, and his son's favorite. His grip tightened around the doll as his emotions threatened to take control.

The static buzz of agitated magic around him began to thicken into a dangerous crackle of power and rage as his anger grew stronger. It was a family condition. His father had it, his father's father had it. And more likely than not, his son would too, one day. If he lived.

Jinnik breathed deep, calming his mind and heart as he'd been trained since his powers began to truly manifest and grow in strength when he was only twelve, just a few years older than his son. Slowly, the dangerous magic receded back into the visla, but only just.

He forced himself to look at the room with a clear mind, pushing emotion aside, at least for a moment. Then he saw it. A single, sealed note on the small table placed in the middle of the room where it could not be missed.

He picked it up. Not a speck on the envelope, not a drop of blood or smear of soot. This had been left for him *after* his son was taken. He turned it over and stared at the seal. One he knew all too well.

Jinnik strode from the room, jaw tight as he headed to his personal study. He would open it there, and then he would plan what to do next.

A bit of motion caught his eye and he stopped and turned, his gaze falling on what he had missed when he entered. A column had tumbled in the fray, and beneath it a Tslavar mercenary lay pinned. His injuries were severe, but not fatal.

"Please, help me," the man asked, exhausted from days of struggle to pull free of the enormous weight.

"Help you?" Visla Jinnik said, the angry magic crackling around him once more. "Oh, I'll help you."

He raised his hand, focusing his power, and released it with one barking spell. "*Hokta!*"

The green man didn't even have the opportunity to scream as he was crushed into an unidentifiable bloody pulp.

Jinnik lowered his arm. An arm that was not wearing a konus or slaap. This was his own power, not that stored in any magical device like the unpowered needed. It had been a fair expenditure, but not enough to completely deplete the crackling, angry excess magic buzzing around him.

But the violence had helped. At least a little. And slowly, the magic began to pull back into his body. He had killed the one witness he could have interrogated, but with the letter in his hand, there would be no need.

For now, he needed to sit and to think. And once he had a plan, then, and only then, would he would act.

CHAPTER TWO

"Mop that shit up! And make it quick!" Darzus growled at the resort's newest laborer. "I swear, Binnik, you're fucking useless!"

"On it, sir. Yes, yes. Right on it!" the man replied, hurrying off with his bucket, mop, and rags, as well as the barely powered konus the maintenance manager had provided him when he started.

It was a shit job.

Literally.

Cleaning up after guests and making sure the waste was all disposed of properly and the pipes unclogged. The slim band of the work konus on his wrist contained just enough stored magic to help with the finishing touches of a cleanup, or to activate the emergency removal protocol spell for truly big issues.

But today, it was used for freshening the air after Binnik had manually removed whatever clog might have been causing the backup.

In this case, a Baringian wedding party had gotten a little too festive in the bridal suite and attempted to see just how much the novel waste system could suck down. It was not the first time, and it would most certainly not be the last.

Things backed up and overflowed often in the facility. But that was why such an extensive cleaning and maintenance staff was on hand, and why Binnik had been accepted for the new job on the spot.

In a galaxy where magic handled everything, including making the toilets flush and their contents disappear and rematerialize in the waste removal area far away, the resort's quaint and old-timey ways were a nostalgic throwback to many centuries prior. And the wealthy paid a hefty premium to experience it.

There were other novel aspects besides the antiquated waste system. Fountains that used pipes to spray water rather than spells, for instance. And a lift to the first five floors that utilized an odd counterweight system to raise the platform, rather than a magically powered lift disc.

Of course, for anything over the fifth floor, lift discs were used. Novelty was one thing, but courting a plummeting death merely accessing one's suites was not anyone's idea of a fun vacation.

It was one of the most exclusive and difficult resorts in which to acquire lodging on all of the beautiful world of Grandall, and that was saying something. The main cities were the playground of the wealthy and powerful, full of hotels, spas, and resorts offering anything and everything their patrons could desire.

And here, in the capital city, this was the most sought after of all. To acquire a room, let alone a suite, would cost what some made in a year, and for VIP chambers, mere coin would not be enough.

Power brokers and influential people frequented those hallowed grounds, recreating in resplendent luxury, while the peons below went about their dull daily lives. It was the most exclusive of air they breathed, surrounded by their peers.

But someone still had to clean up the shit. And one of those someones was poor Binnik.

The man wore the dark, patterned uniform of the lowest of service staff, designed to hide the stains and smears acquired in their daily labors. Unlike the finely dressed guest assistance staffers, Binnik and his ilk were the bottom of the social ladder, and as such, they were ignored by all. All but their tyrannical manager, that is.

It was the type of job one took as a last resort. A last resort, within a resort, as it were. It was also the perfect cover for an assassin preparing for a most audacious hit.

Hozark had been in position for nearly a month playing the part of Binnik the sewage worker. The master assassin had settled into the roll with ease, and he had even added a few additional enhancements to his normally repugnant uniform. Namely, a lingering odor of feces, slightly stronger than the rest of his compatriots.

That, combined with his appearance as the lowest of the low, put him in the perfect position to do what he needed for his pending job. Being a sanitation worker in this place had made him more invisible than any magical shimmer cloak ever could.

And all without setting off any hostile magic detectors in the process. For, in addition to being exclusive, this place was also more secure than some fortresses. Weapons of any kind were strictly forbidden, and magical items brought by any but the guests and their guard staff would be confiscated and the offending bearer thrown in jail.

So here he was. Unarmed, alone, and mopping up shit.

It was grunt work, and hard labor, but his wiry muscles were more than up for the task. And his labors had allowed him to case the entire facility from the inside, giving him nearly free rein not only in the hallways, but within even the most exclusive of the suites and facilities.

Within three days he had the basics of the guard positions, patrol patterns, and shift changes committed to memory. By the end of the second week, he had discerned the location of every ward, trap, and surveillance spell in the resort.

And best of all, he was ignored. Treated like less than a person by patrons and upper-level staff alike. And as he worked, invisible to them simply by the nature of his job and apparent social status, they talked. They talked and talked, and spoke with a careless ease that made him privy to a great many secrets likely thought too sophisticated to mean anything to the shit cleaner's peasant ears.

So Hozark listened. And he noted. And he gathered up many pieces of the puzzle he and the rest of the Wampeh Ghalian were digging into. Namely, who within the Council of Twenty had been so brazen as to target a master of the order of assassins, and why.

The attempt upon Master Prombatz had failed, but only just. The unlikely twist that he had given his contract to an aspiring young Ghalian trainee as his final test before becoming a full-fledged member of the order had been his saving grace.

Aargun, the young aspirant, had been captured rather than Prombatz, and while the master assassin was gravely injured in the process, it was Aargun who suffered the most.

He had not faced mere tortured. That would have been expected of any who captured an assassin, and was a reality they were all aware could befall any of them. But, rather, he had been experimented on. Drained of much of his blood, his eyes and tongue removed to prevent him seeing his captors or speaking of the experience.

Aargun was rescued, eventually, in a brazen attack on a Council stronghold, but he would never heal fully. And all that Hozark and his comrades had learned in that rescue was that Visla Torund, who they had thought to be behind the plot, was merely a lower-level player. It was Visla Ravik, it seemed, who was actually pulling the strings.

Or maybe not. The name Maktan had been called out in the

last breath of an emmik as he lay dying in their friend Laskar's arms. But it made no sense. Visla Maktan was the least offensive of any of the Council of Twenty. And as they investigated him in depth after that incident, he kept coming up clean.

Or *relatively* clean. Because, despite all appearances, something about Visla Maktan stank, and it wasn't the shit on Hozark's boots.

There were dangling threads that just begged to be pulled at, and when he tugged, something unexpected happened. Maktan's name would pop up in unlikely places. Never with great details, though. Always vagaries and brief mentions. But *something* felt off.

And Hozark wanted very much to find out what that was.

He, and the rest of the order of Wampeh Ghalian, had never taken sides in conflicts, always working as impartial, and extremely expensive, assassins. They were not easy to engage, and they did not accept every contract offered, nor could most afford them.

But since the Council's capture of one of their own, and in such an unusual circumstance, the order had begun taking far more of an interest in Council activities than before.

And when a job involving targets related to the Council of Twenty-related arose, the Wampeh Ghalian were now accepting them more often than not.

That was how Hozark had wound up covered in filth and cleaning up after a good many Council-affiliated guests, acquiring quite a sizable amount of intelligence in the process.

But that was all in preparation for his actual job. The real target. A rather horrible woman by the name of Oxalla Slahn.

She was a facilitator for the Council of Twenty, and a great many had fallen, if not directly by her hands, due to her actions or words. She was one of the key parties who made sure the Council's many off-book, nefarious dealings were handled in a timely manner.

A keeper of secrets.

And it was that knowledge that made her such a prime target.

It also made her one of the most heavily guarded women in twenty systems.

"Done, sir," shit-stained Binnik reported to his superior. "It was just Goramus fruit clogging the pipe."

"Goramus? How the hell does that clog the pipes?"

"Well, they managed to fit twelve of them in there, somehow," he replied with a good-natured chuckle. "But I got them all out, and things are working smoothly. I did need to use my konus to shift the deeper ones out to the waste field, though. It took a fair amount of power, but I thought it best, as the rooms were about to become occupied again. Could you recharge it?"

His supervisor snatched the konus from his wrist and gave him a newly powered one. "Good thinking, Binnik. Well done. Get things working and stay out of the guests' way," he said. "Take this one for now. It was just topped off."

"Thank you, sir," the disguised assassin said, then headed back to work.

On his way, he noticed there was a flurry of activity in the reception area. More than usual. And something unusual. Guards of a far different sort than typically accompanied their visitors were sweeping the area, while plainclothes agents casually meandered among the guests.

Of course, the master assassin noted them all, just as they noted him. But they paid him no further heed, especially the ones who were close enough to smell him.

It seemed Oxalla Slahn had finally arrived. Or, her advance entourage had, at least. It was time for the games to begin.

CHAPTER THREE

Hozark, also known as Binnik the shit mopper, had spent weeks upon weeks of careful preparation for this moment. All that study, the countless hours of menial labor, all in furthering his disguise, was now going to finally pay off.

The first wave of guards had been thorough with their rapid survey of the lobby and reception area, a number of their ranks splitting off into every adjacent space to ensure no hidden threats were lurking.

As they did so, the plainclothes agents meandered about, milling among the guests and staff, casually casting their scanning spells to ensure no blades, slaaps, or other weapons were being concealed.

Denna Oxalla Slahn, though she typically eschewed the honorary title of denna, was not a loved woman. She had been responsible, directly or indirectly, for a great deal of suffering to the people of dozens of worlds, if not more. Protestors and the like were commonplace wherever she went. And, occasionally, something worse.

In her case, there was a good reason for all of the guards.

Hozark had to admit, it was a well-executed bit of security

theater. And theater it was, because judging by the visible weapons these men carried, as well as the cut of their uniforms, they may have *looked* impressive, but they were in no way the woman's top guards.

Those would be close to her at all times, keeping a sharp eye out for potential threats. And they would be far better armed than this. Heavy-duty slaaps and konuses, he anticipated, as well as enchanted blades, no doubt. And that was saying nothing of their martial skills.

Highly trained fighters, each of them, for certain. Possibly even former gladiators, given the Council's ties to the brutal games. Whoever they were, the men and women were no trifling matter, even for a Wampeh Ghalian.

Another wave of protection began to enter the reception area. Their uniforms were more ornate and clearly for show. This was the grand entrance portion of her entourage, it seemed, and their attire shouted out her wealth and status.

A great many races were in Oxalla Slahn's employ; a multicolored and multi-species mix of great diversity. There was even a Fakarian among them, the amphibian's blue-green skin contrasting nicely with their uniform, which had been carefully tailored to allow for their powerful tail.

Several of them possessed customized outfits, actually. From the ridged backs of the Orgalun warriors, complete with bulging shoulders and thick necks, to the pair of tentacled Yagutsi with the paralytic, but not deadly, venom carried within each suction cup, the guards' uniforms fit perfectly.

A moment later, a duo of slender Magani bodyguards joined the party, walking in with the eerie grace of deadly ballerinas. Their race was unassuming at a glance, but upon closer inspection, possessed unusual spines several inches in length that protruded from their elbows, knees, and heels, making them particularly nasty when it came to hand-to-hand combat.

And by the look of them, they were quite ready for a fight, if need be.

Hozark, however, had no intentions of fighting them. In fact, he was at the very far end of the space, nowhere near the goings-on. Just another lowly peon staying out of the way of the upper-class guests as he went about his chores.

A slight shift buzzed through the guards, regardless of their position within the hierarchy. The regular patrons would not have noticed it, but the tiny change in their posturing signaled one key thing to Hozark. They were linked by a silent skree system. And someone had just notified them all that their boss was coming.

That subtle stiffening of the back, a holding of the head just a little higher, chest out and shoulders back, doing their best to look intimidating and alert. For Oxalla Slahn expected nothing less from her minions.

At long last, the woman herself finally made an appearance, the tall, lithe, palest green-skinned woman striding into the place as if she owned it. But as wealthy and powerful as she was, even the great Oxalla Slahn couldn't have afforded to buy out this particular establishment.

And even if she could, it was owned by one of the more powerful vislas in the system. One who had no interest in selling. And, conveniently, one with whom she had an ongoing, mutually beneficial arrangement.

"Ah, Denna Slahn," the concierge said, gushing warmth and welcome from his every pore. "It is so wonderful to have you with us again. Your regular suites are ready and have been prepared, as per your usual specifications, of course, and the chefs will be preparing your favorite dishes this evening, compliments of the house."

She smiled at him, as one would a lesser creature whose sole purpose was to serve her needs. "I would first like to visit the spa. It has been a long trip, and I have need of your strongest masseuse."

"Of course, Denna Slahn," the man replied with a little bit too much gusto.

But ass-kissing was his job, and he was so good at it that it seemed he might lose his head up in some dark nethers one day, if he wasn't careful about it. He turned to his chief of staff.

"Have the spa cleared for Denna Slahn immediately," he barked.

"Uh, sir?" the man said, taken off guard. "The Badarian envoy is currently utilizing the healing mud baths."

A brief look of both fear and anger flashed across his face. This was not good. Not good at all. But compared to Oxalla Slahn, the powerful envoy was as intimidating as a puppy.

"Ah, yes, of course," the concierge replied as calmly as he could manage. "Please inform the good fellow that a very, *very* important guest has arrived and will be needing use of the facilities. And please, offer him my apologies. His rooms and meals are on the house today as a token of my appreciation." He turned to the Denna. "All is in order. Please allow my staff just a few minutes to ready the spa facilities for you. And I will personally fetch our strongest masseuse to tend to your every need."

The new arrival had observed the exchange with some interest, and, as she was getting what she wanted, continued on her way, apparently satisfied with the man's quick resolution to what would have otherwise been a problem.

Not her problem, though. But most certainly his.

Hozark had to admit, the fellow may have been a paid sycophant, but he had just pulled off an impressive bit of maneuvering of difficult and demanding guests. Say what you would about the demeaning nature of his position, the man was quite efficient at keeping the workings of the resort running smoothly, even in the most trying of situations.

Oxalla strode across the gleaming stone floor with a confident grace, her closest guards flanking her several feet away on either side.

"You're a murderer!" a woman shrieked from the crowd that had lingered to observe the woman's arrival. "You killed my husband!"

Rotten fruit was hurled, flying straight and true, right at her head. Her security detail had not discovered the threat with all their magical scans because it wasn't really a threat. Not one of damage or injury, at least.

But if she had become smeared with rotten produce, more than one of her guards would certainly have suffered the consequences as surely as the attacker would.

Hozark watched with great interest as the fruit stopped a meter from the woman, its arc arrested mid-flight by an invisible magic shield, before it withered and turned to dust.

That was one thing he had not been expecting. Some defenses, certainly, but a personal protective shield of that power? He began to wonder if perhaps someone had tipped her off that she might be in jeopardy.

But her team handled the situation with the same cool efficiency they showed when performing their initial sweep. No flash of additional weapons, nor hidden troops spilling out. It seemed to have truly been a one-off attack by an angry protester.

The screaming woman was grabbed nearly the instant her improvised projectile had left her hand, hauled off to face a fate likely less than that of her deceased husband. But, then again, she'd just attacked Oxalla Slahn *in public*, so there was also a very good chance an example would be made of her.

Throughout the entire ordeal, which only lasted mere seconds, Oxalla did not slow or alter her stride one bit. She was a cold and confident bitch, and given what Hozark had heard of her going into this job, it didn't surprise him one bit. In fact, he expected no less from the woman.

But the shield would be an issue, possibly making his task more difficult than he originally anticipated. He continued on his way across the outer perimeter of the chamber, leaving the others to deal with the thrashing woman and the mess she was making as they hauled her out.

He had work to do, and not the resort employee kind.

CHAPTER FOUR

"Binnik! Where the hells are you?" the evening shift manager shouted.

"Here, sir," Hozark replied, putting down the implements he had been cleaning and hurrying over to the man.

One look at the poor manager and anyone could tell that something was clearly wrong by his nervous fidgeting and the deeply concerned look in his eye.

"We've got a problem. Oh shit, oh shit. This is not good."

"What problem, sir?" Hozark asked, knowing full well the first, tiny part of his plan was underway.

"It's Oxalla Slahn."

"The woman who came in a few hours ago? She seemed nice. And tall," he said, sounding every bit the innocent bumpkin he'd been portraying for weeks on end.

"*Nice*? You called her *nice*? Have you never heard of Oxalla Slahn before?"

"'Fraid not. Why? Should I have?"

The manager ran his hands through his hair. "Never mind. Maybe it's better if you don't know and just get this done."

"Get what done, sir? You still haven't told me what it is you need."

The manager realized he was losing it, and in front of a far lesser employee. The shit scrubber, no less. He took a deep breath, pausing to run his hands down the front of his immaculate management tunic, smoothing out some imaginary wrinkles.

"Denna Slahn's assistant called down to inform us the waste system in her suite is having an issue."

"Oh, well, it's a good thing there are three of them, then. I can fix the broken one first thing in the--"

"It is her own private restroom, and she will not do with sharing the facilities lesser staff uses. You've got to go up there right now and fix this."

"But, sir, that's Skardrick's job. I'm just the apprentice. I mean, I've learned a lot about--"

"Skardrick isn't here. He's home sick. Some kind of terrible food poisoning that laid him up in bed all day."

"That's terrible! I'm so sorry to hear that. Why, I just saw him last night, and he seemed fine," Hozark said with mock concern. "I should visit him and bring him some soup or something."

In reality, the timing of his sharing a casual meal with the man and his unexpected gastric distress was anything but coincidental. A few drops of Astralgar extract in his wine had been all it took. Not the option of choice, but given the circumstances, Hozark had to make do with what was at hand while leaving no magical residue or traces.

"Never mind bringing him soup. Haven't you heard any of what I've been saying? Denna Oxalla Slahn's private restroom is backed up, and you have to go fix it."

"Oh, well, as soon as I--"

"Now, Binnik!"

Hozark jumped as if terribly startled by the manager's

reaction. "Oh, uh, of course. I'll head up immediately," he said, grabbing tools in a flustered hurry and rushing toward the lift disc.

"Wait!"

"But you said––"

The manager threw a slender konus at him.

"I already have my konus. Darzus gave me a fresh one earlier," he said, showing the band on his wrist.

"It's not for cleaning spells. It'll let you get into her suites without being stunned. Or worse."

"I don't understand," Hozark said, understanding full well.

"She's a high-profile guest, get it? The highest. And her security detail always takes extra precautions, like multiple layers of defensive spells and wards. Without that pass-konus, you wouldn't make it one step inside those rooms."

Hozark turned the slender band over in his hands with mock fascination. "Whoa, that's crazy."

"Not as crazy as things are going to be if you don't hurry up and get up there."

"Right. I'm on it!" Hozark said, then rushed for the lift disc, slipping the pass-konus on his wrist as he went. Work smarter, not harder, he mused.

All was going as he had expected, and with the useful little band he now wore, Hozark wouldn't have to worry about disarming and countering all of those nasty little spells Oxalla's team had put in place.

Or at least most of them. Undoubtedly, there would be a few little surprises in place they hadn't told management about. He'd expect no less of a skilled bodyguard team like hers.

The normal security the property already had in place was no problem. He'd already modified the existing spells and wards weeks ago. They'd still work on everyone else, mind you, but Hozark had a free pass within those walls.

The lift disc took him up high in the building to the most opulent set of suites within its walls. It was also the most difficult to access and most secure of them. Tools in hand, the cheerfully oblivious worker stepped from the disc and out into the corridor, right into the watchful gaze of a half dozen security personnel lining the hallway on either side.

"Hey, fellas," he said with a good-natured smile. "Oh, sorry. And ladies," he added when he saw the barbed-limbed Magani bodyguard he'd seen earlier among the group. "I'm just here to fix the pipes. Did they call up and tell––?"

"You are expected," the Magani woman said as her associate scanned him for weapons. "And you are late."

"Sorry, there was a bit of a misunderstanding, and––"

"No excuses! One does not keep Denna Slahn waiting."

"Ooookay then. I guess I'll just get to it, shall I?"

No one moved.

"Uh, is it okay if I open the door, then?"

At that moment, Oxalla's assistant opened the door from the inside.

Ah. Hidden communications even here, Hozark silently mused.

"The denna has been kept waiting," the woman said with a glare that could melt icebergs, then whispered a disarming spell for the door wards. "Bring your tools and do what needs to be done, then remove your stink from these chambers."

"Jeez, it's just part of the job. No need to be rude," Hozark said, exaggeratedly sniffing himself. He then stepped into the suites, whereupon the door was shut behind him, its wards put back in place.

From what he could tell, the security team was barred from entry. Oxalla felt completely safe once inside her rooms, and only her personal aide was to be anywhere near her once she had retired.

Hozark put on a happy smile and forced out a jaunty little

whistle. "So, I'd say show me the problem," he said, sniffing the air. "But I think I can smell it from here," he said with a laugh.

Her silence clearly indicated that he was the only one amused. With a little shrug, he headed into the resplendent restroom to start his work. And with that, he would move his plan to stage two.

CHAPTER FIVE

The smell emanating from the restroom chamber was not as strong as Hozark had anticipated.

He had been meticulous arranging the little dissolving packets he had affixed deep within the pipe system, ensuring their magical bond holding them to the metal would not trigger any alarms. But as for Oxalla's sense of smell, well, he simply couldn't be sure just how sensitive it was.

Given her rather sheltered existence, free from the difficulties and unpleasantnesses of normal people's lives, Hozark had opted for a fairly strong release of smell, but not so much as he might use for a regular city dweller. She would take to her rooms, freshen up, and then, a few hours later, notice a smell.

By that time, there would be a very slight blockage in her private toilet facilities. Simply a sponge-like piece of plant matter, carefully placed, and easily removed, but more than enough to make her call for maintenance.

Or have her aide call, as the case would most certainly be. Actually contacting the help was not the sort of thing Oxalla

Slahn did. It was simply beneath her, and she had people for that.

Naturally, the aide would be a trusted person, the one soul allowed to stay close to her at all times, tending to her every need and whim. A thankless job, no doubt, but one that brought with it great power.

And speaking of power, as Hozark walked through the vast suites Oxalla Slahn now occupied, he noted there was no trace of naturally occurring magic. Yes, there were plenty of powered devices in her chambers, but the woman herself, and her aide, were both unpowered beings.

He had expected as much, based on the intelligence the Wampeh Ghalian network of spies had acquired for him during his preparation. But, sometimes, on rare occasion a truly powerful visla could utilize their own power to mask itself, making them appear quite benign, when in fact they were anything but.

Denna Slahn, however, did not seem to be utilizing any such tricks.

"Hey, that's not as bad as I thought it would be," Hozark said.

"It is foul, and disgusting, and you will remedy the problem at once," the aide said, glancing nervously toward the nearby chamber's closed door.

Her employer was in there. And they would have to pass through her inner sanctum to reach the restroom. The suite had been designed that way on purpose, giving whoever took the main rooms absolute privacy and separation from others, if they so wished.

"Denna Slahn," the aide said as she quietly knocked on the door. "The repair person has arrived to handle the problem. May I show him through?"

There was no reply for a long moment, then the door slid open. Standing before him in an outfit that simply screamed wealth and power, was the tall woman herself. She glanced at

Hozark for a second, her disdain for the mere worker clear in her look. Then, she turned and walked back across the room without a word, leaving the door open.

"Come, quickly," the assistant said, ushering him through her personal space and into the closed restroom.

Hozark had been mistaken. The smell was actually quite strong, but it seemed that the woman's aide had managed to cast a very rudimentary blocking spell, containing the majority of the stench to within the room once the door had shut.

Now that it was open, however, the spell was broken. Apparently, this sort of magic was not the woman's strong suit. But no matter. She wouldn't have to worry about it much longer.

"Wow. Okay. Now *that* is something," Hozark said, playing his innocent Binnik role to the hilt. "I can see why you guys were in such a rush. I'll get right to it."

"Do so. And when you complete your task, you are to depart at once. And do *not* disturb the denna. Is that clear?"

"Yeah, sure. But where will you be?"

"I will be right outside the door. Now, do your job and get out."

"Sheesh. Fine. I'll just get to it, then," he said, feigning mild offense, then shutting the restroom door and loudly spreading out his tools.

He knew the assistant was tempted to stay and watch him work, despite her attitude. The novelty of this resort's many unusual non-magical systems was fascinating to all who stayed there, including the guests' staff. *Actual* pipes to transport waste rather than magic? It was unheard of anywhere but here these days. And it was fascinating.

But there were appearances to be maintained, and class distinctions to uphold. Her kind, even as a servant of a different sort, did not mix with his.

The door to the master chambers shut. He was alone now. And Oxalla Slahn was in the nearby study. Unguarded. Of course, she still possessed her very effective personal protection spell, which he had already seen in action.

That was likely why her guards had felt so comfortable leaving her alone with the pathetic worker so near and only her personal attendant nearby. The man clearly had no weapons, and if he were to be foolish enough to attempt to attack her, a horrible demise would befall him.

It was also the reason her personal guards were stationed outside. Once inside her suites, she had her own protection around her at all times. Denna Slahn was perfectly secure. Or so she believed.

Hozark banged around with his tools for a few minutes, then cracked the door open, peering out into the adjacent room. The aide was there, but her boss was not. She was likely in the next chamber.

Perfect.

"*Occlustra hantsa*," he said with the faintest whisper, quietly casting the smallest of muting spells on the far doorway.

It was a tiny bit of magic, and one of the few he was allowed to pull from the work konus provided to him. A simple spell provided to the staff to help them keep the guests from being disturbed whenever they were doing work near an occupied chamber.

And now, it would keep any outside the door from hearing a thing.

Hozark quickly purged his stench spell, making himself fresh and pleasant. He also removed all but a trace of the stink within the restroom, simply flushing the small vial of solvent he had in his case down the pipe. It only took a minute before both the blockage and foul odor packet he had placed were washed away.

He then stepped out into the chamber.

"Hey. Could you show me what exactly the problem was? I'm looking at this thing, but it seems to be working fine."

"It was most certainly *not* working fine," the assistant said. "You smelled it when you arrived."

"But that cleared as soon as you opened the door. Are you sure the lady didn't just have some powerful gas or something?"

"You *dare?*"

"Hey, just a logical question in my line of work. Anyway, I need you to show me exactly where the problem was so I can fix it."

The woman hesitated.

"Or is it your boss we need to ask?" he added, knowing full well that the aide was not allowed into Oxalla's private restroom. She would have to fetch her employer.

"One moment," she said, then crossed to the shut door at the far end of the room.

"Uh, excuse me? Denna Slahn?" she said, gently knocking on the door. "The worker has a question. I apologize for the interruption, but he says it will help him repair the problem with your facilities."

There was a long silence that hung in the air as he waited. This was the one weak spot in his plan. The woman's whims. But, hopefully, the allure of the building's unusual systems would entice even her.

Finally, the door opened.

"You dare disturb me?" she said with a cold stare, yet one that hid a slight curiosity.

The *worker* needed her? And the unusual systems would be laid bare for her to see their inner workings? She was annoyed, yet intrigued by the novelty.

Yes, this would work just fine.

"With me," she said as she strode across the room and into the restroom, her aide in tow.

"I'm sorry to disturb you, Denna Slahn," Hozark said. "But I'm working on the plumbing--that's the network of pipes in the unit that make the system function--but I can't seem to

27

see any problem with it. In fact, it seems to be working just fine."

"It was *not* working just fine," she hissed as she eyed the unusual shapes of the pipes he had exposed. "Are your senses so dulled that you could not smell that foul stench?"

"I mean, there's a little bit of an odor. But that's natural when I'm working on the pipes. But could you maybe show me exactly where the problem was?"

"It was the whole thing!"

"I just need to know where. Could you point it out?"

The woman's ire was rising, quickly eclipsing her curiosity. "It was there. *There*, you fool!" she said, leaning in close, jabbing her finger at the open pipe.

As if on cue--because it was--a great stream of shit and waste water spewed out of the pipe, erupting with geyser force, coating her from head to toe.

"Wha-what in the hells have you--?" she began to shriek, ready to go into a full meltdown.

Hozark didn't hesitate, delivering a rapid stunning blow to both Oxalla and her aide. He then removed a vial from his work kit and poured a few drops into the ears of each of the women.

It would absorb instantly, leaving no trace, and the poor victims would simply wake with a massive headache in about six hours.

He would be long gone by then.

Oxalla Slahn's ego, ire, and overconfidence had been the last ingredient Hozark had needed for his plan to work. There was simply no way he could have reached her through her personal protective spell. The bubble around her extended out a full meter, deflecting and destroying anything coming her way.

But it was also tied to its possessor's will, leaving things she reached for unscathed. And when she had leaned in close to point out the problem to the stupid worker, she had brought him *willingly,* though unwittingly, into her space.

And now she lay on the hard floor, her clothing, likely worth more than her staff earned in a year, coated with shit.

But that wasn't enough.

Hozark summoned up more and more feces and filth from the pipes, piling it on top of the unconscious woman, covering her from head to toe. He then pulled up the simplest of spells. One no one thought to prevent the staff from casting. Why would they? What harm could it possibly do?

With a little grin, Hozark uttered the words that cast the backup waste removal spell. The one only to be used when there was a serious time issue at hand that couldn't wait for manual repair. The one that removed filth and waste and deposited it far across the city in the shit heap stored within an underground chamber.

In a flash, the pile of shit was gone, and with it, Denna Oxalla Slahn. The most guarded woman on the planet.

It was a kidnapping by feces.

Hozark quickly cleaned the rest of the chamber and put everything back into order, leaving no clue as to what had happened. He then placed the aide on a couch in the outer waiting area, staging her to look as if she'd just fallen asleep on duty.

Hozark gathered his tools, did a final check of the rooms, then walked to the front door.

"Okay, okay, I get it," he said defensively as he stepped outside, closing the door behind him.

The guards glanced at him curiously.

"Well, it's all fixed, but boy is she mad. Is your boss always like that?"

No one dared answer.

"I swear, that woman's got an anger issue. I mean, she said the next person to stick their head inside that door would lose it. She doesn't mean that *literally*, does she?"

The guards' looks made it clear that she very well may have.

"Well, whatever. I'm done here. You all have a lovely evening," he said, whistling merrily as he casually headed back down the hallway toward the lift disc.

The persona he was playing was false, but the smile on Hozark's face was not an act. This was likely the first time a kidnapping had been carried out this way.

Snatched by shit.

He was actually kind of proud of himself for that one.

Spirits high from a job well done, Hozark stepped onto the waiting disc and descended to the lower floors, where he would clock out as if nothing had happened at all. Then he would trot off to the hidden poop heap to retrieve his stinky prize.

CHAPTER SIX

Oxalla Slahn woke up with a pounding in her head. It was far worse than when she had overdone it on a few bottles of vintage Sikorian Rislik, though that hadn't been the really good stuff. But this? This was just miserable.

The pounding of her pulse in her ears was more than annoying. It was downright painful. And the room felt far brighter than it should have been. And the floor didn't seem right. Wasn't there a fine rug on the—

Oxalla sat bolt upright, her eyes wide and senses sharp as a surge of adrenaline flooded into her body. Her *naked* body, she quickly realized. This was most certainly *not* her suite in the resort. It was a smallish room, sparsely furnished with a table and bed, both firmly attached to the floor, and a door at either end.

It was only then that she noticed the man sitting quietly against the far wall, observing her with a calm stare. He was wearing plain, clean clothes with no identifying markings, but she realized she recognized him.

"You're that shit cleaner," she hissed. "What in the hell have you done? And where are my clothes?" she demanded, rising quickly to her feet.

"You really don't want to do that," Hozark replied. "I suggest you sit down before you––"

Oxalla felt her legs go weak and the room tilt as she fell back to the ground.

"As I was saying," he continued, "you should move slowly for the time being. It will take a little while for your equilibrium to return."

The pale-green woman glared pure hate at him as she realized her situation.

"Coward. You need to drug me to feel like a real man?" she said, spitting at him, though the effort made the room spin a bit more.

"Oh, it was not drugs that rendered you helpless," he said. "They were merely employed to keep you quiet for a time. You do go on so, and we could not have that."

There it was again. That damn calm smile creeping onto the edges of his lips. The man was in total control of her, and she knew it. For once, the most feared woman in several systems was at another's mercy.

"So, what now?" the naked woman asked, barely covering herself with her long arms. "You plan to use me for your gratification, then?"

Hozark stared at her with disquieting silence for a long moment.

"I have no such plans for you, Denna Slahn," he finally replied.

It was at that moment that he saw the faintest flicker of disappointment in her eyes.

Aah, so that's how she is, he realized. *A powerful woman with a proclivity for domination.*

It was in no way uncommon, though it tended to be with consent that those types of power-play scenarios unfolded. But she seemed to prefer it a bit more dangerous than that. And likely rougher, from what he could tell.

But Hozark wasn't one to kink shame anyone. Lord knew he had seen far, far stranger things in his day. Used people's secret urges to gain access to targets on more than one occasion, in fact.

"Drink this," he said, sliding a cup of hot tea to his prisoner.

"What is it? Poison?"

"If I'd wanted you dead, you would be," he noted. "This is Gorram root. It will help alleviate the negative effects of the compound in your system."

She stared at the cup a long moment, debating whether or not what he said was true. But she was alive, and at his mercy. Had he wished to do her harm, he could have at any time, yet he chose not to. Perhaps, she might be able to swing this situation to her advantage yet.

But she would need a clear head for that.

"Thank you," she said, taking the offered cup and raising it to her lips.

The fluid was hot and surprisingly sweet, not bitter like she had expected it to be. And, as it made its way to her growling stomach, she realized her head actually did feel better.

Oxalla rose from the floor, slowly, and took a seat on the low bed, making no effort to cover herself.

"So, you drugged me, then stripped me for your own amusement, I see?" she said with a piercing, critical gaze. "What a banal and so very *male* thing to do."

Hozark chuckled. "It was for your benefit as well as mine," he replied. "You were rather, shall we say, *unpresentable* after our last encounter. I thought a thorough cleaning was in order before we proceeded, for both our sakes."

"And now?"

"Now we can talk."

Oxalla stretched her naked body, making a show of it as she

leaned back against the surprisingly comfortably warm wall. At least her temporary prison was properly climate controlled. She also noted her little display had not budged her captor in the slightest.

"What? You think you will learn my secrets? Oh, you don't know how many have tried. But you'll not get anything from me," she said with a rebellious little laugh.

Her captor smiled a most unnerving grin. He was confident. Far too confident. And a little twinge of uncertainty settled into her stomach.

"Oh, my dear, but I already have," he replied, staring deep into her eyes. It was a trick she was fond of herself, but this time, she was the one who looked away.

The shit cleaner—which was obviously not his true profession—rose and retrieved a small box from the shelf formed in the surface of the wall itself. He returned to his seat, then opened it for her to see.

Vials were neatly lined up in a row, their contents carefully arranged by color, some of the liquids gently bubbling against the glass of their containers. The man smiled as she stared at the collection.

"Yes, indeed. You told me a great deal, in fact," he said, closing the box and setting it aside. "Marvelous things, these elixirs. Why, when used by expert hands, they get people to admit to pretty much anything. And believe me, these are expert hands."

To her credit, Oxalla remained silent. Many would have blurted out a great many things in a panic, but she remained tight-lipped as she assessed her situation, given the ever-increasing information she was gleaning from her captor.

"So, if I've told you all you wanted to know, why am I still being held? A ransom? If so, you know my accounts are more than good for it."

"Yes, you are a woman of significant wealth."

"And power."

"Yet here you are."

"For now. But know this. When we are done with your little game, I will have my people hunt you to the ends of the galaxy and make you pay for what you have done."

Hozark grinned. "I do not doubt it. Though women in your current position do not normally make threats as you do."

"I am no ordinary woman."

"Apparently."

Oxalla's eyes narrowed. There was something odd about this man. About this whole situation. What her captor's endgame was, she couldn't quite put her finger on. But she was a shrewd woman, and one of considerable skill in the ways of subterfuge and deceit. Soon enough she would know his weakness. And when she did, she would exploit it to the fullest.

"You obviously know who I am," she said, relaxing her posture further, as if she hadn't a care in the world.

All the better to mess with the man's head. Oh yes, she would get the better of him yet.

"And if you know who I am, then you also know who I am affiliated with. Who I work for."

"Yes, I do. And about that, it was really quite fascinating what you had to say about more than a few of them. Most interesting, truly. I mean, the Council of Twenty does have its share of difficult members, no doubt. But Visla Ravik? Really, Denna Slahn, you can do better than that."

Despite her best efforts, her cheeks flushed a slightly darker shade of green.

"It was a purely transactional arrangement. And nothing you can use to blackmail me, or him, for that matter. He required a team of smelters, and I provided them to him. End of story."

"And yet, there is more to that tale."

"You may choose to believe so, but you're grasping at straws."

"Straws like your secret friend? Your dear Maktan?" he

replied. "I must admit, I was surprised to learn he was involved in your machinations."

She blanched, her cheeks going pale at the name. Oh yes, there was definitely something going on with the visla. But even in her legitimate shock, she remained tight-lipped. Though it seemed almost to be out of fear rather than cocky avoidance.

"I don't know what you're talking about."

He knew she was lying, of course. But her reaction alone was confirmation enough.

"Please. Lying does not suit a woman of your stature. And we both know that Maktan is neck-deep in this."

"I have no idea what you're talking about," she repeated, that look of concern deepening behind her scornful glare.

Hozark spent the next half hour carefully toying with his captive. Hinting at associations, trying to get her to reveal more about Maktan's role in all of this. Between him, Visla Ravik, and the late Visla Torund, that made up a considerable chunk of the Council of Twenty's more powerful vislas.

They had been creating weapons, yes, she knew. And Torund had been working closely with Ravik, spearheading the efforts. But Maktan? No matter how he tried, she was not any more forthcoming, and the clock had run out.

He had been hired for a job, and, unfortunately, he only had so much time for these games. But at least they had been somewhat productive.

Hozark rose from his seat, collected her empty cup and the little box of colorful vials, and stepped out into the corridor, casting a powerful spell behind him, sealing the room tight with a magical barrier, though it was one that allowed sound to pass through the opening.

"So, was that really the best you've got?" she asked with a cocky grin, rising and striding to the seemingly open doorway.

She knew the spell was in place to prevent her escape, but that wouldn't stop her from making her point, and she stood tall, confident, and stark naked before her captor, her every cell shouting out her defiance.

He had captured her, yes, and perhaps gleaned *some* information. But she still had secrets, and eventually, she would have her revenge.

"Alas, our time is up," Hozark replied.

Oxalla laughed, her contempt for the man she still saw as her inferior clear on her face. She was Oxalla Slahn, fixer for the Council of Twenty. A great many owed her favors of no small measure. And when she was finally free, this little man would pay for his trespass.

"Oh, you pathetic creature. All of that effort, and for what? A little sack of coin, which might seem substantial to you, but is no more than pocket change to my people. And once it is paid, there will be no escaping my wrath."

The man on the other side of the barrier simply stared at her, saying nothing. She smiled, sure her words were hitting home. And she meant to make good on her threats in no uncertain terms. And from what he'd seen in their short time together, he knew it too.

"So, how much, then?" she asked with a haughty grin. "What ridiculously insignificant amount of coin will you be asking for me?"

A tiny smile creased Hozark's lips.

"Oh, my dear woman. I was not hired to *ransom* you."

A single word triggered the spell opening the far door in her chamber.

The door that opened out into space.

The look of utter shock as she realized what was happening was gone as fast as she was, sucked out of the opening into the freezing void. Hozark sealed the door once more.

She would die relatively quickly, nude as she was. The cold would likely claim her before the forces of the vacuum, though some species were more tolerant of it than others.

He could have made her end less unpleasant, had he desired. As a master assassin, he possessed countless means to do so. But this woman was a malevolent blight, and one well deserving of the nature of her demise.

He had been hired to end her, and so he had. But, sometimes, meting out a little bit of justice in the act was a pleasant perk of his job.

Hozark hummed to himself as he tucked the little box containing the harmless vials of colorful cleaning solutions into a storage bin, pleased at how well the ersatz potions had served their purpose.

Then, with the satisfaction of a job well done, he headed for command to set the course to his next destination.

CHAPTER SEVEN

Xymotz was a particularly dangerous place to visit.

It wasn't because of the residents, though, although they were most certainly an extremely rough and hardy bunch. But given the unique nature of the difficult access to the deadly world's lone city, and the unlikeliness of any making a clean escape if they did anything particularly bad on the surface, people tended to behave themselves.

The thing about Xymotz was that it wasn't a normal planet. Not by any stretch. It was a gas giant. One that had failed to condense into a sun. It might not have made it all the way to solar status, but not for lack of trying. And the intense pressure and heat at its core had coalesced a ball of elements and given it a small, dense world at the center of the swirling gasses.

Of course, visiting the world meant near instant death for any who were foolish enough to attempt to land on its surface. If the storming mists didn't tear you apart on approach, the heat would melt you and your craft into molten slag.

And if you somehow survived both those, the gravitational pressure would crush you to a fraction of your size once you passed the halfway mark to the core.

It was a deathtrap. And that was why it was a perfect place for a rather quiet little hidey-hole for those in need of a safe harbor in tumultuous times.

Centuries upon centuries of magic had been laid upon the place, cast by powerful users little by little, pulling the magic force of the gaseous world's mists into the mix, using them to help reinforce the spells.

It took ages, but a narrow conduit to the surface was eventually formed. A slim funnel of safe space leading to the solid ground below. It was there that additional spells were quickly put in place to buttress the tenuous connection the corridor had made with the surface. And from there, an ever-strengthening shell of protective magic was set in place, within which the small settlement of outcasts and runaways took root.

It was here that the legendary swordsmith Master Orkut had taken refuge, having not so much faked his own death, as merely allowed that rumor to stick.

In reality, he was trying to stay far from the notice of the Council of Twenty. Not just for his own safety, but for the safety of his family, for he was one of the very few living who could craft a vespus blade.

It was he who had made Hozark's glowing blue sword, the vespus imbued with a great power when wielded in the hands of a Ghalian master. The weapon could cause much damage in even a layman's possession, but in the hands of a Ghalian, it could not only cut, but also store, channel, and redirect the power the assassins had stolen from their victims.

And now he was in hiding, protecting his family with his absence. His son, it seemed, possessed his father's rare gift, and Orkut wanted to do all he could to afford him a life free of risk of the Council ever coming after him. And part of that meant going far, far away.

It was there with Orkut that Demelza had returned, once again setting to work helping the bladesmith as she had before, slowly earning credit and goodwill toward his making her a sword of her own. Not a vespus blade, mind you, but a weapon crafted by his hand nonetheless.

She had performed more than admirably during her time spent working with Master Hozark, and the amount of distress they had caused the Council had pleased the swordsmith greatly. As such, in addition to merely gaining further respect from the man, his willingness to set to work at the forge on her behalf was clearly increasing.

Of course, her partnership with Hozark had been at Orkut's demand in the first place. Part of the price she would have to pay should she wish to acquire one of his creations, just as it was likewise a requirement forced upon Master Hozark as the final price for his vespus blade.

The thing was, Wampeh Ghalian always worked alone. But this unlikely partnership had wound up becoming a very effective arrangement. And with Hozark's trusted pilot friend, Uzabud, and his new copilot, Laskar, they had accomplished what none of them might have individually.

But for now, she was back with the old swordsmith, doing his bidding, and helping in any way he needed. But there was not much that actually needed doing, most days, and with all of that time to kill, and on an incredibly remote world, no less, he decided to take her under his wing in a sense and train her.

Not in mere swordplay, which she was quite skilled at, but in the art of recognizing and adapting her style to the actual design of blades themselves. Their shape and function. Strengths and weaknesses. How to best use an individual blade's shape and style against its wielder.

No matter how good anyone might be, all trained in swordplay in a way that focused on the user's skill. But he was showing her not how to best the wielder of a weapon, but how to defeat the blade itself.

Two-handed, one-handed, thick or thin, all of them behaved

differently, yet predictably, no matter how skilled the user might be. And he was going to teach her those weaknesses to her benefit.

"Better," the old man said, appraising Demelza's form as she moved through a series of combatives.

"Good enough to best Samara?" she asked.

She'd been training harder than ever since she had fought Hozark's former lover to a standstill. Well, not quite a standstill, but she'd survived longer than just about anyone ever had, and word of that had impressed Master Orkut. But that only went so far.

"Oh, my dear Demelza," he said with a laugh. "I know you managed to survive against her, and even held your own for a rather significant amount of time. But ready to beat her? Not by a long shot."

"No?" Demelza asked, deflating slightly.

"No. But remember, she is one of the best your order has ever seen. Now, put down your weapon and take these," he said, handing her two cups of water.

"Thank you, Master Orkut, but I am not thirsty."

"I did not think you were," he replied with a curious smirk. "Hold the cups. Arms out. And don't spill a drop. I will be back soon."

With that, he left her alone in the training space.

"Holding cups of water?" she grumbled. "What sort of training is this? I am a Wampeh Ghalian."

But she obeyed the man, holding the cups out with extended arms, not thinking much of the task at first. By the time he returned, however, her arms were on fire, shaking from the effort to keep so small a weight aloft. But Demelza did not budge, forcing the energy within her to flow through her arms as well as her torso, locking her arms in place.

Master Orkut took one of the cups from her hands and downed it in a gulp. "Drink."

Demelza's arm trembled as she tried to bring the cup to her lips, her arms not wanting to do her bidding any longer. But she managed, and after draining the cup, looked to the swordsmith.

"Now what?" she asked.

"Well, well. You may have some potential yet," he said with a chuckle. "Come along. I'm sure I can find you something to do."

CHAPTER EIGHT

The next morning, the assassin woke on her cot feeling worse than she had in years. Not since her early days of labor in the order's training house as she worked her way to full Ghalian status had her muscles ached so.

And Master Orkut had achieved all of that with little more than cups of water and a few other seemingly benign activities.

She had been with him for only a few weeks at this point, but having completed his initial grunt work, the training she had undertaken when that list of tasks had run out was surprisingly brutal.

Demelza pushed herself up, propping herself on her elbow then slipping her feet to the floor. She rolled her neck with a loud crack.

"Oh, that is not pleasant," she mused quietly as she began the daily practice of loosening her body at first light.

Her shoulders felt as though they were made of rocks. Broken rocks that had been pieced back together with a heavy, binding cement. And connected to them were a pair of arms as sore as she'd ever felt them. Exhausted, like the time she had clung to the side of an emmik's estate's stone wall for two hours before slipping inside and completing her contract.

Her back was strong, though, and the aches and pains, while unpleasant, were not the harm-causing variety. Demelza rose on sturdy legs and immediately dropped into a series of squats and press ups, forcing the blood to flow into her knotted flesh, restoring its flexibility and spring.

She was still a young woman, and the pains from the rigors of training would melt from her soon enough. To be replaced with fresh ones, no doubt, but still. Five minutes later, her pre-work routine was completed, and she slipped into her loose training attire.

Demelza was a thick woman, but not from lack of hard work or indulging in a life of luxury. She was a skilled assassin, and despite her curvaceous appearance, she could move with the speed and grace of a dancer. And dance she did. Often, in fact. It was one of her favorite infiltration disguises, the bronze-skinned gypsy-like woman of dance and frolic.

Of course, it was magic that colored her pale white skin that way, and carefully selected spells and clothes that rounded out the disguise. But the dancing was all her. One simply could not fake the ability, nor the nimble step that a true dancer possessed.

But this was not an assassination, and she would most certainly not be dancing today.

"All right, then," she said, stepping out of her chambers and picking up the two empty buckets already waiting at her door. "Time to begin."

The route to the magically replenished well on Xymotz was an easy one, and she ran it quickly, her arms held out to the sides, an empty bucket in each of them, as Orkut had instructed her when she first started his tasks.

Because of the hot, dense nature of the unlikely colony in

the center of the gas giant, there was no precipitation, nor any naturally occurring water of any kind. But enough of the requisite magic to produce it did live in the swirling clouds, and it was from there that the residents had cast generations of spells, pulling and condensing it from the mist.

The well was more of a storage pit, in that regard. A place to deposit overflow from what they had drawn into the large cistern feeding the city. And it was there that Demelza would dip her buckets, filling them to the top before carrying them back to the training area with outstretched arms. By the time she got there, the stiffness of the morning had been washed away by the fresh hell of newly aching shoulders.

And then the day's work truly began.

A variety of swords lay out for her use. Each one different in length, heft, and design. Some were designed for heavy, brutal combat by brutish men. Others were fine and sharp, devices for precise slaughter with a delicate touch. And others still covered every type of violence in between.

Training with a master bladesmith afforded her quite a selection, indeed.

Her task with them, however, was an unusual one. Master Orkut had her cut wood. Where he even acquired the wood on a planet with no vegetation beyond the crops the settlers had forced the soil to accept was anyone's guess. Likely something he'd traded an arriving ship for, but why, no one knew.

It wasn't for the cooking fires, nor for the flames fueling his forge. Magical fire did not require wood to burn, and the spells to ignite and sustain them were both minimal in the power required, and one of the earliest things youngsters learned when they received their first konuses.

His task was simple. Reduce a set number of the logs to pieces, utilizing only the blades at her disposal. It seemed an easy enough thing for one as fit as she was, so she swung the heaviest of the swords hard, breaking the wood within a few strokes.

Easy at first, it turned out. The woman's arms quickly wearied from the impacts, and she soon found herself forced to switch to the lighter, more slender blades, sufficing with removing smaller pieces of the logs with lighter blows.

After her first day of it, Orkut had asked her how it went as he surveyed the small pile of chopped wood.

"Well enough, Master Orkut," she said. "Though, I think they will need a good sharpening after all of that."

Orkut surveyed her work and nodded. "Not bad. Not good, but not bad."

"Not good? But I reduced a great many of them to pieces, as you instructed."

"Yes," he said, examining the dulled blades. "But you were inefficient. *That* is why I wanted you to first attempt this task without further direction."

"I do not understand, Master Orkut," she replied.

The old man bent and placed a large log upright. Demelza almost moved to help him, but stopped herself. This was Master Orkut, and he was much, *much* stronger than he appeared.

He picked up two of the swords from the selection. Not the heavy ones she had used to force the wood to do her bidding, but a pair of slender blades. One was so slim she had worried she would break it if she used it for his task. The metal was razor sharp, but it did not seem appropriate for chopping wood.

The other sword wasn't much larger, but its design was different. A wedge-shaped blade rather than a razor's edge taper, and a thicker back edge of the blade, giving it more stability.

"I think those might take a while," Demelza noted.

The old man merely smiled at his foolish pupil. He then moved in a flash, the thinner blade whipping to life, quickly notching the wood in a flurry of minor cuts that shaved away a surprisingly deep groove in but a few dozen strokes. The other blade then sprang to life, driving down with a sharp, quick blow, its wedge-shaped edge striking true, landing in the deepest part of the notch made by the other sword.

With a crack, the log split. It didn't fall apart to pieces, as it would have after many blows with the largest of the swords, but it had split. And with a tenth of the effort.

Demelza stared, amazed. He had done what she had, but in a fraction of the time, and with the least assuming of the weapons. And all without breaking a sweat. Orkut watched the expressions on her face with amusement.

"I have a different task for you now. Come."

It was not what she expected.

One hundred needles were laid out on a cloth. And next to them, a spool of thread.

"I am not a seamstress, Master Orkut, but I will do my best."

"You are not to sew, Demelza. You are to thread each needle. Come find me when you are done with your task."

He walked away, leaving her to her work. With aching arms and tired hands, she picked up the first needle.

"This should be fast," she mused with a grin.

After two dozen, her hands began to cramp. All the chopping of wood had left them overtaxed from the exertion. By the fiftieth, the pain was like the needles were embedded in her hands, not held between her fingers.

By the hundredth, the effort to get the little piece of thread through the tiny eye was tantamount to crushing rocks with her bare hands––a task he had her attempt every day, though all she ever managed to do was squeeze them.

She forced herself to ignore the pain and shakes and complete the task. Then it was on to whatever fresh hell he had in mind.

Ingots.

Ingots of all manner of metal. Some ordinary, others rare,

and others still, enchanted with some form of power or another. Heavy, solid ingots. And it was Demelza's job to move and sort them for him.

She did so, making neat piles, then carried the raw ore to the forge at the man's request, standing near the intense heat of the crucible as he carefully created his proprietary alloys, imbued with varying degrees of his magic.

It went on like this for weeks, and though she had already been incredibly fit on her arrival, Demelza's muscles gained a new degree of resiliency. One that would keep her arms from wearying in lengthy swordplay.

She still had her womanly shape—a small waif, she most certainly was not—but the hard labor had toned the muscle beneath her curves to whip-steel strength.

Finally, Master Orkut stopped her in her work one day.

"I have received an interesting bit of information," he said. "And you are to deliver it."

"A courier run? I will prepare my ship. Where am I to deliver it, and to whom?"

"Oh, you know whom, and you know where," the man replied. "Tell Master Hozark an old friend of mine needs help. He is to hurry, and you are to accompany him once more."

Demelza maintained a stoic expression, but she smiled on the inside. Though Ghalian worked alone, her time partnered with Master Hozark had been an amazing learning experience, and it had put her well in the good graces of Master Orkut as well.

And, to be honest, she simply liked Hozark and his unusual spacefaring accomplices.

"I shall depart at once," she said.

"Wait."

"Yes?"

"Take these," he said, handing her the long box he was

carrying. "I expect you to return them when your task is complete."

She knew the weight of the package as soon as she hefted it, well familiar with the blades within from her weeks of training.

"I will bring them back, Master Orkut," she replied. "And thank you."

CHAPTER NINE

Master Hozark had been in the training house on Sooval's third moon for nearly a week when Demelza came for him. The slim envelope she carried with Master Orkut's seal upon it was safely tucked in her inner pocket, awaiting the master assassin's eyes only.

The facility was as all Ghalian training houses and meeting places were. Safe, anonymous, and robustly fortified. It was also smack dab in the middle of a tranquil farming community, which was something of an anomaly for Ghalian locations.

But here the students were put to work in a manner a bit different from most other houses. Namely, in addition to learning the deadly ways of the Wampeh Ghalian, they also worked the land, growing their own food as well as being provided a convenient way to practice the use of a cover story from their earliest days there.

These were Wampeh, obviously, but all put on the guise of farmers, after sufficient preparation by the instructors. And as of yet, none had ever suspected the mild-mannered youths and their elder guardians to be anything more than a tranquil bunch who merely worked the land.

The cover story also provided a convenient excuse when mishaps occurred, as they were wont to in training. Bruises and cuts were simply laughed off as just another little incident while working the land or herding the beasts.

Hozark had chosen this place for no particular reason after he'd met with Master Corann. The head of the Five, the overseers of the Ghalian order, had agreed he should enjoy a little downtime once he relayed the intel he had uncovered during his recent job.

At the end of the day, he just liked the way this particular facility smelled. Fresh. Clean. Natural. None of the false scents and lingering perfumes one was bombarded with on more "civilized" planets.

Demelza's surprise arrival was treated as simply another Wampeh cousin come to visit the farm and lend a hand with the coming harvest. And while her ship did possess shimmer-cloaking abilities, as did most Ghalian craft, to all who observed the vessel as it landed, it simply seemed as if it were any other craft. Exactly as the Ghalian intended.

She breathed deeply as she walked the short distance to the farmhouse and attached bunkrooms and workspaces that hid the true facilities beneath the ground. On the surface, literally, it was just another farm. But deep below, intense and deadly endeavors were underway.

Master Hozark was taking a more passive role in the training in this particular facility for a change. Observing rather than teaching, at least for the moment. And on this day, a group of the newest recruits were getting their feet wet, so to speak, learning the first of many difficult lessons that would fill their days and nights for years to come.

All of them were young, between the ages of eight to twelve, and fairly diverse in size, shape, and gender. Their one common trait was that they possessed the Ghalian gift. That rarest of abilities that only a fraction of a percent of all Wampeh were born with.

The gift that an even smaller fraction of those ever learned to utilize and control. And if they could, and if they happened to be made of the stern stuff needed of them for the lifestyle, they might even eventually become an elite assassin of the order. A Wampeh Ghalian.

It was the power that gave them an edge. Rare even among their kind, the ability to steal the power from another. Not with spells or clever runes, but in a much more primal way.

They stole power by drinking a power user's blood.

And once it was taken, they could then use it as if it were their own. It was what made the pale assassins some of the most feared creatures in the galaxy, and the mere sight of their fangs slipping into place could send the most fearsome of men running.

This batch of youths, however, were green. Not in coloring, but in abilities and life experience. It was how they all arrived at the training houses, eventually.

Across the systems, a network of Wampeh Ghalian spies and scouts kept an eye out for the first telltale manifestations of the power in young Wampeh. They were spotted young, most often just before puberty, when the gift began to truly show itself. And if it seemed they *truly* had the gift, and if they showed promise, then they would be acquired, though that occurred in many different ways.

Sometimes, it required a visit with the child's parents, which typically entailed an envoy telling the family their child had been accepted into an exclusive academy, with full tuition paid for.

Most of the time, the parents would be thrilled beyond belief and the child was soon acquired. Not always, though. Some families were reticent, proving quite difficult at times.

Of course, for orphans, it was far, far easier.

Hozark watched the youths stumble through the rigors of early body awareness and fight training. He'd been one of these aspirants once, himself. Young, green, without a skill or a clue to rub together. It had been a particularly difficult time in his life, and he might not have survived it if not for a young girl named Samara, who had arrived just a few days before he had.

The two became fast friends, and with each other's support, they had quickly risen through the ranks. They trained together, studied together, and had, for a time, even been lovers, which they remained, off and on, well into adulthood, and well after they had become full-fledged Ghalian assassins.

She pushed him, and he pushed her back, and together they had risen high within the order. But despite what others might whisper, they were only friends. Friends with a special understanding, but not a bonded pair. That was something Wampeh Ghalian simply did not do, though the rule was not written in stone. But they were as close as anyone could come without crossing that unspoken line.

But then Samara had died. Killed on a contract gone wrong.

Or so they had all believed.

Ten years she had been dead, until, one day, she showed up again in the middle of a contract, a new thorn in Hozark's side, fighting him nearly to the death as she protected members of the Council of Twenty.

And she had been popping up more and more, it seemed, especially after someone on the Council targeted a Ghalian master.

It made no sense.

For one, the Wampeh Ghalian held no alliance to the Council, and more often than not, they took contracts specifically to stymie their power grabs. For another, the Council, while cocky and bold, was not so foolish as to do something to bring the wrath of the order upon themselves.

The Five had deemed it most likely that it was only a few members of the Council of Twenty jockeying for power within their own ranks. How targeting one of the Ghalian masters played into that plan, they had not yet uncovered, but the Council's members stabbed one another in the back so often they could make a career out of that alone.

But the Wampeh Ghalian were patient, if nothing else. And they would find out what was truly going on, eventually. The only question was how long it would take. In the meantime, they would carry on.

"Plant your feet beneath your hips," Hozark called out to a young boy who had just abruptly found himself on the dirt. "Your center of balance, your very foundation, is in your hips."

He strolled closer and placed his hands on the youth's shoulders, squaring them above his legs. He then pushed him slightly, forcing his body to react and regain its balance without conscious thought.

"There, do you feel that? That is one of the most basic lessons you will be learning. How to center yourself. An unbalanced opponent is a dead opponent. Do you understand?"

The youngster nodded.

"Good. Now, back to your training."

It was about as good as the younger aspirants could expect from him. Hozark was an amazing teacher for the older groups, showing them the fine points and nuances of their deadly skills. But when it came to the younger kids, he was simply never very good, despite having been one himself, once.

An older boy jogged into the training space. "Master Hozark? Someone is here to see you," he informed him.

"Here? No one knows I am here," he said, wondering if he might need his weapons.

"She says a Master Orkut sent her. *Again.*"

"Demelza," Hozark realized with a grin. "I will be with her momentarily."

The boy trotted off to tell their guest to please wait for the master, leaving Hozark with his thoughts a moment.

Hozark didn't expect it, but he found himself smiling. Strangely, he'd been looking forward to this inevitable reunion.

CHAPTER TEN

"It is a fine blade," Hozark said as he admired the perfectly balanced length of metal in his hand. "And this one? Masterful," he said, effortlessly throwing the accompanying dagger into a nearby target's bullseye. "Master Orkut has prepared you well, I see. And a good thing. You have more than earned his respect after all you have done."

Demelza suppressed her blush. "They are only on loan. One day, I hope to possess Orkut-crafted blades of my own, but for the time being, these will more than suffice."

Hozark walked to the target and pulled the dagger free, then threw it to Demelza with no small amount of force. A Wampeh Ghalian, she snatched it from the air, resheathing it with a little grin.

"Looking sharp. Your reflexes are improved, I see. And they were already quite impressive when last we traveled together," Hozark noted, handing her the sword, rather than throwing it as well.

"Master Orkut has had me performing some rather *unusual* training exercises of late."

"Whatever they are, the effects are noticeable. And I also see your wrists appear to have strengthened," he added, glancing at her hands.

Hozark's perception was far greater than a normal person's. Even more than your average Ghalian assassin. As one of the Five, a master of the order, it had to be.

"A result of some of his more unusual routines," she said.

"Unusual? Such as?"

"Well, for one, he had me holding cups of water."

"For hours, I assume?"

"Indeed."

"Oh, I remember that lesson far too well," Hozark said with a little chuckle as he thought back to his own days under a different master's tutelage. One who also favored some of the older training methods of a long-dead sect of warrior monks.

He had continued his training in unusual fighting styles even after completing his time in the training house of the Wampeh Ghalian. When he and Samara were finally out in the worlds completing contracts and liaising when time permitted, they would often seek out masters of the more obscure arts to add even more to their considerable repertoire.

"What else did he have you do, pray tell? Perhaps some pole standing?"

"Of course. Much as we did here as trainees, but armed with a long blade, and with Master Orkut flinging things at me."

"Which you reduced to much smaller things, I assume?"

"Of course. It would disgrace the order if I had done any less."

"Well said, and quite true. But let me see your hands," he said, taking her hands in his, studying her palms with great curiosity.

The muscles were more developed, he noted, but not just the larger ones used for brute strength. The finer musculature had also seemed to have become more defined since he'd seen her last.

"Rocks," she said.

"Rocks?"

"Yes. Rocks. He had me squeezing rocks. Sometimes for hours a day."

"A favored training technique of the Rugen Marauders, if I am not mistaken. You know, their six-fingered elite guard have few equals in the known systems."

"So I have heard."

Hozark assessed his friend with a keen eye. She'd developed as a fighter during the time they spent together hunting down those responsible for targeting Master Prombatz and his young student. But now, it seemed, she had leveled up, thanks to the efforts of Master Orkut.

Hozark drew his sword, a gleaming blue vespus blade, made by the same man's hands. With calmness of mind and a fair bit of effort, he forced the blade's magical glow to diminish until it was nearly invisible to the naked eye. He then flashed an impish look at Demelza.

"What do you say? Are you up for it?"

She grinned and spun her sword in a flurry of motion, coming to a halt in the ready position. "I am *always* up for it."

Hozark's little smile was the only warning she had before he launched into an attack, his sword flashing through the air with a deadly whistle. Demelza, however, had expected the move and was already weaving her way clear while her own blade rang out against his in a deflecting parry.

The two began circling one another, taking small swings from time to time, testing one another's defensive reactions and boundaries.

"Master Hozark and the new lady are fighting!" one of the young aspirants informed the others in an excited hush as he raced into one of the nearby practice areas.

"What was that?" their teacher said, looking up from his instruction. "You know not to interrupt training."

"I'm sorry, sir. You're right, sir."

"Then to the pole with you. Left foot only. And stand atop it until you are told to come down."

"Yes, sir," the youth said, then paused. "It's just, Master Hozark and the woman who arrived today are fighting in the sparring arena. And he is using his vespus blade."

The teacher did not show surprise. A Wampeh Ghalian is always in control of his emotions. Or at least the outward expression of them. But this was an opportunity too good to miss. Master Hozark had been a bit reluctant to instruct the younger students, but if not by hands-on training, he could still teach them quite a lot by their simple observation.

"Hold that order," he said. "Disregard the pole. You did well. Now, class, come. We are going to watch one of the greatest living swordsmen of the Ghalian at work."

Hozark and Demelza both had a fine sheen of sweat on them when the small group of students entered the arena and moved silently to the walls. Both noticed the new arrivals, of course, but they had been immediately recognized as students and gauged as no threat, allowing the pair to continue their fight without missing a beat.

If anything, they upped their tempo just a little.

It was a master class in swordplay, with some of the most impressive and unusual techniques being displayed, to the great joy of the young students. Oohs and aahs occasionally escaped their young lips, the stoic, silent nature of the Ghalian having not yet been completely drilled into the recent arrivals.

With a flick of the wrist, Hozark opened a little cut on Demelza's left arm. Nothing a simple healing spell wouldn't fix after practice. He moved again, feinting a low strike but cutting high, drawing blood on her right as well.

The two locked eyes, sharing an amused smile. This was the Ghalian way. Train as hard as you can, knowing your wounds will be healed afterward. And more importantly, the more you sweat and bleed in training, the less you die in battle.

Hozark shifted his stance, alternating to a style that Demelza was not entirely familiar with. But Master Orkut's lessons rang out in her head, the result of hours upon hours of repetition driving them home.

Do not fight the wielder. Fight the blade.

Anyone else would have felt the cold sting of vespus metal when Hozark made a quick little lunge, but Demelza instinctively pivoted. Pivoted in a way that actually managed to take the master Ghalian by surprise, and try as he might to adjust mid-stroke, the young woman's blade made contact, drawing blood as it grazed his chest.

The students gasped.

Hozark held up one hand, pausing the combat. He looked at the cut and then at the woman who had dealt it to him. It had been a long time since any but Samara had managed to touch him in single combat with a blade.

"Nicely done," he said. "*Very* nicely done." He turned to the students. "No one is infallible. Not even one of the Five. You have learned a lot today about swordplay, but that lesson is even more important. *Anyone* can fall, no matter how skilled they may be, as Sister Demelza just demonstrated with her most unusual style."

"Thank you, Master Hozark."

"No, thank *you*. This is a valuable lesson for the youths," he replied. "Now, you all get back to your training. Demelza and I have much to discuss."

The students all filed out of the room, a slight buzz about what they'd just seen in the air around them.

"Come here. Let me heal those," Hozark said, sliding on a konus powered especially strongly with healer's power. "I've never seen that technique before. Most unusual."

"It was something Master Orkut showed me," she replied.

"He said, do not fight the sword's wielder, but the sword itself, for all blades have certain ways they move and react, no matter what the person swinging it may be trying to do."

Hozark smiled, then broke into a little laugh. "Oh, that is marvelous. Orkut, you surprise me yet again."

He finished repairing the wounds he'd given his friend, then turned the konus to his own bloody chest. All in a day's training, he mused. And he'd been much more seriously wounded on many other training sessions in his early years.

But being in a Ghalian training house meant all of the tools of their order were at his disposal. No need to use up the stolen magic still flowing in his system from the last power user he'd slain. Instead, he kept that reserve completely intact, instead drawing from one of the many healing devices kept on the premises.

"So, Demelza, I know you did not come here merely to enjoy a bit of sparring with me, though that was indeed most enjoyable."

"No. I have a message from Orkut," she said, pulling a small envelope with the bladesmith's seal on it. A little bit of blood was smeared on the edges. "Oops. Sorry," she said with a little chuckle.

Hozark grinned and opened the letter, quickly reading the contents.

"Orkut says we are required at once. A favor that he owes a very powerful friend. One who will pay us handsomely, and a man of great resources."

"That doesn't sound so bad," Demelza said.

"And it will be the Council we will be up against," Hozark added.

"Oh. In that case, perhaps it might be at least a little bit bad," she corrected.

Hozark's brow furrowed slightly. "You know, everyone seems

to be having issues with the Council of late, and not just us. But why *this* man? And why now?"

"I do not know. I was simply told to come fetch you and to fly you to wherever it is we are supposed to go. The location was to be included in that letter."

"It was."

"Master Orkut also said we are to enter the facility under cover. No one is to know we are there."

"As is our usual way. Very well," Hozark said.

"So, what's the layout? Did he tell you that much?"

"It is a residential estate tower. Very opulent, from what I can tell."

"Access point?"

"The best ingress will be the lone floating garden located outside of his main chambers."

"Floating gardens, eh? They really must be wealthy. That's a serious amount of magic to maintain," Demelza mused.

"Indeed. But they only possess one at the moment. Other gardens are being built, but the completed one is the only place strong enough to support our shimmer ship."

"I assume we'll be picking up Uzabud and Laskar on the way?"

Hozark pondered a moment. "No, I think not. We do not yet know if we will be needing his assistance. And he is currently recreating with Laskar on Tyalius. We should leave him alone for the time being and let him have his fun."

CHAPTER ELEVEN

The wet smack of the fist bouncing off of Bud's face echoed in the stone chamber. He was tied to a chair, which was, in turn, firmly secured to the floor. There would be no overturning it and scrambling to his feet to escape, as he had already done once before.

Bud was a slippery one, but this was one bind he would not so easily maneuver out of.

Another punch, this time to the gut, sent the wind out of his lungs with a painful whoosh of forced air. The goon at the other end of that meaty fist stepped back to watch the poor man gasp for breath as his diaphragm spasmed from the blow.

Put simply, Bud was being beaten to a pulp.

This was supposed to be a vacation. Some R&R. A chance for him and his copilot to get some much-needed downtime to recharge their exhausted selves after some pretty significant adventuring with their Wampeh Ghalian friends.

Of course, they'd taken a couple of minor smuggling jobs on the way to the resort world. But neither had been anything significant, and certainly not anything that would have resulted in the current state of affairs. No, that had been entirely the product of a bit too much alcohol, and a bit too much bravado on the former space pirate's part.

The pained wheeze of Uzabud's attempts to catch his breath lessened as his lungs finally relaxed and filled with air. A tiny sigh of relief escaped his lips. Just as a fist contacted them yet again.

"Oh, come on already! At least let me catch my breath!" Bud whined, spitting blood onto the floor.

"No rest for you, friend," the man said. "Boss's orders."

"Seriously? It wasn't even my fault. I mean, how was I supposed to know she was his wife? It was an honest mistake."

"You were found *inside* his wife."

"Well, yeah. But have you seen her? I mean, can you blame me? And if she was married, why didn't she say anything?"

The man said nothing, merely rolling his shoulders to loosen up. Beating a prisoner was tiring work, after all.

"Wait a minute. This isn't the first time she's done this, is it?"

Again, the man said nothing, but a slight twitch of his eyebrow told Bud all he needed to know.

"If this is a regular thing with her, then their marriage is what needs to be worked over, not me. So why are you stuck down here getting all sweaty and tired over something that was obviously not my fault? It's not fair to either of us."

Whether or not the hired muscle sympathized with him was anyone's guess, but he was certainly going to do his job, whatever his personal opinions might have been.

Another punch to the gut left Bud retching in pain. There was no point in laying on more blows until he had regained his composure, though, so the meaty-fisted man took a step back and poured himself a glass of water while he waited for the captive to recover his composure once again.

Bud was no stranger to fights, and this was in no way the first, nor would it be the last, time he would be on the receiving end of an angry fist. But torture was still something he did his best to avoid.

Bar brawls and the like were one thing. This was something far less common. And he was not amused.

"Really, can't we work something out?" he said as he regained the ability to speak. "I'm a trader. Surely there's something you must want. I've got my fingers in a lot of things."

"Like the boss's wife," he replied, another punch smacking off of Bud's face.

It sucked, being beaten like this. But Bud had to console himself that at least this was a good old-fashioned ass kicking with fists rather than some cruel torture with all manner of nasty spells. Now *those* were the worst.

The poor pilot was preparing himself for the next round of blows when he was granted a most welcome reprieve. A rather buxom and quite tall serving wench in a flowing gown and rather heavy makeup carried a tray of refreshments into the room.

"I was sent to bring you something to eat, and a bit of chilled Azlip juice. Beating a prisoner can be thirsty work, after all."

Uzabud turned to look at the visitor as best he could from his poor vantage point tied to a chair. Something about her voice was familiar. But with all the beating and whatnot, his senses were a little bit foggy at the moment. The way she was positioned, he couldn't get a good look, though he did see a small pile of tempting food, and some frosty cold refreshments.

"I have water enough for my needs," the man said, grabbing a snack from the tray. "But I *will* take you up on one of those pastries."

He downed the first in a few large bites, smacking his lips as he ate. Bud hated loud eaters, but wisely kept his mouth shut.

"Not bad," the large man said, taking another and shoving it in his food hole with gusto.

Again with the awful noises. Bud almost wished he would start beating him again, just to make the sound stop.

"Are you sure you wouldn't like some of this nice, refreshing Azlip juice? It really is a fantastic palate cleanser, and it does wonders for your libido."

Bud cocked his head. He'd never heard *that* about Azlip juice.

"Nah, I'm fine with my water," the man said.

"Well, that's a pity," the serving wench replied, then threw a vicious punch to the man's throat.

He coughed and sputtered, gagging from the blow, unable to call for help, and likewise unable to cast a single defensive spell. Without the ability to form the words, no matter how practiced he was with a spell, it simply would not work.

The tray rang out a loud gong as it met the side of the man's head, dropping him to the ground in a crumpled heap. Bud watched in amazement as the woman then crouched and gagged the unconscious man, then quickly bound his hands and feet.

"You should have taken the juice," the woman said, now in a much deeper voice.

A voice Uzabud knew well.

"Laskar?"

"Hey, Bud," his copilot said as he set to work untying his friend.

"Took you long enough. And what the hell are you wearing?"

"A disguise, dumb ass. And if you hadn't gone and gotten yourself thrown in the deepest cell in the place, I wouldn't have had to pull this together and it all would have gone a lot faster. You really pissed that guy off, didn't you? What did we say about the man running things on this planet?"

"Steer clear. I know."

"And yet, here we are. Not cool, Bud."

"But did you see her? I mean, come on, man."

"And you knew full well she was married to the most feared man in the system, yet you just had to go and––"

"Oh, give me a break. You know you would have if you had the chance," Bud interrupted with a pained smile as he rubbed his rope-bruised wrists. "She just had eyes for me, is all."

Laskar relented and shared the grin. "Well, maybe. But that's not the point," he said as the bindings around Bud's ankles came free.

Uzabud rose to his feet, wincing in pain and clutching his side as he stood.

"Oof, I think he may have broken a rib."

"We can get it fixed once we're out of here and far, far away from this system."

"Yeah, right. Uh, Laskar?"

"Yeah, Bud?"

"About that. It looked like this place was pretty well guarded when they brought me in. Exactly how many more guards do we have to deal with out there?"

"Oh, so *now* you care about the odds."

"How many?"

The horribly disguised man hesitated a moment. "Seventeen," he finally said.

"Shit."

"Sixteen, if you don't count this guy," he said, nudging the man at his feet.

"Oh, now I feel so much better. *Those* odds are a cake walk," Bud grumbled. "Man, we are so screwed."

Laskar pulled a pack from beneath his flowing gown and tossed it to his friend. "No, it's okay," he said with a ridiculous grin. "I have a *plan*."

CHAPTER TWELVE

"You call this a plan?" Bud grumbled as he adjusted the enormous fake breasts Laskar had hastily fashioned to fill out the pilot's gown. "This is ridiculous. No one will buy it."

"They will. I got in, didn't I?"

"Yes, but you were coming *in*, not trying to go *out*. And you were carrying food. Everyone is nicer to people with food."

"I'm telling you, it'll work. Now, come on, hold still. I've almost got it."

The two men had moved the downed goon from the floor to the chair his former target had been tied to. Now it was his turn, though not for a pummeling. Though Bud might have been tempted to land more than just the punch or two he meted out on the man as he began to rouse, they simply didn't have the time for proper retribution.

And, truth be told, Bud really didn't hold it against the guy. He wasn't kidding when he said he was just doing his job. And with a boss like his, it was best to not ask too many questions.

Of course, being found trussed up in his own torture cell would not go over well. Bud punched him once more, reasoning the additional bruising now might spare him a worse fate later.

He wanted the man hurt, sure, but not dead. That would have been a bit much for something as relatively benign as this had been. Yes, the beating had sucked, but he'd suffered worse in his day.

That is, unless that eventual fate was on the menu for him had he stayed a captive. Then he might have considered something a bit more Draconian. But without proof of that, he was not going to add cold-blooded murder to his long list of criminal history.

In any case, the goon needed to be restrained, and the chair did provide a convenient, secure means of keeping him from raising a ruckus. And if there were some sounds of struggle that happened to make their way out of the chamber, it would appear as if it was just another beating underway. Nothing to see here. Move along.

Laskar adjusted the false bosom within Bud's dress one more time, then stepped back to admire his handiwork, like a painter assessing their masterpiece. He stared a long moment, then gave a satisfied nod.

"Oh yeah. That's perfect."

Bud hefted the bulges filling out his gown. "Did you need to make them so big? This is ridiculous. They don't even look real."

"They look real enough. Trust me, I've seen my fair share."

"Are you bragging? During a rescue?"

"Not bragging," Laskar said defensively. "Just stating the facts."

"You're ridiculous, you know that?"

"Ridiculously *amazing*, you mean. Admit it, I'm a most impressive man."

Bud sighed. Laskar had been a rather insufferable egoist as long as he'd known him, and now it looked like there would be a new cockiness feather added to that cap.

"Come on. We've got an amazing and death-defying escape to complete," Laskar said, moving for the door.

He opened it and peered out into the hallway. There were three guards there, and all of them pretty big. But he and Bud had one thing they didn't. They had a serving tray.

Oh, and the element of *surprise*. That too.

"Hey, give me a hand in here," Laskar called out in the gruffest voice he could manage.

"He didn't sound like that," Bud hissed.

"Now you tell me."

"You didn't say you were going to be doing a shit impression of this guy," Bud shot back, hurrying into position on the other side of the door. "Oh, hell. Give me that," he said, snatching the tray from the man's hands.

"What is it?" the nearest hallway guard said as he stepped inside the room.

His eyes had just fallen on his bound associate when the metal tray rang out against his head. But this one had a thicker skull than the other, and he only fell to one knee. He was down, yes, but not out.

"Shit! Close the door!" Bud said in an urgent whisper.

Laskar quickly closed it, hoping it would muffle at least some of the sounds of Bud bashing the stunned man repeatedly with the serving tray. Finally, a half dozen blows and one dented tray later, the guard was unconscious. Bud quickly bound his wrists and ankles and placed a gag in his mouth, then dragged him across the room, stashing the slumbering man where he wouldn't be seen by any stepping through the doorway.

"Anyone hear that?" Bud asked.

Laskar peeked out of the door. Apparently, the room possessed some sound-deadening spells, given its use as an occasional torture chamber.

"They're just standing there. No one heard a thing," he replied. "Hey, come here a second."

"What is it?" Bud asked as he walked back to the door.

"You're lopsided," Laskar said, then grabbed the enormous

fake boobs and shifted them back into alignment. "There, that's better."

"If we survive this, I swear, we tell no one."

"Are you kidding? This is arguably my best plan yet."

"Exactly my point. So now what, Mr. Best Plan Yet?"

"Now we take out the rest of them, make our way to the main bar, flirt with some swarthy mercenary types, then effect our escape right out the front door."

"You make it sound so simple. We're going to wind up in a massive brawl, aren't we?"

"Oh, ye of little faith," Laskar replied with an overconfident laugh. "Now, come on. We've got an escape to make."

The bar fight wasn't exactly epic in its magnitude or violence, but the sheer destruction being wrought was quite impressive nonetheless. The two women who had been at the center of its outbreak had been rather homely, their faces overdone with makeup and their feminine walk in need of a more womanly sway.

But the men paying them great attention hadn't been staring at those. They'd paid far more interest to the enormous bosoms hiding within their gowns, and, like a present sitting before a child, they had not wanted to wait for drinks and sweet talk to unwrap them.

The taller of the two had slapped one of the men with surprising force. In fact, she nearly knocked him out with her open palm. But while that had given the man a momentary pause, those watching her found that display of spicy fire in her blood most delectable. In no time, a half dozen other suitors had joined the hunt.

Things quickly devolved into an all-out bar brawl, complete with tables through windows and chairs broken over men's heads. And that was saying something, for the furnishings of the establishment were quite robust, specifically in case of such an incident.

A tumbling sea of fighting men blowing off steam churned from the inside of the tavern to the street outside. And there, more joined in the fun. And for this particular group of men of action, *this* was fun.

Fists and feet flew, a violent froth whipping out from the whirling mass of combatants that occasionally connected with one of the amused bystanders. Of course, that would, more often than not, turn that bystander into a participant, and their friends, too, would join into the fray.

"Is this what you call a quiet exit?" Bud asked Laskar as he struggled free from an amorous drunkard who was so focused on his chest that he'd failed to notice the objects of his interest had shifted to the entirely wrong place.

"Hey, it's working, isn't it?" Laskar replied, dropping the groping letch with a quick punch to the corner of his jaw. "I do think we need to get to the ship as soon as we can, though."

"Oh? Why the sudden interest in doing the logical?"

"No reason," Laskar said, motioning down the street.

It was difficult to see at first amidst all of the fighting, but then the shapes became clear.

"Shit. Council goons. And here, of all places," Bud realized. "I thought our vacation was going to be far away from them."

"So did I. But I guess they've got their hooks into this world too," Laskar mused.

"Okay, fun and games are over. We *really* need to get out of here, and I mean *now*," Bud said as he watched the riot-armored Tslavar heavies wade into the fray, stunning combatants with cudgels, fists, and even stun spells.

Yes, it was *definitely* time to go, lest they wind up going from one man's basement torture chamber to a Council prison cell.

Bud and Laskar pulled the remainder of their disguises free

and left them in a pile on the street, where they would be trampled into a dirty mess by the riled-up crowd.

Dodging punches, kicks, and even some outstretched tentacles from one of the downed patrons, their suckers grasping at any who ventured close enough to be snared, the two pushed for the edge of the boiling sea of combatants.

After far too long for either of their taste, they were free.

Leaving the raucous crowd behind them, the pair took off at a full run and did not stop until they were safely aboard Uzabud's mothership.

"Hang on. This is going to be a little bumpy," Bud said as he slammed the hidden Drookonus in place, powering the ship with its Drook magic and jumping it into the sky.

It was an abrupt way to take off, but given the Council's presence, he thought it prudent. Laskar, for all of his ridiculous talk, was at his copilot's seat plotting a jump as soon as they had entered the ship. In most things he could be quite a loud-mouthed fuckup, but when it came to flying, he was a seasoned pro.

"Talk to me, Laskar. We have a jump course?"

"Ten seconds," he replied.

Bud noticed a Council ship was approaching fast from the distance. It was likely coming to help quell the trouble, but he really didn't want to stick around to test that theory.

"Laskar? We've got company."

"Just a few more seconds."

"We may not have a few more—"

"Got it!" he blurted.

Uzabud did not wait a moment longer, engaging their jump spell before they'd even cleared atmosphere, though the practice was frowned upon. But that wasn't his concern. Freedom was. And with his obnoxious partner's help, they were free indeed. Free, and getting as far away from this entire system as they could.

CHAPTER THIRTEEN

The Wampeh Ghalian assassin's shimmer-cloaked ship floated invisibly in the frozen stillness of space. It revealed no lights, emitted no skree transmissions, and left no trace of itself whatsoever.

Unless someone were to happen to fly directly into it, the craft would never be noticed.

It had been there for hours, quietly watching the comings and goings in and out of the atmosphere of the planet below. Craft arrived and departed on a regular basis, but as of yet, no Council ships had made an appearance. Nor had any over the last day and a half the system had been under surveillance.

Hozark and Demelza were not bored, however. The pair were well trained, and on a mission, and patience was most certainly a Ghalian strong suit. It was one of the many traits that made them the greatest assassins in the galaxy.

They had arrived in the system under cover of a fully engaged shimmer cloak, exiting their jump at the very outskirts of the solar system. Though this ship remained invisible the whole time, shimmers so large as would hide a ship of this size did not typically work in outer space.

It was believed that it had something to do with the way the vacuum of space reacted with the magic, though none had ever discerned precisely why. But with the talents of not one, but two Ghalian helping feed the spells required to maintain the cloak even in the void, the camouflage remained solidly in place, hiding them from all eyes, even as they flew closer to the edge of the atmosphere.

"Anything?" Hozark asked calmly from his pilot's seat.

Demelza checked her spells once more, reaching out and testing the strings of magic she had cast out into the space around them.

"Nothing," she replied. "We appear to be alone."

Hozark pondered a moment. "We shall stay a while longer, yet," he decided.

"Understood," she replied, then settled back into her routine, gently casting trailing spells to tickle any nearby magic, then reeling them back in, searching for a hit.

So far, however, she had come up empty every time as they made headway on their creeping flight.

Their final approach had been a gradual one, even though their destination was clear as soon as they had arrived, a tiny dot far out in front of them many planets closer to the sun.

But they would not rush this. *Could* not rush this. They simply had no other choice, despite the request coming from one as trusted as Master Orkut.

The search for hostile vessels hiding out in the low gravity of any one of the system's moons, or perhaps in orbit around one of the less-populated worlds, was a necessity, not a luxury. After what had happened to Master Prombatz so recently, it was something all Ghalian were doing when entering into a new contract.

The means by which Master Prombatz and his poor aspiring Ghalian student were ambushed, the pair caught entirely by surprise by a Council hit squad, were now known to the order.

And with that in mind great lengths had been gone to in order to ensure such a thing would not occur again in the future. But it had been a costly learning experience.

Aargun, the youth who had been captured, would never be the same again, and his was now a cautionary tale burned into the mind of every Ghalian brother and sister in the galaxy.

Vengeance had been taken, however. Master Hozark and his friends had tracked down the sender of that first contract and ended his life. Visla Torund, was his name. And he was a member of the Council of Twenty. But even as he fell, another rose.

Visla Ravik was his name, and even with Master Corann's considerable power, as well as her dangerous use of a claithe—one of the rarest of magical weapons, and one even a master Ghalian would never use unless absolutely necessary—he had managed to escape. An escape he made along with his most unusual of bodyguards.

Samara.

Hozark and the others had slain almost all present that day, but not her. She had fought Demelza to an easy standstill while her visla attempted to end her former lover and their mutual friend.

But Corann's claithe proved too strong, and with Demelza distracting Samara from the visla's plight with some surprisingly sound swordplay, Hozark had managed to get close enough to drive his vespus blade through the man's chest, draining him of much of his power before the light in his eyes flickered and went dim.

Chaos had ensued in the aftermath, and Samara and her new visla had managed to escape in the confusion. But something strange had come out of the whole ordeal. A new name would be added to the list of fingers pulling strings. Another man behind the curtain, though this one was a shock to all who heard his name.

Visla Maktan.

The man wasn't exactly foppish, but as far as members of the Council of Twenty went, he had seemed about as benign as one could ever be. A powerful visla, no doubt, but also one seemingly absent the bloodthirst and craving for power that his counterparts possessed in such large amounts.

And yet his name had been the dying words of a slain emmik on the day of that terrible battle. Spoken, but the man was nowhere to be seen. He had slain his victim, leaving him to die in Laskar's arms before he could say another word. The man was slippery, and apparently far more of a threat than any had realized.

The Ghalian faithful paid special attention to his activities from that point forward, their spies monitoring as much as they could of the man's movements. But he was a visla of substantial magic, and no simple disguise would allow any of them to get near him on short notice. Thus, a rapid infiltration to gather more intelligence had been an impossibility.

And now there was some new mystery afoot. Something that had brought Hozark and Demelza together once more. A mission at the request of Master Orkut himself. For the swordsmith to ask such a thing, knowing full well it would put him in their debt, meant it had to be something serious.

It also meant the man they were going to meet was someone of considerable power. But exactly what kind of power was anyone's guess.

They'd scanned and surveyed, watched and waited, for well over a day and a half before Hozark finally felt there were no threats lurking in the stars. There might be some nasty surprises waiting for them down below, but out in space, at least, they were clear.

"What do you say, Demelza? Shall we head down and meet this mystery employer our mutual friend so wished for us to help?"

She took one final read of her magical survey spells. All were still absolutely clear of any Council ships.

"I believe we are as safe now as we will ever be," she replied. "It is clearly not a trap. At least, not from space."

The master Ghalian nodded his agreement. "Then it is decided," Hozark said, setting a course for atmospheric entry. "Let us go and make our new friend's acquaintance."

CHAPTER FOURTEEN

Hozark's approach to their contact's location was a master class in Ghalian stealth. He eased the ship through the outermost shell of the exosphere, making sure to do so at such an angle and speed that he generated the absolute minimum amount of heat possible, keeping their craft invisible.

The spells he poured on top of that deft flying were the icing on the stealth cake, ensuring an utterly smooth, and totally unseen, arrival within the world's atmosphere.

Once within its confines, he then gradually released the additional spells and focused on their approach.

The ship flew slowly. Painfully slow for any non-Ghalian who would have been with them. But for the patient killers, this was the way. The only way.

By the time they arrived at the luxurious estate tower, they'd not only avoided any observation from the air or below, but they had also enjoyed enough time to fully examine their surroundings as they descended. So far as their expert eyes could tell, this was not a trap.

"Not many ships in the landing site near the estate," Hozark noted.

"Surprising for such a wealthy area," Demelza said. "These are rather elite towers, though I see the one we are to meet our client at appears to be both the tallest, and the most luxurious. A lot of coin went into that."

"And a lot of magic," Hozark added, nodding to the multiple floating gardens under construction.

One, however, was complete, and serenely hovering just next to the uppermost floors.

"I will set us down over there," Hozark said, then took them into a gradual descent until the shimmer ship was hovering just above the surface of the garden.

The two assassins pulled their personal shimmer cloaks about themselves and stepped out of the ship. A pair of invisible killers leaving an invisible transport, and all without any being the wiser. Carefully, they moved toward the estate itself, sensing for traps and wards with their magic.

Both Hozark and Demelza had fed on power users not too long ago, and both still possessed fairly significant amounts of residual magic within them. They were both using their konuses, however, keeping the internal stores as an emergency backup, just in case.

You never knew what might be waiting for you inside a strange new estate, for example.

With utter silence, the pair entered the building, easily bypassing a tripwire alarm spell and closing the warded door behind them, leaving everything exactly as it was. They started walking, taking note of the telltale signs of a fierce battle as they moved.

The property had been cleansed and scrubbed, a great deal of magic used in the process to remove all traces of blood and gore. But they were trained killers, and not all clues had been so thoroughly washed clean.

A speck of blood here, a chipped wall there. A heavy table whose legs had been repaired by a master craftsman, but one who couldn't entirely hide the damage done to it in the conflict.

Whatever had happened here, it was a battle to the death, and that was something both were certain there had been a lot of.

On they crept, moving farther into the building. They were to meet the mystery man or woman in the study at the end of the hall. And luck was on their side. The door was open.

The shimmer-cloaked assassins padded through the doorway in utter silence and surveyed the room. It was tastefully decorated, heavy furniture carefully placed, but not to a degree that suggested an overt display of wealth. The art, likewise, was not on display to impress, but, rather, for the enjoyment of the owner.

Apparently, the client was a person of taste.

"Thank you for coming," a voice said, carrying across the room with an energy all its own.

Hozark and Demelza turned silently. Both were still completely hidden by their shimmer cloaks, yet the man seated at his desk had seen them, and with little effort, apparently.

A visla, no doubt. And an immensely powerful one at that, judging by the ease with which he'd just spotted the pair.

And yet, this man was not a member of the Council of Twenty. In fact, this was someone neither had ever heard of. It was quickly becoming apparent, that the reason for that was because the man wanted it that way, not by any oversight of their own.

Hozark removed his shimmer, joined by Demelza a moment later.

"I am Hozark. This is Demelza," the Wampeh master greeted the man. "Master Orkut requested we visit you with great haste, and we have come as quickly as we were able."

The man nodded, and as Hozark and Demelza walked closer, the barely hidden distress just beneath his cool façade became apparent. He was upset, and from what they could tell, just barely holding it together.

"I am Visla Dinarius Jinnik," he said, his puffy eyes lingering on each of them, as if assessing their worth.

It was a name neither knew. Of course, there were hundreds of inhabited systems in the galaxy, containing thousands of worlds. It was only natural they might not have heard of him. Though with the amount of power he possessed, it was notable in its unlikeliness.

"It appears there was quite a fight here recently," Hozark said, his eyes casually gauging the man.

"Yes. Quite a fight, indeed," Visla Jinnik replied, picking up a child's toy from his desk, staring at it with a sad look.

A slight crackling of magic formed around his body. A static discharge of power that was seeping out of him entirely of its own accord.

Hozark cast an imperceptible glance Demelza's way. She'd seen it too. Now *this* was something new. A massively powerful magic user with a potentially catastrophic overflow problem. He dreaded the thought of what might happen when the man became truly upset and his self-control failed.

Another thought flashed through the Wampeh's mind. A power user with this sort of problem had likely experienced a few difficulties from it over the years. But what if there was a way to help control it? To reduce the overflow.

Of course, Hozark also doubted the man would entertain the idea of being slightly drained by a Wampeh Ghalian from time to time in order to keep it in check, but perhaps he would. In any case, this was definitely not the time to broach the subject.

With his power, it seemed unusual the man would have gone to such lengths to contract the Wampeh Ghalian to do his dirty work. In fact, given the barely contained anger clearly bubbling within him, Hozark thought perhaps a little bit of violent payback was precisely what this man needed.

They had invaded and defiled his home and loved ones in a most heinous manner. Turning them to a bloody pulp would be a cathartic release.

But his was not to question the man's decisions, only to do as Master Orkut had asked of him. He moved closer to the visla, staring him straight in the eye with the calm confidence of his kind.

"Master Orkut trusts you, Visla Jinnik. And we trust him," he said. "He sent us to find you, and we have come. So, tell us. Whom do you wish eliminated?"

Visla Jinnik pushed his seat back and straightened his back, the slouch of days of grieving forced from his body with every cracking vertebrae.

"Eliminated? Oh, my dear Ghalian, that's not what I'm hiring you for," he said with an almost amused look. "Nothing so pedestrian."

"What is it that you require of us, then?"

"I want you to find my son, Master Hozark. I want you to find Happizano and rescue him from the Council of Twenty."

CHAPTER FIFTEEN

The Wampeh Ghalian did *not* take sides in wars, and it was beginning to feel like one was brewing. They also most certainly did not perform rescue operations for kidnapped children, but here they were, helping a powerful visla whose enemy was a common one, it seemed.

"Most unusual," Hozark said as he and Demelza slipped into their shimmer cloaks and made their way onto the floating garden beside Visla Jinnik's home.

While Jinnik had been aware of their arrival, it was still important no one else learned of it. Vital, in fact, for if the Council of Twenty was truly holding his son as he described, it was all but certain they had agents observing the visla round the clock.

"Most unusual indeed," Demelza agreed as they stepped out onto the fecund soil of the magically supported gardens. "If what he says is true, then it would seem the Council is going to great lengths to acquire his powers to their side."

"But to what end? That is a disturbing element to all of this. There is no open warfare between the Council and any others at present, yet they go to this extreme to persuade the man to bring his considerable power to their side."

"And from what he said, his family has always remained independent of the Council, much as Visla Balamar had been for so very long."

"Yes," Hozark said. "But in this case, with a far less destructive conflict between them. Jinnik lost a tower full of men and a child. Balamar lost an entire estate, city, the lands surrounding it, and all the residents within. Jinnik should consider himself fortunate his is not a quarrel of that intensity."

"But he lost his only son. The lone heir to his bloodline. The boy seems to mean everything to him."

"Indeed. He is the only link remaining to the woman he loved, and for that, he cherishes him even more. I feel it is almost fortunate his wife passed so many years ago. I would wager the Council would have left her remains behind as an incentive otherwise. The child is the leverage they seek. And it would seem he is going to have to play their game, at least for now, while we remove their leverage from the equation."

"Agreed," Demelza said as they reached their cloaked ship and stepped into its waiting safety. "So, we are on a rescue mission, it would seem. How novel."

"We did rescue Laskar not too long ago," Hozark noted.

"Yes, but that was for Uzabud. And Laskar is part of our team. But this? This is something different," she said, shedding her shimmer cloak and taking her customary seat. "So, where do we begin, Master Hozark?"

"Begin? Why, right here, of course."

The ship entering the atmosphere was clearly visible to any who cared to observe it, just as its landing at the facility near the visla's estate was likewise plain to see for all.

The tall man and his womanly companion who exited

seemed to be just another couple come to visit for a shopping excursion in the well-to-do city, nothing more.

It was a disguise without a disguise. Hozark and Demelza even went so far as to not even shift their skin tones to hide their Wampeh nature. On this planet, there was a fairly large Wampeh population, and all but the most nefarious of sorts simply took them as another pair.

Why would a normal person have reason to fear a Ghalian attack, after all? And besides, those kinds of Wampeh were incredibly rare. And if you did happen to see an actual Wampeh Ghalian, odds were, it was too late anyway.

Hozark and Demelza had flown a fair distance away, fully cloaked and invisible, then made their arrival in full view, returning to the scene of the crime yet again, but this time visible to all.

The ersatz couple landed and exited their ship with the seemingly oblivious wonder so many had on their first visit to the city's shopping area. The towering estates of the wealthy were something of a novelty, as most upper class tended to possess more sprawling parcels on other worlds.

Here, in this dense city, however, vertical was the way to go. The natural layout with nearby hills and rocky crags had formed a cradle of sorts that simply led to that type of development. The two smiled and gawked a bit, then set off into the city to see whatever sights caught their eye.

The path the two assassins took was a carefully planned one, yet one that seemed utterly natural. Every shop, cafe, or street vendor they stopped and lingered at longer than normal also had a strategic position. One that would have allowed them to see at least some aspect of the conflict at the visla's tower nearby.

Talk of the city, its beautiful region, and unusual architecture inevitably led to a curious query about the tallest of the buildings in sight.

"Oh, that would be Visla Jinnik's," they would be told.

"He must be a very powerful man to possess such an estate," was Demelza's usual follow up. "I noticed some work being done to it when we were strolling past it earlier. Is the family doing renovations? I bet it will be magnificent when they're done."

At that prompt, most related the same story, or a variant thereof as seen from their particular vantage point. A group of unmarked ships had dropped down to the landing area right outside the building and attacked it. They must have been robbers looking to plunder the estate while the visla wasn't home.

"Oh? That was good luck on their part," Hozark would interject with faux shock as he urged them to share more information.

"It really was. If the visla had been home, there's no telling what he might have done to them."

"So, he's a violent man?"

"Not at all. A very peaceful one, in fact. But his power can be a bit erratic. It was the same with his father. And if he gets riled up, well, sometimes accidents do happen."

Everyone had shared that information as well, in one way or another. The visla was, it seemed, more or less the man they'd taken him to be on their first meeting. But these people knew him, and his family, and that sort of unguarded intel was far more useful than any first impressions.

What they also learned was that the alleged robbers had attacked the house with overwhelming speed and numbers. It was simply something the guards and staff couldn't defend against.

All day long the couple walked the streets, chatting amicably with locals and gaining useful intel in the process. By the time they'd had a romantic dinner at a restaurant that just happened to look directly at the visla's tower, the picture was quite clear, and their serving staff was more than happy to fill in any gaps in the details for their good-tipping guests.

The two went back to their ship that night, opting to sleep there rather than one of the establishments in the area. They could have, of course, but there was simply no need to draw this out any longer. They had the information they needed.

"Someone knew he was out of the system," Hozark said as they went over what they'd learned within the secure environs of their ship. "From what everyone said, no one would be foolish enough to have attempted this when he was home."

"But his staff appeared loyal. And he said his personal flight crew have been with him for many years. An inside job does not seem terribly likely in this case."

"I agree. It feels much more like something we ourselves experienced so recently," Hozark mused. "When Master Prombatz was ambushed."

"You think the meeting that he was out of the system on was scheduled as a ruse?"

"It is looking quite likely. He often traveled with his son, but this was a visit to a particularly rough world to meet an emmik who wished to discuss the possibility of him helping tame some unrest. It would not have been a trip on which he would have brought his son."

"Indeed. And the boy was home with his tutors when the attack occurred. Right around the time the meeting was taking place, conveniently," Demelza noted. "It would seem this is a highly likely theory."

"Meaning we must speak to this emmik and learn exactly how this meeting came to be called, and at whose request. I fear we may find ourselves not liking the answer. This feels much like the work of Visla Rovnik," Hozark noted.

"Or even Maktan, though I'm sure he has a good alibi, once again."

"The most slippery of them always do."

It was an interesting conundrum. The visla had been pressured by the Council for a long time to join them. In fact, they had even courted him to even be one of the Twenty one day when a spot opened up, though that had undoubtedly angered the aspiring power users waiting in the wings with their claws sharp and knives out for their opportunity to seize that prize.

But he had declined. So they sought to convince him to at least lend his considerable power to their causes. And, yet, he had still steered clear of their machinations. He had no issues with them, but he also had no desire to become embroiled in their affairs.

And his son had just turned eleven. Just about the age his powers should be starting to truly manifest. This was an important time for the father and son to bond and spend time with one another

Yes, there were tutors, but they could only do so much. The rest, the elder Jinnik would teach his boy. How to best manage his budding power, as well as the finer points of spellcasting, just as his father had done for him.

And now the Council had taken the boy. Taken him and left a note in his place. The visla would be called upon from time to time to do a service for the Council. To lend his power to their causes. And in exchange, the boy would remain unharmed. But the question remained. Was this the Council as a whole, or was it Rovnik or Maktan manipulating from behind the scenes?

It didn't matter to the boy's father. Surely a demand would arrive at some point, and he would do what his son's kidnappers wished, for now, anything to keep the boy alive. But as he did, his Wampeh agents would be hard at work, finding his son and rescuing him.

And when he was free and safely back at his father's side where he belonged, Ravik, the Council, or whoever was ultimately responsible, would be made to regret what they had done.

CHAPTER SIXTEEN

Groll. It was a shitty name for a shitty planet, and it suited the place perfectly. Hozark and Demelza had barely taken a step off their ship before realizing precisely why Visla Jinnik had been lured to this particular place.

It was distracting.

It was filthy.

It was dangerous.

But looking around at the bustling crowds and active landing areas, something else was also clear. This place had potential. Not as a lovely place to live or vacation. Not by a long shot. But a commerce hub? Oh yes, it could serve that purpose admirably. Because Groll, shitty as it was, happened to be ideally situated between an unusually large number of commerce worlds and fabrication moons.

For one such as Jinnik, it would have been a tempting project, and one that would not only allow him to flex his magical muscle a bit, but also significantly expand his family's wealth and holdings in the process.

In fact, the more they looked around the capital city, the

more Hozark was of the opinion that the meeting could even have been legit.

But one thing caught his attention. Namely, that despite his initial impressions, and the somewhat filthy degree of apparent disarray surrounding them, Groll actually seemed to be working well in precisely that commercial and industrial capacity.

Judging by the manner and number of craft coming and going with regularity, and the bustling commerce of the open markets, the place really didn't *need* the attentions of a visla, let alone one of Jinnik's power.

"A diversion," Hozark said, confirming their initial thoughts.

Demelza nodded. "I would tend to agree. This place is a bit of a dump, no doubt, but a dump that appears to be functioning quite well as a commerce hub, albeit one that is admittedly also something of a mess."

"So, Jinnik was definitely lured here to leave his estate unguarded," Hozark said. "Most interesting. Let us go and visit Emmik Ozman and see what she has to tell us of their meeting. And more importantly, who it was that coerced her to offer up a portion of her thriving, and undoubtedly lucrative, business to Visla Jinnik."

Emmik Ozman was a stout, gray-skinned woman with a particularly strong set of flexible appendages upon which she ambulated, and an equally robust but longer group of them on her tubular upper body. Not tentacles, though. More like the multi-jointed structure of a tail, only prehensile, capable of carrying her about in a rippling wave, as well as manipulating items around her.

The two assassins found her holding court within a squat but rather ornate building. A government office of some sort, it appeared. They quietly entered and asked for Emmik Ozman's whereabouts. Everyone knew her in this place, so locating her was quite easy and directions were forthcoming.

They made their way to the main chambers, where she was presiding over a small group of traders. By the sound of it, they were having a minor squabble regarding the overlapping territories in which they were vending their wares. It was a heated discussion, no doubt, but all deferred to the emmik's authority. Likely a good thing, judging by the magic they felt wafting off of her.

She might have only been an emmik, but she was a strong one. And those individuals quarreling were non-powered to a one, each relying on a konus for their minor casting abilities. Had she so desired, she could have likely struck down the lot of them with just a few well-placed spells.

But she was diplomatic in her role as overseer of this place, and that meant *not* smiting anyone who rubbed you the wrong way. Things tended to go poorly when that was one's policy.

The confab was not a terribly lengthy one, but it did drag on a bit longer than either of the Wampeh would have liked. But there was little they could do to speed things along, and this was definitely a time for casual subtlety rather than brash motivation.

At long last the group had come to an understanding of a sort and disbanded, each feeling equally screwed by the deal. A sign of everyone being treated the same, in Ozman's book. That was the nature of compromise. You're all screwed a bit. Deal with it and carry on.

"Who the hell are you two?" she asked, walking over to the two who had been quietly observing the proceedings for so long. "I've never seen you around here."

"Ah, yes. We are associates of Visla Jinnik," Hozark replied. "He asked us to do a little followup with you, if you don't mind."

"Jinnik, you say?" she asked, an eyebrow askew. "Pull the other one––I know there's no way you're with that one."

This was a bit surprising. They'd expected at least a modicum of cooperation from the woman, but all they were getting was irritated pushback.

"Why would you say that?" Demelza asked sweetly.

"Oh, you can stop with the bullshit niceties, sweetheart. That crap won't work on me. And besides, I already told that shit clown to take his greedy plan and shove it."

"I-I'm sorry, perhaps we're operating on the wrong footing here. I understood it that you *invited* the visla to meet with you to discuss his possible involvement in furthering the commerce of your world."

"Oh, I invited him all right. But that's all I had to do. Invite him. You think I would actually let anyone dig their claws into my hard work? Not likely. I built this up from nothing, and no way I'm letting some high-falootin' rich kid snob slide up in here and sink his teeth into my precious. No way, no how."

"I must not understand this correctly. We were simply to gather further information on the trade numbers, you see. But if we're mistaken—"

"Oh, you're mistaken, all right."

Hozark stepped in, putting on his best concerned accountant face. "This won't go over well with the actuaries. Not at all," he groaned with faux concern. "Why in the world would you have invited him all the way out here if you weren't serious about the opportunity?"

At that, Ozman laughed. "Because even I have to be careful where the Council of Twenty is involved. They leave me alone, for the most part, but they still take their pound of flesh. And when they say jump, unfortunately, we all have to ask how high."

"The Council? I thought this meeting was your idea," Hozark pressed.

"Mine? Oh, you sweet, ignorant man. The only reason I

contacted Jinnik was because I was asked to. Well, *told* to, more like it."

"Told? But who told you to do such a thing? You seem quite in control of your affairs."

"I don't know who was behind it. All I got was a simple little note on Council parchment, in an envelope with a Council seal. One of those godsdamned anonymous validity seals any of them could have sent. But the seal was legit, and I know better than to poke at that slumbering giant. They wanted me to talk to the visla? Fine, I'll talk to the visla. But nowhere did it say I had to do business with him."

"Who delivered it to you?"

"I didn't see. It was just waiting for me on my desk."

Hozark glanced at his associate. "Well, then. It would appear we have had our time wasted with this pointless voyage. Come, we may as well leave this place. There is obviously nothing more for us here."

Demelza nodded and followed him out of the building into the streets.

"Don't let the door hit ya on the way out," the boisterous woman called after them.

"This is all too familiar," Hozark said when they were a block away. "Mysterious, anonymous Council notes? It is like what we found in Emmik Drazzix's papers."

"Though that man had been killed. Drained, no less. Do you think Samara might have been involved?"

"There's no telling," Hozark replied. "It is one of the infuriating aspects of those seals. Any member of the Council can utilize one. And for precisely this reason. Plausible deniability. *Someone* sent that letter with an official seal, but there's simply no way to determine who it was, and it will be a tough road to follow in our efforts to track them down."

"But there will be a trail. No matter how difficult to find, we will eventually succeed."

"I sincerely hope so," he agreed. "By the way, I assume you have noticed the heavily bundled individual following us."

"Of course. They have been with us since we left the emmik's presence," Demelza replied.

"Indeed," Hozark said, then changed direction, heading, not toward their waiting ship, but into a winding, dark alleyway.

Demelza followed close behind, the two disappearing down the twists and turns. Hurried footsteps softly echoed off the alley walls as their pursuer increased their pace to keep up.

"Hello, friend," Hozark said menacingly, bodily slamming the person against the alley wall, holding them aloft.

Their feet were off the ground, and a bit too easily for their bulk, he noted. Their pursuer seemed to be more clothing than person. He pulled back their headwrap, revealing not a man, but a woman with pale violet hair and pinkish skin.

It was her eyes, though, that truly caught his attention. Demelza saw them as well. Sparkling eyes that caught the light and reflected as if they had galaxies trapped within them.

It was an unusual trait, supposedly of exceedingly rare magic. One they had both only ever heard old wives tales about but never actually seen in person. However, this scrappy young woman didn't seem to have a clue as to how to manage her power. In fact, judging by the way she squirmed and struggled, but without calling upon that magic, it was quite possible she was unaware she possessed any at all.

Hozark and Demelza shared a curious look. This was not what they had been expecting. But the strange woman had been following them, and had to have a reason.

Hozark slid his fangs into place for effect and flashed an intimidating smile.

"Let us have a little talk, shall we?" he said, then hauled her off in a rush, headed for the darkest part of the alley, where they would be certain to not be disturbed.

CHAPTER SEVENTEEN

"Take your hands off of me! I'll gouge your eyes out!" the slender woman threatened, squirming in Hozark's solid grip.

Her hands, however, merely grasped at his forearms, refraining from any attempts at his eyes or face. As agitated as she was, even she realized tearing into a Wampeh Ghalian was *not* a good idea.

"You really should calm down," Demelza said, stepping close to her comrade and the woman he held aloft, pinned to the wall. "You will find that cooperation will lead to a much longer life."

"You threatening me?" the young woman spat with a glare that looked as if it could melt flesh. And if she'd actually been in control of her unusual power, who knew? Perhaps she could.

"Merely stating a well-documented fact," Demelza replied with a look of her own. One chilling in its calm certainty.

She then cracked a little smile, her fangs sliding into place as well. The young woman was dealing with not one, but two Wampeh Ghalian, and if that wasn't enough to get her to calm down, who knew what would.

"I'll snap those pointy bits right outta your face hole, you stupid--"

Hozark shoved a cloth in her mouth. Apparently, she was unimpressed by the Ghalian pair.

"Most unusual," he said with an amused chuckle. "I have a strange feeling that this is *not* a Council agent."

Demelza's lips twitched with mirth. "I believe you are entirely correct in that assumption," she replied. "But what do we make of this one? Was she sent to follow us? A spy? And if so, for whom does she work?"

Demelza turned her attention directly at their captive. "Who do you work for?"

Hozark pulled the cloth from her mouth.

"That's disgusting! You have any idea how unsanitary that is? A rag? Really?"

Given her filthy appearance, the objection to a simple strip of cloth was almost comedic in its intensity.

"Answer the question, woman. Who do you work for?" he demanded.

"Woman? My name's Henni, thank you very much."

"Fine. *Henni*, who do you work for? Why were you following us?"

The violet-haired woman hesitated, a flash of uncertainty in her eyes, quickly replaced with cocky bravado.

"I was following you for your coin. Duh. Two shiny-clean types like you? Yeah, you're bound to have a little something for the taking."

Still suspended in the air, she reached into her pocket and took out a small pouch of coin. The same pouch that had been on Hozark's hip when he grabbed her.

"A pickpocket?" he said, taking the pouch from her hand with amusement. "And a good one at that. Did you see that, Demelza? I did not even feel her hands at work."

"Nor did I see them," she replied. "Quite a skilled thief, though admittedly, a rather smelly one."

The two Wampeh shared a look that spoke volumes. It was

clear this street urchin was not a threat. But as a resident of this world, and one who dwelled on the streets near Emmik Ozman's grounds, she might quite possibly have information that would be of use to them.

"Tell me, Henni," Hozark said, handing the pouch of coin back to the thief as he gently lowered her to the ground. "How is it you wound up on the streets like this? You seem to be intelligent enough, and you certainly have skills with your hands."

Henni looked like she might bolt, but the strange man had given her the coin back, and for some reason, she actually felt safe around him and his odd companion. On a whim, she decided to stick around. At least for the time being.

"I'm stuck here," she said, the quickest glimpse of grief flashing across her face. "Just trying to scrape by and come up with enough coin for food."

"You didn't answer the question," Demelza said, noting just how thin the young woman was as she shifted her bundled clothing back into place.

She was malnourished, but not to the point of sickness. Not yet, anyway. But she was certainly not on the Council's payroll. Not living like this.

"I escaped the people who captured me," Henni said, her fingers absentmindedly running across her neck as she spoke.

It was then that the two assassins got a clear look at the burn mark ringing her neck just above her collarbone. A control collar. She had been a slave. And yet, somehow, she had forced the collar off.

Maybe, she could harness her power after all. Or perhaps it had been a fluke. In any case, she had acquired quite a set of burns for the effort.

But she was free, and that mattered above all else.

Wampeh Ghalian as a whole abhorred slavery and often went to great lengths to relocate slaves freed in the course of a contract, providing them safe refuge far from the reach of those who might seek to capture them once more.

Of course, they could not free every slave. The galaxy was run on their power, for one. Drooks for ships, Ootaki and others for powering magical devices and all manner of spells.

But when they could, the Ghalian would save a few. Making a difference one life at a time. It was an unusual dichotomy for an order of elite assassins, and one that would undoubtedly have shocked any who learned of it. But as they dealt with so much death and pain on so regular a basis, life held a particular value for them that others simply could not appreciate.

"You've been on these streets a long time, haven't you?" Hozark asked.

"You could say that."

He studied the skinny, filthy young woman. Looking as she did, *smelling* as she did, she was invisible to most people. Shunned. Avoided. Something beneath even the lowest of the traders and mercenary scum who frequented the markets and brothels.

And for that, she had an advantage. She was camouflaged, in her own way. Something Hozark was quite familiar with.

"Perhaps we got off on the wrong foot," Hozark said. "I am Hozark. This is my friend Demelza. We were just heading to get something to eat. Would you like to join us?"

Henni looked at him with distrust clear in her eyes. She'd had similar offers in the past, especially when she had first taken to the streets when she broke free from her captors.

Demelza and Hozark recognized that wary look in her eyes.

"You have nothing to fear," Demelza said, holding her hands up, her fangs already receded and her smile normal and non-pointy. "Just come join us for some food. I'm sure you could use a hot meal right about now."

Henni's stomach didn't growl loudly. It would have needed to have recently had food in it for that reaction to have occurred.

But the look in her eye spoke louder than rumbling organs could.

"My treat," Demelza said, turning to walk away, trusting the violet-haired girl would follow. "You know anywhere good to eat around here? We're new to the area."

Henni slipped into tour guide mode with startling ease. Something about this strange pair of Wampeh did quite the opposite of scare her. She didn't know why, but they actually put her at ease.

Despite their fangs and initial threats, she knew in her gut they did not mean her harm. It was quite possibly the safest she'd felt in she couldn't even remember how long.

"Yeah, there's a little spot just around the corner and up two streets. Noodles and broth. Filling and cheap, and Bintu, the owner, he's a good man. Doesn't rip you off and give you small portions."

"Then let's go see this Bintu. I know I could really do with a good meal right about now. Couldn't you, Hozark?"

"Oh, yes. That sounds great. And I am sorry I grabbed you so roughly, Henni. You startled me, is all," he said with a warm grin.

"That's okay," she replied, falling in with her new friends.

They walked to the dingy little restaurant and took a nice and secluded table away from other patrons. Not only to put Henni at ease, but also so no one would be able to eavesdrop on their conversation.

"Tell me, Henni. This place has a lot of ships and visitors come and go, right?" Hozark asked as he sipped his bowl of soup, which was, as she had told them, actually quite good.

It seemed those hole-in-the-wall restaurants were the same on all worlds. Secret nooks of quality cooking.

"Yeah, a lot of people come through here," she replied, already on her second bowl.

"Slow down. You'll give yourself an upset stomach," Demelza cautioned as their new friend dug in with gusto.

The conversation turned to the arrivals around Emmik Ozma's place in recent days. Specifically the days prior to Visla Jinnik's receiving the invitation to come speak with the emmik. Henni had indeed been an observant, yet invisible part of the landscape at that time.

And she had seen things.

All that remained to do was figure out what exactly it all meant.

CHAPTER EIGHTEEN

The meal and casual chat with the possibly insane pickpocket had turned from an impromptu little intel dig into a full-fledged information dump.

It seemed that in the process of scraping by and stealing from pretty much anyone she could to survive, Henni had gotten close to a great deal of people, and she had heard a wealth of conversations. All of which she had somehow locked away in that somewhat scrambled noggin of hers.

But all of her oddities aside, the girl was good. *Really* good. And she was observant as hell. It made both Hozark and Demelza wonder what she might be capable of once she managed to recover from the horrors she had undoubtedly lived through in her relatively short life.

"Henni, I have a proposition for you," Hozark said, having already gotten the silent nod of agreement as soon as he had flashed a questioning look to Demelza.

She'd known what he was thinking. Hell, she had been thinking the same thing. This one was something special, and if they could help right her mental ship, she could become a truly great asset.

"I don't do that kind of thing," the young violet-haired woman said, a flareup of the prickliness they'd seen when they first encountered her quickly rising, but leveling off rather than spiking. "Nope. No one can make me. I'll steal, but I'm not for sale."

Demelza could only guess what might have happened to the girl in her enslaved life, and the possibilities that flashed through her mind raised her ire. She quickly moved to smooth over the situation and calm the girl.

"That is not what Hozark meant," she said with a warm smile. "Not at all. We will not let anyone do anything to you, and I hope you understand that I mean that with all sincerity."

Henni looked at the two Wampeh, and her perceptive eyes read the looks reflected in theirs. No, they would not. In fact, these two seemed to already be rather protective of her, though they'd just met her.

How exactly she knew that, having only been in their presence a short while, Henni couldn't say. It was just a thing she did. The reason she agreed to join her former pickpocketing targets for a hot meal. Sometimes she could read a person's unguarded feelings. Not power users, mind you. At least, not the really strong ones. And often not regular people either. It was hit and miss.

She had no idea how or when her gift would kick in, but at the moment it told her one thing. These deadly people would fight to protect her, though even they didn't know exactly why.

"Okay," she replied, relaxing back into the steady slurping of her bowl of soup.

Hozark continued his thought, but this time with a bit more careful phrasing. "What I wish to ask of you is this. Would you like to come with us as we follow up on what you have told us today? You would be of great help identifying the individuals you say you saw sneaking into Emmik Ozman's grounds."

"You want me to come with you?"

"That is correct."

"You want to take me away from this place? Take me off of this rock?"

"If you prefer to remain, we understand. It is just that we feel——"

Hozark was cut off by the small woman's arms thrown tightly around his neck in a tearful embrace. It took his Ghalian self-control not to instinctively pull a weapon as she did. But instead, he just held the warm, stinky bundle of the gently sobbing girl.

Demelza gave him a little smile. The smell would wash off. The girl's gratitude would not.

Finally, Henni released her grip, her sparkling eyes wet with emotion.

"What do you say we finish up here and get back to the ship?" Hozark asked as the girl wiped her eyes and nose with the back of her hand. "We've got some clothing aboard that should fit you, once you've cleaned up."

"You have hot water?"

"Of course. That is a common spell for any ship's washing facilities."

"I can't remember the last time I got to use hot water," Henni said, her tears threatening to well up once more.

"Then let us settle up here and get to the ship," Demelza said, rising from her seat and tossing a few coins on the table. "I'm sure you'll feel much better once you've had a hot shower and a good night's sleep. The quarters are not spacious, but I am sure you will find them quite comfortable."

"I get a *room*?"

"Of course," Demelza replied.

"And a bed? An actual bed, with a real pillow?"

"Naturally."

Now it was Demelza's turn to find the slim woman hugging her tight, her arms wrapped around her as best she could. A little flash of amusement creased the corners of Hozark's eyes. It seemed both of them would need to be laundering their clothing after this unlikely encounter.

And it would be entirely worth it.

Henni led the way to their ship as they wove through the dimly lit streets and alleyways. The girl had a knack for finding the easiest path, and though they knew full well where the ship was and how to return to it, their new friend was a local. And a resourceful one at that. One who knew all the shortcuts and back ways.

"How is it you know precisely where we are parked?" Hozark asked. "Were you following us since our arrival?"

"Oh, nothing like that. But you said I would get my own room. And since there are two of you already, and you're clearly not together––"

"What makes you say that?" Demelza asked. "Most automatically assume a man and woman traveling as we are to be a couple."

"Oh, please. It's so obvious you two have zero attraction for each other. I mean, you like each other, clearly, but it's more of a professional thing, if that makes any sense."

"Perfect sense," Demelza replied with a little grin.

Henni, it seemed, was even more perceptive than she'd initially realized. It wasn't a magic thing, though. It was just her natural way of being observant. Of seeing beneath the superficial acts people put on.

"But that doesn't explain your knowing where we left our craft," Hozark said.

"Oh, that. Yeah. Since it has to have at least three sleeping chambers, that means that it would have a decent-sized command center. And that means a cargo hold and probably a few other little additions, seeing as you're Wampeh Ghalian and all. So, for a ship that size, and since you were so interested in Emmik Ozman, the closest suitable landing site that was also relatively tucked out of the way would be this one," she said as they emerged from the alleyway into the far end of the rows of parked craft.

"Clever girl," the master assassin mused. "Come along, then. Let us leave this place. We have work to do."

They climbed into the ship to prepare for flight, but Henni paused in the doorway, looking back on the dirty world as emotion flooded her once more. Her eyes were shining, but not from tears. Power swirled within those limpid orbs, and the tiny galaxies sparkling within seemed to come alive with her swelling happiness.

"Come on, Henni. You are free of this place," Demelza said. "Let's get you settled in."

Henni took a final glance, then turned her back on the shitty world of Groll. She was finally free, something she'd only dreamed of for so long. And more than that, she was with friends.

Once the grime had been thoroughly scrubbed from her body in the sheer bliss of the craft's hot water shower, and her old bundles of clothes tightly sealed in a storage container, Henni settled down in the privacy of her own room on the first real bed she'd lain on in longer than she could remember.

And then, as the ship quietly flew on to their next destination, the exhausted young woman felt the stress and always-present alert anxiety of her existence finally loosen its grip, and with a relieved sigh, slipped into the most tranquil, deepest sleep imaginable.

CHAPTER NINETEEN

The exhausted young woman had been sound asleep for nearly three hours when Hozark and Demelza convened in the command module of their ship.

Both were wearing fresh attire, not so much from a desire to change into something more comfortable for the flight, but because the smell of Henni's joyful embrace would take a decently strong spell to remove from their clothing.

Fortunately, the young woman had washed away all of those months, or possibly even years, of filth as soon as she'd boarded, and her damn-near biohazard clothing had been safely sealed and tucked away in the cargo storage area.

Demelza would have preferred burning it with fire to ensure the completeness of its removal from existence, but Hozark held her back. He felt it would be wise to keep their guest's outfit in case it might be needed in the future.

That degree of filth and stench simply could not be mimicked by most spells, and ensconced in that bundle of cloth, the young woman was as good as invisible to most. And that might come in handy.

Of course, they both hoped she would prove to be as effective in clean clothes as she was in dirty ones. It would certainly make traveling with her a lot easier.

"You know, I think this one has quite a bit of potential," Demelza mused as they plotted their next jump.

Tracking down leads was busy work, and while the Ghalian spy network was diligently running down possibilities, with the sheer quantity of coin advanced to them by Visla Jinnik, it would be foolish not to use some of that to bring to bear every resource at their disposal.

Hozark sat deep in thought, his fingers steepled as he pondered the unusual circumstances by which they had come across their passenger. She had a gift. Possibly several. But with her traumatic shock, that element of unpredictability made her something of a wildcard. But at least she was a wildcard on their side.

"I wish we had the time to have one of our specialists work with her," he said, turning to Demelza. "She truly is a disturbed young woman."

"Yet strong. Strong and self-sufficient."

"By necessity."

"Which does nothing to change her proficiency at surviving."

"I wouldn't dream to suggest it did. I was merely pointing out that the origins of a good many of her skills and tricks were likely rather difficult circumstances. In fact, I wouldn't be surprised at all to learn she had been in more than one do-or-die type situation in her past."

"The look in her eyes? Yes, it seems likely."

"And about those eyes," Hozark said, voicing what they had both been thinking. "You saw the stars in them, Demelza. The sparkle. It was not a figure of speech in her case."

"It has always been a rumor. I never believed I would

actually see anyone with the anomaly. But could it mean she truly does have unknown powers?"

"Time will tell, my friend. But it seems clear that if there is a gift that accompanies those eyes, Henni is not yet aware how to utilize it."

"Perhaps we can help teach her."

"If only we knew the first thing about them ourselves," Hozark replied. "But for now, we keep a close watch over our little friend and do what we can to help her fit into her new role while she is with us."

"She had a very solid lead on the one who likely left that note for Emmik Ozman," Demelza said. "That was an impressive bit of intelligence gathered by a young, untrained woman. I think with our help, she will fit in just fine."

"Indeed. And now, we have a great deal of work to do. The visla's child is out there somewhere, and we have a task to complete."

"I think it is likely time we summon Uzabud and Laskar, wouldn't you agree? I have a feeling we will be needing their assistance in the coming days."

"More likely than not," Hozark concurred.

He retrieved their long-range skree and sent a message to the former pirate, wherever he may be. Then they waited.

The nature of a skree's magic was simple. It communicated with other skrees within its magic's range. Typically the same solar system, but occasionally all the way to extra solar bodies, if they weren't too far out.

For longer contact, however, a long-range skree was required. It used a great deal more magic, and relied on both its own densely packed spells, as well as the piggybacked repeater nature of the other long-range skrees it would ping off of.

It was that cooperative nature of the devices that made them so costly and rare. Most simply didn't have the coin to keep one active, knowing others might sap some of its magic with their own communications. But for the wealthy, it was not a concern. And the Wampeh Ghalian were wealthy indeed.

It took some time for them to finally receive a reply, but eventually they heard Bud's voice come over the device.

"You want us to come join you for what? To go to a party on Ripsala?" Uzabud said. "I mean, sure, we love a good party, and we'll bring all the usual fun stuff with. But we're a pretty long way out. It's gonna take us a bit of time to get there. Plus, we've got a few loose ends we need to tie up here before we head out. But we'll join you just as soon as we're able. And thanks for the invite!" he said, ending the transmission.

Of course, there was no party, nor would he be bringing along the accoutrements one would associate with festivities. But knowing the Council of Twenty possessed a secret backdoor into the supposedly secure and impenetrable skree network meant that on the exceedingly rare occasions a Wampeh Ghalian utilized a skree, it was done with a predetermined code system to ensure none were the wiser to their communications.

Bud and Hozark had long ago come up with a basic series of predetermined messages, and by now they were quite comfortable utilizing them if need be. And at the moment, given the distance between them and how hard it would have been to send one of the Ghalian messengers personally, it was definitely a need-be situation.

Hozark tucked away the specialized skree in its holding compartment and turned to the star chart beside him.

"It seems it may take him a bit longer than we anticipated," Demelza said, looking at the chart as well. "What do we do until then?"

"Until then?" Hozark said. "We have coordinates of the possible deliverer of the emmik's note, yes, but we need Bud and Laskar for that."

"So, we are stuck waiting?"

"I think not," he replied. "What of the armed forces that were employed for the strike on the visla's estate? Think about it. Unmarked uniforms. Tslavar mercenaries for hire. And a Council-sanctioned action, no less? Why, it seems obvious. Only a very few places where one could easily arrange such things. And one of them is relatively nearby. We're going to Azlaht."

CHAPTER TWENTY

Azlaht. It was a thriving hub for acquiring pretty much anything you could possibly want or need, legal or otherwise. Weapons, recreational spells, even dangerous magic was sold in the many sprawling marketplaces there.

The Council tended to turn a blind eye, as was so often the only way an underground black market of that sort could remain operational. It was because the power players *allowed* it. And they had their fingers in the pot as well. No business was transacted that they didn't get at least a small piece of, in one manner or another.

Especially the mercenary trade.

The Tslavars were a brutish race. One fond of, and prone to, violence regardless of their employment by the Council. But as the favorite mercenary enforcers of choice to carry out the Council's plans, a great deal of the green men and women had served under Council of Twenty orders. And more often than not they enjoyed a bit of leeway in their other, non-Council affairs for it.

There was a rumor in the wind, but many believed the Council was quietly attempting to make the Tslavar fleets into an exclusive extension of their own reach. If no others could hire the mercenaries, or at least the majority of them, it would give the Council a great deal of leverage.

If successful, they could then flex their collective muscle across a wider range and conduct their affairs from afar, all without requiring the risking of their own people's lives, which they tended to value far more than mere mercenary contractors.

And Azlaht was one of the vital hubs for the mercenary trade. One Hozark felt might provide them with some much-needed answers.

Hozark took his ship in a quick loop around the planet, mirroring the orbits of a great many other craft that had arrived there recently and were deciding which of the commerce zones they would be landing in. Unlike many worlds, Azlaht did not have just one capital city. It had power hubs across all continents, but no one person or group ruled them all.

For that reason, the Wampeh would have to make several stops on this world to accomplish their plan. And after an hour watching the traffic to and from the surface, Hozark selected the first.

He took the ship down in a rapid descent, snatching up a prime landing site as a larger Tslavar ship took off. It was a perfect place to start, and right in the middle of the mercenaries' stomping grounds within the city itself.

"This is a rather dangerous part of the region," Hozark said to the young woman now an impromptu part of their crew. "And you have only just been freed of your former home. Stay here and regain your strength. We shall return shortly."

Henni, washed, rested, and clothed in nondescript but clean attire, stretched in the doorway of her room. Without that additional layer of grime, her violet hair shone with renewed health, even in the ship's normal lighting.

"I'll come with," she said. "I can help."

"I'm sure you can. But the initial effects of a single night's sleep can be deceiving. Build your strength and energy. There will be plenty of time for excursions in less-dangerous regions."

"I'm used to dangerous," she protested.

Hozark flashed a look at Demelza.

"We know you are, Henni," Demelza said. "And you are a tough woman, indeed. I have every confidence in your abilities, as does Master Hozark. But what he is trying to tell you is that while we would gladly have you join us on this outing, our disguise is one that your presence would make difficult to maintain. We shall be acting as a married couple in search of our child. And I'm sure you can understand, two distraught parents makes a much more convincing act on their own."

Henni's attitude shifted, lightening immediately. She turned to Hozark.

"Why didn't you just say so in the first place?"

"Forgive my lack of clarity," he replied.

Demelza headed for the galley. "Would you like some food while we are away? You must be hungry after such a long rest."

Henni's eyes spoke as loudly as the rumble in her stomach. Demelza smiled warmly.

"Come. I will show you where the rations are kept."

"I know where they are," Henni said, scooting ahead of the Wampeh and down the corridor to the galley.

Hozark let out a low chuckle. "It appears our guest has already made herself right at home."

"That she has. It is nice to see her rebounding from her hardships so quickly, though we both know it will take more than a bath and good night's sleep to heal some of those wounds."

"I agree. But it is a start. Now, let us feed the girl and prepare for our task. This promises to be an interesting excursion."

The pale couple walking the avenues and alleyways of the

bustling commerce hub looked rather out of place. Too clean. Too polished. And definitely too weak. The uncomfortable glances they cast at the ruffians around them only reinforced the impression.

These offworlders had no place on a world like this, and the local talent smelled them like a shark could find a drop of blood in an ocean. But there were a lot of sharks, and some were bigger and badder than others. They all noted one another, and a silent game of chess began, to see which of them would scare off the others and claim this prize.

The couple seemed completely oblivious to the machinations unfolding around them as they walked deeper and deeper into the marketplace, right toward the most dangerous part, in fact. The area even the biggest and baddest steered clear of, for the sharks that resided *there* had something they did not. Council backing.

"I think this is the place," the man said in a thin, reedy voice.

"Should we go in?" his wife asked.

The lurking men and women silently willed them not to, but to no avail it seemed.

"We must. For the sake of our boy," the man replied, then strode right into the place they shouldn't have. The place even the toughest avoided.

They walked right into the Tslavar mercenaries' den.

All eyes turned to them when they stepped inside. To say they stood out would be an understatement. Pristine attire and foppish manners were not something the Tslavars were known for.

"Excuse me," the man said.

The crowd stared but ignored him. If, by ignored, you meant sized up for an easy target.

"I said, excuse me!" he repeated with a little more force, though his thin voice wavered as he did. "I am looking for whoever is in charge of this place."

A towering mountain of a man with a latticework of scars crisscrossing his deep-green skin rose from his seat to his full height. He knew his role well, and the way he unfolded and loomed over the visitors showed he had done this on more than a few occasions.

"What tha hell do you want, little man?" he growled, his fingers idly tapping the pommel of the comically large dagger at his waist.

"Um, yes. Uh, are you the one in charge here?"

"I am."

The man looked scared, but the woman nudged him. The Tslavar appreciated her curves with an obvious leer. Just his type. She blushed and positioned herself slightly behind her husband.

"Then I have a proposition for you," the man said, plucking up his courage.

"A proposition? I see something I might take ya up on," the man replied, his colleagues joining him in a disconcerting chuckle.

The man and wife shared a worried glance, but the woman's back straightened, and she stepped out from her man's protection.

"We want you to do a job for us," she said, trying to be brave.

"I bet you do," the Tslavar replied, again with that same overt leer.

"We want to hire you to find our boy, Happizano. He has run away, but we fear someone may have taken him from the streets."

"You hear that? They want us to play nanny," the man said, roaring with laughter. "Oh, dearie, you really are in over your head, aren't you? You have no idea who you're dealing with."

"I think we do," the man said, producing a hefty bag of coin from his pocket. "And rumor is, you're the best at what you do."

"Damned right I am."

"Then find our boy," he said with a surprising flash of bravado.

He threw the bag to the man, who snatched it easily from the air. He looked inside. There was a significant sum held within. The Tslavar glanced at his men. All were thinking the same thing. Take these fools and part them from every coin and valuable they possessed.

"There is a significant amount more to be paid upon the delivery of information leading to the recovery of our son," the man said.

The mercenary's glance halted his men's advances.

"More? How much more?"

"Five times that amount if you provide us accurate information about our son's whereabouts. Ten times that amount if you also find who took him."

That was a significant sum for so little work. Easy money, in fact. The mercenary nodded to his men, and they returned to their casual posturing.

"And if we do find the boy? How much to bring him back?"

"He ran away from home, but even if he has indeed been taken as we fear, we still must win his trust before he will come home with us willingly. Just tell us where he is, and we will come to him as parents to convince him to come home."

"And then?"

"And then you may do with those who have taken him as you wish. And you will be paid well for it," the woman said with a flash of motherly anger.

It only made the Tslavar like her more. Curves and *fire*? If things worked out, maybe he would take her anyway. *After* they were paid, of course.

"You've got yourself a deal," the man said.

"Thank you. You don't know how much this means to us!" the man gushed.

Long-range skree contact information was given, as was

additional coin for the expense, then the man and his wife departed.

"Can you believe that pathetic waste of flesh has a woman like that?" the Tslavar said to his men with a laugh. "Well, my boys, it looks like we've got a little side job to do."

CHAPTER TWENTY-ONE

Walking back through the rough streets, no one so much as lay a finger on the couple whose cleanliness made them stand out like a pair of diamonds on a dung heap. They were easy targets, and likely a pretty decent payday, but word had already been spread. These were not to be touched. They had business with the Tslavars.

That didn't stop the greedy stares, though, along with more than a few lustful ones. Not until they had stepped back into their craft were the two offworlders free of the intense scrutiny.

"Well, that went rather well," Hozark said with an amused chuckle.

The poor tough guys in town had no idea what would have befallen them if they had actually given in to their desires and attempted to rob or harm the seemingly harmless pair.

"Yes, it was quite productive," Demelza agreed, shedding her weakling charade as easily as taking off a coat.

"Their leader was certainly taken with you."

"It never ceases to amuse me how the slight reveal of cleavage can muddy men's minds so," Demelza said with an amused grin. "I think I will play that up again at the next stop. It seemed to be a wonderful distraction."

"I am sure our Tslavar friends will be quite appreciative."

Hozark and Demelza walked to the galley for some refreshment before heading off to the next commerce hub on their planned route. They would visit a great many of them before their work was done. And the Tslavar thugs they would hire in each of them would do their dirty work for them.

The Ghalian spy network was robust, and they were certainly hard at work searching for Visla Jinnik's boy, but with the hefty advance the visla had paid, it made perfectly good sense to use some of that coin to hire the Tslavar mercenaries who tended to work on Council endeavors to do some of the legwork for them.

After all, who better to make inquiries among the ranks of Tslavars than a group of their very own comrades? Men ignorantly doing the bidding of the Wampeh Ghalian, and against their own friends and employers, no less?

"It seems our little guest has something of an appetite," Demelza noted when they reached the galley.

The girl hadn't exactly raided the place, but judging by the state of the foodstores that had been readily accessible, having a seemingly limitless supply of food was something the chronically underfed young woman was not about to take for granted.

"I fear she will have quite an upset stomach," Hozark said, noting exactly how much Henni had ingested.

"I would not be surprised if she hid some within her quarters," Demelza replied. "It seems a natural instinct for one so recently removed from her previously precarious circumstances."

"A valid point. In any case, we will need to perhaps secure some of the rations, if for no other reason than to keep her from causing herself unintentional gastric harm."

"I've got a strong stomach," Henni said as she trotted into the room and headed straight for the bread storage container.

She grabbed a thick slice, then took some fresh fruit preserves they had sourced a few worlds back and spread them on thick, eating the treat with obvious relish.

She was like a little fusion reactor, with her ability to ingest massive quantities and convert it into her seemingly boundless energy.

"So, was it fun?" she asked.

"Fun? We were infiltrating a dangerous Tslavar group and tricking them to do our work against their own best interests," Hozark said.

"Yeah. Like I said. Fun."

The Wampeh chuckled. "I suppose one *could* say it was fun. Dangerous, yes, but a pleasant outing, for certain."

"Cool! I wanna go with next time!"

The assassins shared a look.

"Henni, I know you are used to the rough streets of Groll, but this is a different sort of world. And the risks are many, and not the type you are used to."

"So? Everywhere's dangerous, you guys. And I know I can help."

The two assassins knew far too well what having an unpredictable element like the young violet-haired woman embedded in an operation could do to their whole plan.

She had survived on Groll, sure. But this was different. This was an active deception plan, and a somewhat delicate one at that. Henni's impulsive and rather lippy nature could cause far more damage than she realized, and fast.

"Come on. You can't lock me in here forever!"

"Henni, it has only been an afternoon," Hozark said.

"You know what I mean. I need to be out doing something. I'm gonna earn my keep!"

"You are welcome here with no payment required," he said. "This was not a condition of your coming with us."

"But I *want* to help."

"Again, your enthusiasm is appreciated, but you are not obligated to put yourself at risk."

"Hozark is right," Demelza said. "Just stay here and relax for a bit. We should be done on this world relatively shortly."

This was *not* what the young woman wanted to hear. The thrown piece of bread stuck to the wall, leaving a trail of preserves as it slowly slid to the deck.

"If you don't take me with, then dump me here!"

"We are not dumping you, Henni."

"If you don't take me with, I am going to trash this ship. You don't think I will? You know I can."

Hozark sighed. *This* was the sort of thing that he did not need on board his craft. But one worked with what one had, and he had a moody young woman of unknown abilities on his ship. And she was pissed.

Reluctantly, he accepted the reality that Henni was going to have to be let out, one way or another. He just hoped he could do so in a way that would not negatively affect their plans. The girl was erratic and would have to be steered clear of any sensitive dealings, but she did have skills.

"All right, Henni. You make a valid argument," Hozark said. "And we actually *could* use your particular expertise. But only if you're up for it. This will be a difficult task."

"I can do it. I'm part of the team!" the girl chirped.

Hozark was not fond of the increasing frequency that word was being used of late, but he let it slide in the interest of minimizing the girl's potential damage.

"Yes, you are," he said. "And you have a *very* important job to do."

It actually *was* an important job. If she could manage to do it stealthily, that is. But that was something she was actually pretty good at back on Groll.

Hozark tasked her with being their scout on the ground. Their secret eyes and ears. While he and Demelza played the part of distraught parents hiring the Tslavars to find their son, Henni would watch and listen and report back all that she learned.

It was something they would do repeatedly, as each of the different cities across the planet were essentially their own domains. And the big dogs of each tended to stick to their own turf, where they controlled things with an iron fist.

Of course, the Tslavars did still know quite a few of their brethren––especially the power players––but the odds of them sharing that they'd scored a lucrative side gig were slim.

Even if they did discuss it, all that would do is put both parties on higher alert to complete the task first and claim the remaining payment for themselves. If the strange couple had paid the same sizable deposit to another Tslavar captain, then they must truly have a lot of coin at their disposal.

And coin spoke louder than words. On top of that, knowing there was another on the job would be quite an incentive. More often than not, a little competition was just what a man needed to motivate him to go that extra mile.

"Prepare yourself, Henni. We will arrive in our next landing site shortly."

"On it, Captain!" the young woman said with glee, then raced off to get ready, whatever that entailed.

Hozark flew them to the next of the main cities at a somewhat hurried pace. His landing was likewise a bit rushed, all the better to maintain the impression of someone operating on a ticking clock. From the moment they were visible as a speck on the horizon to the time they vanished into the sky, they were playing a part, and everything they did had to reinforce those performances.

They would set down and head off into the city, making themselves visible, as they'd previously done. All attention would be on them when their little friend would sneak out of the small access hatch at the opposite end of the craft. If done properly, no one would notice a thing, and she could go about her task with ease.

"What in the worlds?" Demelza said, wrinkling her nose in disgust.

"What?" Henni asked as she strutted into the command center.

"Oh, no. No, that is not what we had in mind," Demelza said, eyeing the foul bundle of clothing Henni had recovered from its sealed storage bin. "We will have to burn those."

"Hands off!" Henni hissed. "No one messes with my stuff. These are mine!"

"Believe me, I have no wish to put my hands anywhere near those rags."

Hozark chuckled. "She does have a point. She will be not only invisible, but actively repulsive with this outfit."

"So I keep them, right?"

"Yes, Henni. You keep them, but you bathe as soon as we return. And those stay sealed in storage when they are not in use, understood?"

"Deal."

"All right, then," he said, walking to the door with Demelza at his side. "Let us begin."

CHAPTER TWENTY-TWO

The leader of the Tslavar mercenary band in the next city they arrived at was a gargantuan woman named Blatzik. For a woman to lead so rough and ready a group of hired killers truly said something about her drive and abilities, for while gender often played no role in a person's career, in this particular line of work, men tended to rise to the top.

The violent, aggressive, and dangerous ones.

When Hozark and Demelza saw Blatzik, they immediately placed her in the "threat level high" category. What she would have had to do to reach this pinnacle could only be guessed. Likely because those who might have been able to talk had been slaughtered and fed to the Bundabist corralled in the pen outside. To underestimate her would be true folly.

Her men and women were as loyal as they were dangerous, and, unlike the previous location's hub of Tslavar activity, the mercenaries in this place were all on their best behavior. At least, inside of Blatzik's base of operations.

Hozark had anticipated another, "What the hells do you want?" line of greeting from the Tslavar welcoming committee, but instead, all he got was a cold, calculating stare that took in both he and his alleged spouse. He fidgeted and shifted his weight from foot to foot, acting unsettled under the woman's intense gaze.

Demelza simply looked down at the ground in front of her. Lowering the eyes was a demure posturing that would be taken for subservience by many, but it served another purpose. For with her eyes gazing down, but ahead, the assassin's peripheral vision could easily count and track the others in the room.

But they had not come to fight. They had come to hire this woman and her crew.

"Uh, we thought this was the place to come to hire the best tracking crew on the planet," Hozark said, a faint waver in his voice. "Should we go?"

Blatzik spoke at long last.

"Oh, you're in the right place, all right. But what I can't figure out is what a pair of upper-crust socialites like you are doing in my turf. You can't be here for trade. You haven't brought a thing with you. And you don't look like couriers. So tell me, why are you on my doorstep?"

"Doorstep?" Hozark asked, confused. "B-but, we're inside."

"It's a figure of speech, little man," Blatzik replied.

She then shifted her attention to the buxom woman this pathetic male had somehow landed as his own. Not bad, and curves in all the right places. On top of that, she seemed solid beneath her feminine exterior. Blatzik thought this one could be a *lot* of fun. But first, she had to find out their true reason for coming.

"Well? Speak up. Why have you come here?"

Demelza read the woman's gaze quickly, as had her partner, and they silently shifted their plan accordingly without so much as a word or a glance.

"If I may speak, we have come because we need your services," Demelza said.

"My services? Oh, dear, you have no idea what services I can offer you."

Demelza's cheeks flushed deep red––a nice trick she'd practiced for years––but she continued.

"Yes. It is said that you are the best on this planet. In this system, for that matter. And we need your help. Our son has gone missing. At first, we were certain he ran away. You know how boys can sometimes be," she said, her gaze locking on the intimidating woman's eyes. "But it is looking as if he may have been abducted."

"Abducted?" Blatzik asked. "You get a ransom demand?"

"No."

"Then why do you think he's been snatched up? Seems out of character to kidnap a boy and not ransom him."

Hozark took a timid step forward. "I had a local investigator from our system ask questions. He had to spread a lot of coin, but eventually, word of him was received. He'd been seen in the company of rough men. He doesn't have any friends like that. I'm sure he was taken."

"Or ran away precisely because he wanted to be with those 'rough men,'" the Tslavar said. "In any case, why is this my concern?"

Hozark nodded to Demelza. She pulled out a hefty bag of coin and timidly walked close to the sturdy Tslavar woman. "We will pay well to find our boy," she said, handing the pouch over.

Blatzik weighed it in her hand.

"A sizable sum, indeed. But not nearly enough for what you're asking."

"There is more if you are successful. Five times that amount if you provide us accurate information about our son's whereabouts. Ten times that amount if you also find who took him," she said.

That got the woman's attention. It was a lot of coin for so little work. Sure, it would be time consuming, but she had crews running across the systems. It wouldn't cost her a thing to simply have them keep a look out for the boy in the process.

"Well, then," she said, leaning closer to Demelza. "It looks like we've got ourselves a deal."

With that, the couple gave the woman their skree contact and made a hasty exit. As they walked, they sniffed the air. Even dulled senses could have picked up that particularly pungent aroma.

"She is close," Demelza said quietly as she and Hozark walked back toward their ship.

"Yes, I can smell her too."

"We really must at least clean the stench from her rags, if we can't burn them entirely."

Hozark's attention shifted, his shoulders stiffening slightly. "Darling, you've been so brave during this ordeal. Please, go back to our ship and rest while I handle one last task before we depart."

"Are you sure?" she asked.

"Yes. Now that we are allied with Blatzik, I am confident all will be okay."

The mention of their ties to the Tslavar boss immediately sent any who had any thoughts of assaulting the woman as she walked back the remaining distance to the ship on her own change their minds. Blatzik was one they did not want to cross, no matter how tempting the score.

"Very well, my love. But do hurry back to me."

"I will not dally any longer than needed, my sweet."

Demelza continued on her way, while Hozark turned down a side alley leading to a small marketplace of sorts, following the sound of boots all the while. Many boots, and all of them in an angry hurry. They were pursuing someone. And from the smell lingering in the air, he knew who it was.

This was getting more and more complicated. And he was going to have to act fast.

CHAPTER TWENTY-THREE

Hozark walked as quickly as he could without drawing attention to himself. At least, not any more than his appearance already did. He was disguised as a fancy man, but this was almost certainly going to call for far less foppish behavior.

Unfortunately, he found himself constrained by their recent operation's disguise. Looking as he did, he simply could not be seen engaging in violence. Not after the show he and Demelza had just put on.

It would ruin their cover, and not only in this city, but potentially the others they visited as well. Word would get out, and no one else looked like they did.

Hozark casually veered across the marketplace toward the animal and food vendors. As he passed, he cast a little spell. One that knocked free the gate of the Bundabist pen in the closest market stall. On top of that, he threw in a quaint little spell he rarely had use of. The one that gave the sensation of stinging insects.

He quickly applied it to the animals, and the agitated beasts wasted no time making a raucous escape. It was what he needed. Attentions shifted, even if just for a few moments, and in the confusion, Hozark lifted a long, filthy cloak from one of the animal herders' stands.

He had made sure none were looking his way, of course, then slid it on in a flash, and in an instant, he had vanished down the alleyway, his makeshift disguise in place as well as it could be.

The sound of racing boots was close, but less in number now. Whoever they were chasing must have either been cornered or caught, and the pursuit had finally come to an end.

Close ahead, around just a few more turns of the alleyway, a deep voice was saying something in a very angry tone. Judging by the grunts of the owners of the other boots, what he was saying rang true with them all.

Henni, what have you done? Hozark wondered as he came upon the group of angry men.

The violet-haired girl was there at the far end of the tiny dead-end alley, her back to the wall, a small, yet dangerous-looking blade flashing in her hand. She was waving it in front of her, keeping the men at bay, though the stench of her clothing might have served the purpose just as well. At least, in most circumstances.

Whatever she had done, it must have been bad, because these fellows were more than ready to get up close and personal. Hell, they were even looking forward to it.

The most vocal of the angry mob seemed to speak for the rest of them when he quite loudly voiced his outrage.

"Bitch, give me back my blade. That was my father's!"

"I don't know what you're talking about," Henni shot back. "What blade?"

"What the hell are you talking about? You're waving it around in your hand, you little whore."

"I am *not* a whore," she shrieked, slashing at the man.

Apparently, he had touched a nerve, but the others quickly

jumped in, all yelling at once about the things of value that had gone missing from their persons.

The thing about Henni was, she was an exceptional pickpocket. Possibly better than Hozark, even. But she lacked the restraint to know when *not* to take something. She was impulsive, and that led to bad choices. But a crowd this size? There was no way she had stolen all the items she was being accused of taking.

Somewhere in the city, more than one thief was resting easy now that their crimes had been foisted off on the offworld criminal. A brutish man lurched forward and swung a stout club at the violet-haired girl. It missed her blade hand, but it caught her other arm with a sickening crunch.

Henni shrieked in pain, but the man moved in for the kill.

"I'll take that," Hozark said, snatching the cudgel from the man's hand just as he was about to deliver another blow.

"You with her?" the man growled, his and the crowd's anger rising.

"No. But this is merely a girl, and surely––"

A hot spray of blood splashed across the nearest attackers. The club wielder had tried to land a surprise attack on the interloper with a hidden blade. A hidden blade Hozark had seen before the man had even reached for it. When it had finally been drawn and swung at the newcomer, simply taking it from him and turning it against its owner had been child's play.

And now the man lay bleeding on the ground. Nothing fatal. Hozark did not want to kill any of these men and women. But an example had been made.

Unfortunately, the mob had the mentality of, well, a mob, and rather than back off in realization they were up against someone who would actually fight back, and efficiently at that, they only ramped up their aggression.

Henni shrieked as another man grabbed her roughly by the

broken arm. He was dead before he hit the ground, the blade taken from the previous assailant lodged hilt-deep in his eye.

"Enough! Leave now, while you still can," Hozark growled.

"He's with the thief! Get him!" an outraged woman yelled in a shrill cry.

"Damn it," Hozark sighed, then set to work, fending off attackers from all sides, and coming at him with a wide assortment of weapons.

Two large men charged with makeshift pikes. Really, they were just broom handles that had been snapped to a point, but the effect would be the same. Namely, a big hole in you if you misjudged their trajectory.

Hozark spun aside, breaking one in half with his boot, and pivoting sharply, grabbing and driving the other length into a woman attacking him from the other side. She dropped in a screaming heap, the rod protruding from her belly.

She would live. Probably. But Hozark still had a great deal of attackers to handle, and in a very tight space.

Elbows flew, and debilitating knees dropped into oncoming attackers' thighs, cramping them painfully and taking them out of the equation. But still more came, believing that they had the advantage because of their numbers.

They couldn't have been more wrong. But Hozark was doing all he could to spare the poor yokels, but with odds like these, it was taking much of his skill to avoid landing fatal blows.

Then a pair of hands managed to grab his cloak, tearing it free with a sickening rip, revealing his disguise.

"It's the offworlder!" someone called out.

"Damn," was all the Wampeh said.

He could not be found out. Their mission depended on it. And that meant one thing.

Hozark yanked the weapons from the nearest attackers' hands and ended them immediately with them, spinning into the others with no hesitation or hint of fear. He moved quickly, shifting his position to block the lone exit to the alleyway. It took a moment for the angry mob to realize what was happening. And by the time they had, it was far too late.

The master assassin moved in a blur, blades slicing through the vital parts of man and woman alike until only two in the alley remained standing among a sea of dead and dying. With the help of his practiced hands, the wounded quickly joined their friends on the other side.

Hozark yanked a relatively blood-free cloak from a corpse and covered himself. "Come."

The taller man ushered the filthy street urchin from the alleyway as fast as they could move, and once they were clear, they vanished into the crowded marketplace. Hozark stole a few more cloaks and coverings as they moved, changing his appearance and the girl's several times before they turned toward their ship.

"My arm," Henni sobbed. "He broke my arm."

"And you are fortunate that is all. It could just as easily have been your skull."

"Bastard!" she said, spitting on the ground as if it were the man's corpse.

Hozark grabbed her firmly by the shoulders, taking care to avoid her injured arm.

"Henni, you cannot steal like that. Those people did not have to die."

"They attacked me!"

"And with cause," he replied with an exasperated sigh. "Listen, and listen well. You must be careful."

"I am."

"You were *not*. I understand your habits, and you are indeed a talented thief. But you *must* be cautious."

"I almost never get caught."

"And yet, you were. But I am not talking about your being caught. While that is bad, what you have done is worse. You could have put our marks on guard. You could have even cost us all the work we've put in on this world. Do you understand?"

Henni grumbled like a moody tween, but she wasn't a foolish girl. She did understand.

"And when you do steal, never take anything your mark will miss. If you do, they will be on guard, and that makes doing anything far more difficult."

Henni was willful and proud, but after a long moment, she quietly apologized.

"This is water under the bridge," Hozark said. "But learn from it, and do not repeat your mistakes. Now, we must separate. I will cause a little diversion that will allow you to enter the ship. I shall then join you shortly."

Hozark ducked into a doorway and shed his cloak, then stepped into the nearest stall and began haggling over a gift for his wife. He got loud. The merchant got louder. Soon it looked like it might devolve into a brawl, but the offworlder was pathetic in his fear and quickly scurried back to his ship.

A ship that a smelly young woman had just snuck back aboard.

Demelza immediately saw the specks of blood on his boots. Others had missed the detail in the commotion outside, but she was a Ghalian.

"Trouble, I take it?"

"Henni," he replied. "We will have some work to do with that one."

"I feared as much. So, what now?"

"We rendezvous with Bud and Laskar."

"It will be good to have their skills backing our attempts. But we need to plan our next steps. The boy is still missing, after all."

Hozark sat and eased back in his seat, a little smile tickling the corner of his lips.

"I do have an idea," he said. "But I fear our poor friends will not like it."

CHAPTER TWENTY-FOUR

The flight to the rendezvous point with the former pirate and his gregarious copilot was a relatively uneventful one. At least, it was after Demelza had decontaminated Henni's filthy attire and sealed it in a sturdy storage bin in the cargo bay.

She hadn't killed it with fire, though she'd threatened to. Hozark had joked that clothing wasn't alive anyway, so there was nothing to kill, though Demelza's point about Henni's garb possibly being an exception to that rule had been one he couldn't really argue. In any case, once they had cleaned up their impulsive little guest, they set their course to meet up with the others.

Henni was a bit quieter once she had bathed and settled into the growing comfort of her familiar quarters aboard the ship. Demelza had sat her down for a girl-to-girl talk in hopes perhaps a bit of female camaraderie might help put her more at ease.

But that wasn't her strong suit, and neither was it Henni's. The girl did show an understanding of what she'd done wrong though, and even more surprisingly, a bit of remorse at the lives lost because of it. Perhaps the little rapscallion wasn't such a feral beast after all.

"We shall be with you in three hours," Hozark skreed their friend. "We have a new destination and will be departing for it shortly after we join up. And a little heads-up, we are now traveling plus one."

"New crew?" Bud asked.

"Not exactly. You will see when we dock," Hozark replied.

"Way to be mysterious, man."

"Trust me, Bud, it is easier than explaining."

"Whatever. See ya in a few hours."

"I look forward to it."

Hozark cut the skree conversation and plotted their final two jumps. Soon enough his poor friend would have to deal with the difficult young woman in person.

The rendezvous point Hozark had relayed in his coded message to Uzabud was a small moon in the Londrus system. It was an unpopulated solar system consisting of rather hostile planets that were utterly uninhabitable. And the sun's rays were draining to magic users. For that reason, no one ever visited the region.

But Hozark and Bud had discovered a small moon at the outskirts that had a convenient orbital path. One that kept the dark side permanently facing away from the sun and its draining rays. It was a perfect meeting point, and one they'd used plenty of times.

"There he is," Hozark said to his companions as they exited their final jump.

"Where? I can't see anything," Henni said.

"There. The dot on that moon," Hozark said, pointing out the tiniest of reflections revealing the craft.

"Oh, wait. Now I see it. Wow, that's a beat-up ship."

"Do not let Uzabud hear you disparage his craft," Demelza said with a chuckle. "He is quite fond of it."

"I don't know why. It's hideous."

"And has served us well for some time," Hozark noted. "Now, come. Let us introduce you to the others."

He took the shimmer ship in low and landed atop the much larger craft, applying his magical docking and umbilical spells that would bind them to the ship and provide a safe, breathable accessway aboard.

There were several other small ships fastened to its hull, as was Bud's usual practice. You never knew what you might need, and aside from landing and battle craft, there were also a couple of junkers as well. Sacrificial vessels, should the need arise.

Bud was a firm believer in the adage that it was better to have it and not need it than to need it but not have it.

"All right. Follow me," Hozark said, leading the way into the waiting ship.

They found their friend waiting for them on their arrival.

"Hey, you guys! You made it!" Bud said, welcoming his friends with open arms. His eyes shifted to the violet-haired woman skulking between Hozark and Demelza. "Who's the new girl?"

Henni ignored him and pushed right past, nearly knocking Laskar down as he joined the new arrivals. Moments later, the sound of food storage bins being flung open rang out from the galley.

"Uh, did I miss something, or is there a small, violet-haired person apparently ransacking our foodstores?"

"Henni is her name," Demelza said. "And she is with us now."

"New crewmember, then?"

"Not exactly. But she is flying with us for the time being."

A loud crash rang out.

"What the hell is she doing?" Lasker grumbled, taking off for the galley.

The others followed close behind. Henni, it seemed, had

found the supply of dried Maringus fruit and was happily stuffing her face. The novelty of easily accessible food was not wearing off. Not by a long shot.

"Is she going to be earning her keep?" Laskar asked, aghast at the way she was devouring their supplies. "She's tiny, but damn, look at that."

"Seriously," Bud agreed. "Hey, slow down before you choke to death."

"I've been eating my whole life. I'm not going to choke, weirdo."

"Eating your whole life? Ha! Could have fooled me. You're skin and bones," Bud shot back.

Laskar seemed skeptical of the new addition. "You have any skills, girl? You gotta earn your keep if you're flying with us."

"I've got skills coming out my ears. What about you, pretty boy?"

"I'm the best damn pilot in forty systems."

"Second best," Bud corrected.

Henni rolled her eyes. "Is that one always so self-aggrandizing?"

"Hey, I'm just telling the truth," Bud replied with a broad grin.

Demelza leaned in. "You had better, Uzabud. She's an intuit."

"Really?"

"Look at her eyes."

Bud and Laskar looked closer and realized that, indeed, she might actually be a very unusual and rare variety of power user.

"She can read my mind?" Laskar asked, clearly a bit freaked out.

"No. Not exactly. But she does possess a strong intuitive power," Hozark noted. "It is hit and miss, though."

"Huh," Laskar said, relaxing a bit.

Bud, however, was transfixed. Once he'd taken a proper look at her eyes, he couldn't look away.

"What are you staring at, creep?"

"Your eyes."

"Creeper."

"I am not. It's just, I've never seen anything like them. Did your parents have the same thing?"

"I don't know. I was taken when I was really little."

"Taken? Like, by slave traders?"

Hozark tried desperately to make eye contact with his friend to signal him to stop this line of questioning, but Bud blustered ahead, going so far as to reach out and pull open her collar, displaying the burn around her neck.

"Hey! Hands off, creeper!" she said, smacking his wrist.

Bud turned uncharacteristically serious. "I'm sorry. I had no idea."

The intuitive young woman could sense he truly was.

"But how did you get the collar off? How did you get free?"

"I don't remember, exactly."

"Well, you know, we can get that healed, if you--"

"No. It's a part of me. And no one changes me. No one."

"Okay, okay. It was just an offer," he said, retreating as best he could.

"Enough, you two," Hozark interjected. "We have a great deal of work to do. And I am truly sorry, Bud, but you are definitely not going to like it."

CHAPTER TWENTY-FIVE

Bud hated the cold, and Moolar was, using his particularly colorful description, "A fucking cold and desolate ball of pure misery."

Naturally, he was thrilled when he learned it was their destination.

Yet, when they arrived, it wasn't the pilot who griped the most. He was bundled from head to toe in the warmest garb he possessed, and in his instance, the expression, "There is no bad weather, only bad clothing," truly applied.

His dislike of being cold had previously led to the acquisition of a fair amount of the finest, warmest garb available. Hozark had even contributed a fair amount of coin to their purchase, as it had been one of his prior jobs that required them, which had made the pricey expenditure somewhat less painful.

And now it was paying off.

It was again one of those cases of better to have it and not need it than need it and not have it, though Bud did everything in his power to avoid freezing climes.

Laskar, on the other hand, had decidedly *not* been prepared for their unpleasant destination, both physically and mentally. And even though the Wampeh outfitted him with warm attire, his complaining made Bud seem absolutely stoic.

"It's so cold I can't feel my face," he whined almost as soon as they stepped off of the ship.

The landing site was obscured by the swirling snow, which was pretty much a constant on this world, but they still had to set down far enough away from the nearby city where their target held court to avoid notice. His name was Arvin, and he ran one of the toughest operations in the nearest five systems.

And it looked like he was the one who had delivered the mysterious Council note to Emmik Ozman. Or, at least, so their intel suggested. But until they spoke to the man directly, they simply would not know for sure. Unfortunately, that would not be so easy.

The recreation establishment he ran was the hottest spot in town, as well as the warmest. All sorts visited it to get out of the cold, and unlike so many of the places they had visited of late, this was actually frequented by more than just unscrupulous mercenaries and pirates.

Music, food, drink, entertainment, all were available within those walls, and any who acted up were removed with great prejudice. Rumor had it, the truly offensive ones were even fed to the giant Obanta that roamed the icy tundra.

Those were essentially snow-white, bipedal beasts, but magical in origin, made of powered ice, formed by the world's unusual, innate magic. Ice that looked like white fur, like a Yeti, but with a much worse attitude. And they were quite omnivorous, eating pretty much anything, or anyone, who stumbled into their grasp.

"Did you see that?" Laskar asked, turning abruptly to the right. "Was that an Obanta?"

"Relax, Laskar. They do not typically attack large groups of travelers. At least, not unless they are particularly hungry," Hozark replied.

"But what if it *is* hungry?"

"Then, perhaps, we might have a problem."

"Wonderful," their copilot said, pulling his hat lower on his head against the cold.

Interestingly, Hozark noticed that while the snow was sticking to the others, it seemed to be slowly melting from Laskar. Apparently, he had decided to use the tiny amount of magic within him to fend off the cold.

It was actually pretty impressive, his unexpected little trick. Not everyone could manage that spell, and for one as weakly powered as him, it was quite a feat. He was just full of surprises, it seemed.

"How much farther? I can't feel my toes," he whined.

"And here I believed Uzabud's intense dislike of the cold would have meant *he* would be the griping one," Demelza said.

"You all bitch too much," Henni said. "Less whining, more walking."

With that, she powered on ahead of them, plowing through the snow with a singular purpose. She was a dynamo, and one they would all do well to emulate in this instance.

The little woman was bundled up from tip to toe, just a slit for her sparkling eyes visible providing access to the depths of her coverings. At least she had fabricated her outfit from clean materials, so her stink would not alert anyone––or *thing*––of their approach.

"Shouldn't we have her wait for us?" Bud asked.

"Do not worry, she is fearless. And this is what she does," Hozark replied. "Why she is part of our group, at least for now. She is somewhat unstoppable in this respect."

"It is true," Demelza added. "When she wants to, she blends in and hears things as well as most Ghalian spies I've met, though she does it all without formal training."

An echoing bellow rang out through the swirling winds.

"Obanta?" Laskar asked, his eyes wide.

Hozark listened intently for a moment, pinpointing the direction of the sound. "Yes. But captive ones are employed as guard animals near the city. Not only do they keep unscrupulous types on their better behavior, they also tend to hold other Obanta at bay."

"A territorial thing?" Bud asked.

"More or less."

"I don't care what they're doing. I just want to get out of this cursed cold!" Laskar said. "If we can hear them, we must be close, right? I can't see shit in this damn snow."

"Yes, Laskar. In fact, had you been looking ahead instead of focusing your energies on complaining, perhaps you would have noticed what is directly before us," Demelza said.

He squinted his eyes, focusing on the shapes becoming clear up ahead. And the snow seemed to be lesser there. As if a degree of magic was keeping it somewhat at bay, preventing massive snow drifts from covering all in sight.

"Is that a town?"

"Very good, Laskar. It is, indeed. And if you talk less and listen more, you may even hear the faint sound of music coming from our destination."

The miserable man actually heeded the recommendation and ceased his whining long enough to make out the telltale sounds of festivities.

"Is that where we're going?"

"Indeed, it is," Hozark said.

"So what are we waiting for?"

"Just one thing," the Wampeh replied. "And here she comes."

Henni seemed to appear out of nowhere, though her trick came not from a shimmer cloak, but simply her innate ability to stand where the light and natural environment made her less visible. It was probably entirely subconscious how she did it. And it was likely what had kept her alive so long.

"Hey, guys! So, there are twenty-two visible guards inside, seven near the VIP section, four at the door, and the others spread out across the joint."

"What do you mean *visible*?" Bud asked. "The crazy chick makes no sense."

"I'm not crazy, creeper. I was just being thorough. If you'd let me finish, that is."

"So finish."

"I *am* finishing," she shot back. "As I was saying. Twenty-two visible guards, but there are also five security types in patron attire."

"How can you be so sure?" Bud asked.

"The way they move. The stuff they're drinking. They're nursing their drinks. And what they ordered is pretty weak stuff. And they keep scanning the crowd, but casually. Pretty obvious, though."

"Damn," Bud said, impressed.

Hozark slapped him on the shoulder. "You see, my friend? *This* is what she excels at."

Laskar seemed unimpressed. "Great, there are guards. We knew that would be the case anyway. Can we please just get the hell out of this cold and into that nice, warm building?"

"That we shall," Hozark said, undoubtedly brightening the man's spirits. "All right," he said, turning to the others. "Let us get inside and see what we can see."

CHAPTER TWENTY-SIX

Calling the transition from their trek across the freezing tundra to the cozy interior a night-and-day difference would not have been an exaggeration. When Hozark and his team stepped in through the magical force curtain keeping the snow and cold out when the doors opened, what they found was so utterly opposite of the outer conditions, it was staggering.

The heat felt almost tropical compared to what they had just come in from. And the patrons were all lively and in fantastic spirits. They were also quite scantily clad for the world they were on. But here, in this place? Less was more, and the dancing patrons were shiny with a thin sheen of sweat.

The smells of roast meats, grilled root vegetables from the subterranean, geothermally heated grow rooms, and the musky pheromones of the partying patrons mixed together to give the place an incredibly inviting and cozy feel.

Of course, there were also spells in place, subtly enhancing the effect. Something Hozark and Demelza had noted the moment they stepped inside. But that was the only magic in play, it seemed, and it was of no threat to them. Merely a way to keep the clientele happy and encourage their prompt return.

Some of the more private seating areas were frequented by somewhat debaucherous patrons, many engaging in acts that, while not explicit, were nevertheless clear in where they were going. But for that, Arvin's establishment conveniently offered private rooms, rentable by the day or the hour.

Or by the minute, for the more overly excitable, though he sold a special ointment to help with that as well.

Arvin was a businessman, and quite a clever one, regardless of his mob boss lifestyle. He was shrewd, and not one to fall into the stupid strong-arm thug games of so many of his lesser peers. He projected class and confidence from his VIP booth where he held court over his establishment, his personal guards stationed around him.

Another sign of his more cultured, and also more intelligent, manner of running things was the nature of his guards. While those at the door and on the floor––including the plainclothes ones––were rather large and intimidating, the ones serving as his own retinue were not hulking beasts, but rather, men and women of far smaller, normal builds.

Hozark and Demelza knew full well that size meant nothing when it came to martial proficiency, and Arvin's employment of calm, confident, and even-keeled guards to work closest to him showed he was a man who had learned that fact as well. Again, a comfort in his environment that belied his unusual grasp on the reins of power on this world.

"That's him," Henni said quietly, nodding slightly toward the guarded man.

"Are you certain that is who you saw at Emmik Ozman's establishment?" Hozark asked.

"I never forget a face."

"Well done. See what you can find out about this place, but be careful. And, Henni, be *subtle*."

"Will do," she said with an upbeat grin, then shed her

bundles, revealing a rather form-fitting and skimpy outfit that blended right in with the other patrons.

Again, she was becoming invisible in plain sight, vanishing into the churning crowd of patrons.

Hozark turned to his friend. "Bud, please keep an eye on her. But from a distance. She is good, but trouble does seem to find that one at times."

"Will do," the space pirate said, mimicking the young woman, then dropped his heavy garb at the coat check and danced off into the mass of revelers.

"Laskar. Go work your magic on those tough-looking fellows nearest the bar. Those are Arvin's plainclothes guards. We wish for them to stay where they are, so buy them some drinks and keep them occupied."

"How do I do that?"

"You are the one always bragging about how charming you are. Impress me," Hozark said, stealthily slipping the man a bag of coin to help complete the task.

Thanks to Visla Jinnik's deep pockets, this sort of operation was far easier than it might otherwise be, as the promise of free alcohol tended to grease the wheels of new friendships easier than almost anything else.

Demelza's cleavage was the other thing that could help sway people's attention, but for this particular plan, she was buttoned up high and staying at Hozark's side.

"So, just buy them some drinks? That's it? Not even the women over there? That kinda sucks, Hozark," Laskar said, a little disappointed.

"Perhaps. But when the time comes, I need you to give us a distraction. A sizable one, if you can."

At this he perked up slightly. "How will I know when?"

"Oh, you will know. We shall make it abundantly clear."

"Well, all right then. I guess I'm off to get a bunch of thugs drunk. Oh, joy," he grumbled, then headed off toward the bar.

Hozark turned to his partner, who had shed her outerwear and was ready for the next step of their task.

"Shall we?"

"Let us begin," she replied.

Hozark and Demelza adopted a casual air, but one of official business nonetheless. To any watching, it seemed they were enjoying the sights and sounds, but still had work to do.

They approached the elevated VIP section, stepping close to Arvin's table. Hozark had to hand it to the man's staff. They were subtle, yet quietly efficient in positioning themselves between him and their employer, all without seeming intimidating or aggressive in any way.

The very picture of high-end security.

Hozark moved casually, with his hands clearly visible, adopting the posture of a harmless man. Demelza, likewise, was non-threatening in her demeanor, though either could take the guards out relatively quickly. It would not be easy, though. They were obviously highly skilled professionals. But, ultimately, the Ghalian won out more often than not.

"Arvin?" Hozark asked.

"That's me," the man said. "What business do you have here? You're obviously not patrons."

"Uh, no, we're not. We're friends of Daruvius Kahn," he replied, using the name of a well-known smuggler who frequented this particular part of space.

The Ghalian spies had informed Hozark that Daruvius had been seen several systems away, so there was no chance of his showing up and spoiling their way into Arvin's inner circle. Unfortunately, the spies were not privy to one important fact.

Arvin bristled at the man's name. "Daruvius? That scum owes me coin! And a lot. You have some nerve coming here and saying his name."

The security detail, while outwardly just as relaxed as before, had shifted their posturing to one of heightened readiness. A layman wouldn't have noticed it, but the Ghalian assassins saw the change as plain as the switch from night to day.

"No, you misunderstand," Hozark said with a big, friendly grin. "That's why we're here. He knows he screwed up with you, and he wanted us to deliver this to you with his apologies."

Hozark reached into his inner pocket, moving carefully so as to not set the security staff into motion, and drew out a hefty bag of coin. It had originally been intended to use for bribes and any other issues that money would smooth over, but it seemed that now meant something other than they'd initially expected.

But the Ghalian adapt and improvise as easy as breathing.

Hozark handed the coin to the man, his staff closely watching the hand reaching toward their employer. Arvin took the bag and hefted it in his palm.

"Feels light. *Very* light."

"And Daruvius knows it. This is just a token of his apologies. The full amount, plus an additional interest payment, will be coming to you as soon as he is able. He wanted us to tell you that he deeply regrets his actions, and he'll do whatever it takes to make things right and repay his debt."

Arvin opened the pouch and looked inside. It was a substantial sum, even if not all he was owed.

"You say this is on top of what he owes me?"

"Yes. And it also does not include the interest he will pay as well," Hozark replied.

Arvin tossed the coin pouch in his hand, enjoying the heft more than before, a smile growing on his face. This was looking to be a far more profitable day than he'd expected.

"Smart man," he said, his countenance shifting to a far friendlier one.

"If I can say, sir, this is quite an impressive place you have here," Demelza chimed in. "Really amazing what you've done.

Great music, a fantastic vibe, and the bar looks amazingly well stocked. As good as any I've ever seen, in fact."

Arvin's face cracked into a pleased smile. Flattery was another sort of coin he was always happy to receive.

"It is, isn't it?" he said. "Come, sit with me. Have a drink."

"Really?"

"Why not?" he said, hefting the small bag. "It's on you, after all."

Hozark looked at Demelza, and a moment of "should we?" passed between them. Of course, that was all for show, but the overt look helped cement their act.

"Well, okay. Thank you, Arvin. You really are a great host."

The two assassins slid into the seats beside him and ordered up strong beverages. Three of them. If they were drinking, Arvin would have to join them. Soon the trio were engaged in a quite refreshing bit of casual conversation, and the proprietor found himself increasingly enjoying their company.

Hozark looked around the establishment with an amazed expression on his face. In reality, he was clocking the locations of all of the guards, as well as noting where Henni, Bud, and Laskar were. The latter was hard at work plying the security detail with drinks. And under his charming assault, they'd actually been partaking more than they should have while on duty. That he had spiked the bottle with a particularly potent extract also didn't hurt.

Soon they would move on to their next steps. But for now, they would continue their ploy until the moment was right. And when it was, they would move, and with speed.

CHAPTER TWENTY-SEVEN

In an unusual twist of events, Arvin was happy to find that he was quite unexpectedly having a surprisingly good time with his guests.

Normally, when people sought him out, it was because they were social climbers, eager to seek his favor and backing in one way or another. But these two truly did not seem to care about those things.

They were just having a good time, engaging in pleasant conversation and equally pleasant liquor. It was refreshing, to say the least.

The man had said his name was Orkin, and he proved to be a most excellent storyteller and fellow of infinite jest. And his buxom associate, Liana, was likewise a delight to have at his table. Little did Arvin know he was carousing with two of the deadliest killers in all the known systems.

The proprietor was getting progressively more relaxed, and with that came an increased openness to talk about all manner of things with his two guests. That they had spiked the bottle of alcohol as soon as it had arrived at the table never occurred to any of the security staff, for the two visitors were drinking it as well, keeping pace with their inebriated employer.

Little did they know that both Ghalian were employing the clever little spell that took any liquids passing their lips and rematerialized it a hundred meters away, out in the snowy tundra.

Of course, had they wished it, they could have simply poisoned the man with ease, then been safely off world before he even felt the first cramps of his impending demise. But that was not the task for the day. Not for this one. He had valuable information, and they were going to extract it.

The plan was to get him alone after worming their way into his good graces. Once he felt a particular fondness for the pair, a fight would just happen to break out, spilling over to all areas of the establishment.

Their boss would be drunk. Very drunk, and not really capable of defending himself, so, naturally, his security detail would sweep him away from the commotion to his personal safe room.

If all went according to plan, the two Wampeh would be invited along, with Arvin intending to keep his new friends from harm's way in his safest bolt hole. But the man would be anything but safe there.

Once they were alone, he would give up the answers they sought, having been incapacitated by a quick stun spell, then dosed with more elixirs to the point he would likely talk about anything and remember nothing.

It was a difficult maneuver in that it took time to coax information from a victim in this manner. But, if done properly, none would be the wiser, and the poor loose-lipped sap would not recall anything they had said.

His security detail would be standing guard outside of the chamber, leaving him with the seemingly unarmed and harmless visitors within. And when they finally took their staggering, drunken leave of him, he would simply appear to be sleeping off the effects of one hell of a bender.

Hozark and Demelza clinked glasses and took another drink, laughing merrily and keeping up their act. But their eyes met, relaying their shared assessment with a glance. The plan was going according to design. And with perhaps another bottle finished between them all, Arvin would be primed for the next stage of their mission.

The staff was always close when Arvin was in the building, so Hozark flagged down the nearest one and ordered them another bottle. It was all going perfectly. Perhaps a bit too perfectly. Something was always bound to go wrong, but no one could ever guess exactly what it would be.

In this case, however, Henni would have been a good bet.

The violet-haired young woman was having a fantastic time, making the rounds of the place, eavesdropping on any conversations that seemed of note, while lightening a few pockets along the way. She had heeded Hozark's warning, however, and was only taking coin and other items that would not be missed by their owners.

It was the most fun she had had since she couldn't remember when, and she even paused in her work to simply let loose and be, enjoying the warmth, her cleanliness, and the freedom she felt in this new place with her new friends. For the first time in ages, she felt her guard begin to lower, just a bit.

A stocky man with slicked-back hair of the deepest blue bumped into her as he passed, jarring Henni from her moment of grace. She spun and pushed back instinctively, shoving the man off-balance despite her diminutive size. The adrenaline surge had given her a start, and now she was ready for a fight.

But Hozark had said to stay unnoticed, and with great effort, she forced herself to ease off the aggression throttle and calm down. Unfortunately, the man she had shoved was not similarly inclined.

"What the hell do you think you're doing?" he growled in a very menacing way.

He was not about to let that slight pass, it seemed, and he moved for Henni quickly and with open aggression. Bud saw the whole thing unfold and was actually impressed the girl had managed to control herself as she had, but he pushed through the crowd toward her regardless, just in case.

The reason had just become readily apparent, in the form of a blue-haired man with a bone to pick.

Bud shoved harder as he tried to reach the outsized girl. "Out of the way!"

But before he could reach her attacker, Henni did the unexpected. Rather than cower and run, as the larger man expected, she launched herself through the air with a piercing shriek, spinning as she flew, landing a brutal kick to the man's cheek.

He shook it off as best he could, but the people around them had already reacted to the sudden outbreak of violence in the way people in crowds so often did, despite having no reason to.

They joined in.

Uzabud leapt into action. Not so much because Henni needed his help, but because he didn't know what else to do. There was a whirlwind of fists, feet, and elbows flying around him, and to attempt to be the calm in the center of that storm would be a sure-fire way to lose a few teeth.

His old pirating ways were never that far below the surface, and when it came to melee brawls, pirates really were the best, and Bud had been one of the better among them. And here, outnumbered as he was, this promised to be fun.

He ducked a punch, kicking the attacker in the groin while simultaneously snapping out the opposite direction with his fingertips, catching a would-be assailant in the throat, making him gasp for breath.

Shifting on the balls of his feet, he changed direction and

followed up with a headbutt, putting thoughts of breath far from the man's mind as he slumped to the ground. Another attacker was flying his way, and Bud spun to face them, his fist already in motion.

Abruptly, he pulled back, barely missing Henni's face. The smaller woman, on the other hand, struck him square in the solar plexus before realizing who was in front of her.

"Same team! Same team!" Bud gasped.

"Oh, shit. My bad."

"Ya think?"

"Stop whining. You'll be fine," she said with a grin and a wink, then jumped back into the swirling fray.

It had seemed like the brawl was going to be a small, contained affair, when Laskar saw Henni and Bud involved.

"That's got to be the sign," he reasoned. But what was he supposed to do?

Without another moment to ponder that question, he took a swing at the nearest of the guards he had been drinking with, punching him square in the face. The stunned man looked at him with shock as his nose started to bleed.

"What the hell? Why would you do that?"

Laskar didn't have the chance to reply as the question was followed up with an immediate punch, returning the favor. Laskar simply rolled with it, swinging wildly at patron and security alike, and in no time that section of the crowd was engaged in an all-out brawl as well.

The energy had shifted, and the two distinct fights quickly blended into one large rumble.

"Get in there and stop this. Now!" Arvin shouted to his staff. The nearest guards joined the fray, but the personal security detail simply pulled in a little closer, creating a perimeter around Arvin and his guests.

Hozark flashed a glance at Demelza. This was too soon, and Arvin was not nearly drunk enough for their plan. The security detail wasn't whisking him away. In fact, he wasn't fleeing at all. He wanted to fight.

Arvin reached under the table, his hand emerging with a skree to call for even more help. Hozark, however, put his hand on his arm, stopping him.

"What are you doing?"

"We should let this play out," Hozark replied, hoping the man would agree.

Unfortunately, seeing damage inflicted on his property sobered him up somewhat, and he didn't.

"My bar, my rules," Arvin said, pulling his arm free.

Hozark sighed. "Well, don't say I didn't try."

Before Arvin could ask what the hell he meant by that, he found his head violently slammed down into the table, knocking him out cold. The sound, along with the sight of their boss facedown and unconscious, sent the private security team into action.

The slim woman nearest Hozark pulled a blade from a hidden sheath, lunging for his heart. Even as he disarmed her and rendered her unconscious, he had to admire her tactical prowess. She had foregone the obvious weapon at her hip, pulling the secret one instead, saving both time and distance required to strike.

However, against the master Ghalian, she simply didn't stand a chance. But Hozark had no desire to kill such a talented fighter. She was only doing her job, after all, and she was not a Tslavar. So he merely rendered her unconscious before turning his attention to her comrades.

Demelza was already in motion, and two of them lay writhing in pain, grasping their broken limbs a moment before she kicked them to sleep. Hozark quickly took out the remaining threats, then turned his attention to the all-out brawl that had spilled across the entire establishment.

None of these men and women were targets. Just

unfortunate victims of bad timing. The wrong place at the wrong time. And given the time constraints at hand, and the very real possibility their friends might wind up seriously harmed in the fray, the two Wampeh set to work in earnest.

They moved through the crowd like a tornado of fury, disarming, disabling, and pounding to unconsciousness all who crossed their path. And that meant pretty much everyone.

Bud, Laskar, and even Henni stopped their fighting at the sight of the two Wampeh Ghalian cleaning up the place with such brutal efficiency, all three suddenly feeling woefully inadequate. They'd never seen them work like this, and it was a sight to behold. They were good fighters, no doubt, but the two Ghalian were just so much better.

In barely a minute, all lay unconscious or wishing they were. A few patrons had scrambled out into the night, but that could not be helped.

Hozark looked at their copilot. "Why did you strike those men, Laskar?"

"I saw the sign," he replied.

"That was most certainly *not* the sign," the Ghalian master groaned. "That was simply Henni being more than a little overenthusiastic."

Henni, her mouth bloody from battle, smiled broadly and gave a cute little wave. Injuries be damned, she was having a blast.

It was such an unexpected sight that they all found themselves chuckling at the diminutive woman. For her size, she could certainly fight.

"What is done is done," Hozark said, striding over to the unconscious form of their target and hefting him over his shoulder with surprising ease, then heading for the doors. "Come. We move on to Plan B. And I fear we haven't much time."

CHAPTER TWENTY-EIGHT

When Hozark snapped off two table legs before departing, then grabbed a length of rope from one of the unconscious patrons' snow-covered conveyance parked outside of Arvin's establishment, Uzabud had absolutely no idea what his friend was up to.

The captive was, well, *captive*, and with the five of them and one of him, there was simply no way he would be escaping any time soon.

"Henni, would you mind? I wish to keep my hand unoccupied," he asked, handing the young woman trotting at his side the coiled rope.

"Sure thing. I've got it," she said, slinging it over her shoulder.

He shifted the unconscious man slumped over his shoulder and pushed on, heading for the expanse of white nothingness that marked the edge of the inhabited area. Henni and the others followed quietly, not just to keep their egress unnoted, but because they were deep in thought about what had just happened. What they had just seen.

Their friends had taken out dozens in a minute, and non-lethally at that. It was a reminder that, while they were their friends and colleagues, the two Wampeh were also something else entirely.

Henni stumbled as her leg caught a loop of the rope. With all of the bundled layers she was wearing, it kept slipping off, forcing her to constantly readjust as they walked.

"Here, give me that. I'll carry it for you," Bud said, intending to make up for his failing to protect her when the fight broke out.

Unfortunately, all he did was aggravate the young woman.

"I don't need your help. What, do you think I'm not capable?"

"No, no. Nothing like that," he said, backtracking as best he could before the dynamo of a woman truly lit into him. "I just wanted to help, is all."

She glared at him, only the sparkling orbs of her eyes visible through the bundling wrapped around her head. What expressions she was making underneath all of that were anyone's guess, but her gaze had a hard edge.

"I don't need your help. I don't need anyone's help," she said, continuing along in Hozark's footsteps as he pushed on into the white.

Laskar stepped closer to his partner. "Damn, Bud. That one *really* hates you."

"Thank you, Laskar, I noticed."

"No, man. I mean, like, really, *really* hates you. More than that Umarian gal you met on Trakkal, even."

"That was just a fling. She knew it as well as I did."

"It didn't seem that way when we were leaving," Laskar replied with a chuckle, muffled beneath his bundled clothing. "Did you ever get that scar healed?"

"Not yet. And it was just a fork. Seems like a waste of coin for something so insignificant."

Laskar chuckled. "Whatever you say, boss."

His spirits were greatly improved with the pleasant addition of a little bit of petty thievery that had become a part of the day's agenda. With all of the patrons of Arvin's place out cold on the floor, they wouldn't be needing the plentiful coats and cloaks stowed at the entrance, and Laskar had taken his pick.

Where he was freezing on their arrival, now he felt perfectly comfortable out in the icy tundra. Of course, he didn't know how long they would be out there, so it was always possible the misery might make a return appearance if they stayed out long enough.

But Hozark had a plan. And that plan did not involve trekking too far from the town. In fact, not too long after they headed out into the ever-falling snow, they found themselves outside of the town proper, but still quite near to its periphery.

Close to its guard beasts.

The roar of the Obanta had been a somewhat distant sound when they'd made their arrival, but now, much to Laskar's distress, it appeared to be getting louder. And that meant *closer.*

"Uh, Hozark? Where exactly are we going?" the man asked, a slight waver of fear in his voice.

"Just up ahead, Laskar. We shall be there momentarily."

The ice beast roared again, and this time it was close. *Really* close.

Hozark nodded to Demelza, who slid a konus she'd liberated from one of the slumbering guards back at Arvin's place onto her wrist. It was a pretty substantial piece of magical gear, she noted now that she had a moment to better look at it. It had been quite fortunate there were so many people involved in the fight, lest the guard be tempted to use it, even in those close quarters.

Demelza uttered a few arcane words and cast a minor force spell, pushing back the snows around them, leaving the group in a tiny bubble of clarity within the flurries. That was when they saw it.

The Obanta was almost invisible, its icy-white shape blending perfectly into the swirling snows. If not for the flat-trampled area around it from the beast's agitated pacing, one might even walk right within its reach and not realize it until it was too late.

"Here," Hozark said, stopping just outside the packed snow.

The others stopped just behind him and waited. A tense silence crackled through the air, waiting for *something* to happen.

The beast lunged at him silently, long, cold claws outstretched as it tried to snatch the Wampeh and make him its meal. But Hozark had stopped outside its area of danger, and the magical collar around the beast's neck violently pulled it back to within its prescribed boundaries.

"Holy shit!" Laskar blurted, falling back over his own feet as he frantically backpedaled.

"It's okay," Bud said. "Look at the collar. It can't get us."

Henni dropped the rope and reached down.

"What are you doing?" Bud asked. "You're not actually going to--"

The snowball flew from her hand, traveling with impressive accuracy for one as bundled up as she was. Its path was true, and the snowy burst as it hit the Obanta in the face enraged the beast even more.

"Come now, Henni," Demelza said. "Let us not torment the poor beast."

"But it wants to eat us."

"Yes, but can you blame it? It is simply its nature. We do not need to be cruel to a beast in unfortunate circumstances, even if it does wish us harm."

Henni thought about it a moment, shrugged, then picked up

the rope and walked over to where Hozark had placed their captive on the snowy ground.

"You still want this?" she asked.

"Yes. Now is the appropriate time," he said, taking the rope from her. "Uzabud, Laskar, will you please give me a hand here?"

The two men walked over to the Wampeh and found themselves somewhat puzzled at what he was doing.

"Uh, why are you stripping him?" Laskar asked. "Bud, why is he taking off Arvin's clothes?"

"I am preparing our friend for a little talk," Hozark said. "And if you would be so kind as to help speed the process, perhaps we might finish here sooner than later."

Bud and Laskar squatted down and set to work helping the assassin remove their captive's clothes. All of them. Demelza and Henni shared an amused look as the men pulled off the man's underpants. It might have been cold out. Even *really* cold out. But that still wasn't much of an excuse.

Demelza kept her stoic demeanor and straight face, but Henni pointed and laughed. The men, however, just continued their work, refraining from any comments about the chill in the air, or growing rather than showing. With the violet-haired imp, it would have merely amused her more, most likely.

"Now, help me get him in position," Hozark said, moving the nude man and tying his wrists securely, then fastening the rope around his body.

Demelza stepped closer, the Obanta roaring and swinging its claws futilely as she passed just outside of its reach.

"Right here will do perfectly," Hozark said, pointing to a spot just within their magical bubble.

Demelza nodded and focused her mind. Then she pulled the magic from the konus and spoke the words, using a common spell but in a most uncommon way, as Hozark had instructed her. In no time at all, her work was done.

"Excellent," the master assassin said.

"Uh, guys? What the hell are you doing?" Laskar asked.

"Doing?" Hozark said, pulling the rope tight. "We are interrogating, of course."

Laskar was confused, but a moment later all became clear. "Oh, that poor bastard," he said with a malicious grin. "If that doesn't make him talk, nothing will."

CHAPTER TWENTY-NINE

"What—where am I?" Arvin asked as the waking spell jerked him back to consciousness.

"Hello, sunshine!" Henni said, then slapped the man across the face.

"Ow! You little bitch! I'll have you cut to pieces and fed to the––"

At the commotion, the Obanta lunged forward, letting out an angry roar as it did. Its restraining spells held it back, but the deadly claws slashed through the air less than a foot from the confused man's face. A warm trickle of urine ran down his leg as his bladder released from sheer terror.

Henni trotted back to her waiting friends.

"He's awake now," she announced.

"Yes, Henni, I know. That was the purpose of the spell," Hozark said. "You did not need to slap him to rouse him."

"Oh, I know. I just wanted to," she replied with a chipper grin.

She and the others had shed some of their layers as the protective spell holding the elements at bay was actually becoming a bit warm inside with so many bodies present. Or, if not warm, it was not freezing, at least.

The small, magical flame that Demelza had cast was also raising the temperature, ever so gradually. The flickering light made the crystals of the snow dance in a brilliant display that mirrored Henni's unusual eyes. And the Obanta's icy fur likewise gleamed from the illumination.

The captive man slowly moved his head, surveying his difficult situation. He was bound at the hands and feet, and had several loops of rope tied around his body, like some kind of kidnapper's shibari.

The two table legs had been carefully placed between his knees and tied in place, the wood above and below the joint effectively splinting his lower extremities and preventing him from bending his legs, let alone walking. Yet he was standing, somehow. Supported by a tug from behind.

He turned, carefully, to ensure he did not accidentally fall forward into the Obanta's reach, and saw how he had been bound. Terrified as he was, Arvin had to admit, it was a clever bit of handiwork. The trailing end of the rope ran from between his shoulders and back to a tall, thick ice stake driven into the frozen ground.

It wasn't a normal rod, but more of an icicle in shape, growing thicker at the top and tapering down to a point. It was that wider aspect that was holding the rope firmly in place. It was solidly constructed and could likely hold his weight indefinitely.

If not for the small flame nearby, that is.

The magical fire was positioned not so close as to immediately melt the icicle. But the tiny drips of water periodically falling from it told the bound man that it would melt through it eventually, in time. And when it did, he would fall forward into the Obanta's reach.

A flash of chill crept through Arvin's body as the urine cooled against his leg.

The realization that the cold he felt was not just a strong breeze cutting through his clothing, but because he was completely nude made his entire body prickle with goosebumps.

In this place, freezing to death was a very real possibility if you weren't careful, and more than one drunk had crossed the rainbow bridge after losing their way in the white.

But these people could have killed him, yet they hadn't. It confused the trussed-up man, no doubt, but as his senses sharpened as the spell continued to do its work, waking him but also purging the spiked alcohol from his system, his self-control kicked back into gear. Despite the conditions, he was doing his best to hold it together, the assassins noted.

Hozark watched impassively as the man's eyes finally cleared and his wits returned to him. Arvin glared at the Wampeh with hate in his eyes but said nothing. He looked at the motley group of captors, clearly doing mental calculations about his odds and how he might get even with them.

Though the man was rather deplorable, despite his somewhat cultured façade, and had become a captive for very good reason, Hozark nevertheless admired the fellow's gumption.

The assassin shifted on his feet, making the snow crunch loudly for a moment to focus Arvin's attention solely on himself without needing to speak. That accomplished, he slowly walked over to the bound man until he was nearly face-to-face with him.

Staying outside the Obanta's reach, of course.

"Right about now, you are asking yourself, 'What did I do to deserve this? Why me?'" Hozark said with a voice utterly terrifying in its calmness. "But none of that matters."

Bud had seen him interrogate plenty of people in their day,

but it never ceased to give him the willies the way he could just turn it on like that. And damn if the man wasn't good at being scary. And in the most subtle of ways. But sometimes, more overt action was called for.

Hozark smiled at his captive, but did not allow his fangs to slide into place. This wasn't *that* kind of an interrogation. At least, not yet.

"What does matter, what is actually the important question you need to be asking yourself, is, will you freeze to death first, or will the flame melt that ice and the Obanta get you instead. Honestly, I do not know which outcome is more likely, but if you speak clearly and honestly, perhaps we will not need to find out."

"Please, I'll give you whatever you want. Take your coin back––"

"We already did."

"Then tell Daruvius our debt is cleared and he owes me nothing. Just let me go."

Hozark let out his well-practiced chuckle. The one that said he knew far more than you did, and you were in far deeper shit than you could possibly imagine.

"What makes you think that is of interest to me?"

"You were sent to handle his debt. So let's make a deal."

"That is where you are mistaken," the Wampeh said. "I do not even know this Daruvius Kahn."

The realization quickly dawned on Arvin that this situation was far different, and far more serious, than he had originally believed. This had nothing to do with old debts and run-of-the-mill subterfuge. Something else was at play, but for the life of him, he couldn't guess what. Of course, when you commit as many atrocities as he had, that sort of thing just came with the territory.

"What is it you want? Coin? I have plenty in my offices, and it's all yours."

"I do not seek coin."

"Then what?" the man asked, confusion in his eyes.

"I merely wish for you to speak the truth. My business with you ends there, if you are completely honest with me."

The rope slid an inch along the melting ice rod's slick surface, jarring Arvin and making the Obanta resume its hungry pacing.

"Anything. Whatever you want to know, just ask!"

"Very well," Hozark said, gesturing for the small young woman with the unusual eyes to stand by his side. "What I wish for is that you answer me this. You delivered a sealed note to Emmik Ozman. A note from the Council of Twenty."

"I did. Yes, that was me!" he blurted.

"Of this I am aware. But, as you know, it was sealed with an anonymous validity seal. What I wish to know is who had you deliver that note? Who within the Council of Twenty sent it?"

Arvin's demeanor perked up. This was something he knew the answer to and would have no problem revealing whatsoever.

"It was Visla Ravik," he said. "He came here and hired me to make the delivery. Paid good coin too."

Hozark looked down at the little violet-haired woman at his side. Her sparkling, galactic eyes were slightly squinted as she looked at the captive with an intense stare.

"He's telling the truth," she finally said, her facial muscles relaxing and her usual mischievous demeanor slipping back into place.

"Wait, you can really do that?" Laskar blurted out in shock, despite Hozark's running the interrogation.

"With this one? Yeah. He's actually really easy to read. Not like a visla or anything," she replied.

Bud stared at the girl with a mix of wonder and concern. They really did have a reader among them. But if Hozark was right about her, then only those not on guard against that particular skill would be susceptible. And Uzabud had no desire to have anyone picking around in his head.

Hozark drew a wicked blade and held it up in front of the captive man's face. He paused, letting the flickering light from the magical flame dance across the metal. Then, slowly, he began slicing the ropes until Arvin was free.

The man fell to his knees, his legs unable to function just yet after being bound in such a manner. It would take him several minutes before he could walk, no doubt, but Demelza's flame spell he crawled toward in hopes of getting warm would last at least that long.

Hozark loomed over the nude man. "We know where you reside. And you know what we can do. Our eyes and ears are everywhere, and you cannot avoid them. Do not speak another word of this again and you will be free to live a long and happy life. Do we have an understanding?"

Arvin looked up at Hozark, and all the fight had gone from his eyes. "It's a deal," he said meekly.

Hozark didn't say a word. He just turned and walked away. The others immediately fell in with him.

"Wait! What about my clothes?"

"They are gone. But you are accustomed to this world, and I would wager if you move fast enough you can make it back into town before any lasting damage is incurred."

With that, the assassin and his team stepped out of the magical bubble and disappeared into the whiteout.

Normally, leaving someone to fend for themselves like that with no clothing out in the cold would be a death sentence, but Arvin knew this place, and as he was with the trapped Obanta, he could extrapolate which way town was, even if he couldn't see it.

But the walk––or run, as the case might be––would not be pleasant.

The five travelers trudged along in the deepening snow,

making their way back away from the town to where their ship lay waiting. They were making good time when Hozark abruptly stopped. The others did so as well, instantly alert at the sight of his slipping the blade from his hip.

He stared out into the white, squinting to see anything in the windswept snow, but nothing was visible.

An enormous claw lashed out from the snowy camouflage, barely missing the Wampeh as he jumped back, his blade already flying through the air into the snowy nothingness. But it wasn't nothing, and the blade flew true. The bellow of the wounded beast confirmed his accuracy.

"Holy shit! An Obanta!" Laskar said, pulling out a blade for each hand, spinning around, desperately surveying the blurred white with wide-open eyes.

Hozark also had a blade in his hand. One of the several secreted on his person. He cautiously walked forward into the snow, peering at the small spattering of blue blood already disappearing into the icy crystals.

He resheathed his knife. "It is gone," he said.

"How can you be sure?" Laskar asked, knives very much remaining in his hands.

"Obanta do not hunt when outnumbered like this. It must have been extremely hungry to even attempt such a thing. And now that it has felt this prey's sting, it will not be back."

"But what if it does return?" Uzabud asked.

"Then we deal with it," he replied. "But I have no desire to harm the creature. It is wounded, yes, but from the amount of blood spilled, I believe it will recover. It meant us no personal harm. It is just a beast, doing as beasts do."

Henni reached out and tugged on Hozark's sleeve.

"Yes?"

"What if it finds Arvin before he makes it back?"

Hozark just smiled at her and turned toward their ship.

"Oh," the young woman said, then quickly fell in behind him.

In just a few minutes they were back in the safe warmth of their craft, and once they had all had the opportunity to clean up and enjoy a hot shower, Uzabud lifted them off of the freezing world and up into the very different cold of space.

They had a new destination. A new target. And Visla Ravik was his name.

CHAPTER THIRTY

The flight from the icy ball of misery that was Moolar made Uzabud happier by the moment, with his mood improving the more distance they put between themselves and the uncomfortable world.

He had performed well, but the sheer hell that was being cold to that degree had made him even more gun-shy of their next destination. Hozark was a bit quiet about where they were going, and in Bud's experience, that could mean anything.

More often than not, trouble.

This time, however, Hozark's reticence was for a different reason. He was trying to pinpoint the location Visla Ravik was actually using as his current base of operations. Sure, he had a main estate that he called home, but as one of the Council of Twenty, he was away from home as often as he was in residence, and that meant he could have taken Visla Jinnik's son anywhere.

Young Happizano could be at any one of a vast number of facilities by this point, and if they infiltrated the wrong one and were seen, their odds of retrieving the boy alive slipped greatly. And his powerful father would not be amused by that whatsoever.

And as for the visla, word had reached Hozark that Visla Jinnik had indeed been out with the Council of Twenty's forces, deploying his magic at their command, helping them secure troublesome colonies and worlds.

He had no choice in the matter.

If he didn't play along, his son's life would be forfeit. So, with a heavy heart, the man who never wanted anything to do with the Council was suddenly one of their pawns, albeit a pawn more powerful than nearly all of their members.

But what troubled Hozark was a strange bit of news about those goings-on. While Ravik was involved, the Ghalian spy network had not picked up word of the other members of the Council participating in his little raids.

It was entirely possible that he was simply given free rein to carry out his task without the rest of the Council needing to divert resources from their other endeavors, but the nature of the silence was troubling. The lack of chatter. How it seemed almost as if Ravik was acting on his own. Or, if not on his own, with the help of someone who had been very, very good at staying behind the scenes.

Ultimately, it was a quandary that would not see its resolution until they had rescued the boy and returned him to his father. Only then could they truly engage and get to the bottom of the nefarious plan, whatever it really was.

Uzabud set them down on a small, fecund world to rest their Drookonus and resupply their foodstuffs. Henni, despite her diminutive size, ate like two full-grown men, and Laskar was very loudly pointing out that they could quite possibly run low on supplies if things required them to stay out for a prolonged time with this very hungry extra mouth to feed.

It wasn't even a question of her proving useful to the team and paying her own way. It was just the sheer quantity she ate that concerned him. When they were alone, the copilot mentioned his concern once more.

"It's not normal, is all I'm saying. I mean, that girl eats more than you do, Bud, and I've seen you put it away."

He could speak freely, as Henni was off with Demelza practicing some fighting techniques that might better work with her size handicap and speed advantage. When an actual Wampeh Ghalian offered to give her lessons, the over-enthused young woman leapt at the opportunity, almost literally, in her excitement.

That meant that the boys were alone for a while, and they did have a few things to talk about while their intel network did their thing.

"Perhaps it is her unusual magic," Hozark pondered. "I am sure you both noticed it. There is something about her, though she does not seem able to properly control her skills, for the most part."

"Hell, from what I've seen, she doesn't even know what she can do," Bud added.

"She can read minds, man. That's some creepy shit."

"Are you gonna start calling me creepy now too?" Bud grumbled.

Laskar laughed. "Nope. That's entirely the girl's domain," he replied.

"She cannot read minds, Laskar. How many times do I have to tell you?" Hozark asked. "Yes, she is an intuitive woman, but that is all."

"That you know of. You've seen her eyes. You know what the legends say."

It was true, Hozark had indeed seen the girl's eyes. Big pools of emotion that just so happened to sparkle as if they contained hidden galaxies within. There were stories about an incredibly rare fluke of nature within some innate magic users that gave them exceptional powers. But those legends were hundreds of years old, and exactly what type of gifts those people were purported to possess had been lost to time.

And for all they knew, Henni might simply be a somewhat troubled young woman who just happened to have rather striking eyes. Or she could be something entirely different. But there was no sense in fretting about it now. Not when they had a job to do, and a pressing one at that.

"Whatever the case may be with Henni, there is nothing we can do about it at this time, so let us do what we *can do* and continue on our way," Hozark said. "Bud, if you set us down by that main farming community, I'm sure we can obtain more than enough supplies to carry us through whatever we may encounter, regardless of our young friend's appetite."

"You've got it," the pilot said, then took them in for their approach to the largest of the agricultural hubs they had seen while leaving orbit.

There were indeed vast fields of all manner of produce being harvested year-round on the pleasantly warm world. For Bud, it was a wonderful change from their prior stop. Laskar was also in good spirits as they headed out to acquire supplies, their pockets heavy with Ghalian coin.

Hozark had been generous with them after their recent ordeal, giving each an extra amount to spend on whatever morale-boosting goodies they might see fit to acquire. They'd done well, after all, and a happy crew was an efficient one.

That, and sending the two off on a shopping expedition gave the Ghalian master the freedom to do what he had *really* directed them to this world for.

Hozark quickly purchased a variety of rations for the voyage, all of them coming with the requisite spells stopping their spoilage for a short time.

He paid a bit extra and had the spells added to even the foods likely to be eaten immediately. One never could tell, and there was nothing quite so annoying as the smell of rotting food in a sealed ship in space.

That handled, he directed the porters to deliver the goods to their waiting craft, then made his way to the grain threshing facility. A tall silo stood casting its shadow across the fields below where men and women of all manner of species worked the soil with their specialized magic.

Small floating conveyances kept their knees—or tentacles, as the case might be—from suffering the abuse of constant contact with the ground as they pruned and managed the vegetation the old way, by hand.

There were spells that did what they were now doing, but out here, where time was abundant and magic was not, a little bit of sweat was far more logical an expenditure than valuable magic.

"Quite a day," Hozark said to the old woman resting in the shade of the silo, drinking some Arambis juice to refresh her energy.

"It is," she said. "Thank the gods for our good fortune."

"You are fortunate indeed," he replied. "But all that is beautiful is not necessarily good."

"An assessment of a wise man," she said.

"Or a tired one. Obstacles are often exhausting, after all."

"Ah, but the obstacle is the way," she replied with a little nod.

The passphrase was an old one, and one of many the Ghalian spies had at their disposal. But Hozark was a student of the classics, and for that reason he had decided upon this particular one.

The woman fanned herself and took another drink. "Can I offer you some refreshment?"

"That would be wonderful. Thank you for your hospitality."

"It is my pleasure," she said, pouring him a glass and stepping close. "Zargota," she said, naming the world the spy network had determined Visla Ravik was now using as his primary base of operations.

"The boy?"

"Unknown," she replied. "But other factors may be in play.

Corann fears the rumors may be true of another Council member in play."

"I guess we shall find out soon enough," Hozark replied, then finished his juice and handed her coin for her troubles. "Thank you for your help," he said.

"Safe travels," she replied, the message delivered. She then went back to work, not knowing how long it would be until her services would be called upon again.

CHAPTER THIRTY-ONE

Zargota.

Of course they knew the world. Anyone with any familiarity with the Council of Twenty knew the few dozen worlds they tended to utilize as their favored bases of operation.

There were always their actual homeworlds, of course, but with the frequency with which their powerful leaders were out expanding the reach of the Council, more often than not, they stayed at one of their peripheral estates rather than living full time aboard a ship.

And Zargota was one such location.

Visla Ravik had slipped up. He didn't know it yet, but by heading to one of the better-known worlds within the Council's realms, he had given the Ghalian spy network something of a rarity. Namely, an easy target to find.

"You're sure that's where he is?" Laskar asked when Hozark relayed the coordinates to him.

"I am certain."

"So, why the secrecy? I don't know why you didn't want to tell us where we were going until we got there. I mean, Moolar was cold and sucked, but Zargota? It's pretty benign if you ask me," Laskar said.

"You have visited Visla Ravik's world in the past?"

"Of course. It was a pretty long time ago, but it's a great stopping point to resupply and have a little fun. And Ravik runs a tight ship, so there's never any craziness or drama in town."

"Some might call that a bug, not a feature," Bud noted. "Drama is what gives a place character. Charm."

"If by character you mean scars from bar brawls and lingering rashes from questionable encounters, then sure," Laskar retorted.

"Yep," the former pirate said with a broad grin. "Like I said. Character."

"I am afraid we will not be spending enough time there for you to partake of any recreation," Hozark said. "Nor would you wish to after we have freed the captive and made our escape. Given the effort that went into not only snatching the boy, but also keeping the true identity of who commanded his kidnapping hidden, I feel confident we will be needing to make our departure in a most timely fashion."

Henni had been listening to the conversation from a seat along the wall, quietly taking in all of the facts and concerns of the upcoming adventure while she powered down a bowl of hot soup. She still had a tiny bit of a residual chill from the outing on Moolar. A lingering issue from the lack of body fat she carried as a result of her rough life on the streets of Groll.

But she was filling out, albeit slowly, and as she returned to normal young woman proportions, the somewhat frantic way she ate her food had finally slowed to an almost normal pace. She still inhaled it, and in great quantities, to be sure, but no longer like a starving beast.

Henni tipped the bowl back and slurped the remainder of her soup loudly.

"Aaah," she said, burping, then licking her lips with satisfaction.

"Charming," Bud grimaced.

"Bite me, creeper," she shot back, then turned her gaze to Hozark. "So, I have a question."

"Yes?"

"What if this Ravik guy was actually hired by someone else?"

Laskar laughed. "Oh, my poor little street urchin, he's a member of the Council of Twenty. No one tells him what to do."

Henni bristled at his tone. "What about someone else in the Council, then? Someone stronger than he is? You considered that?"

"The Council members are backstabbing, power-hungry assholes, but it would be pretty hard for one of them to get another to do something like this without the others being involved," Bud noted. "Word is, some of them even have eyes and ears within the others' ranks."

"Pretty standard spy stuff, right?" Laskar asked.

"Yes and no," Hozark said. "But they do make frequent power moves behind one another's backs. And temporary alliances of a secret nature have been known to occur, though typically to gain personal power, not to coerce a non-Council visla to do their dirty work."

"Which is what I am still curious about," Demelza noted. "To what end is Visla Jinnik being used? We have heard he is quelling uprisings and performing basic power plays for the Council, but that seems beneath a man of his power. They could have sent anyone to do that. But Jinnik? It does not make sense."

Hozark pondered her words a long moment. He had wondered the same for some time now, but no answer had presented itself, regardless of how much digging he had done. Visla Jinnik was under the Council's thumb, no doubt, but whatever the real play was, he had one thing going for him the Council had not counted on.

He had hired the Wampeh Ghalian to retrieve his son before submitting to his servitude. And when the boy was returned and safe, there would be a reckoning.

But for the time being, he did what any concerned parent would do. Namely, anything he had to, to keep his son alive. And for the moment, that meant he was the hammer swung by the Council's hand. A tool with no say in his use.

Soon, hopefully, that would change.

"We will be flying into the system and making our approach as just a normal trading vessel stopping off to gather a few supplies and take some shore leave before continuing on our way," Hozark said.

"Why not split up like we usually do? Come at them from all sides?" Laskar asked.

"The likelihood of there being multiple scouting craft in the system is high, as this is Ravik's current base of operations, and Uzabud's ship would draw attention if it touched down minus some of the craft mounted to its hull."

"Can't you just shimmer cloak them?"

"Mine, yes," Hozark said. "And Demelza's as well. But to do so through a jump while docked to this ship would use an excessive amount of magic, and we would be foolish to attempt to engage them once we are within likely observation range."

"So just use the magic. I mean, you guys have resources galore. It seems like the perfect time to use them."

Hozark knew it seemed like a simple solution to all problems. Using a shimmer was indeed a wonderful tool to keep from being seen. But they had spent a lot of power recently, and to travel cloaked for long periods and distances drained it even faster, especially in space.

It was a lesson the young Ghalian aspirants learned in their flight training. Save your resources when you can, and do not use them without great consideration. Not because they shouldn't be used, but because you never know when a true, urgent need for them might arise.

But Laskar did not know just how much power they had expended in their recent adventures, nor would he. None but Hozark and Demelza knew the actual status of their reserves.

The reality was, yes, they could shimmer cloak their ships, and for a decent amount of time, but neither had fed in some time, and they were running on a limited amount of power. And to engage a shimmer of that nature was a draining endeavor.

That, however, would not be relayed. To all outside of the order, it would always seem as though the invisible ships could appear at any time, anywhere. It was part of the Ghalian myth they wished to continue.

"We have the magic, Laskar, but the goal of this incursion is not to spread our numbers and make our escape more difficult than needed."

"More difficult? It should help us."

"They do not expect us, and they are in their home element. That means that while security is tight, their guard will nevertheless be down. The overconfidence of the powerful. If we spread our numbers, the likelihood of losing a craft should something go wrong increases."

"You think that because this is Ravik's home base they won't be ready for us?" Laskar asked.

"There is no intelligence stating otherwise," Hozark replied. "They do not know that we know they are behind this plot, and they are blissfully unaware we are coming."

CHAPTER THIRTY-TWO

"What was that you were saying about them not seeing us coming?" Bud asked his Wampeh friend through gritted teeth as he spun his ship into a steep dive toward the small moons orbiting Zargota.

"Jump us out of here!" Henni shrieked as powerful magic buffeted the ship's defensive spells.

"We can't. They've cast a blocking net. If we try to jump, we'll be torn to bits," Laskar said, his eyes glued to the display in front of him.

"Then use the ship's defenses and blast them!"

"What do you think I'm trying to do?" he shot back.

"So do it!"

"We are in an evasive maneuver kind of situation here. It's not as easy as you make it sound."

"Hang on," Bud warned everyone. "This is gonna get a little uncomfortable."

He dove the ship in a tight spin, evading the craft hounding his every move. For just a second, he even managed to pull clear of them enough to give Laskar a moment to shift his attention back to the jump spells.

"We clear to jump?" he called out.

"If you can hold it steady for––shit. No. They adjusted."

The pressures within the craft were all kept relatively neutral whether within space or in atmosphere. Gravity stayed the same at pretty much all times, as the ever-running spells were designed to do. It was one of the first things that had been devised when space travel had been accomplished.

But in severe combat situations the forces generated were sometimes extreme enough to put too much of a strain on those spells. And on those occasions, they would sometimes fail.

This was one such occasion.

The spells had backups and would start to re-engage, but the sensations the sporadic shifts in gravity caused were utter misery for those aboard. Fortunately, the vacuum of space typically provided a buffer of sorts for most maneuvers, but Uzabud was heading straight into the gravity of the small moon nearest them. It wasn't full gravity as one would find on a planet, but there was enough to perhaps serve his purpose.

"What are you doing?" Henni asked, her sparkling eyes watering as her stomach churned from the unfamiliar, violent forces assailing her body.

"Giving them a little something to think about," he said, powering into the moon's gravity. "Hozark, prep the chaff and whatever else we can spare."

The Wampeh leapt into action, the shifting gravity throwing him against the walls as he moved. Even his exceptional reflexes and strength couldn't overcome the forces they were being subjected to.

He raced through the ship, gathering personal items, foodstuffs, and even a corpse that had been kept in cold storage for years for just such an occasion. All of them were then hauled on a floating conveyance down the corridor to the site of the umbilical spell leading to one of the craft on the ship's hull.

Hozark opened the inner seal. It did not look good. The

chaotic flight and barrage of deadly magic, combined with the ship's failing gravitational systems, had all pushed the spell to the limit.

There was a tube of breathable air leading into the Kanarian shuttle––that had been mounted there longer than he could remember––but there was no telling how long it would hold out.

But there was simply no choice.

Hozark took a pair of powerful konuses from the items he'd gathered and bound them together, speaking the words of the unusual spell that would link their power in a deadly feedback loop.

As soon as that was accomplished, he clambered into the failing umbilical and began loading all the things he'd collected as fast as he was able. The personal effects were first, and the corpse came last. It was already beginning to thaw a little, but that was of no concern.

If he didn't hurry, nothing would matter at all, for they would all either be dead or captured. If it was the latter, the former would be sure to follow shortly anyway.

The last of it in place, Hozark sealed the ship and dropped out of the umbilical spell's corridor of safe space just as it failed. He cast as fast as he could, sealing the accessway with a powerful spell, and with no time to spare. Had he been but a few seconds delayed, the lack of air caused by the sudden decompression would have prevented him from articulating the spell. And if that had happened, they all would have perished.

Hozark didn't have time to think about that. A violent blast of magic rocked the ship and sent him into the wall, hard. He scrambled to his feet and raced back to the command center, securing himself in his seat as quickly as he was able.

"What is that?" he asked of the multi-colored splatter on the far wall.

"Sorry," Henni replied, her normally pale-pink skin having taken on a decidedly greenish hue.

"You get it done?" Bud asked, ignoring all else but his evasive maneuvers.

"It is loaded."

"How long?"

"Forty seconds," Hozark replied.

"It'll have to do. I just hope we *have* forty seconds," Bud grunted as he pulled the ship into a sharp bank as they approached the moon's surface.

Henni's head slumped forward, the g-forces causing her to black out. Laskar began to see stars, but he knew the old trick of clenching your legs and buttocks to keep the blood from fleeing your brain. He stayed conscious, but only barely.

Two of the pursuing ships slammed into the moon, their crews apparently unaccustomed to handling the unexpected forces at play. It was a last-ditch attempt by Bud, and it had bought them some time.

Being the personal fleet of a Council of Twenty member, and a visla, no less, one would have expected them to have had a bit more training to handle these sorts of things. But Demelza watched them with great interest from her display, as several more of the pursuing craft abruptly began drifting in an erratic manner.

"More of them are out of commission," she called out. "For now, anyway."

"Twenty seconds," Hozark called out.

Bud banked hard again, taking advantage of the temporary gap in the enemy's swarming attack squadron. "Laskar, do we have a jump window?"

"I don't know," the woozy man said. "They're trying to re-establish the blocking net."

Bud gritted his teeth and dove them straight toward the

moon at even higher speeds than before. "Fuck it. Hozark. On my mark."

"Ready."

"Laskar, jump when I say."

"What?" the man said, on the verge of passing out.

Demelza assessed the situation and immediately leapt from her seat, racing to Laskar's console, where she grabbed on and held tight.

"I've got it," she called out. "We've got a window."

The enemy ships were closing in once more, the functional ones swarming and the others quickly regaining their senses. Bud had pulled away for a moment and was flying straight for the moon's surface, but they would not fall for his trick a second time.

"Five seconds," Hozark said, his mental countdown always accurate whether fighting a dozen men or fleeing in a ship about to slam into a moon.

At the last second, Bud pulled up hard. His ship shook violently from the amount of power its Drookonus was expending. The device was glowing hot from the power dump, but this was all or nothing.

"Hozark! Now!"

Hozark cast the release spell immediately, detaching the shuttle containing the charged konuses.

"Demelza! Jump!"

She was not as proficient as Laskar in emergency plotting and jump execution. He was a pilot and navigator, while she was an assassin. But necessity was one hell of a motivating factor. Demelza engaged the jump just as the shuttle craft slammed into the surface of the moon right behind them.

Just as the two konuses exploded in a massive blast of magical destruction, sending debris containing personal effects, supplies, and even body parts scattering about the surface of the moon.

The ship was gone. Destroyed by their own foolish tactics and their pursuers' deadly magic.

Or so it seemed.

CHAPTER THIRTY-THREE

The spacecraft that exited its jump in the middle of nowhere had done so abruptly, and with an unusually strong bit of magic. The space around it crackled with the overflow of dangerously discharged power before settling back into its normal inky blackness.

The term "middle of nowhere" was particularly apt in this instance, as the ship had jumped not to one of the myriad systems in the galaxy, but to that empty space where nothing dwelled.

The darkness between the solar systems.

It hadn't been intentional. An emergency jump to whatever coordinates were available had been all there was time for, and Demelza had done her best to simply get them out of the mess they were in as fast as she was able.

But in the process, Uzabud's ship had been flung to a place utterly devoid of light and life.

People would venture into the black from time to time. It was perfectly normal, and even needed at times when the jump between systems was particularly long. But to do so unintentionally was never anyone's choice. Yet here they were.

Uzabud was the first to question their circumstances when he roused from the abrupt nap caused by the pressures of what might very well have been his final maneuver had he failed. He quickly scanned the area, trying to get a fix on where they were and what their status was.

Hozark was already up, kneeling beside his fallen friend. Demelza had not been strapped in when they jumped, which was normally not a problem. But with the forces of Bud's daring maneuver in play, she had been rudely slammed to the deck the moment the jump engaged.

"What––" she said as she began to wake.

"Slowly," Hozark said. "We are safe. Take a moment and gather your bearings."

She did as he asked, slowly taking stock of her body. She seemed intact, but the throbbing told her she would have a decent bump on her head, and quite an ache to go along with it. But it appeared that aside from that, she was all right.

"Oh, my stomach," Laskar said, unslumping in his seat.

Hozark was about to move to check on him when quite abruptly he and Demelza quite abruptly began floating. A few moments later, they were dropped back to the deck.

"Ouch," she grumbled with annoyance.

"Bud, the Drookonus," Hozark called out to his friend.

The pilot wasted no time, quickly pulling the magical device free. It was still orange-hot from the excessive power that had been pulled from it, thin wisps of smoke trailing up into the compartment's air.

"Ouch! Shit, that's hot!" he said, dropping it to the deck with a loud thunk.

The sound woke Henni. The violet-haired woman slowly raised her head, taking a deep, pained breath. Even more than the others, the rigors of their escape had taken their toll on her wee body. She immediately passed out once more.

"Where the hell are we?" Laskar mumbled as he cleared his

head and looked at his console. "What happened? Who jumped us here?"

"That would be me," Demelza said, rising to her feet. "And as for where we are, I haven't the faintest idea."

"I'm sorry, you what, now?"

"I found the first clear pathway I could and jumped us. You had passed out, and we were about to be killed, so I was left with few options."

"But we're in the middle of the black. There's nothing around us. Like, *nothing*."

"Not intentionally, I assure you. When the blast erupted behind this craft, it was just as the jump was being cast. There was konus magic in that event, and its eruption pushed us far out of line with the intended jump."

"That would explain the fried Drookonus," Bud mused.

"Likely," Hozark said.

"Are you all missing the fact that we're drifting in the black?" Laskar said, once again pointing out their dilemma.

"But we are alive, so at least there is that," Demelza said before abruptly floating in the air once more.

"Bud, will you please see to that?" Hozark asked, floating beside her.

"On it."

The pilot pulled from the konus embedded in his command seat and reached out to his ship's many spell systems. It took a minute to pinpoint the breakdown, but soon enough he had managed to right the ship's gravity spells. For the time being, anyway.

"Okay, that should hold for a bit, but we've got some problems."

"What kind of problems, Bud?"

"The kind that mean we can't jump."

"We're stranded here?" Laskar said, a shrill note of panic creeping into his voice.

"Not stranded. Not exactly. But the gravity is spotty, the ship needs a top-to-bottom check to ensure the hull's integrity, and the Drookonus is fried. So yeah, we can't jump. Not now, anyway."

"But Hozark has an extra Drookonus."

"Did you miss the part where I said we need to check the hull? There's way too much stress that is put on the ship by flight to use one now. I mean, for all we know, it's the magical shielding that's keeping the air inside. And if that fails and we haven't patched any hurt the ship may have incurred, we're screwed. And I mean the dead-and-floating-in-space kind of screwed, if you catch my drift."

Demelza walked to the slumped-over young woman in the far chair and checked her for a pulse.

"She lives," the assassin said, then gently rubbed the nerve point on Henni's neck to stimulate increased blood flow to her brain.

A moment later the typically perky woman roused once more, but slowly, and with watering eyes.

"What happened?"

"We survived," Demelza said.

Henni's eyes finally focused and she looked around at her shipmates. All were well, it seemed.

"Oh, shit. I'm so sorry," she said, spying the splatter on the far wall. "I'll get a rag," she said weakly as she fumbled with her seat restraints.

Bud rose and helped her to her feet in a rare display of concern. "Go lay down. We'll take care of it. Demelza, would you see her to her room?"

"Of course. Come along, Henni. Let us get you to a bed to better regain your energy."

"Okay," the violet-haired girl said, allowing herself to be led down the corridor.

"Now I know she feels bad," Bud said. "No way she'd have gone along with that normally."

Hozark gave him a curious smile. "You surprise me, Uzabud. I did not think you had it in you."

"Hey, she may be an annoying little shit, but she's part of our team, right?"

The Wampeh nodded once.

Bud walked around the command center, running his hand over the ship's smooth interior. "She performed well, this old girl," he said. "Not designed for those kinds of forces. Not by a long shot. But she got us out of there in one piece."

"But to where is the question," Laskar noted. "I'm going to have a bit of work with the star charts, I fear."

"Then get to it," Bud replied. "Hozark and I are going to get started going over every bit of this ship. She seems all right, and we're alive, but you never look a gift Malooki in the mouth."

"Of course not. They'll bite," Laskar joked.

"Not quite how it goes, but good enough," Bud said with a grin. It seemed his copilot's snark was returning, and that meant he would be okay. "Come on, Hozark, we've got work to do."

The two men walked the ship they knew so well, each focusing on opposite sides of the compartment or corridor they were passing through. They both wore powerful konuses, hoping they would not be needed, but ready to use them if necessary.

Either one of them could make a survey of the ship on their own, but with damage and decompression a possibility, having backup was the wisest move. It also allowed them to discuss the surprising turn of events that had led them to this point.

They had reached the galley when Demelza joined them, likewise wearing her strongest konus for the task. She reached out with her magic as did the others, probing the craft with specialized spells, seeking out any flaws or weaknesses.

Normally, that bit of magic was used to either sabotage or infiltrate a craft. But now the pair of assassins were using it for a far different purpose. Fortunately, thus far, at least, the craft had seemed to be intact and unharmed. But they still had a long way to go.

"That was a lot of ships back there," Bud said as they swept for damage.

"Indeed," Hozark agreed.

"No, I mean a *lot* of ships."

"I know what you are getting at, Bud, and I agree. This is not a fight we wish to engage in, nor one we could win with our limited numbers."

"Not just that, though. That wasn't normal. We jumped into that system and made a normal approach. There was no reason for that many of them to have been standing by. They came at us as soon as we were close. And to cast a jump net to keep us there? That spells out just one thing."

"I agree, Bud. They obviously were tipped off that we were coming. Or that someone was coming, in any case."

"Arvin?" Demelza asked. "We did let him live."

"I do not think so," Hozark said. "He did not strike me as the sort who wanted to give up his comfortable lifestyle. And if he did make it back to town in one piece, he was very well aware that any negative actions on his part against us would result in very serious ramifications. He would have had to give up all he had. And I do not believe he would do that."

The others considered that point. It was a sound assessment of the man.

"If not him, then whom?" Bud asked.

"With all of the stones we have been turning over in this search, I am afraid anything is possible. And now we are in a difficult position, almost certainly unable to approach Zargota without detection."

"Yeah, even if they bought our fake death, which we did

quite expertly, I might add, they'll still be on high alert for some time," Bud said.

"But we did gather an important clue in this encounter," Demelza interjected. "And one that may well mean we do not have to return to Zargota at all."

"Oh?" Hozark said. "Explain."

"When we were in combat, I noted something unusual about a few of the attack craft that were pursuing us. When their pilots lost consciousness their slowed movements allowed me a better look."

"What did you see? They just looked like a bunch of assholes trying to blast us out of the sky to me," Bud said.

"Did you not see the markings on the ships?"

"Markings? No, sorry. I was too busy trying to keep us from getting shot down."

"Which we all appreciate. But I did get a good look, and they were not just Ravik's Council ships. Several of them bore the markings of Emmik Urtzal."

Bud looked confused. "But he's a low-ranking emmik. Not even a key player in Council affairs. Why would he have ships there?"

"An excellent question. I would be willing to wager they were not there by accident," she replied.

A faint smile began to form at the corners of Hozark's lips. "The man craves power, and what better way to curry favor than to help out one of the Twenty? There would be no reason for them to be present unless he was somehow involved."

"Exactly. And if Visla Ravik knew a rescue attempt would be coming to his base of operations--"

"He wouldn't want to keep the kid there, just in case," Bud said. "Holy shit. Do you guys know what this means?"

The two assassins most certainly did.

"Yes, Bud," Hozark replied. "It would seem quite likely that young Happizano Jinnik is not on Zargota at all. He is likely with Emmik Urtzal."

CHAPTER THIRTY-FOUR

The process of inspecting and repairing Bud's ship took nearly twelve hours, even with Laskar joining the party once he had finally figured out where they were out there in the middle of nowhere.

Apparently, while the hull remained unbreached, some sections of the ship's superstructure had become stressed to the point of damage. Not failure, but weak spots had sprung up, and they needed to be addressed before they dared fly into potentially hostile space again.

The process was relatively simple. It was just time consuming. And now that they had a better idea of where Visla Jinnik's boy was *truly* being held, they wanted to get moving far sooner than later. Unfortunately, the repairs would take as long as they did, and there was no way around that.

"With the damage the overloaded Drookonus did when it crapped out in that most spectacular fashion, I would estimate we'll be able to fly at about eighty-five percent efficiency until we can get this old girl in for a proper overhaul," Bud said when they finally powered the craft up and tested it with a very short jump.

"Okay, so it'll take us a bit longer, then. But at least it'll hold together, right?" Laskar asked.

"Yeah, she'll get us where we're going. I just sincerely hope we don't run into any significant problems along the way."

"You and me both," his copilot agreed.

"Did we jump?" a groggy-eyed Henni asked as she padded into the command center.

"We did. You feelin' any better?" Bud asked.

"Yeah. How long was I out?"

"Over twelve hours. It would seem the wear and tear on your body was a bit more intense than we had originally realized," Demelza said.

"I don't do good with that kind of thing," Henni said. "Not that it's a regular occurrence, but I remember when I was a girl, I would get sick a lot from it."

"Why would you get sick from travel?" Laskar asked.

"Oh, they didn't use the good spells in my part of the ship. Didn't want to waste precious magic, you know."

They had all known their newest guest had gone through some rough times and had even been enslaved, but now it appeared as if she had an even more difficult past than she'd let on.

For her to have been kept in such conditions meant the cruelest of slavers. Not the kind who cared one bit about their cargo. People died in those conditions, and regularly. While Ootaki or Drooks would undoubtedly get preferential treatment, anyone else would be seen as having the same value as a pack animal, if not less.

Hozark and Demelza were Wampeh Ghalian, and their order had a very, very negative outlook on slavery in general. That this had happened to one of their friends made it even more repugnant.

Laskar took it in stride, as was his laissez-faire way. But Bud felt a visceral rage bubble up within him. Annoying or not, the idea that this poor little woman had been abused so terribly made him want nothing more than to punish those responsible, likely leaving a trail of their remains as warning to any who would think to copy their actions.

You can take the pirate out of his fleet, but you can never take the pirate out of the man.

Uzabud quickly got his anger under control, turning his attention back to the task at hand, but the vein on his neck was still visibly throbbing.

"You ready, Laskar?"

"Yeah. Just say when, Bud."

He double-checked their systems. "Jump."

It took fourteen jumps spread out across a far longer period than they'd have liked before they reached Emmik Urtzal's system. Tempting as it was to push themselves and make it in eight, Bud knew full well he had to go easy on his ship until it had been properly repaired.

"This time we take the shimmer ships," Hozark said. "Demelza and I will do a recon of the emmik's domain. You stay well clear of his homeworld. We likely have the element of surprise, but given what happened back at Zargota, we must be prepared for anything."

"Can I come?" Henni asked.

"I am sorry, little one, but not for this mission."

"Come on, I want to help."

Hozark glanced at Bud. "But you will serve us so much better here, keeping an eye on our friends, standing ready if they need assistance. All Demelza and I will be doing is flying around and reconnoitering the location. Why, we probably won't even set down."

"Really?"

"Of course," he lied.

There was no way he and Demelza would not gather intel on the ground firsthand if they could safely do so. Even if it wasn't safe, in fact.

"Skree us if you find anything," Laskar said.

"The skrees appeared to have been damaged by the surge of magic during our escape. I fear they will need to be replaced."

"Well, that's just great. What if things go to hell on us?"

"Then we improvise," Hozark replied. "But first and foremost, we must know what exactly we are dealing with. For this emmik to have become involved with the likes of Visla Ravik, there must be more in play than we know."

"Why's that?" Laskar asked.

"Because Urtzal is a low-level player within the Council's organization. He has little to offer aside from his service and loyalty. Power-wise, he is nothing of note, though he has enough to be an emmik, of course."

"So what's in it for him?" Bud asked.

"He has aspirations, my friend. And men who aspire to be more will often sell their souls for the opportunity for advancement. In this case, by helping Ravik, he may very well be positioning himself for a stronger position within the Council's ranks once Ravik makes his move. Whatever that may ultimately prove to be."

"But why take the kid to go through all of this? I mean, I get it, his dad's really strong. But Ravik has him doing ridiculous little jobs. Things way below his abilities."

"I do not know his reasoning, Bud. But I hope to find out. For the moment, however, we must focus on the immediate task at hand," Hozark said, making his way to the door. "Demelza and I will return shortly. Remain prepared to move quickly."

The two Wampeh took their shimmer-cloaked ships and left their friends at the far edge of the system, well out of harm's way, once they had confirmed there were no lurking attackers as there had been at Zargota.

Hozark and Demelza had agreed upon a rendezvous point on the surface before they had launched. While their personal, Ghalian skrees within their ships were more robust than the ones aboard the mothership, they did not wish to risk communications over them.

It was the real reason Hozark had told Laskar the other units were damaged. They were, to a degree, but more than that, he did not want the impulsive man blurting out something that might be overheard. For if Visla Ravik was truly backing Emmik Urtzal, then the lesser caster might have been clued in to the skree system's hidden back door, and *any* unexpected skree calls might draw attention.

The two Ghalian killers landed at opposite ends of the city Emmik Urtzal called home. It was a warm planet, with an almost desert climate, but lacking the deadly heat waves and burning sands. The skies were a cozy orange hue from the twin suns, one yellow, one red, and the native architecture and paint scheme complemented it perfectly.

The buildings were all rather low and wide, rather than tall and narrow. On this world, no one, it seemed, had bothered to develop magic-heavy towers when they could just expand laterally. Even the emmik resided in a relatively short estate, though his encompassed far more land than those who lived under his control.

Hozark left his ship fully cloaked atop a sturdy building, the craft remaining in a low hover and ready to fly at a moment's notice. If all went to plan, Demelza would be doing the same across the city. He wore his shimmer cloak, camouflaging himself before slipping invisibly to the streets below.

It was a fairly bustling environment, with the usual assortment of floating conveyances and porter carts, all carried by their cushions of magic. Hozark slipped behind a small stable and adjusted his appearance to match that of one of the more common races present. Orange skin and hair replaced his own, and with that in place, he stepped out into the street once more to better interact with the locals as he gained intelligence.

It quickly became apparent, by both the wares he saw for sale, and the stench in the air, that animal products were a strong suit of this place, whereas the marketplace was rather devoid of fresh produce. Meat was to be had readily, but greens commanded a premium. Not the sort of place he would wish to stay any length of time, but a short visit was precisely what was planned.

He cut through a fabric dying neighborhood on the way toward Emmik Urtzal's estate. The colors were being expertly applied to the raw fabric by casters with an impressive grasp of their particularly specialized magic.

Any other day, Hozark would have taken a moment to enjoy their display of artisanship, but today he was on a ticking clock.

It took nearly two hours to properly survey the area on foot, but by the time he and Demelza met up at the small square in front of Emmik Urtzal's home, both felt it had been well worth the time.

"A fascinating world," Hozark said. "Did you notice the lack of control collars here?"

"Yes. It is actually both surprising and refreshing seeing a place devoid of slaves, yet under Council control."

"But you realize what will happen if Emmik Urtzal is moved up in rank within their organization. The policies of the Council will trickle down, and this world will also become polluted by the taint of slavery. Look at these people. They do not realize how fortunate they are, for under different leadership, a great many would go missing, sold off to those in need of slave labor on other worlds."

"But if we retrieve the boy, we make Urtzal look bad. And if that happens, there will be no promotion for him," Demelza noted.

"If he keeps his head," Hozark added. "Come, we must return to the others. I have a plan."

CHAPTER THIRTY-FIVE

"I'm sorry, you want to do what?" Laskar asked.

"You heard him," Bud replied.

"Yeah, I heard him. I just can't believe he actually said what I thought I heard him say."

Hozark looked the worried man in the eyes. "I understand your concerns, Laskar, but given the layout of this particular estate, as well as the rather spread-out nature of the city itself, I feel we are not presented with any better options."

"Hozark is right," Demelza agreed. "And you should be pleased to be able to land so close to the target."

"The guards will get us."

"Not if you do as I say," Hozark said. "It is a simple matter of accessibility and covering the distances required to make our escape once we have found and rescued the boy."

"If he's even here, you mean," the copilot griped.

"What's with you, man? You're even bitchier than usual," Bud asked. "We've got a good plan, and if all goes smoothly, we should be in and out without raising a single alarm."

"When does anything ever go smoothly?"

Henni paused from her snacking and chuckled. "He's got a point, you know."

Bud sighed. "Fine. But come on. These guys do this for a living."

"Well, technically, we do not perform rescues for hire, as a rule," Hozark noted.

"Yes. We are more the silent assassination types," Demelza added.

Laskar shook his head. "I'm telling you, this whole plan is too dangerous. All this infiltration and sneaking around? You should just grab the kid and run. There's no telling what this emmik might have up his sleeve if he was willing to risk taking on Visla Jinnik."

"And we intend to do just that. To an extent, anyway," Hozark said. "We will split up and seek out the child once we have penetrated the compound. It will be a fast pass through and an even faster exit, if we can manage it."

"Ugh. Fine," Laskar griped. "So, I assume you'll need to be ready to take off immediately?"

"Yes. We will be up against something of a time crunch, I fear."

"Then I'm your man. I'm a fantastic pilot——"

"As you keep saying," Demelza noted.

"Well, I am. And if this is going to be a hurry-up-and-run-away kind of situation, you'll want someone to be with the ship, keeping it prepped and ready for takeoff."

"Are you seriously pussying out on us?" Bud asked. "I thought you loved this sort of thing."

"I'm just being realistic about the situation. Hozark said it himself. You said it yourself. The place is too spread out for multiple ship landings to be effective if we have to make a fast escape. If we're going in with just one ship, then it should be ready at all times."

"He does make a valid point," Demelza said.

"See? She gets it. You won't be able to run all over town trying to get out of here. You'll need the ship close. And if you need an emergency pickup from the rooftop? I'm your man."

Bud and Hozark had actually been thinking about just that possibility, but had decided the probability of requiring one would likely be slim to none. But given his current state of agitation, Laskar might well prove to be more of a liability on the ground than not.

"Very well," Hozark said. "I think this is a reasonable suggestion. And you *are* a rather talented pilot. With Bud working the building from the inside, it will be good to have you covering our backs."

"What about me?" Henni asked.

"You will be with Uzabud."

"Aww, but I'm better by myself."

"Gee, thanks for the vote of confidence," Bud griped.

"The truth hurts, don't it, creeper?" she shot back.

"Bud knows the plan. Once we land, we will make our entrance under cover of shimmer cloaks. This emmik is not remotely powerful enough to detect us. Then you will make your entrance. Are we good?"

"All set," Bud replied.

"Excellent. Then, if you'd please take us down, I think it is high time we begin this operation."

The central most landing site in the city was quite close to Emmik Urtzal's estate. This had been a conscious choice on his part when he came to power. Not only did it make his seat of power the same place as most higher-class travelers would arrive, but it also gave him quick and easy access to his ships should an emergency necessitate them.

He was paranoid of attempts on his life, and having a quick escape path was one of his pet concerns. Of course, a pair of assassins would actually be in his home on this very day, but he was not the target. And if all went according to plan, he would never even know they were there.

Bud set down the ship in a somewhat snug space between several of the emmik's own vessels. As they landed, Demelza got a better look at the crafts' markings, confirming without a doubt that these were from the same fleet that had attacked them at Zargota. Not the actual ships that had been part of that attack, but additional craft from the emmik's ranks.

"You gonna be okay here all by your lonesome?" Bud asked as he and the others headed for the door.

"I'm golden," Laskar replied with a cocky grin. "Ready and waiting to bail your asses out and get us as far from here as possible."

"Good times."

"Oh yeah."

"All right, then. I'll see ya on the flip side," Bud said, then stepped out to join the others.

To all observing, the only people to exit the newly arrived craft were a man and his petite female companion. A pair who, after asking directions of one of the nearest guards, made their way toward Emmik Urtzal's estate.

What they did not see was the pair of shimmer-cloaked Wampeh Ghalian who stepped out directly after them, the invisible pair making quick time to the emmik's property.

The security at the entryway was relatively lax. There were plenty of guards, of course, but they had the demeanor of men and women who had spent far too much time with nothing exciting to do. As a result, they were not nearly as attentive as they should have been.

A pair was randomly scanning entrants with their specialized spells, but it looked as if they were being conservative in using the magic and only actually cast the spells once in a very long while.

It was security theater, essentially, but it was enough to deter most who might have any unsavory thoughts and sticky fingers. The display was, however, by no means enough to even slow the cloaked assassins for so much as a moment.

In no time Hozark and Demelza had passed all of the checkpoints and were deep into the property's grounds. They stayed close as they moved until they reached a T intersection in the hallway.

"May fortune smile upon you, Brother," Demelza quietly said.

"And may your hunt be a success," Hozark replied.

The two shimmer-cloaked Wampeh then split up and went in opposite directions to search for Visla Jinnik's son. So far, it was going as they had planned. If he was anywhere within those walls, they would find him. As for Bud and Henni, while their entry might be difficult, Hozark was confident their charade would be successful.

They would be fine playing it up for the guards. What he was more worried about was the duo's interactions with one another.

CHAPTER THIRTY-SIX

Given that neither Bud nor Henni possessed the power or skill to use a shimmer cloak, their entry into Emmik Urtzal's property was, by necessity, going to be a different type. A far more direct approach, but one neither of them was particularly happy about.

Dressed in some of his nicest attire, Uzabud walked through the main doors to the emmik's compound, heading straight for the nearest member of the house staff.

The older woman who was overseeing the workers saw them coming and cracked a knowing smile. On his arm was a stunning young woman with violet hair and sparkling eyes. The way they looked at one another, it was clear they were deeply in love. And that meant just one thing in this place.

"Bonding?" she asked as soon as they opened their mouths to make their inquiry.

"Why, yes," Bud said. "How did you know?"

"I've seen many young couples in love in my time, dear. And with the emmik being the highest authority on the world overseeing the sacred bonding of two beings, it has been my pleasure to be party to many such happy unions."

"Yep. That's us," Henni said. "Toootally in love, me and him. Yeah, he really is the best."

Where the man appeared a relatively strait-laced sort, the girl seemed a bit strange. But who was she to judge?

"Sadly, the emmik is not available for a few days, I'm afraid. But if you wish to make an appointment, I'm sure we can fit you in for a ceremony as soon as his schedule clears. It shouldn't be more than four or five days, I would think."

"That sounds lovely," Bud said with an innocent and bright-eyed smile.

Henni had to give him credit. The guy could act. If she didn't know better, she'd never have guessed he was a smuggler and former rough-and-ready pirate.

"Could you please point us in the direction of the office that handles those appointments?" he asked.

"Of course. Just go through those doors over there, then turn left. At the end of that hallway, you take the stairs up one level and turn right. The fourth door on your right is where you need to go. Ask for Atilda. She handles all of the bonding-related issues."

"Thank you so much," Henni gushed, reaching out and actually squeezing the woman's arm warmly. "You've been such a help."

The couple headed off, following her directions. The woman caught the eye of the security detail by the entryway and waved the pair through.

"Such a nice couple," she said, then returned to her other duties.

Arm in arm, Bud and Henni walked down the corridor and took the stairway, as they were instructed. Once they were out of sight, however, they promptly separated, letting go of each other with haste.

"That went well," Bud mused.

"Yeah. Nice acting," Henni replied.

"You too. Quite convincing."

"Because I'm *good*, and people are gullible," she said. "Not like I'd ever actually want to bond with a creeper like you."

"Hey, this creeper helped get you past security and into the building. And he also happens to own the ship you're so comfortably living aboard, thank you very much."

"Doesn't change a thing," she shot back.

"Ugh, as if I'd ever want a pain in the ass like you. Just shut up and come on. We've got work to do. Hozark and Demelza should already have cleared the bottom level and moved to the top. We'll meet them in the middle."

"Yes, I know the plan," she snarked. "Go on, then. Lead the way."

Bud shook his head and sighed, then headed off down the corridor, his ersatz bride in tow.

Moving through the upper levels like an invisible breeze, Hozark and Demelza quickly scanned every room, cell, and hidey-hole they came across, hoping to find Jinnik's boy. So far, they had covered much of the building at speed, avoiding the guards in their shimmer cloaks as they searched high and low.

Hozark had something of a lead on Demelza in the searching department. His proficiency with the shimmer cloak was exceptional, and he could move at full speed without any catching sight of him. Demelza, on the other hand, was forced to slow her pace when close to bystanders.

Hozark had shown her a few tricks to improve her shimmer cloak use after their last mission together, and she had proven quite adept at them, and was incorporating them in her current use. She was still nowhere near as good as he was, though, she hoped she might be one day.

Both the Wampeh had opted to carry their full complement of

weapons on this incursion. Given what had happened so recently, and adding the fact that they would be cloaked by shimmers, they were free from the scrutiny that a normal disguise might face.

As such, she wore the blades lent to her by Master Orkut, and Hozark carried his vespus blade strapped to his back.

It was he who finally stumbled upon a young boy in an upper corner chamber. The quarters actually seemed quite comfortable, all things considered. It appeared the boy was either a well-treated prisoner, or the wrong one, in which case Hozark would have no choice but to stun the youth to protect from his presence from being discovered.

Hozark looked at the boy closely, having entered the room without him so much as noticing the intrusion. He had a pale violet complexion, even lighter than Henni's hair. His father did not possess these colorations, but from what Hozark had learned of the man's deceased wife, it seemed the boy took his coloring from her side of the family.

He couldn't have been more than ten or eleven years old. The right age for the target. This had to be Happizano.

"Excuse me," Hozark said, shedding his shimmer cloak. "I do not mean to startle you, but are you Happizano Jinnik?"

"Duh," the boy replied.

"Excuse me?"

"I said, *duh*. Now go away."

"You must come with me," Hozark commanded.

"Screw you."

Hozark quickly realized that this youngster was one of *those* kind of kids. The kind that reinforced why he'd never wanted any of his own.

"Your father sent me. I've come to bring you to him, but we must leave at once."

The boy looked at him curiously a moment. "How do I know you're not lying? Everyone around here lies."

"I can understand your caution, and it is wise. However, I have a token to prove I am on his errand."

Hozark reached into a small inner pocket and removed a folded page. On it was Visla Jinnik's seal. The boy was not impressed.

"And? Anyone could have taken that when they broke into our home."

The assassin sighed. "You have a choice, young Jinnik. Do you wish to walk, or would you rather be carried?"

The boy was about to mouth off in protest when the strange man flashed a pointy-toothed smile. *Then* Happizano realized who he was dealing with. *What* he was dealing with.

"Uh..."

"I thought so," the Wampeh said. "Let us make a quick adjustment, so you are not so conspicuous."

He pulled from his konus and cast a very, very basic disguise spell. One of the simplest and least invasive he knew. It would not last long, and it only changed the boy's complexion from violet to orange, but it would not hurt at all, and given their rocky start, he thought that to be the best option to go with.

He stepped back and looked at his handiwork. It wasn't fantastic by any stretch of the imagination, but it would have to do.

"Good enough," he said, then quickly adjusted his own coloring to match the boy's. "Now, with me, and hurry."

Hozark led the way, sweeping the hallway for hostiles while appearing as casual as possible. Just a man and his son walking down the corridor. Nothing to see. Nothing worth noting.

They took the stairs heading down toward the main entryway. It was the most exposed and heavily trafficked of the potential exits. But it was also a direct line to their ship. And from what Hozark had seen while they were making their entry, the guards were interested in who was coming in, but they were paying no mind to who was going out.

"Hey, there they are!" a young woman's voice called out.

"Yes, I see. Keep it down."

"You keep it down."

"Woman, you'll be the death of me," Bud grumbled.

"Keep up with that lip and I just might be," she shot back.

Happizano looked up at Hozark, a bit concerned.

"They're with you?"

"Yes. Though they are typically more professional in their behavior," he said, loud enough to make his point clear to the quarreling pair.

Henni and Bud both clammed up, each silently blaming the other for Hozark's displeasure. But whoever's fault it may be, there was a job to do.

"You two need to take the boy back to the ship," Hozark said.

"Wait, what are you going to be doing?" Bud replied. "And where's Demelza?"

"She is still engaged in the search. And I have one more thing to check. The emmik's personal offices. There may be further useful intelligence there as to what they truly plan for Visla Jinnik. The opportunity is too good to pass up."

"What are they doing to my dad?" the boy asked, a flash of concern darkening his face.

"Nothing much. But now is not the time to discuss that. We will have plenty of time once we are well clear of this world," the assassin replied. "Bud, if you would, please."

"Right. Come on, kid. Follow us."

"And Uzabud. Do hurry. The spell will only last approximately five minutes longer, give or take. We do not want him shifting back to his natural coloring before he is far from these walls."

"We're on it," Henni chirped. "Let's go!"

CHAPTER THIRTY-SEVEN

The faux lovers and the orange boy they had not arrived with made for the exit in a hurry. They were so close to achieving their goal, it was tangible.

"Hey! You two!" a voice called out as they rushed across the lobby area toward the beckoning light of freedom.

They turned. It was the woman who had helped them when they arrived.

"We have to say something," Bud said in a stage whisper as they steered over to greet her.

"Hi!" Henni said, all smiles and sunshine. "Yes, we found the right place. Thank you so much for all of your help."

"So, she was able to get you scheduled?" the woman asked.

"Yes. We're to be bonded in nine days' time," Henni replied.

"Oh, that's wonderful. You know, I can tell you two will make it last. I've seen hundreds come through these doors, and I'm never wrong."

"From your lips to the gods' ears," Bud said, tamping down the frustrated scream that he felt welling up inside of him. "Well, we really must be off. Things to do, people to invite and all that."

"Yes, much to do," Henni agreed. "Thank you again for all of your help."

They turned to leave and had taken a few steps when the woman spoke again.

"Wait a minute. Didn't you two come by yourselves?" she asked, a curious expression on her face.

"Oh, you mean *him*," Bud said, clapping the boy on the back with a big, friendly smile. "This is our neighbor's son. She knew we were busy and trying to get a date locked in, so she sent him here to get come information for us about what options we might have. It was a lovely gesture she hoped would take a little off our plates."

"Your neighbors did that for you?"

"We have always been quite close with them," Henni noted. "And when their boys were young, I babysat them for a spell."

"How utterly delightful. It's so rare to see that true neighborly care these days. I mean, you're young folk, but back in my day, it was so much more common to help one another without even asking."

"We really are lucky," Bud agreed, mentally counting down the minutes until the boy's magical disguise would fade away and their charade would be up. "Well, it really was fantastic chatting with you, and thank you again for all of your help. But we really do need to get him back to his parents. I think he's been gone far longer than they'd expected, and they must be a bit worried."

The woman smiled warmly. "Of course. I know how it is to have a young one out in the world. You two take care, and congratulations again."

Bud and Henni smiled and waved, ushering Happizano ahead of them as they moved casually, but quickly for the exit.

"How long?" she asked.

"A minute, tops," Bud replied.

"Shit. We're not going to make it."

"We *are* going to make it. Come on. Kid, you go in front," he said, gently steering the boy to the lead of their departing group. "This is going to be a wonderful ceremony!" Bud said loudly as they approached the guards. "I think we may even have a visla in attendance!"

He was talking far too loudly, and people were looking. Including the guards. But that was what he wanted. The more they looked at him, the less they would be looking at the boy, who had already begun slowly changing back to his normal skin coloration.

Bud had dropped the V word. Visla. And for someone to have a power user of that magnitude attend one of their ceremonies, they must be quite important. All eyes were on the supposed lovebirds, and Happizano stepped through the exit and out into the orange glow of the city's light unmolested.

He was also nearly entirely back to his normal coloring, but he was in the lead, and facing away from the guards. So long as he didn't turn around, the guards would have no idea who had just walked right past them to freedom.

Bud closed the gap once they were clear of the exit and placed his hand firmly on the boy's shoulder, steering him toward the waiting ship's landing area.

"Do not look back. Just keep walking. I'll direct you," he said, quietly. "Henni, keep an eye out for––"

"I know."

The little woman had already begun her scan, casually moving in front of the kidnapped boy, watching the crowd for any sign of recognition or threat. They didn't have too far to go, but anything could happen before they were safely aboard their ship.

They moved quickly, an impromptu unit functioning far better than any might have imagined. The necessity of the situation had forced them to cooperate, and in that one, blessed moment, they were operating as smoothly as any team.

· · ·

Still inside the estate, the leader of the group had cloaked himself in his shimmer once more and was making his way quickly through the most private chambers of the emmik's estate. He was a man on a mission. A secondary mission, after the rescue of the visla's son.

Emmik Urtzal was a piddling little nobody. So why had he so suddenly become a trusted co-conspirator in this little plot? Something was going on. Something far from normal.

If Visla Ravik had brought Urtzal into the mix, it would make sense that they would have shared forces in their ambush at Zargota. But to elevate the man to a near equal status, allowing him to be the one to keep the young Jinnik secured, well, it was beyond unusual.

Unless someone even more powerful than Ravik was pulling the strings. Someone dictating their actions with an entirely ulterior set of motives. It was a great mystery, and it was seeming to tie in to more than one loose thread that was just begging to be pulled.

What would come out in the unraveling, though, was anyone's guess.

Hozark felt for wards and traps as he approached the emmik's private offices. Nothing touched his sensing spells as he passed through the door. With eyes trained for this sort of thing, the master assassin scanned the room, looking for any signs or clues that might give him a modicum of clarity as to the real machinations behind these overlapping and increasingly wild plots.

Someone was manipulating power users, and not just the visla. Ootaki and Drooks alike had been used for some strange tests. Zomoki had been experimented on and slain. And even a young Wampeh had suffered a similar fate. While it was highly unlikely the emmik knew of these events, it was looking like he was tied in with people who did.

And Hozark was going to find out how.

The exposed spaces held nothing of use. He searched high and low, but nothing was conveniently left out in the open for him. It rarely was, but on more than one occasion, he had actually stumbled upon crucial items with a little help from blind luck.

The safe was easy to locate, and its warding spells almost child's play to disarm. But all that was inside was some coin, a few charged konuses, and some image discs that appeared to contain blackmail images of a few high-ranking members of the planet's elite.

It was becoming clearer how Urtzal managed to maintain a grip on this world despite his rather middling power. Hozark shifted his search to the large desk that sat at the far end of the room. It was an ornate piece of furniture, and it possessed a small amount of magic, the maintenance spells it was imbued with keeping the wood at a permanent glossy luster.

Unlocking the drawers was not an issue and barely took two seconds for Hozark's practiced fingers. He slid the central compartment open slowly.

"Can it be?" he wondered as his eyes fell upon a validity seal. There was simply no way a non-member of the Council of Twenty would be allowed to utilize such a powerful item. Not powerful magically, but because of what the seal could make its recipients do.

Hozark reached out to pick it up.

The trapping spell slammed into him with blinding force, locking his limbs in place, stopping him from moving so much as an inch. Hozark was unable to even speak, rendered helpless by his inability to cast a single spell. His eyes, however, still worked.

He peered down at his shimmer cloak. The magical trap was stripping away the protective camouflage, leaving him exposed in the chamber. The power was shocking in both its strength as well as its specificity against Ghalian tricks of the trade.

And worse than that, Hozark realized, this was no emmik's magic. This was a visla's. And it was very strong. And very recent.

A great deal of magic had been poured into this ingenious trap. Not in the room, not in the door, not even in the wards on the desk itself. This was a carefully disguised trigger spell connected to a massively powerful catch-trap. Whatever visla had set this was not only incredibly powerful, but strangely familiar.

Hozark relaxed his body against the spell. Fighting it would do no good. He needed to use his mind, not his muscles if he hoped to escape. But what of this magic? It was as if he had––

Suddenly, it dawned on him. Where he had sensed this power before. The secret weapons smelting operation on Garvalis. Where he had once before fallen prey to this same magic user's clever traps.

Despite his dire situation, Hozark nearly smiled. It was a break. Information. Something that tied all of this together. Now all he had to do was live to tell the others.

CHAPTER THIRTY-EIGHT

Footsteps ringing out in a corridor normally wouldn't concern the master assassin. He was one of the Five, after all, and was wearing his shimmer cloak, no less. He had dealt with far worse than a small group of guards on countless occasions.

And yet, today, they might quite possibly be his end. It was almost amusing in how ridiculous it was. For one of the greatest assassins in the galaxy to fall in such a manner. But he had been outplayed. Tricked and trapped by a very, very clever visla.

And now he was frozen in place, unable to cast even the slightest spell, let alone reach the vespus blade riding on his back.

Seven guards rushed into Emmik Urtzal's offices, weapons at the ready. Obviously, there was a magical alert also tied to the trapping spell, Hozark noted, ever watchful and aware, even as his doom closed in.

The men were Tslavars, all of them, and Hozark had a feeling this lot would just as soon slay the Wampeh Ghalian as capture him for questioning. They could always say he had nearly escaped the trap and they were fighting for their lives, after all. And with a Ghalian assassin, who would doubt them.

With his shimmer cloak failing, they saw the man clearly. And, as he had been ready for a fight, his vespus blade was partially exposed for quick access should he need it. Their eyes fell upon the faintly glowing weapon.

"He's got an enchanted sword," one of them said, drawing his own blade.

"Aye. And when we're done with 'im, there's no need for anyone to know about it. We can fetch good coin for a Ghalian's weapons on the black market."

"Even split?" another Tslavar asked.

"Even split. Now, come on. Let's slice us off a piece of Ghalian, shall we?"

The man's head parted from his body and fell to the ground in a sickening, wet thud. The line of the cut was clean and precise, made by the fine blade seemingly floating in the air.

A moment later, the stocky Wampeh wearing a shimmer cloak slid it from her head and released her grasp on the spell. They had threatened Master Hozark and planned to slay him in a most cowardly manner. She *wanted* them to see her when she took everything from them, and the gleaming blades in her hands were nearly humming in anticipation of her bloody work.

Master Orkut's weapons were undoubtedly the finest she had ever been fortunate enough to wield, and every cell in her body cried out in longing for a fight. An opportunity to free these beautiful, deadly pieces of art to do their terrible work.

"Well?" she said, cocking an eyebrow at the six remaining Tslavars.

If they had been wise, they would have sent one for backup while the others tried to keep her trapped, or at least slowed her down. But these were overconfident men, and a five-on-one fight seemed like plenty good odds to them.

They weren't.

Demelza spun into action, sword in one hand, long dagger in the other, the pair slicing through flesh and armor alike. The closest of the Tslavars fell to one knee. Not because he was kneeling, but because his other leg had been cut off mid-thigh. His cries ended abruptly when her dagger pierced his skull as easily as a soft gourd.

The remaining four attacked her all at once, hoping to overwhelm her with their superior numbers. But Demelza was used to fighting multiple opponents, and far more skilled ones than these.

Frozen as he was, Hozark nevertheless happened to be positioned in such a way as to see his friend fight, and he was pleased to be treated to quite a show of Ghalian prowess. Demelza had been training. Hard. And now it was showing.

She was fighting the blades, not the wielders, and with her new, adapted style, she was almost toying with the men, prolonging the fight a moment just to allow herself the opportunity to try a few more of her new moves.

But they were on a timetable, and Master Hozark was in a precarious position, so she feigned a stumble, drawing the four attackers in close for the kill. Little did they realize, the killing would be theirs. Her sword flashed out in one direction while the dagger swung an arc in the other. Seconds later, she and Hozark were the only living beings in the room.

"Master Hozark, hold still. I will free you."

His eyes spoke volumes of both appreciation and mirth.

"Ah, yes, of course. You have no choice but to hold still," Demelza said as she began carefully countering the layers of catch-trap spells that had snared one of the greatest assassins alive.

It was a time-consuming endeavor. Far too time consuming for either of their taste, but there was little that could be done about that. Slowly, however, Demelza loosened the strands of power binding her friend and mentor.

"This is far stronger magic than Emmik Urtzal is capable of," she noted.

"Mmmhmm," Hozark replied.

"Let me see about that bit," she said, pulling free the bonds over his mouth.

They were particularly robust, and well-crafted. Whoever had set the trap knew full-well that their captive could cast deadly magic even while bound. And so they had ensured they would be unable. It was a masterful bit of casting, Hozark grudgingly admired.

"It is the same magic I sensed back on Garvalis," Hozark said when the final thread locking his jaw shut was removed.

He moved his mouth a moment, loosening the tight muscles.

"Garvalis? What could Urtzal have to do with that? You said those were weapons manufacturers."

"I know," Hozark replied. "And yet somehow this man is somehow tied up in all of that."

He pulled power from his konus, forming the words of the unbinding spells he knew so well, layering them atop Demelza's castings. It was still a lot of work to free the rest of his body, but with two of them working together, it would at least be faster progress.

"What of the boy?" Demelza asked.

"Located and retrieved. He is with Uzabud and Henni, returning to the safety of the ship as we speak."

"Then our work here is done," she said, when the validity seal caught her eye.

"Don't," Hozark warned. "It is the trigger to this spell. A very clever trap laid for any who knew what it was, and how utterly wrong it was for it to be here."

"Fascinating," she said, turning her attentions back to the bound assassin. "Then we need to get out of here sooner rather than later. Someone will notice their trap has been sprung. And I mean more than just those guards."

"Agreed," Hozark said, redoubling his efforts to free himself.

"At least the boy is safe, so that is one less thing to focus on for the moment."

CHAPTER THIRTY-NINE

Bud and Henni had made great time back to the ship once they'd cleared the dangerous area just outside the emmik's compound. And for his part, the visla's son had done well, keeping his face pointing straight ahead, away from the prying eyes behind them that might notice his shifted skin color.

He looked like himself again, which was dangerous, but aside from the emmik's lackeys, none of the regular citizens of the city would have any reason to take note of him. He was just another boy, out for a walk with what were likely his babysitters or guardians.

"Is *that* your ship?" Happizano asked as they made a beeline for Bud's craft.

"Yep. Ain't she a beauty?" he said with pride.

"It's a wreck," the boy replied. "You expect me to fly in *that*?"

Bud bristled. "Would you rather go back to your cage?"

"I almost think it would be better," the boy groused as they stepped into the ship's open door.

"That can be arranged if you don't watch it," the ship's owner replied. "Laskar, we're back. Prep for liftoff as soon as the others join us," Bud called out as he entered the command center.

Laskar did not reply. In fact, he was not even there.

"Laskar, where the hell are you?" he demanded over the ship's internal skree comms. Again, no reply. "Damned things must be busted too," he griped, then set out to find the flaky copilot.

Bud returned five minutes later with a worried look on his face.

"I can't find him anywhere."

"What do you mean?" Henni said, a look of concern flashing in her eyes.

"I mean exactly that. He's not here."

The violet-haired young woman had a pair of blades in her hands in an instant, ready to do violence, if needed.

"Where did you get those? We went into Urtzal's place unarmed. Did you grab them, like, literally as soon as we were back on board?"

"A girl's gotta be prepared," she replied. "And something is not right. The tall guy's not here, and that was his *one* job."

"I'm tall too."

"He's taller."

Happizano stepped between the two. "Excuse me, but is this an actual rescue? Do you guys even have the slightest clue what you're doing?"

"Shut it, kid. I've rescued bunches of people over the years," Bud replied.

"Could've fooled me."

Henni spun and lunged, her twin knives flashing out as a shadow entered the doorway. Laskar caught her by the wrists and flung her aside, a shocked look on his face.

"What in the actual fuck, Henni?" he blurted.

The small woman rose from the deck where she'd landed and picked up her blades. "I thought you were a bad guy. I trust my instincts."

"Well, they were obviously wrong. Jeez!"

Henni dusted herself off, but her scowl was slow to clear. Happizano was standing stock-still, shocked by what these strange people seemed to take as a normal occurrence.

"She just tried to kill him."

"Yeah, it happens. Don't dwell on it, kid," Bud said. "And as for you." He turned to Laskar. "Where the hell were you? You're supposed to be here keeping the ship ready for a fast dustoff."

"I was," Laskar protested. "But some of the emmik's city guards came to examine our cargo. We landed too close to his personal estate, Bud. I told you so. And as a result, they were checking us out."

"Shit."

"Yeah. Shit. So I did whatever I could to buy us a bit more time."

"How did you manage that?"

"I stepped out to greet them with that fake manifest in my hand and bought them a drink at the bar just across the landing site while we went over it. A bunch of drinks, actually. And the good stuff."

"And they went with it?" Bud marveled

"For now, at least. Come on, it was Bud's lesson number one. Remember what you told me when we first partnered up?"

"Shut your mouth and fly the damn ship?"

"Ha. Funny. But no. You said a little bribery goes a long way. And it did."

"So, we're good?"

"Yeah, we're good. Now we just have to wait for Hozark and Demelza to get back and——"

A shrill alarm rang out through the air, the sound even making its way into the ship.

Henni craned her neck to try to see what was going on. "What the hell?"

"The estate alarm," Bud said, jumping into his pilot's seat and casting the activation spells from his Drookonus. "They'll lock down the landing area any second now. Everyone take a seat. It's time for Plan B."

"What's Plan B?" Henni asked.

"We get the hell out of here and, hopefully, they meet us in the air."

"But their ships are still mounted to the hull."

"I know. But they're Wampeh Ghalian. If there's a way, they'll manage it," he replied, then took off as casually as possible before making his way up into the sky.

Hozark and Demelza made expert use of their shimmer cloaks as they bolted from Emmik Urtzal's estate, but she was still not able to properly use it at a full run, so they were forced to pause far more often than they'd have liked as they raced for the exit.

The trapping spell had been strong, and it had been thorough. No one could have escaped it on their own, but with Demelza's help, Hozark had actually managed to break free. But in so doing, they triggered a fail-safe spell. One that was shocking in its very presence.

No one used them for traps of this nature, and for someone to have left one deeply embedded, waiting for the impossible to happen, told them both that they were dealing with a far shrewder opponent than they'd previously imagined.

The two assassins were fortunate that whoever had set the trap did not appear to have clued in the main body of the estate's guards. If they'd known it was likely a Ghalian was in their midst, they'd have undoubtedly double or tripled their security measures and sealed the grounds entirely.

Fortunately, the cloaked pair were able to slip out through a lesser-used delivery entrance they had noted during their first run-through of the property looking for Jinnik's son. There was still a significant security presence, but timing it just right, they were able to sneak past the guards and escape into the bustling city.

Clear of the compound grounds, both shed their shimmer cloaks as soon as they found a secluded place free of prying eyes. They immediately cast their disguise spells, altering their complexions to a deep bronze, just in case. If anyone was looking for a Wampeh, they most certainly did not fit the description.

Hozark mentally clocked the time since he'd been captured. Bud was undoubtedly off-world by now, shifting his focus to keeping the kid safe as soon as he heard the alarm. That meant Plan B.

"We are going to have to find our own means of escape," he said as they moved toward the landing area.

"Your thoughts?" Demelza asked.

"There are a great many craft here, but most are locked down. Only the emmik's ships are free to move. I think we should avail ourselves of his generosity, don't you?"

Demelza liked that idea very much, and as soon as they arrived at the rows of ships, she immediately began surveying them for the best prospect.

"The third from the end," she said. "I sense power from it, and there is only one man nearby. Thankfully, he does not appear to be paying much attention to the craft behind him."

"Yes," Hozark said. "He appears to be quite interested in the clamor coming from the emmik's compound. But that will not last. Come, we must move quickly."

The two made their way behind the lone sentry and silently boarded the ship, all without raising any alarm or suspicion. And they were in luck. Demelza had been correct in her initial scan. There was a Drookonus still in place, though it felt as though it had been recently drained a fair amount.

It would have to do.

"Strap in," Hozark said as he sealed the doors and cast the spells lifting the ship off into the air.

Now *that* got the sentry's attention. In no time, a handful of pilots raced to their ships, all of them ready to pursue the thieves. Hozark pushed hard, casting the drive spells just to the edge of breaking the Drookonus and leaving them adrift.

It was nowhere near as strong as the ones he was accustomed to using, and it took constant attention to not overtax the lesser device. The ships from the surface that were streaking up toward them, however, did not appear to suffer any such handicaps.

They were fully charged, and they were ready for action.

"Demelza, defensive measures, please."

She nodded and set to work directing their limited shielding resources to block the incoming attacks. The ships on their tail were trying to disable, not destroy them, and that was a lucky break.

But they both knew that any time now the dead guards would be found within the emmik's compound, and when word of that reached their pursuers, the spells were all but guaranteed to turn deadly.

"What sort of offensive power does this ship possess?" Hozark asked, dodging a flurry of spells as they tried to knock out his Drookonus.

"Not much, I am afraid," Demelza replied. "This craft seems to have been recently returned and was awaiting a refresher to its power stores."

"Then we are in for a very difficult fight, indeed," Hozark said, gritting his teeth as he spun the craft one hundred eighty degrees, flying right at the pursuing ships. "Now would be a good time to utilize what little we have."

Demelza was already casting the spells as he spoke, and the magic she was sending out at those ships was most decidedly not meant to stun. One of the craft took the full brunt of a spell, halting in place as its shielding cracked from the unexpected magic.

This was not like spells they had previously defended against. This was stronger magic. More deadly. And one of their own had just fallen victim to it. The remaining craft immediately ramped up both their defensive shielding as well as their offensive attacks.

Hozark flew like a man possessed, dodging as best he could with the underpowered craft. Demelza, likewise, was casting for all she was worth, but they were simply out shipped and out gunned, magically speaking. A trio of spells rocked their craft. Seconds later, a thin wisp of smoke abruptly rose from their Drookonus.

"We cannot continue like this much longer," Hozark noted with grim certainty as the attacking craft looped for a closer assault.

They had performed as well as any could given their circumstances, but, it seemed, that was simply not enough. No one could will victory from defeat, no matter how strong their desire.

Two of the attacking ships suddenly burst to pieces, targeted by a fierce and powerful barrage. The remaining craft were sent fleeing, where they would regroup and face this new threat.

Bud pulled his mothership close--right under the stolen attack craft, in fact--and Hozark quickly cast his docking spells, latching to the larger vessel. He and Demelza wasted no time descending into the familiar safety of Bud's ship.

Hozark then overloaded the failing Drookonus and released the spells, sending the craft speeding off into space. A moment later, as the other craft made their moves against it, the ship blew to bits, just as Laskar initiated the jump and took them to safety.

"We could have sold that!" Bud whined when his friends entered the command center.

"It would have given us away, Bud," Hozark replied.

Of course, the pilot knew that, but nevertheless, the loss of a valuable and free bit of salvage––or in this case, theft––hurt all the same.

"What kind of a rescue do you call this?" Happizano griped from his nearby seat. "The rescuers need rescuing? That's just sad."

"You would be wise to watch your tongue," Hozark said. "We have risked much, and a little gratitude would serve you well."

"Yeah, right. You're not my dad. You can't tell me what to do," the boy snarked.

"Oh, I like this one!" Henni said with a laugh.

Hozark sank into his seat and pondered the situation they were in. This was going far, far worse than he'd imagined.

"Hey," the boy said. "I know this is fun for you and all, but I'm hungry. Get me something to eat."

Hozark looked over at Bud and sighed. Yes, indeed. *Far* worse.

CHAPTER FORTY

"Take me home! Take me home, now!" the tantrum-throwing youth hollered, his voice carrying throughout the ship.

"We cannot do that just yet," Hozark said. "I have told you over a dozen times thus far. Our destination is wherever Visla Jinnik is at this time. Only he can properly protect you. And we have not confirmed his whereabouts as of yet."

"So take me home. That's where he always winds up. Even after those big trips he takes without me."

Bud flashed his poor Wampeh friend a sympathetic look. The boy was proving to be more of a handful than they'd anticipated, and his frequent and rather vocal outbursts were beginning to wear on everyone's nerves.

Unfortunately, they could not simply drop the youth off at his home estate and be done with it. For one, he had already been taken from that very place when his father was away. For another, if the visla was still off on Council business, returning him to the scene of the crime without his father's protection would be courting disaster.

He had been freed, and they intended to keep it that way. Now all they had to do was find his father. But that was proving more difficult a task than anticipated. It seemed that whatever the reason for bringing him under their control, the Council was moving Jinnik around frequently, sending him on errands all across the systems.

And now that this low-level emmik had been wrapped up in the affair, and with a booby-trapped validity seal to boot, it was looking very much like whatever was going on, the real reason for Jinnik's acquisition was yet to be revealed.

"Listen, kid. We want to get you home. Really, believe me. The sooner you're back with him, the better for all of us. But for the moment, you've just gotta tough it out while we figure out some things."

"Like what? Hell, I can tell you how to get——"

"It's not about where home is, okay? Just trust me on this."

"Why should I trust you? Any of you?"

Bud flashed an exasperated look to his friends, but they weren't stepping into this. It was his turn to have the same conversation for the umpteenth time.

"Because we rescued you. How many times do we have to say it, kid?"

"I told you, don't call me kid."

"Yeah, but what's your name? Hapinasasomething?"

"Happizano."

"Yeah, I'm just gonna call you Happy," Bud said with a mischievous grin.

"Do *not* call me that."

"Why not, *Happy*?"

The boy's violet face began to redden. "My father is going to kill all of you," he hissed.

For a youth of ten or eleven, he was certainly a handful, and not in a cute and amusing way. Hozark leaned in close.

"Your father is the one who hired us to rescue you, as I have told you multiple times now. I suggest you come to terms with that sooner rather than later, young Jinnik. It will make your time with us far more pleasant."

Happizano deflated just a little. The wear and tear of being kidnapped, held hostage, and then rescued by this unlikely and motley bunch of misfits had strained him to his limits.

"Why didn't he come for me himself?" he said quietly.

No matter what a royal pain in the ass he was being, they all felt some degree of sympathy for the kid. It sucked, they knew. And all he wanted was to see his dad again.

"Listen," Hozark said, resting his hand on the boy's shoulder in a rare display of tenderness. "Your father is a good man, and he cares about you very much."

"But he sent you instead of coming himself."

"Yes, he did. But that was also to keep you safe."

"My dad's strong. He could take them on."

"Yes, but sometimes the true strength is in holding oneself back."

The boy looked at him, more than a little confused.

"I'll clarify," Hozark said. "The people who took you might have done some very bad things if your father came for you himself. By the time he found out where you were, there is no telling what the Council of Twenty might have done."

"The Council?" Happizano said. "But he hates the Council. Or, at least, really dislikes it. I mean, he's always felt that way. It's why he stays away from all of their stupid parties and gatherings, even though they invite him all the time."

"Yes, we've heard that they have courted your father for some time. But that is why he had to have us come to get you. So he could keep you safe from future reprisals."

"Reprisals?"

"When someone is angry at what you have done and wants to do something bad to you for it," Hozark said.

"It means *revenge*, kid," Laskar chimed in.

"Don't call me kid," he grumbled. "And don't call me happy!" he quickly added.

"Okay, okay. But Happizano is kind of a mouthful. I'm with Bud on that. How about Hap? Does that work for ya?"

The youth thought about it a long moment. "I guess," he finally said. "It's better than Happy, at least."

Laskar beamed wide. "I totally agree. And Hap's a cool nickname. Makes you sound badass."

Henni raised a brow but kept her mouth shut. Whatever it took to calm this little terror was fine with her.

"So, Hap is recovered, and that means Jinnik will be free to do to his kidnappers whatever he sees fit," Bud mused. "Oh man, once we get his kid back to him, I would hate to be one of the people who did this. That guy's got power to spare, and I have a feeling someone is going to be very unhappily on the receiving end of it."

"Demelza, would you and Henni please show our guest to the galley and provide him with whatever he wishes to eat?" Hozark asked. "It has been a difficult time for him, and I'm sure he must be hungry."

Demelza caught his drift.

"Come along, Hap. Let us get you something to eat, shall we? And then I shall show you to your quarters and provide you some fresh attire, if we have any that will fit you."

She and Henni rose and began walking, as if expecting the youngster to follow and never even considering he might play stubborn and refuse. The ploy worked, and Hap found himself tagging along with the women as they headed toward the galley.

"Now that we are alone, let us revel in a moment of quiet," Hozark said with a sigh of relief.

"Man, that kid's a piece of work. You sure his dad really wants him back?" Bud joked.

"Indeed he does. And I have to say, your thoughts on what

will befall those who took his boy are likely not far from the truth. Someone will be having a very, very bad day," Hozark said.

"So, what now? I mean, I suppose we can just hang out in the luxury of a visla's estate and eat all of his food while we wait for him to come back," Bud said. "We can protect him from there if we bulk wards and defenses on key access points."

"Yeah, that's actually not a bad idea," Laskar agreed. "If he comes back anytime soon, that is. But if he doesn't, at least we'll be living in style."

Hozark pondered the idea. The Ghalian spy network would be hard at work pinpointing the boy's father regardless. And if they were to stay with him at his home, not only would that put the boy at ease, it would also mean he had several bodyguards to help keep him safe.

It wasn't a perfect plan, but it was good enough. And for the moment, good enough would have to suffice.

"Very well, then," Hozark said. "Set a jump course. We shall take the young Jinnik home."

CHAPTER FORTY-ONE

Uzabud took the cautious route to young Happizano's homeworld, making sure to stop at nearby systems so Hozark and Demelza could do a bit of intelligence gathering before making their final return.

If they could suss out a bit more information prior to the visla's return, then the joy of his son's rescue would only be compounded by the knowledge of whom he could punish for his absence. But no one seemed to know a thing, or if they did, they were all being quite tight-lipped.

It was a somewhat frustrating process, and that, combined with Hap's incessant whining, made their next decision easy.

"We may as well just take the brat home," Bud said, finding refuge in the galley after the boy had yet another meltdown. "I don't know how much more of this I can take."

Hozark sipped his cup of herbal tea as he commiserated with his friend. "He is a handful, I will agree."

"Handful? Understatement of the century," Bud replied with an exhausted sigh. "I mean, the kid is wearing me out with his incessant bitching. You'd think he would be grateful we saved his ass. But no, instead he's not satisfied with his food, or his bunk isn't soft enough, or why haven't we taken him home yet? It's maddening, Hozark. Seriously, half the time, I just want to space the kid."

"But you are far too kind a soul to do that, aren't you, Bud?" Hozark said with a wry grin. "But rest easy, my friend. Our next stop shall indeed be our passenger's last stop. And once his father returns, we shall be on our way, the favor to Orkut repaid."

"And our pockets significantly heavier with coin," Bud added.

"Well, that too, of course," Hozark agreed. "Has Laskar prepared the course for the final series of jumps?"

"Dialed in and ready to go. When you give the word, we take the kid home."

"Then consider this the word. Let us offload our obnoxious cargo, shall we?"

"We're getting rid of Henni too?" Bud joked.

"Very funny, Bud. Now, come. Let's get the boy home."

"Something feels off," Demelza said, staring at the glowing orb that would so soon free them of their unwanted passenger. "You sense it, do you not?"

"Yes. Something does not seem right," Hozark agreed. "I cannot pinpoint it, but there is definitely something. Bud, settle into a low orbit around the nearest moon, if you would be so kind."

"The moon?"

"Yes. I am going to take my shimmer ship to the surface and reconnoiter a bit before we bring young Happizano home."

"You think it's another trap?" Laskar asked.

"I am not certain. But I do know that something about this feels off. And I have learned to trust that feeling when it arises."

"Well, be quick about it. When the kid realizes how close to home we are, you know he's going to become an even greater pain in the ass than he already is."

"Of course. And I do pity you being stuck up here with him whilst I scout."

"Just hurry back, okay?"

"I shall. Hopefully this is nothing, but it is always best to verify," Hozark said as he walked to board his cloaked craft. "I will see you soon."

Within three minutes he had detached from Bud's mothership and was making a stealthy approach to the globe below.

As powerful as he was, if Visla Jinnik was home, he would be able to sense the invisible ship, if he wasn't distracted. However, as he was offworld at the moment, Hozark felt confident he was arriving unseen.

Even so, he landed a fair distance from the visla's estate tower. All the better to approach by foot and get a proper feel for the pulse of the city via its residents' unguarded daily interactions.

Hozark had his shimmer cloak with him, but decided to don a disguise for this approach rather than expend magic on his shimmer.

In addition to saving power, the more traditional method would also allow him to remain visible, though disguised, which meant interactions with the locals. Interactions during which he could glean a great deal of interesting information.

Hozark casually strolled the streets, taking a circuitous route to the Jinnik estate and listening in to the chatter of the locals. There wasn't an overt problem being openly discussed, but there seemed to be a tension in the air.

He felt the energy of the people around him, gently reaching out with his konus's help.

Yes, there it was again. That unease. Something felt *off* here, but he couldn't quite put his finger on it. As he approached the visla's tower, however, the picture quickly became more clear.

The estate looked much as it had before, but now another of the floating gardens that had been under construction was magically suspended beside it, apparently completed since his and Demelza's last visit.

But there was something more. Craft were parked in the landing area beside the tower, and shapes could be seen moving about the garden. It looked like there were a few men, up there, whom he could make out fairly clearly, even from a distance.

And from the look of them, they weren't the visla's people. These appeared to be Council goons. If that proved to be true, it could mean only one thing. They had occupied the place.

Hozark knew they needed far more information than that, now that the unexpected had reared its ugly head, so he drew close to the visla's tower and waited. Soon enough, one of the property staff exited via the service entrance to run an errand.

Hozark followed the man, closing in as he took a turn conveniently near an alleyway. The poor man disappeared from the footpath with barely a squeak, his slumbering body carefully tucked into a dark nook within the alleyway, where he would not be found.

A minute later, Hozark emerged, with a new uniform, as well as a new face.

He made a point to linger for a little bit before heading back to the entrance. Any who had seen the man whose face he was now wearing leave would wonder why he had returned so soon otherwise.

When he did finally approach the estate, he gained access with ease, and without a single question being raised.

But once he was inside, his own questions would be myriad.

CHAPTER FORTY-TWO

Once inside the tower, Hozark changed his appearance to that of a generic face he kept in his toolkit of disguises.

He had no real knowledge of the man he'd just pretended to be, and it was often easier to gain access by bullshit and bluster than it was using an identity that might not have the clearances he needed.

And then there was the fact that the poor man, of whom he had only made the most preliminary copy for his infiltration, was known by those he would encounter on the way. That could get sketchy.

Moreover, if word that he and his team had recovered the boy had made it here, any Wampeh would be suspect.

His own pale complexion simply would not do.

So Hozark became a stern-faced, olive-skinned, ball-buster of a man. One who took his job seriously, and who made others uncomfortable by his professionalism.

He had found over the years that the strict adherence to rules tended to make this persona unpopular. It also made people want nothing to do with him, pushing him through checkpoints quickly to go finish whatever it was he was doing without much scrutiny at all.

Sticklers for rules wouldn't break them, after all, and those actually enforcing them might get called out for not doing so properly. The nitpicker types were just the sort to actually know their job better than they did. The kind who took joy in correcting the slightest of mistakes.

It wouldn't work everywhere, of course, but in a recently occupied estate, and one owned by a very, very powerful visla no less, a person of that sort would likely be given a wide berth.

And this visla was now working for the Council, or so it seemed. No one would know it was under duress, but that worked to his advantage. For all intents and purposes, this was still the visla's home, and if he was under that man's umbrella, the newcomers would treat him with a degree of deference.

Hozark grabbed one of the packages from the sorting table where deliveries were made. They had already been checked in and were now simply waiting for distribution within the estate.

Not much was arriving these days with the visla off world, but that would make any delivery for the visla even more pressing. That, in turn, would be a free pass to almost anywhere in the building.

Hozark pulled from his konus and layered what appeared to be a complex seal on the container, then walked straight out into the foyer of the ground floor.

When last he was in the building, his entrance had been made from high above, via the floating garden beside the structure. This, however, was a bit more complicated.

Multiple security personnel were patrolling the area. And they were definitely not the visla's people.

They wore the uniforms of his staff, but Hozark could see the difference in posture and the look in their eyes as clearly as if they were wearing flashing signs that read, "Council Goon" on them.

It was not an overt occupation. That was not the point here. This was merely the Council making sure they had a handle on this place, keeping up appearances while ensuring the facility remained under their control. Just a subtle presence, though, and one most would not question.

"Where are you taking that?" one such Council guard asked as Hozark crossed the open space toward the lift discs.

"I am making a delivery for the visla," he replied.

"Those get left down below at the receiving area. You don't have clearance to go to the upper floors."

Ah, he was *that* type. The kind who enjoyed flexing his middling power, Hozark mused. This would almost be fun.

"What's your name?" Hozark demanded.

"What?"

"Your name. Give me your name."

"Who the hell do you think you are to speak to me like that?"

"Your name. Are your ears plugged? I need to know who it was that diverted a direct delivery from Visla Agnatz to Visla Jinnik," the assassin replied. "You can clearly see this is a specially sealed container, and you should also be well aware that this type of delivery is not only a priority-one in nature, but it also must remain in the proper chain of custody until such time as it is properly handed off at its final destination. Now, again. What is your name?"

The guard hesitated, and in that instant, Hozark knew he had him.

"Uh, I don't know about all of that. But you're not supposed to——"

"No. *You* are not supposed to. Not supposed to be accosting staff performing their duties. You're one of the newcomers, I see. Tasked with the ground floor security detail, I imagine. And that group is focused at the entryway, as they are supposed to be. But *you* are all the way over here, overstepping and harassing the *real* staff, and if you think I'm going to be punished because *you* want to interrupt my work, then you've got another thing coming. Now. Your name."

Hozark had long practiced the cold stare he now fixed on the man. It made all but the most hardened men squirm. And this was no seasoned soldier. He was just a security guard riding high on his modicum of power. And that balloon had just burst.

People were starting to look. Or so the cornered man believed. Any second now, this could turn humiliating.

"Uh, there's no need for that. You just take that and deliver it where it's supposed to go. And be snappy about it," he said, a bit louder than necessary, to be certain those nearby heard.

He hadn't been browbeaten by a delivery person. He was the one giving orders. And his order was to carry on and deliver that package.

It was almost funny how easy the man had been to manipulate. For now, with his rather vocal command to carry on, which everyone heard, Hozark had free rein on this level, all the way to the lift disc across the foyer.

The security detail there had just seen his interaction with their compatriot and stepped aside.

"Thank you," Hozark said curtly, the words having none of the courtesy typically associated with them.

The disc took him up to the visla's personal levels. The same level Hozark and Demelza had infiltrated. The one where they had met the visla and accepted his unusual job.

He stepped off the disc and made a straight line for the visla's offices. There were regular staff on this floor, but none of the newcomers to be seen. It appeared the bulk of their presence was at the less important areas of the building, though Hozark was sure a few of them lurked around these levels as well. He had seen a few on the floating gardens, after all.

But here, he could relax his posturing. At least for the moment. With the visla's actual staff, a kinder persona would elicit far more information.

"Hey, what's going on with all the extra security downstairs?" Hozark asked a pale-green woman tending to the potted plants dotting the open living space.

She turned to find a warm, open face smiling at her. Fine tendrils wafted from her temples and jawline, pulling additional oxygen from the atmosphere. The perfect type to be caring for the vegetation, Hozark mused.

"What are you doing up here? This is a restricted access level," she said.

"Oh, I know. I was told to bring this up here myself and not let it out of my sight until it had been delivered to the visla. Or, in this case, whoever would take charge of it until he gets back."

"What is it?"

"No idea. It's from Visla Agnatz and is for Visla Jinnik's eyes only. See the sealing spell?"

"Of course."

She had noted the magic as soon as she lay eyes on him. A very astute woman, Hozark noted, and a credit to the visla's staff. But her suspicion could easily be overridden. With the added security at the lifts, there was no way he could have made it to this level without being authorized.

Or so she believed.

And that was the pervasive weakness in this particular security setup. Once you passed a certain point, all just assumed you belonged.

"Come on, I'll show you where you can put that," the woman said, leaving her task for the time being. "I'm Inari, by the way."

"Gorlik," Hozark replied. "Nice to meet you."

"I haven't seen you around here before," she said.

"No, I was hired to work for the visla a few months ago, but this is the first time I've actually been able to visit his estate."

"Ah, a system hopper," she said, knowingly. "That's gotta be a tough job. Always on the move, living on a ship."

Her mouth said one thing, but her tone said another. She

had likely never left this world. Not once in all of her years. And the thought of interstellar travel was quite alluring.

"It can be, sure," he replied. "But I have to admit, there's something wonderful about being able to see the galaxy like that. All of the systems and people. It's actually pretty great, truth be told."

"I can only imagine."

"But I suppose it must be nice here. A quiet life without all of that craziness."

"Didn't you hear?"

"Hear what?"

"There was an attack."

"Where?"

"*Here.* Some mercenary types raided the tower not long ago. Killed a lot of our people. They even made it to the visla's personal chambers before they were stopped."

"That's terrible!" Hozark said in faux shock. "Did the visla smite them?"

"He wasn't here. But Happizano was."

"I don't know who that is."

"His son."

"Oh, shit. Was he okay?"

"Yeah, he's fine. I haven't seen him around lately, though. Word is, after the attack his dad decided to take him with along wherever he went."

Hozark nodded along with the story. So *that* was how the Council was playing it. Most interesting.

"Makes sense," he said. "I can't imagine how worried he must've been."

"I was in the marketplace at the time, but people said he damn near blew out part of the building when he got back and saw what had happened. He's a very powerful man."

"I know. But why the new security staff? I mean, between you and me, they look kind of, well--"

"*Council*?" she said, finishing his thought. "Yeah, you've got that right. It's a bit weird, Council guards in our colors. But rumor is, the visla asked the Council to come help provide security while he was gone, after that incident."

"But doesn't he, uh, how do I put this nicely? *Not particularly like* the Council?"

"You're right on that, so for him to have asked them to come here, it must have been a real concern. Many of our guards and staff were killed in the attack, you know."

"Still, for him to invite them into his home..."

"Well, word is, it was actually the Council who just happened to have some of their people nearby when all of this happened. They're the ones who got Happizano to safety with his father. They even come by to check up on things and make sure we are okay, from time to time."

Hozark had to admit, it was a clever story, and one that not only allowed for the Council lackeys' presence should they be noted, but also explained where the visla's son was. The whole thing was well planned and well played. As seemed to be so much of the case with this strange series of events.

Someone was pulling a lot of strings, and in an incredibly convoluted way. Much was in play, and Hozark was quite sure he didn't know all of it. Not yet, at least.

"Here's his office," Inari said. "I can open the door wards, but only for a minute. Put that on his desk, and he'll get it when he returns."

"Is it okay to leave there?"

"Trust me, no one will touch it," she said, then quietly uttered the spells allowing temporary access.

Hozark memorized them immediately.

It was a courtesy the visla had afforded a few of his staff. The ability to come and go to perform their tasks even if he was not present. But they couldn't linger. If they did, they would trigger his alarms, and who knew what other magical protections he may have hidden in those walls.

Hozark dropped the package on Jinnik's desk and quickly exited the room, but as he had been placing the container, he noticed something out in the open. Something that tied this confusing web of intrigue into an even greater knot.

There was a folded letter, and on it was the Council's validity seal.

There was no opportunity to read it, though. Not with Inari standing right there. So Hozark ignored it, for the time being, and left his odd package.

When the visla did finally return, he would likely wonder why a sealed container of dried root vegetables had been placed in his office, but, if at all possible, Hozark hoped to find the visla well before that happened. And he had a feeling that letter would guide the way.

Inari walked him to the lift disc and shook his hand warmly before returning to her tasks. "I hope your stay is a pleasant one," she said.

"Thanks, Inari. Maybe I'll see you around before we head out again."

"That would be nice," she said with a warm smile as the lift disc began its descent.

He would head out, all right, but it seemed he had more work to do first. And it involved a round trip back up to the top.

CHAPTER FORTY-THREE

Hozark stepped off the lift disc with purpose, striding across the foyer like a man on a mission, his eyes scanning the working men and women with a haughty confidence.

The guard who had so foolishly interrupted him earlier was at his assigned station now, but he was making a conscious effort to avoid making eye contact with the troublesome worker. In fact, no one, it seemed, wanted anything to do with him.

Whispers of his berating of the guard must have spread in spite of the man's efforts.

That served his purposes just fine. Better than that, in fact, for now he was not only within the security perimeter, and therefore seen as already vetted to be there, but he was also avoided.

It was a perfect combination.

Hozark could go wherever he wanted, to a degree. He could probably even ride back to the top on the lift disc if he pushed his luck, but without a package to deliver, that would not be prudent. And though Inari had taken a shine to him, a sudden repeat appearance so soon would cause even her to have questions.

He walked toward the access door to the service area away from the main foyer and tucked in. The building was relatively quiet with the visla off world, and finding a spot to step out of sight and slip into his shimmer cloak was quite easy.

After so much difficulty, a bit of ease was a nice change of pace, even if it would only last a short moment.

The invisible assassin waited by the door several minutes, until a worker carrying cleaned linen passed through on his way to deliver it to wherever it was destined. Hozark followed close behind, exiting through the door in his wake, then peeling off and moving straight toward the lift disc.

He could not simply step on and ascend. Yes, he could easily get around the bored-looking guards standing there, but if an empty lift activated, all sorts of problems would arise. Namely, a swift security response to the confined space.

But with his shimmer cloak, Hozark had a different option. It would take patience, and quite possibly hours of standing still, but he was as well practiced at that as he was at killing in an instant. In fact, a little bit of quiet meditation while he waited beside the lift disc would even provide a lovely refresher of sorts.

It was a Ghalian trick. To slip into a meditative state while remaining alert to what was around them. Akin to having two halves of the mind functioning on parallel, but utterly different, levels at the same time.

But Hozark did not have to wait long. In less than an hour, a pair of Council guards made their way to the lift disc, the cloaked killer watching their every move.

"Making the rounds?" the guards at the lift asked.

"Yep. Same shit, different hour."

"Better watch how loud you say that. I hear the Council might be having one of their agents do a sweep any day now."

"Really? An *agent*? But why?"

"Way beyond my pay grade. But you know how those guys can be."

"Yeah, real sticklers for details," the guard replied. "Thanks for the heads-up," he said, stepping onto the lift disc to join his partner. "Let's get this done. Take us up."

The spell was activated, and the two men rose quickly to the upper levels of the estate tower. Little did they know, there was a third riding along with them, invisibly tucked at the very back edge of the disc.

Hozark had taken a little gamble at the men's destination. The lift disc had been accessed several times while he had been waiting, but those had all appeared to be regular estate workers, and none who seemed to be members of the visla's private staff.

The new security detail, however, were more likely to have full access to the more important areas of the building, and realistically, the middle floors were not of great concern to them. Only the entryway level and the private chambers would be of interest.

The disc ascended in a flash, arriving at the topmost level of the tower, just as Hozark had hoped. The two guards stepped out, but then paused a moment at the lift exit as they scanned the area around them.

It was imperative they move ahead, for if not, the disc could be recalled at any moment, leaving Hozark stuck inside and descending to the wrong floor. On a contract, the assassin would have just stunned the men and hidden their sleeping bodies until he completed his hit. But in this case, he was forced to be utterly stealthy, forced to leave no trace.

As quietly as he could, Hozark uttered a tiny, minimally powered spell. It wasn't a Ghalian tool, nor was it used by any military forces. In fact, it was something employed by children more often than not.

A fart spell.

The guards both sniffed the air, the pungent aroma of someone's bowels filling their nostrils. Each assumed it was the other, and neither wanted to stand in the other man's stink, so they quickly stepped away to get started on their rounds.

Hozark moved off of the lift disc and headed the other direction, walking with complete silence as he made his way to Visla Jinnik's office.

Inari was long finished with her tasks by this time, and no other staffers were anywhere in sight on the floor. It was just Hozark and the guards, so far as he could tell. But a Ghalian was always cautious, and he took a moment to quickly check the nearby rooms to ensure he was correct in his assessment.

Even in a shimmer cloak, one did not want to be disturbed unexpectedly. All it took was one person accidentally bumping into an invisible intruder to set off a chain of events he would rather not have to deal with.

The first set of rooms were empty, and he noted the signs of damage that he had seen on his previous visit had all been repaired. If you did not know a brutally violent battle had taken place here, there was no way you would be able to tell from looking.

He paused at young Happizano's room. It was spotless. All of the scattered toys were neatly put away, and, more importantly, the blood of his tutor had been thoroughly cleansed from the floor. But it was *too* clean. It did not feel like a young boy lived there, but more like a staged scene attempting to give that impression.

It mattered not. The boy was safe, and that was what was important.

He left the youth's room and continued his sweep. As he suspected, the floor was indeed empty, save those two guards, and they would soon be finishing their rounds.

It was funny, in a way. The Council had sent a group of uninformed men to guard the estate after the vicious attack. But what they didn't know was they were guarding it from their own forces.

Voices caught Hozark's attention. The security team, it seemed, was moving a bit faster than he had expected. The clock was ticking. Hozark focused his senses on the magic in the air and made his way to the visla's warded door.

How long he would have inside the room was a big question mark. A variable he had no way to know the answer to. Inari had told him to be quick about it, but if she or another staffer had chores to do, say, cleaning or delivering materials, one would think at least a few minutes would be permitted.

But in the interest of safety, Hozark reduced his time to just one minute. He would get in, read the letter, get out, and get back to his ship. That was it. Sheer elegance in its simplicity.

But simple was never truly simple, in his experience.

Hozark pulled up the words Inari had spoken in his mind. He, and the others of his order, were almost freakish in their ability to retain spells like that. But it was not a quirk of neurology or chemistry, but simply a skill they had trained into them from their earliest years.

A Ghalian assassin was a killer, no doubt, but they were also some of the greatest intelligence gatherers in the galaxy. And that knowledge had to be collected, then retained, and all in a manner that would be undiscoverable should they be captured and searched.

Their minds, however, served as the perfect repository. A hidden vault of information that could never be stolen. And that storage space was now offering up the means of entrance into the visla's office.

Hozark took a long moment to focus on the *intent* of the spell. The drive behind it that made it work. Once that was firmly fixed in place, he quietly spoke the words of the spell, releasing the spells warding the doorway from intruders. He reached out with his konus to ensure it was open. It was, and there were no additional spells guarding it.

He slipped into the room and made for the visla's desk. The

container he had delivered earlier was still there, untouched. And just where he'd seen it, the validity seal-bearing letter sat beside it. Hozark paused before moving anywhere near the page.

His recent experience with the seal itself had made him *very* wary of anything related to this quest. He pulled strong magic from his konus and focused on the page, the seal, and everything around it.

There were some magical protections in the room, and even a few catch-traps on the desk itself, but those all appeared to be unrelated to this letter. At least so far as he could tell. The caster of the trap spell had been masterful in his or her use of it, and there was always the possibility that this was simply another layer of incredibly powerful magic he was unable to detect despite his skills.

Hozark took a breath and reached out for the page. Nothing happened when his fingers touched the parchment.

Quickly, he unfolded the note and read the contents, committing every word to memory in an instant. Within were instructions. A demand. A location he was to go to and what he was to do. If it hadn't been clear before, this made it abundantly so. The visla was being forced to do some Council member's bidding against his will.

If he didn't, his son would be killed.

It was an audacious plan, getting a man of his power to do another's bidding, essentially serving as a strong arm for the organization he so detested.

But the anonymous validity seal was confounding. It gave Hozark no lead to go on, no clarification as to who exactly it was who had done this to the man.

But that didn't matter. Not at the moment. What did was that they had to find Jinnik, wherever he was, and return his boy to him. Once that was accomplished, the man would be free to have his revenge, and Hozark and his team would be released to continue their work. To find those behind these machinations.

Forty seconds. He had twenty more to get out before his self-imposed deadline.

Hozark gently re-folded the page, then placed the letter back where it had been resting. He was about to leave when something on the visla's desk made him pause. He only had a few seconds to decide, and that choice was quickly made. He snatched the item from the desk and concealed it within his shimmer cloak as he hurried from the room.

The two guards didn't notice anything amiss when they summoned the lift disc, nor did they feel the slight breeze of the camouflaged man slip past them when they reached the ground floor.

The hidden assassin moved with speed and grace, his shimmer cloak remaining perfectly engaged as he made his way out of the visla's estate and into the city's bustling pathways and thoroughfares.

With the number of people milling about, passing through shimmered as he was would be difficult, as well as an excessive use of his limited magic, so Hozark tucked into an alleyway and quickly shed his shimmer cloak, stashing it in his clothing as he re-emerged onto the path as simply an average man just out for a walk.

It only took a short while to make his way back to his ship, which he promptly boarded and launched into the sky. His friends were waiting for him, and he had much to tell them.

CHAPTER FORTY-FOUR

The shimmer-cloaked craft exited the planet's atmosphere at a slow rate of speed to ensure it did not generate a heat glow that even the powerful spell could not obscure. It was somewhat tedious, especially when Hozark had much to inform his crewmates about, but it had to be done.

The fact that the Council of Twenty had a presence here, albeit a somewhat surreptitious one, gave his flight something of an urgency. But once he was safely in the embrace of the blackness of space, the master Ghalian was able to resume his course with haste.

A quick scan of the ships in orbit revealed that, as he had feared, a few were Council craft circling the globe under the guise of simple trade ships with their landing crews on the surface.

It was just further confirmation that there was no way they could bring the visla's son back home. Not now, anyway. That meant no life of luxury. No classy food. No spa treatments and drinks. None of that was in the cards for the boy now. Instead, they had a hard road ahead of them. One that Hozark knew Bud and Laskar would not be thrilled about.

He flew out to the small moon where his comrades were in a low orbit waiting for his return. Hozark then docked atop the craft, only disengaging his shimmer once he was entirely sure there were no other ships to observe them.

He cast the spell forming his magical umbilical to the mothership and hurried inside.

A whiff of something aromatic greeted him as soon as he stepped into the ship. Someone had cooked. That meant they would likely all be in the galley.

As expected, Hozark found all of his friends sharing a meal. Prepared with fresh ingredients, he noted, wondering if Bud had finally decided to take up his cooking hobby once more.

"Did you save any for me?" he asked as he stepped into the room.

"Holy shit, man!" Laskar blurted. "How the hell do you do that? I didn't even notice you docking to the ship."

"Years of practice, dear Laskar."

Hap was seated beside Henni, and, for a change, he actually seemed to be in decent spirits. It seemed that the promise of going home had pulled him out of his funk to a great degree. Hozark found himself feeling bad that he was to be the bearer of bad news.

He and Bud shared a look. One that said clearly that the boy would not be going home.

"Hey. I baked some dessert. You want some, Hap?" Bud asked, hoping to lessen the blow with sweets.

"Yeah, sure," Hap replied, then turned his full attention to Hozark. "I can't wait to get home. And when we're there, I'll show you guys the garden. My dad just had the first one installed. He said by the time I'm grown, there will be a dozen of them."

Hozark took a breath. There was simply no pussyfooting around the harsh facts. Better to get it out there all at once and let the chips fall where they may.

"I am sorry, Happizano. I truly am. But I am afraid there is a problem."

"What do you mean?"

"The men who took you. They have a presence in your home and around your world. I am sorry, but we cannot safely take you home. Not now, anyway."

The boy's eyes welled up with emotion as he bolted from the galley.

"But dessert," Bud called after him.

"I'm sorry, Bud. But I appreciate your attempt to minimize the trauma," Hozark said.

"Master Hozark, what happened down there? You said there was a Council presence?" Demelza asked.

"There is. Both in orbit, though disguised, and within the estate's grounds themselves, also disguised, though the staff seems to know who they are. They believe the ruse is all for the protection of the property at the visla's request."

"Which we know is a steaming pile of crap," Bud said.

"Hey, what's this about the Council and a visla?" Henni asked.

She had not been present for the earliest stage of this endeavor. As such, there were some finer points she was still not entirely up to speed on. In all the commotion and racing from system to system, bringing the young woman who they'd thought would just be a temporary passenger up to speed had kind of fallen through the cracks.

But now that she was more and more acting as a part of the crew, it would likely be a good idea to fill her in.

"Essentially, the people who attacked Visla Jinnik's home, kidnapped his son, and killed a great deal of people are now on site under the auspices of being invited by the visla to keep his home safe."

"And it was the Council that did it. You're sure?"

"Yes. And if there was any doubt before, there is none now," Hozark replied.

"Oh?" Laskar asked.

"There was a letter on the visla's desk. Not a trap, but merely something he left there as he hurried off to do as it directed him."

"And?" Laskar asked. "You're killing me, here. What did it say?"

"It demanded the visla fly at once to Nefario to assist the local emmik squash an uprising."

"That doesn't sound too––"

"And help them enslave those captured with control collars for use in the slave trade," he finished.

"Oh. Shit."

"Yes, Laskar. 'Oh shit' does sum that up fairly well."

Uzabud didn't like the sound of this one bit. Bad things were afoot, and far worse than he'd previously imagined.

"I assume there was a threat against the kid if he didn't comply?"

"Yes, of course."

"Son of a bitch," Bud grumbled. "By now he's almost certainly moved on from there, so that letter doesn't help us much."

"But it does tell us one thing," Hozark said. "Validity seals are not used often, so we know it was very likely the same person who laid that trap for us. And that was tied to Visla Ravik and Emmik Urtzal. While those two are not directly involved in quelling that uprising, I would wager that if we dig, there will be other similar disruptions ongoing that *do* affect them. And it would be at one of those that we would have a higher likelihood of locating the visla."

"So, we narrow the search to what, a few dozen worlds? It doesn't sound like the most logical idea," Laskar said.

"*We* do not. But the spy network most certainly will. A power like Jinnik's will not go unnoticed, and word will soon leak out. And if we make it known we are specifically looking for that man, I feel we will have a hit relatively soon."

"But why use him on peripheral problems? Why not break him out for the big ones?" Bud asked.

Demelza leaned in. "If I may, I have a theory on that. It would seem, from what we have learned so far, that there is a power struggle at play within the Council. One that they are working very hard to keep silent. If a player happened to acquire a visla of this power to their side, even if by coercion, it would be wise to save that asset for themselves."

Bud nodded in agreement. "I hate to say it, but that makes a lot of sense. And those Council freaks are always backstabbing each other to get more power. I mean, when's enough, enough, right?"

"I would argue, never," Laskar said. "But what do we do now?"

"Now we return to Corann to inform her of what has transpired. She and the rest of the order need to be aware of these goings-on. And while we do that, the spy network will do what it does best."

"And the kid?" Bud asked.

Hozark let out a long sigh. "I will see to him."

"Go away!" Hap shouted through his door.

"Happizano, I only wish to speak with you."

"I said, go away. I hate you!"

Hozark opened the door and stepped inside. "I understand your sentiment, and, given the circumstances, do not blame you one bit."

Hap's eyes were red from crying, and a slight buzz lingered in the air around him. Hozark found that most interesting. It

263

was an unfocused power, but the boy most definitely had his father's gift.

Soon, he would grow into his power and would be an emmik at the very least, though given the familial traits, he might very well even become a great visla, if his power proved strong enough.

For now, however, he was still just a young boy, lost, scared, and unfocused.

"We will find your father, young Jinnik. And we will get you to him. I know this setback is upsetting, but you have my word we are doing all in our power to reunite you."

The boy wiped his nose on his sleeve, but at least his crying had ceased. It had been a rough time for him, no doubt, and this was just one more bump in an already rocky road.

"He was going to teach me some new spells. He said it was time for me to learn the fun stuff."

"And he is a great visla. I am sure he has many amazing things to share with you."

"If I ever see him again."

"You will," Hozark said. "Your father loves you very much."

"Sure."

"I was just in his office, and do you know what he had on his desk? This," he said, pulling the gladiator doll out of his pocket.

"Suvius the Mighty!" Hap gushed, taking the toy and holding it tight.

"He looked at this every day, hoping to have you come back to him. I can promise you, he will not give up hope. And neither will we."

Happizano actually seemed calmed for a moment, and strangely enough, Hozark found himself experiencing an odd emotion for a killer. Empathy.

"I'll tell you what," the assassin said. "Let me show you a little trick."

He pulled power from his konus and directed it to the air

above his hand with a simple spell. "*Arcatis vespool*," he said, the magic flowing out and forming a tiny snow flurry that quickly condensed into an ice cube.

"Whoa. That's cool."

"Here, you try," he said, taking the konus from his wrist and slipping it over the boy's.

It was large for him, obviously, but for one of Jinnik's blood, pulling from a konus should be quite simple. In fact, when he was grown, Hap would likely be able to do the opposite, charging the device as easy as breathing.

But for now, he was just a boy, learning the first bits of how his power truly worked.

"*Arcatis vespool*," Hap said. "*Arcatis vespool!*"

"You must not force it. The key to casting is the intent behind the words, not just the words themselves."

Happizano took a breath and squinted his eyes with concentration. "*Arcatis vespool*," he said.

A tiny snowflake formed above his palm, but no more. But it was something, and with it, his spirits brightened.

"Keep at it, young Jinnik. Practice. And tomorrow, I shall help you further. In the meantime, it is late. Get some rest."

Hap looked up at the Ghalian master. "Hozark?"

"Yes, Happizano?"

"Thanks."

"It is my pleasure, young Jinnik," he replied, stepping out the door. "Until tomorrow, then."

CHAPTER FORTY-FIVE

The following morning—if it was actually morning, one could never tell in space—found the crew in surprisingly good spirits for a group dealing with the myriad deadly, and downright confusing, variables they had faced of late.

But despite losing the opportunity to get some much-needed rest and relaxation at the visla's estate, they were nevertheless well-stocked with supplies, and had a destination dialed in.

It wasn't their first choice, but if they had to pick a second one, visiting the leader of the Five wasn't a bad fallback.

Corann kept a cozy home wherever she was based. All the better to maintain her warm and friendly motherly vibe. It wouldn't be a visla's life of luxury, but she would feed them well, and the beds would be soft and welcoming regardless.

It was a big question mark just how long it would take the Ghalian spy network to discern the likeliest location of Happizano's father. It could take mere days, or it could take weeks. But one thing was certain. Once they had been tasked with this mission, they *would* find him. It was just a question of when.

"Sleep well?" Uzabud asked as the violet-haired girl walked into the galley.

"What's it to you?" she shot back with a groggy yawn.

Her snark was not exactly on point this early in the day, but with better sleep and a significant amount of food, she was actually beginning to look healthy for what was likely the first time in no one knew how long.

As was always the case this early in the day, her hair was something of a mess. The effect only added to her typically off-kilter appearance.

There was something about her. They all felt it. But none could quite put their finger on what it was. One day, Hozark hoped, they would learn the truth of her nature. But for now, that was not a secondary, or even tertiary concern.

"You are looking well, Henni," the Wampeh said as he sipped his usual morning tea concoction. "How has your sleep been?"

"Better," she admitted. "Thanks."

With Hozark, she had adopted a more considerate tone. Not because he could kill her in less than the time it took for her to draw a breath, but because, despite his deadly nature, he had taken her under his protection and accepted her as a part of their odd little group.

She wouldn't exactly call it a family, but these people had a bond that seemed somehow different than other crews she'd flown with.

The Ghalian were bound by their order, of course. But they had been through a lot together, and it showed. The same with the annoying pilot. Bud was a cocky bastard, but it was clear Hozark trusted him implicitly.

Laskar was the wildcard. He was part of the team, but he seemed to grate on everyone's nerves on a fairly regular basis. But he was a good pilot, and a very good navigator, so it seemed his grating nature was given a pass.

In short order, everyone had gathered in the galley and was enjoying a relatively quiet breakfast before digging into the day. Everyone but their newest guest.

"I suppose I'll go wake up the kid," Bud said, sliding up from his seat. "A little food in his belly should keep him from bitching. At least more than usual."

Bud left his mug on the table and strolled out while stretching wide, his shoulders crackling as he did.

"Oof, that didn't sound good," Laskar noted.

"Just working the excess awesome through my bones, is all," Bud said with a grin, then headed off down the corridor.

A few minutes later he returned, a slightly confused look on his face.

"Uh, guys? Any of you seen the kid this morning?"

"Why, Bud?" Demelza asked.

"He's not in his room."

"Perhaps he is in the restroom or bathing compartment," she offered.

"Nope. Checked there too."

Hozark's brow furrowed ever so slightly. "This is disconcerting," he said. "And you are certain he was not merely hiding?"

"Dude, this is *my* ship. I know the nooks and crannies. He wasn't in his room, or anywhere I could see."

"Shit. You think he spaced himself?" Laskar asked.

"There? Your mind went *there*?" Bud asked.

"Just asking."

"He's a kid, Laskar."

"A kinda messed up kid," he replied.

"Enough of this nonsense. Come, all of you. We must search the ship. And I do not mean just the living spaces," Hozark said. "He is relatively small and could be anywhere."

"Aww, shit," Henni said, dropping her food back onto her plate. "Well, I guess it'll taste good cold too. So, what do we do?"

The five of them split up, each with a different part of the ship to search. It was a smuggling ship, and Uzabud had outfitted it with many secret compartments in which to hide contraband, should the need arise. Unfortunately, that also meant there were a very large number of places the young boy could hide.

Bud seemed incredulous that a mere kid could have even found the hidey-holes he had so painstakingly constructed and concealed, but Hozark was firm. They had to be thorough.

It was rather time-consuming, but after nearly an hour the group reconvened in the command center. Each of them empty-handed.

"How is this possible?" Demelza wondered. "He has to be somewhere."

"I'm telling ya. He spaced himself."

"Shut up, Laskar."

"He actually has an interesting point," Hozark said, a curious look in his eye.

"What? You really think he'd do that?"

"Not exactly, Bud. But this line of thinking does give me an idea. I shall return shortly."

Hozark walked the corridors of the large craft until he reached the location of the umbilical spell that connected his vessel to Bud's mothership. He uttered the words to open the seal between both craft.

Happizano was there, seated quietly in the seeming void of space. Of course, there was a magical tube of air connecting the ships, but that was not visible to the naked eye. He didn't even look up at Hozark.

The assassin stared a moment, then let out a small sigh.

"Are you all right?" he asked as he took a seat next to the boy.

Hap did not answer, his eyes fixed on the hull beneath him.

Hozark waited a long moment, deciding what to say or do next. He could simply haul the boy inside, of course. But that would not rectify whatever this situation was, and it could even possibly make it worse.

Finally, he spoke. "Tell me. Why did you choose this place? There are many far more comfortable locations to hide."

Hap slowly looked up and met the Wampeh's gaze. "I was gonna steal your ship," he admitted.

Hozark was greatly amused, on the inside. The sheer gall of the boy. The balls, though they likely had not even dropped yet. It was impressive, and he couldn't help but approve of his young guest's plan. He lacked the requisite skill to carry it out, of course, but nevertheless, he had tried. And that was more than you could say of most.

"You planned to fly home, I assume?"

"Yeah," the boy replied, looking away.

"But you quickly learned that my ship is much harder to force entry to than the umbilical spell, didn't you?"

"Yeah, I noticed."

Hozark chuckled slightly. "My dear boy, you should be proud of your accomplishment. To overcome the spell sealing off this space required a fair bit of magical skill. And had you attempted to access one of the lesser ships mounted to the hull, you might have even succeeded, though that is still not likely. You see, in space, the docking spells are far stronger out of necessity."

"Why is yours harder to get into?"

"I am a Wampeh Ghalian, and my spells are much, much stronger than most."

Happizano said nothing. It wasn't the angry reaction he had been expecting, but he was chided, nevertheless. The Ghalian master was about to invite the boy back inside the mothership when something caught his eye. Something utterly unexpected.

Puddles. Several of them. Tiny puddles of water, in this place, nowhere near any source of liquid. Hozark's interest was suddenly piqued.

"Show me," he instructed the boy.

Hap reached out with his hand, the oversize konus still dangling from his wrist. "*Arcatis vespool*," he said, casting with not just the words but the intent, as he had been instructed.

A swirl of sparkles appeared in his palm, slowly coalescing into a tiny snowball. It wasn't a hard and fully formed ice cube. Not yet. But it was worlds of improvement from what he had been able to do the day before.

Hap placed the little ball of snow on the deck and watched as it slowly began to melt like the others had.

"I am most impressed, young Jinnik. You have greatly improved, and in just one day."

"I still can't get it right, though."

"No one does at first. This is a process, and it takes time. For some, far longer than others. But you have a visla's blood in you, and I believe you will be a great caster one day, if this is any sign of your growing powers."

"You think?" he asked, making eye contact again, at last.

"I do," Hozark said. And he wasn't just giving lip service. If the boy was able to do this with just minimal instruction, he would indeed grow to be a power user of some force.

"So, now what? Are you gonna take me back inside?"

Hozark thought but a moment. "No. You may remain here as long as you like. But when you are ready to come back inside, there is food and drink waiting for you in the galley."

With that, Hozark opened the access and slid through, leaving the boy to his thoughts. He wasn't all right. Not by a long shot. But he was, at least a little bit, less upset. And that was a good place to start.

CHAPTER FORTY-SIX

It took multiple jumps for Bud to finally bring them to Corann's current home turf on the world of Etratz.

Laskar had plotted the most direct course he could, but given the pull on their Drookonus, and the likelihood of encountering Council vessels in some of the more directly accessible systems, they had been forced to take a somewhat circuitous route in the interest of safety.

Once they arrived, though, concerns seemed to melt away. Etratz was a pleasant world, and Corann's bungalow was a truly welcoming place surrounded by other, similar pleasant abodes. It was something of an idyllic locale, and the perfect place for her to set up shop and live unmolested.

Of course, her sweet, motherly demeanor had made her a favorite among the locals, and her neighbors, young and old, often dropped by to visit the kindly woman. And more often than not, she would have fresh-baked treats on hand for the local youth.

And through it all, not a one had the slightest inkling that the leader of the deadliest group of assassins in the galaxy was living just down the path.

Uzabud swung his ship in low over the town, making a casual loop before dropping down at the landing site conveniently near Corann's abode. Of course, that was intentional on her part. Quick access to her ship was always a concern. As well it should be for any master assassin, let alone the leader of the Five.

"All clear?" Laskar asked as they settled into a low hover just above the ground.

"Yeah. No signs of any hostiles anywhere," Bud replied. "Hozark?"

"All is well, my friend. I have reached out to Corann and announced our arrival."

"Wait, I thought the skrees were all on the fritz," Laskar said. "You mean we have working ones?"

"Not exactly," Hozark replied. "The unit built into my shimmer ship is still functional, but only on for a specialized Ghalian spell. I am afraid it would do no good in attempting to contact any outside of my order."

"Ah, shit. I was hoping we'd get our communications back up and running sooner rather than later."

"I am sorry to have raised your hopes. But do not fear. Soon, we should be able to repair our systems."

"I'm just looking forward to some home-cooked meals," Bud said. "She may be the leader of the Five, but damn, that woman can cook."

"Always thinking with your stomach, Bud," Hozark joked.

"Wait, we're visiting a chef?" Henni asked.

"No, Henni. But Uzabud is correct, Corann is quite skilled in a kitchen," Demelza said.

"Then what are we waiting for?"

"We aren't," Hozark said. "Come. We have arrived."

He gathered his small bag and headed for the door.

"You heard the man. Time to offload," Bud said with a grin.

"You'll love this place, Hap. And Corann? She's really, really nice."

The boy didn't seem terribly enthused. But since he'd found his little quiet place in between the docked ships, he had at least seemed to improve his attitude a bit. And with Hozark showing him the ropes, he was picking up a few little spells here and there.

The practice of them gave him something to focus on other than missing his home. Naturally, it was still hard for him, as his father had planned on working on spells with his son.

They'd both been looking forward to the lessons, and they had planned on some quality time as soon as the visla returned from his most recent task. But that had been a decoy to lure him from his home. And then all of *this* happened.

But he seemed to be faring better. At least, so Hozark thought. And while it would hurt until he was back with his father, the boy was making progress, and, perhaps, even a few new friends.

"Hozark! Demelza! Wonderful to see you both!" Corann called out warmly from her seat on her porch as the group arrived.

"Corann," they replied, each of them giving the cheery woman a big hug.

It was all for show, of course. Ghalian assassins were not exactly known for their displays of affection. But here, in public, to all who might observe, she was not a deadly killer, but was the kindest, sweetest, friendliest woman in town.

"And you, Uzabud. It had been too long. And I see you have Laskar with you. I am glad to see you are still flying together."

"He can't shake me," Laskar said with a cocky grin.

"Nor would he want to. Your flying skills are something to behold," she said, turning her attentions to the boy standing beside Hozark. "And you must be Happizano," she said, squatting down to greet him. "I've heard a lot about you. Quite an up-and-coming young caster, I'm told."

"I'm not any good," he replied, bashfully.

"Oh, it just takes time and practice. I'm sure Hozark told you how when he started out, why, he couldn't cast to save his life. And now look at him!"

"Really?"

"Yes, really. We all start out from nothing and build our way up. But look at me, talking your ear off without even giving you a proper welcome. Come and say hello. I'm Corann, and we do hugs around here."

Before he could even think to protest, she wrapped the boy up in quite possibly the most comforting, motherly, and warm embrace he'd ever felt.

"You'll love it here, I just know," she said as she relaxed the embrace. "And who do we have here?" she said as she turned to greet the violet-haired young woman hovering nearby.

"This is Henni. She's flying with us, for the time being," Bud replied.

Corann beamed with joy and moved to give the girl a hug.

Henni's eyes went wide and she leapt back, right into Bud.

"She's a killer," she gasped. "A stone-cold killer. And so many. Hundreds. No, *thousands*."

Corann eased back from her open-armed welcome, but her smile didn't falter once. But the faintest flicker of interest shone in her kind eyes. Despite her most cheerful, sweet, and motherly appearance, Henni had read her like an open book.

"A bit of a reader, that one," Demelza said. "But it is uncontrolled. Sporadic. We never know when it will kick in."

"Fascinating," she said.

"Look at her eyes," Hozark said.

Slowly, and in the most unthreatening manner possible,

Corann leaned in a little for a closer look. Henni's galaxy-containing eyes were sparkling more than usual, but whether out of shock or something more she couldn't tell.

Corann turned back to Hozark with a slightly arched brow. "Oh, my."

"Indeed."

The two were thinking the same thing. The same question they all had at one point or another since bringing the young woman aboard. They wondered exactly what powers this unusual young woman might possess.

"Well, that makes things interesting. You never disappoint, Hozark."

"I shall accept that as a compliment," he joked.

"All right. Let's get you all inside and settled in. I've had rooms made up for you, and there's a big pot of Borangis stew simmering."

As the others settled in, Hozark and Corann set out for a little stroll under the guise of picking up a few things from the local trading post. Yes, they would acquire a few basic goods to keep up appearances, but what the true purpose of their excursion was quite different.

"You are picking up strays now?" Corann asked as they walked back with some fresh fruit and a loaf of bread.

"She was a slave," Hozark replied. "And she somehow broke free from her control collar. The scars on her throat––she was burned when she forced it off."

"That little thing? Amazing. But how?"

"She does not remember."

"An enigma, then."

"So it would appear."

"But tell me of your other news. What have you learned of this plot within the Council of Twenty?"

"We are still unsure of much of it. However, it would seem that Visla Jinnik is now being employed in the furthering of these plans."

"Yes, our spies are attempting to locate his whereabouts. But are you confident returning his boy to him will put them both out of harm's way?"

"No, I am not. But it is clear that the separation is doing the boy far more harm than good, personal safety be damned. I have to believe that with both of their reactions to losing one another, whatever happens, they are best served by being together."

"Even if it means their demise?"

"If it comes to it."

They walked in silence a moment before Hozark spoke again.

"There was a trap, Corann. Powerful. Dangerous. If not for Demelza, I would have fallen."

That got her attention. "What happened?"

"A validity seal was in Emmik Urtzal's offices. I was ensnared, but only after reaching the innermost chambers in the emmik's estate. Someone knew I would make it that far."

"And you say he is acting on Council orders?"

"Perhaps, but perhaps not. This might be an internal power struggle, given there is no chatter about Visla Jinnik now working for the Council. In any case, Emmik Urtzal is obviously aligned with Visla Ravik."

"You are certain?"

"Yes. His ships were assisting Ravik's forces in the ambush waiting for us at Zargota."

"An ambush? And Urtzal in the mix? Interesting," she mused. "So, they definitely knew you were coming. No ambiguity there."

"It would seem so. And while that might be explained by our ongoing endeavors, the fact that the validity seal was a trap, and one of incredible power and complicated casting no less, tells us one very important thing. It is now confirmed. Someone other than Visla Ravik is involved in this plot, and *that* visla is far stronger than any we've suspected."

CHAPTER FORTY-SEVEN

Henni seemed to get over her visceral aversion to Corann by the time dinner was served.

Whether it was a bit of comestible bribery, or just her getting to know the woman beyond the deadly assassin who lurked inside was anyone's guess, but the important thing was she was a bit more at ease.

Of course, as she shoveled down the utterly fantastic stew—as Laskar had declared it to be the finest he had ever tasted—the warming in her belly and energy flowing through her veins might have played more than a little role in her improved attitude.

Even Hap seemed to be doing all right, though the boy was still often found deep in thought.

"He's a pensive one," Corann noted as Hozark helped her clear the dishes.

"Yes. And understandably. But despite what he has been subjected to, he actually appears to be dealing with the situation better by the day."

"Good. It is difficult for a boy to lose his mother, then his father."

"Though we will get the father back," Hozark noted. "And from what I have seen of his power, when Visla Jannik is no longer constrained by the threat of harm to his boy, the Council is going to have a very big problem on their hands."

"That strong?"

"It actually *leaks out of him* when angered," Hozark said.

"You know, we could help him with that problem."

"I was thinking the same thing, but I did not think it was the appropriate time to bring such an arrangement up."

"Obviously not. But he could prove to be a useful ally in the ongoing pushback to the Council's machinations."

"I agree. But first, we must find him."

"Soon, Hozark. And in the meantime, you and your crew may rest here and restore your energy and spirits."

"In no small part thanks to your cooking, Corann. It has always been a pleasure to partake of your culinary works of art."

If she had been the woman she pretended to be, the Ghalian master would have blushed demurely at the compliment. But this was Master Corann, leader of the Five. And she was not putting on airs for Hozark. Not here in her own home, unobserved by outsiders.

"It is an interesting conundrum we are facing, Hozark. Someone is attempting to amass power, and in very, *very* unusual and covert ways. And they are willing to directly attack the order in the process."

"I know. It is extremely troubling, to say the least. A power play, but of unknown purpose," Hozark said. "Speaking of which, how are Master Prombatz and Aargun doing?"

A look of unguarded sadness settled onto Corann's face.

"Prombatz is back to his former self. Healed, full of freshly harvested power from a series of smaller contracts. Not much, but enough to get a good base of power back into his system."

"And Aargun?"

The poor aspirant had been horribly maimed at the hands

of the Council goons who had captured him. Experimented on. Drained of most of his blood, his eyes and tongue removed to keep him in the dark, literally, and silent about the procedures he underwent.

He had survived, but he would never return to Ghalian life. But he was a brother, and he would not only be taken care of the rest of his days, he would be avenged. And Master Prombatz would be first in line for that bit of payback.

"Aargun is as well as can be expected," Corann said. "The pain is gone, and his spirits are improving, but the damage done to him has left more than physical scars. He is, I am afraid, somewhat of a shell of his former self."

Hozark silently dried the dishes, pondering all that had befallen not just himself and his friends, but others in the order caught up in this mess as well.

"I hope to find answers, Corann. And soon. And with them, the means to put an end to whatever is in play and obtain closure for them both."

"Thank you, Hozark. I know Master Prombatz appreciates all you are doing. Now, will you please help me bring some after-dinner sweets to the guests? One would not wish to be a poor host."

The following morning found the weary travelers well rested after a good night's sleep in soft beds with full bellies. Even Henni seemed in better spirits, though she still eyed Corann with caution over her cup of hot herbal tea.

Corann, however, rolled with it in stride. The young woman was a fascinating specimen, and her abilities could prove most useful. If she could learn to control and harness them, that is.

They were just tucking into the breakfast feast Corann had spread out for them when one absence caught everyone's attention.

"Ugh. Again?" Laskar grumbled.

"I'll go get him," Bud said, heading out to find the boy. "You all finish your breakfast. He's almost certainly at his usual spot."

There was a whole city to explore, but Bud had a gut feeling that the boy had stuck with what he knew. And that was the ship he'd spent the past several days aboard. It had become, if not a home, at least a relatively familiar and comfortable environment. One where he had found places to feel safe.

"I'll come with," Hozark said, following his friend out of Corann's bungalow. "The fresh air will feel good."

"Suit yourself," Bud replied. "Maybe we can source some fresh Boramus cheese on the way back. I love that stuff."

"Obviously not for the flavor," Demelza said.

"Hey, it makes you strong!"

"That it is nutritious is not in question. But as for palatability, it is not the most pleasant of foods."

"And you're entitled to your opinion," he said. "But I was raised on the stuff, and look at me––big and strong."

"That's not all muscle, you know," Henni pointed out.

"Totally is," he shot back. "Anyway, come on, Hozark. Let's go find us a kid."

Henni snort-chortled. "You really should work on your phrasing, creeper."

Bud ignored her and headed out, but Laskar couldn't help but laugh. The others, however, politely refrained, though the girl *was* pretty amusing.

"So, you think it'll take long for your people to find the visla?"

"I do not know, Bud, but with the resources at our disposal, I would think that now that this particular man has been brought to our attention, it should not take terribly long to locate him."

"Good. I don't know how much more of Happizano's moody angst I can take."

"You said his name correctly," Hozark noted.

"Yeah, don't make a thing out of it. I just like busting his balls, is all. Gives a kid character."

"He's eleven, Bud."

"Precisely my point. He needs it now more than ever, if you ask me. The formative years."

"Well, given I had daily sessions of knife training at his age, I suppose I cannot argue your logic. At least, not entirely. Though name-calling is not the most productive of methods."

"The kid's gonna be a visla one day, right?"

"Likely."

"Then it's incumbent upon us to try to make him a good one when that time comes. I mean, we have limited time, and a limited influence on him, but if any of this stuff sticks, he might just turn out okay."

Hozark looked at his friend with wonder as they drew closer to his ship.

"Uzabud, my friend, you never cease to amaze me."

"And amuse you."

"Yes, that as well," Hozark said as they strode up to Bud's large ship.

"Okay, I said I'd do it, so hang tight. I'll be right back."

Bud stepped into the ship to go and retrieve young Hap while Hozark took a moment to simply look around and appreciate the beautiful morning. Only, one thing was not right.

"Hey. He's not in there," Bud said, exiting the ship a minute later. "He always goes to that umbilical spot. Weird. I guess he's off somewhere else. But where, is the question?"

Hozark nodded to the pilot. "Look up, my friend."

"What the shit?" Bud blurted out when he realized what Hozark was referring to. The empty space atop his ship where one of his smaller craft had been parked. "Son of a bitch. He stole one of my ships? *My* ships? How dare he?"

"Indeed."

"And more than that, how *did* he? How does a kid that age

even know how to fly? To power a Drookonus? I mean, it was a pretty weak one on that bucket, but still."

"I would think his father likely showed him on the many flights they took together. He is strong, and a quick learner. Undoubtedly, his father taught him a thing or two."

"But even if he knew how to fly, how did he overcome the umbilical spells? Those things should have kept the ships locked down tight."

"I fear that is my fault," Hozark said. "When we discussed his inability to steal my ship, I pointed out that the docking spells were much stronger in space. He obviously took that to heart and was waiting for an opportunity to make another attempt."

"Shit. We've gotta find him, Hozark."

"Oh, indeed," the Ghalian replied. "We must gather the others at once. He cannot have gotten far. Not yet, anyway."

They rushed back to Corann's home and informed the others what had happened.

"He did what?" Henni blurted. "Not cool."

"That's what I said," Bud chimed in.

Hozark stopped in front of the head of the Five. "We will return as soon as we can, Corann."

"Until you do, fly safe," she replied.

"I don't know about safe, but we'll fly fast," Laskar said as they hurried to the ship.

As they were in public and observed by the locals while boarding, Corann then gave each of the visitors a big hug, a massive smile plastered on her face. Henni, however, held back, and the Ghalian master did not press the matter.

She was an unusual one, no doubt, and of indeterminate power. She was an enigma. And while they were away recovering their little runaway, Corann had some research to do.

CHAPTER FORTY-EIGHT

Space was a vast and mostly empty void. That emptiness was a good thing at the moment, as young Happizano had watched, but never actually flown a ship before. Had there been anything remotely near for him to hit, he undoubtedly would have.

Repeatedly.

But he was all alone in the black, doing his best to navigate his way back to his home. For a boy his age, it sounded like a great idea. That is, until the reality of the situation reared its ugly head. After he'd stolen a ship, of course.

The problem was, Hap had no idea *how* to navigate.

Sure, he had seen his father's crew do it––they made it look so simple––and sure, they had let him power up and even steer the ship sometimes. But that was always under their close supervision, the experienced men and women correcting his mistakes and guiding him back on course.

But this was different. He was all alone with no one to fall back on.

It was all up to him, and the pressure was intense. He simply had no choice. From what the others had said, his home was being occupied by some bad guys as well as his father's normal retinue. That was a problem, and step one would be stealing a ship so he could go back.

Surprisingly, Hap had actually done just fine accessing the small craft mounted to Bud's ship's hull. That was the easy part, though. In space, he hadn't been able to access any of the craft's interiors. But Hozark had been right. It was easier in atmosphere. It had proved to be a rather useful tip.

Hap almost felt bad about using the man's attempt at sympathy against him. But he didn't have time for that sort of thing. He needed to get back home to round up his father's loyal staff to kick out whoever the hell was staying in his house. And from there, he would take them out into space and find his dad.

If he could. First, he would have to get home, and that was proving to be quite a lot harder than he had expected.

He had lifted off, albeit in a rather jerky manner, uneasily making his way through the sky and up into space. It wasn't pretty, but he had done it. And from there he managed to fly to the very edge of the solar system, trying, and failing, to activate the jump spell the whole while.

Over and over he made those attempts, and over and over the Drookonus barely acknowledged his efforts.

At the end of the day, and at the edge of the system, it was clear. Happizano was a terrible pilot and an even worse navigator. And adding insult to that injury, he had no idea how to even read a star chart, let alone focus the Drookonus's jump magic if he did.

There was one other thing he quickly learned he did not know. He didn't know how to avoid pirates.

The large, battle-scarred craft had been lurking in the darkness at the edge of the solar system for some time, watching ships come and go, just waiting for a tempting prize to happen their way. It was tedious work, the waiting, but it often turned out to be worthwhile, the targets they did manage to acquire never expecting an attacker from the black void between systems.

When a small vessel was acquired by their scanning spells, they fully expected it to jump away far before it was close enough for them to strike. The angle of the sun was illuminating them at this particular time, and even the most basic of defensive spells would likely have picked up their presence.

But, miraculously, this ship didn't seem to be changing course. It was so unexpected, they actually thought it was a trap. At least for a while. But when the ship came closer and closer, flying somewhat erratically as it did, they pinged its defenses with the smallest of spells, testing for potential weaknesses.

It was then that they realized this was something far more tempting than normal. As incredible as it seemed, this was an entirely undefended sitting duck.

Who would fly without engaging even the most basic of shielding spells they didn't know? Perhaps the ship's built-in konuses were damaged, or the casters were low on their own magic. No one knew. But one thing was certain. This prize was theirs for the taking.

"Go in for the kill, boys!" the grizzled captain commanded with glee.

"Aye, aye, Captain Darvin," his second-in-command replied. "You heard the captain. Prepare to board!"

The pirates raced into action, taking their stations in a frantic yet orderly chaos. They were rough and ready for action, though given the diminutive size of this particular target, there wasn't likely to be all that much action. In fact, it was so small as to be barely worth their time.

But the captain had given them his orders, and they all knew far better than to ignore them. There was a reason Captain Darvin possessed the reputation he had, and they didn't want to be just another story reinforcing his iron-fisted legend.

Poor Happizano didn't have the slightest idea what was

about to befall him. And even if he had, there was simply nothing he could do about it. The ship he had stolen wasn't fast, it wasn't particularly robust, and it certainly wasn't heavily armed.

Captain Darvin's ship swung around the smaller craft as quickly as they could, putting themselves squarely in the small pinpoint of the sun's rays, blinding any potential observer to their presence. At more central worlds this was a relatively easy maneuver, but this far out, the sun was just a dot. A bright dot, but a dot all the same.

It was an impressive bit of flying by any standards, and those at the Drookonus were putting on an impressive show. It was just too bad their intended target had no idea of the display of talented flying being put on so close by.

Captain Darvin focused his intentions on the little craft now in front of them and unleashed his carefully crafted spell, knocking out their Drookonus from afar with a disabling blast of magic.

Immediately, the ship lost propulsion, drifting instead, maintaining its speed in the vacuum, but totally vulnerable. Seconds after Darvin's ship dropped down on top of it, boarding spells, akin to elongated umbilicals, streamed from his craft to the smaller one below.

His boarding party immediately dropped down and began casting their breaching spells. Two of them, one at the front and one at the rear, allowing them to catch the defenders in a crossfire they could not escape.

"Put down your weapons, or we'll chop off yer bloody--" the leader of the team cried out when his boots hit the deck. But those words fell short when he saw the enemy he was facing.

"A feckin' kid?" he said in disbelief. "It's just a feckin' kid?"

"What? Lemme see," the man behind him said, suddenly deprived of at least a little bloodshed.

Happizano was frozen in place, terrified and utterly unsure

what to do. The flashback to his very recent abduction and the murder of his tutor and staff was fresh in his mind, and in the heat of the moment, he simply locked up, unsure what to do.

"Bag the kid. Take him back to the ship. Cap'n will want to have a look at 'im."

A pair of rough hands did just that, scooping up the boy and carrying him effortlessly up through the magically opened breach and into their pirate ship.

"The rest of you," the pirate cried out. "Take all you can grab. The ship is ours!"

With a joyful cheer the pirates set to work, stripping the vessel of every last thing of value, then left it adrift, an empty shell floating in the void. And poor Hap was a prisoner once more.

CHAPTER FORTY-NINE

Uzabud had scrambled their ship up into the air as soon as they could, all while making their departure seem as natural as possible and not a sudden, frantic race for the sky.

Corann had to keep up appearances, after all, and the extra few minutes of delay wouldn't make a big difference in their search.

The sky was big, and space was bigger, and the boy could only go so far with his limited abilities. First and foremost, they would survey the area immediately around Corann's home, just in case Hap had only managed a short flight.

When that came up empty, they then expanded outward to the neighboring regions.

"I do not detect any trace of that ship," Demelza said as she adjusted her spells to refine them for the specific Drookonus that powered it.

Normally, that was simply not possible. Every Drookonus was different, and you had to know one intimately to hope to trace it with a spell. But this was a ship Demelza had plenty of familiarity with. It was one of Uzabud's favorites, and its constant presence had afforded her the opportunity to become quite familiar with its magical signature.

"I do not believe it is still on this planet," she said, having expended all of the tracking spells in her arsenal. "The traces are far too weak. In fact, I would wager that young Happizano managed to escape the atmosphere somewhat rapidly, judging by what I can find."

"So, up we go, without further delay," Uzabud said, then streaked skyward toward the stars.

It was a relatively quick search around the planet. Now that Demelza had a better feel for the traces of the ship's Drookonus, she was able to rule out entire sections of space where there were simply no hits for the unique power signature. The farther out they went, however, the longer it was taking.

The distance between the worlds and moons in the system was, frankly, massive. And the ship could have flown anywhere out in that wide-open nothingness. But Demelza had a trace. It wasn't huge, but it was there, and gradually, as they made their way farther and farther out toward the edge of the system where it dropped off into the *real* black, it was getting stronger.

"He went this way," Demelza said.

"You sure?" Laskar asked.

"Positive. And not far now." She paused. "Something is not right. The power, I felt it growing, but suddenly it stopped."

"Did he jump? Maybe he did know how to do it after all. Clever kid, that one," Bud said.

"No, it is different. Not the same power shift as with a jump. That is always more of a surge. This feels like an abrupt cessation altogether."

Bud and the two Wampeh shared a knowing look.

"He wouldn't have blown himself up. No, there's no way. That Drookonus was way too underpowered for anything like that. At least, not in his hands."

"Then, what?" Henni asked.

"The other option is almost as bad," Demelza said. "For a Drookonus to suddenly stop emitting any power, its vessel would have to be more than just stopped. It would have had to be removed entirely."

"And? Maybe he just pulled the wrong thingamajiggy and took it out."

"That is highly unlikely. A Drookonus requires specific spells to release it from its cradle. And *that* is a particular bit of magic I doubt young Jinnik has ever learned," Hozark said.

Bud looped them around the area where the last traces of the ship's power faded away. There was no sign of the ship, but the former pirate had an idea.

"Demelza. Give me your last four hits for their Drookonus, will ya?"

"What's that gonna do?" Henni asked.

"Just a thought, but it'll show us the rough trajectory when the Drookonus went out."

"But the ship is gone."

"Yes, but you heard Demelza. No surge. Get it? It might not have jumped. It might still be out there."

It was a logical move, for following debris or wrecks. But there was no sign of either here. Just a missing boy aboard a missing ship.

"Here you are, Bud," Demelza said, giving him the last four readings.

"Great. Now, I'll just plot that in and account for drift," the former pirate said. "Aaaand... Holy shit. Guys, there it is!"

"What happened to it?" Henni asked. "It's all messed up."

"Stripped, is more like it," Laskar noted.

"Pillaged, we liked to say in my pirating days," Bud corrected. "And that's what happened here. Seen it a thousand times. But the ship isn't structurally damaged. It's still intact."

"Hang on," Henni said. "Pirates? Like, honest, for-real space pirates?"

"Yeah, pretty much."

"Shit. That's bad."

"Can be. Depends on who it is. Not all pirates are total assholes, you know. Look at me, for instance."

"Terrible example," she replied.

"Uzabud, do you think these might have been friends of yours?" Demelza asked.

"I can't say for sure, but highly unlikely."

"Why is that?"

"Because my ship is still here. I mean, yeah, they did a number on it, but it's still sound. My people wouldn't have left a perfectly good ship like this. Really, no self-respecting pirate would. Not unless they didn't have a place they could sell it, that is."

"What? Like, banned from the markets?" Henni asked.

"Essentially. And if that's the case, they're not just pirates. They're Outlanders."

"Is that some special kind of pirate?"

"Not exactly, though I suppose you could say that, in a weird sort of way," he replied. "Outlanders are people who pissed off the wrong folks. The wrong *powerful* folks. That means they're on pretty much everyone's shit list. Almost no one will trade with them. It's not worth the heat it brings."

"Bud, this kid, he's a visla's son. Don't you think they'll try to ransom him? The family's worth a lot of coin, you know," Laskar said. "I know that's what I'd do."

"A paragon of class and culture, you are, Laskar," Bud said. "But no, I doubt they'll ransom him, so long as he keeps his mouth shut and doesn't tell them whose kid he is. More likely than not, they'll just try to sell him at the next slave market."

Hozark and the others shared a look.

"So long as he keeps his mouth shut," Hozark said with a sigh.

"Oh, hell," Bud said. "We need to find him. And fast."

CHAPTER FIFTY

There was an old saying within the ranks of the rough-and-tumble men and women who called themselves space pirates. "Once a pirate, always a pirate."

It was a familial thing, and though they sometimes fought amongst themselves, to the death at times, a deference and respect was given to their former brethren regardless.

That saying, however, didn't quite hold true for the few who left the fold to become bounty hunters, which occasionally meant hunting down their former brothers- and sisters-in-arms.

Those former pirates were most assuredly *not* still members of the club, so to speak. In fact, if their former allies happened upon them in a dark alleyway, they might very well find themselves on the receiving end of a club of an entirely different variety.

Uzabud, however, was not only still in good standing, he had left the profession with the well wishes of not only his shipmates, but also most of the other pirates he knew from his years of pillaging and mayhem.

It wasn't just that he had always been a good shipmate and skilled pirate, it was also because he was going into a parallel career. One that could prove useful to his friends from time to time.

Uzabud had left to become a smuggler.

He fenced and trafficked all manner of items. Snuck both people and goods into places they would not have otherwise been able to go. And he did it all without backstabbing a single one of his friends in the process.

In fact, it seemed to all concerned that he had never really left, he had simply moved on to a new branch of the same field.

And now, with an Outlander pirate on the menu, it was those old friends he would need to turn to for help. The Ghalian spy network would most likely eventually find their culprits, but this was pirate life they were talking about, and that sort was always on the move and difficult to pin down. By the time you figured out where they were heading, they'd already arrived and left.

On top of that, they didn't even know which pirates they were looking for. Bud had been out of that loop for some time now, and while he still occasionally dealt with his old friends, he was by no means nearly as dialed in as he once was. And that left them just one choice.

"You're seriously gonna call in *pirates*?" Laskar asked for the third time as he plotted their jump course. "Like, actual pirates?"

"Again, yes. What is it with you, anyway? I thought you were up for any sort of adventure."

"And I am. But pirates aren't exactly known for being reliable. Or friendly, for that matter."

"Aww, we're just misunderstood."

"*We*?"

"You know the saying."

"Yeah, but you haven't *actually* been a pirate in, like, forever."

"Doesn't matter. They're still my people."

Hozark watched the exchange with mild amusement. He'd worked with Bud long enough to have seen him call in his pirate friends once or twice, and despite their ruffian ways, the men and women had actually proven to be not only quite friendly, but also very, very skilled at what they did.

Of course, if they weren't, they wouldn't last long in that sort of trade.

"We seem to be receiving a skree message," Demelza said. "But it is from a woman named Lalaynia claiming your children miss their father. Is there something we need to know, Uzabud?"

The pirate laughed as he picked up the skree. "Honey, I've missed you all so very much. It's going to be great holding you in my arms again."

"Soon, my dear," a woman's voice replied over the magical comms device. *"The kids are looking forward to playing with you."*

"And I with them. Are you close by, my love?"

"Very."

"Wonderful. I will see you soon," Bud said, then closed their skree spell.

"You've got a working skree too?" Laskar asked. "What the hell, Bud?"

"Not a normal skree, my friend. It's a hardened one used by a certain sort of people."

"A certain sort of people?"

"Well, *my* sort. Pirates and the like get bombarded with skree-disrupting magic pretty regularly, so we had to have a way to communicate even when attacked like that. It's kind of a trade secret, so don't go spreading it around. But yeah, I've still got my old one for emergencies like this."

"That is all well and good, Uzabud, but who is this Lalaynia, and did she say you have children?" Demelza asked.

"You'll meet them all real soon," he replied with a mischievous grin.

The much larger ship that had rendezvoused with Bud's

mothership made his fairly comfortable space home look somewhat cramped by comparison. His ship was still too big to settle into the pirate ship's landing bay, though, so an umbilical spell bound the two together.

"Okay! Okay! Let go!" Bud said, catching his breath when the strapping, tall woman finally dropped him from her embrace.

"What is it, Bud? You said you couldn't wait to be in my arms again," she said, the swarthy band of men and women at her side sharing in her mirth.

"You didn't have to take that all so seriously, Laynia. And damn, have you actually gotten stronger?"

The pirate captain flexed her arm, showing off her well-defined muscles. She wasn't massive. Not like a body builder or gladiator. But she had a lot of years of hard work and harder fighting under her belt, and it had chiseled her into top physical condition.

"Wow. She's big," Henni said.

Bud laughed at the small woman's awed look. "Guys, this is Captain Lalaynia Demarzik. The roughest, toughest, and finest pirate this side of the shoulder of the Oryahn Cascade."

"You're too kind," she said with a grin. "But not wrong. A pleasure to meet you all. Any friends of Bud's are welcome aboard my ship."

"Thanks for coming so fast, Laynia. We're in kind of a jam, here."

"Hey, if there's promise of some good pillage, you know we're game. And besides, someone got a promotion and couldn't wait to tell you about it."

A wiry teenager strode to the front of the crew of pirates, a pair of raider's bandoliers strapped across his slowly developing chest. What the kid lacked in age, he more than made up for in confidence, and judging by his new kit, his skills were finally catching up to his attitude.

"Saramin? Holy shit! You're a boarding party leader now?"

Bud said, pulling him in for a fierce hug. "Damn, kid, you were just a scrub last time I saw you! Well done!"

"Thanks, Bud. It's been a wild time since the last time you were on a raid with us, and a few openings needed to be filled, so here I am."

"Who'd we lose?"

"Terrik. Brayintz. And Gallfor took a few pretty big hits and is healing up on Dorall."

"More like carousing with whores and drinking away his days while the rest of us are busy working," one of the pirates said with a hearty laugh.

"Well, that's a given. But he's spending a lot of time with the healers, that's for sure."

"I'm sorry to hear about Terrik and Brayintz. Good men, those."

"Yeah. But hey, it's the life, right?"

"Right. Fight or die, as your kind-hearted captain always says."

"So what's this about a raid?" Saramin asked.

"Hold your Malooki, kid. That's a conversation for me and the captain."

She chuckled. "Thanks, Bud. I appreciate the consideration, but my question is pretty much the same. What's this raid all about, anyway?"

Bud's smile faded.

"You won't like it."

"You don't know that."

"I do," Bud replied. "Our target is a pirate ship."

Murmurs of disbelief passed throughout the crew.

"You know we don't do that, Bud," Lalaynia said, her men quickly falling silent.

"Yeah, I know. But this is different. They took a boy under our protection. And there's a lot at stake if we don't get him back."

"You're transporting a boy? What are you into, Bud?"

"Never mind all of that. Just know that it wasn't one of our friends who did this."

"How can you be so sure?"

"Because they left a perfectly good shuttlecraft behind when they took him. Stripped it, of course, but left the ship. You know what that means."

The captain's eyes went a bit harder. "Outlanders. A bunch of godsdamned Outlanders."

"Yep."

"But if that's the case, there's nowhere anywhere near they could offload that cargo. Not for over a dozen systems."

"Nope."

"And they're persona non-grata there and pretty much everywhere in between," she said, realizing what this could mean.

Bud saw the thoughts forming in her head. "If that was the case, Lalaynia, and you were shit out of luck and with that kind of cargo to unload, where would *you* go?"

The look in her eye said she knew damn well where they would go. "Shit. You really think...?"

"Yeah," Bud said. "I do."

"But this could be bad, Bud. I mean, *really* bad. And I think a bit harder to pull off than you're realizing."

"I know," the former pirate said, resting his hand on his Wampeh friend's shoulder. "But we've got something they don't."

"And what's that? A girl, a sidekick, and a pair of Wampeh?"

"Hey, I'm a woman!" Henni protested.

"And I'm not some sidekick," Laskar added.

Lalaynia just raised a single brow in amusement.

Bud gave her a little wink. "Oh, they're not just a pair of Wampeh," he said.

On cue, Hozark smiled, his fangs sliding into place.

"Oh, shit!" Lalaynia said, almost taking a step back. And for a woman as confident as her to do so really spoke to the effect the assassin had on people. "You're Wampeh *Ghalian*."

"Indeed. Demelza and myself."

"*And* he's one of the Five," Bud added, flaunting Hozark's impressive status even among his kind.

"Well, damn. That changes everything," the captain said. "But if they are what you say they are, then it's almost a given where they went."

"Yeah, I know," Bud said. "And I'd bet anything they went to Drommus."

Henni had followed the back-and-forth, but this was all a bit out of her depth. "Drommus? What's a Drommus?"

CHAPTER FIFTY-ONE

Drommus.

It was the crown jewel of dangerous, backwater worlds in this part of the galaxy. Most of the galaxy, actually. An angry, volcanic planet that always seemed just on the verge of eruption. And not just of the geologic type.

It was where the roughest of the rough went when they needed safe haven. A place where even Outlanders were not only allowed, but accepted with little grief, although no open arms. But then, it was far better than the reception the outcast pirates would otherwise receive.

The danger was very real, and non-pirates were simply not allowed. And unlike some allegedly pirate worlds, this one meant it. Even mercenaries shied away, though they were occasionally tolerated for the briefest of stopovers if they had something of true value to trade.

The Council of Twenty had learned long ago that, unlike some other strongholds they had been able to overrun with sheer force and numbers, the residents of Drommus had learned that lesson from the others' example, and they would die before surrender.

And with the deadly and massive spells they had layered within the volcanoes, they meant it. The whole world could be triggered to blow, taking not only the pirate inhabitants, but any ships foolish enough to be within their system.

Once, a Council ship had tried to make a point, taking one of the orbiting pirate craft captive for some foolish and petty offense. A volcano had been triggered, and its geyser of magic-laced magma blasted into the low orbit, the still-hot shards of volcanic glass tearing through the Council ship and the captured vessel alike.

It was an excessive show of force, no doubt, but the point had been made.

Do not. Fuck. With Drommus.

The message was received loud and clear, and from that point forward, no one even dreamed of making waves there. The price was simply too high, and it just wasn't worth it.

But Captain Lalaynia Demarzik not only had safe passage anytime she wanted it, she had something bordering on carte blanche while on the hostile world.

With *her* altercations, the overseers who were generally keeping things from erupting into full-fledged riots tended to look the other way. If Lalaynia was putting boot to ass, there was always a very damn good reason for it.

Fortunately, she was rarely involved in such things. People generally knew better than to rile up the thoroughly dangerous woman. But nevertheless, every once in a long while, some liquored-up idiot would think to try their mettle against the notorious woman.

And every time, they would find themselves on the losing end.

Uzabud had once been an integral part of her crew, and he was still allowed access to Drommus as both a legacy-type courtesy, as well as because of his current smuggler status. He was not, however, given the same free rein that the captain was, and any trouble he got himself into was on his own head.

This time would be different, though. He was flying with his ship being considered a temporary part of Lalaynia's crew, more or less. A partner, if you were to be more specific about it. And that gave him a layer of protection he would not otherwise possess.

Likewise for Hozark and the others, though with Henni's unpredictable nature, he didn't really know what might happen if she pickpocketed the wrong person.

Hozark and Demelza would arrive with the pirate's main ship, while Bud and the others circled to outer areas to touch down and survey for their quarry. One group on the ground, the other leapfrogging by air, hopefully finding the Outlander craft in the process.

Corann had outfitted them with a few new skrees, and with that added tool in their kit, the impromptu rescue party would be able to communicate just about anywhere on the planet. The skrees she had on hand, however, were not particularly powerful, and any messages beyond that range were simply not an option.

But for this mission, they would certainly suffice.

The large pirate ship settled down in the large docking area best suited to handle not only craft of that size, but also that possessed an area for VIPs, of which Lalaynia most certainly was. That didn't afford her much more than a quicker access to the township from her ship, but at least it was something.

And in this instance, when she might need to get to her ship in a hurry, it could make the difference between success and failure. Possibly even life or death, depending how bad things went. And knowing how trouble tended to follow Uzabud, she was quite confident this would lean toward bad, if not outright catastrophic.

But it was worth the chance. There was booty to be had, and a hefty payment from the Ghalian, no less. And doing something that amounted to a favor for the order of assassins was always a good idea. There was no telling when that check mark in the favor column might come in handy, especially in her line of work.

Bud started off by landing a little bit farther away, with all the rest of the rabble and their ships. As expected, it would delay his meeting up with the others, and it was for that reason, it had been decided that he, Henni, and Laskar would start their search from afar, working their way through the outer landing sites and gradually making their way in closer to the others. They didn't know whom they were looking for, after all, and for all they knew, their target could be anyone.

Outlander ships were not overtly flagged as such, though some of them wore their status as almost an inverse badge of honor. But for the most part, you could not quickly discern one at a glance. This would take legwork. Legwork and a degree of subtlety.

"Are you ready, my friends?" Captain Demarzik asked. "Once we touch down, it's a straight shot into the township proper. I'll have my people fan out immediately and start making small talk with the locals. We should have an idea who's landed in the last few days pretty quickly."

"And what about the boy?" Demelza asked.

"We will have to be far more subtle about that part. If word gets out someone's looking for this particular kid, they'll get spooked and either run, which we can handle, or go to ground, which will make tracking them become several fold more difficult."

"So, we will be subtle," Hozark said as they stepped off Lalaynia's ship and onto the hard, black rock of Drommus's surface. "Let us get to it. Young Jinnik is in far more danger than he likely realizes, and time is of the essence."

CHAPTER FIFTY-TWO

Lalaynia and her team were good to their word, and as soon as her ship had settled into its landing spot, they all quickly stepped clear and fanned out into the surrounding areas, quickly making friendly small talk and trying to suss out which of the many ships docked there might be the one containing their prize.

Hozark and Demelza did what they did best on any world. They blended in without anyone noticing a thing. To all who did happen to take notice, they were just a pair of Wampeh pirates on Drommus for a bit of shore leave.

Even his vespus blade, stuck to his back, went unnoticed. Unless he unsheathed it, it would just seem like another sword. So they walked the pathways between the ships. And while they were at it, they happened to drop that their boss was in the market for a few new slaves.

Most who had some for sale were quickly disqualified, either for having been on the planet too long to be their target, or for simply not having the *right* slaves in their possession.

One of the slave pens contained a few Ootaki, and at the

sight of them, Hozark found himself reflecting on the poor captives he had come across in the weapons smelting factory hidden on Garvalis. The same world on which he had briefly found himself trapped by a rather clever pitfall.

Someone had been using them to power weapons, but that was a commonplace use for their magical locks. But on Actaris, where poor Aargun had been held and mutilated, there was something more. Dark work at play, and it had been tied into the goings-on at the Garvalis facility.

What was done at Actaris was something different, though. They had experimented on far more than just Ootaki in that location. Drooks had been mutilated as well in the attempt to take their very specific flavor of magic and force it to bend to their torturers' will.

It seemed doubtful it had been even a moderate success, since their power was so tied to driving ships it had no other use that anyone had ever discovered. But the dead bodies of not just the Ootaki, but also the Drooks showed those making the attempts were more than willing to sacrifice the valuable magic users if it might further their goals.

And then there were the other corpses. A pair of Zomoki, the mighty creatures slain in an attempt to tap into their innate gifts, no doubt. But worst of all, at least for the Ghalian who had discovered the scene, was the young Wampeh they had found, the body discarded with the others like so much rubbish.

People were being killed. Tortured. Experimented on. And as Hozark re-shifted his focus, he was determined that no such thing would happen to young Happizano. Not if he could help it.

"Excuse me," he said to a heavily muscled man standing before a pen containing control-collared Ootaki. "I was wondering, do you have any unshorn Ootaki in your stocks?"

"You think I'd be selling them *here* if I did?" the man replied.

"I guess not. But it was worth asking."

"You might want to check with Ragnak," the man suggested. "His stocks are newer. He might have something more to your liking."

Hozark threw him a coin. "Thanks for the tip, friend."

"My pleasure," the man replied. "Hope you find something suitable."

"Me too."

Hozark and Demelza continued on their way, looking for this Ragnak person. As they asked around to determine where exactly he was parked, it was looking like he might actually be the man they were after. He was a mysterious sort. Not a confirmed Outlander, but definitely one of the pirates on thin ice in these parts. And for Drommus, that was saying something.

It also seemed that his ship had arrived very recently. With that additional bit of information, Hozark hoped that this might actually be the man they were seeking.

"This Ragnak's ship?" he asked when they reached the craft they knew full well was his.

The guard stationed outside the fairly large craft looked the two Wampeh up and down. He was not impressed.

"Who wants to know?"

"We're looking for a bit of trade, potentially," Hozark replied. "If this is the right ship, we'd like an audience with Ragnak."

"The captain don't talk to--"

Hozark casually tossed the pouch of coin up and down in his palm. From the sound of it, there was a fair amount inside.

"I mean, let me take you to see him," the man corrected.

"I said I wasn't to be disturbed!" the bearded man with deep green hair and an even deeper orange complexion said.

Captain Ragnak was a jigsaw puzzle of scars, the souvenirs of his many years living a life of action. He could have had them healed at any time, but he felt they were badges of courage. Plus, they really added to his pirate image.

"Sorry, Captain. These two were lookin' to talk about some trade with ya."

He shifted his annoyed gaze to Hozark and Demelza. "Trade? What sort of trade are you looking for, then?"

Hozark resumed absentmindedly tossing the pouch in his hand. "We've got an employer who is looking for some new house slaves. We heard you just made port not long ago and still had a fresh batch."

"That I do," he replied. "Ezzil, go bring the merchandise."

"Aye, Captain," the man said, hurrying off to fetch the available slaves.

"Have a seat," Ragnak said.

"Don't mind if I do. I have to tell you, it's been a bit of a bust so far. When we landed here with Captain Demarzik, I was told Drommus was the best place for ten systems to find what we needed."

"You're with Demarzik?"

"Yeah."

"Ah, that explains it."

"Explains what?"

"How you two found your way to this part of the township. All the best traders are here. Good captain, that one."

"We think so," Demelza noted.

"But Drommus?"

"Yeah, not our first choice, really. But it's just such a pain, always steering clear of the damn Council and their goons."

"Fuck the Council," Ragnak spat.

"I'll second that. Fuck the council!" Hozark agreed.

"Fuck 'em all to hell! Arr!"

Hozark paused and took a chance on the man's mirth. "Did you actually just say 'arr'?" he asked.

Ragnak laughed, breaking his rough-and-tough façade for a moment. "Ironically," he replied. "It's kind of an inside joke around here. Ah, excellent. Here they come."

A moment later a dozen slaves of all size, gender, race, and color were led in and walked past the newcomers in a procession. None of them were the boy they sought.

"An impressive lot," Hozark said, pulling a bottle of very, *very* expensive Sluvak from his deep pocket and nodding to their host. "Glasses?"

Ragnak's eyes widened slightly at the sight. It was a very rare, and very good alcohol, the likes of which he hadn't tasted in ages. He snatched up three glasses from the small table beside him, and Hozark poured them each a small taste, a bit more for their host, of course.

"A very nice group of slaves," he said. "But our employer is looking for something a bit, uh, *younger,* if you know what I mean.

Ragnak paused, mid-sip. "I do know what you mean," he said with a conspiratorial look. "But this is all I've got at the moment."

"Ah, that's a shame."

There was something behind the pirate's eyes. The way he shifted a little and paused. He knew something, it was clear as day to the master assassin.

"Well, I appreciate your help anyway," he said, then pushed the nearly full bottle of Sluvak toward the pirate. "In any case, a gesture of thanks for your hospitality, between friends. And now, we really should get back to Captain Demarzik. She'll be disappointed to hear we struck out."

Hozark and Demelza rose to leave.

"You know. Now that I think of it, Captain Darvin might have something that suits your needs. He just came in today, and I heard a little talk of his cargo. Nothing confirmed, though. But maybe worth your time to look."

Hozark gave him an appreciative nod. "Thanks for the tip, Captain. We'll check it out. And it was really nice making your acquaintance."

"Likewise," the pirate said. "And remember, 'Arr!'"

"Arr!" Hozark replied with a laugh, then headed out to find this Captain Darvin and see if perhaps he was in possession of their young ward.

CHAPTER FIFTY-THREE

Captain Darvin's ship wasn't exactly what anyone would call hard to track down. In fact, the massive, battle-scarred craft stood out even among the other rather beat-up pirate ships that regularly frequented the docks of Drommus.

As an Outlander, one would expect his craft to have had to forego some of the cosmetic niceties that so many opted for after a few good scores. But this was excessive even for one of that outcast sect.

But, like Ragnak's latticework of scars, the patched-up damage to the pirate ship lent an additional menace to its already imposing air.

The location of the ship, however, was just as rough an area as the men who disembarked it. Volcanic instability had lava flows running all around. They were kept back by a steady stream of magic, but, every so often, a drunken pirate met a very fast, and very hot end when they had a misstep.

Only the lowest of the low were made to set down there, but when they'd come to land, the Outlanders were pegged for who they were and were directed to this most treacherous of landing zones.

But they had expected no less. Outlanders weren't popular anywhere, not even on Drommus.

"You go left. I'll go right," Hozark said, splitting off from Demelza without a glance, totally nonchalant in his redirect around the immediate landing area.

If this was indeed their man, things could spill over and turn the whole area into a free-for-all rumble. It was a powder keg waiting to ignite, and if things might go down that path, it was imperative they had backup standing by, ready to step in.

But first, a bit of reconnaissance was in order.

Demelza made initial contact with a rather gregarious band of raiders who were taking a bit of recreation, roasting some utterly unidentifiable animal over an open flame.

Their ship was a small affair, and they seemed to be a newer bunch to the pirate game. As such, they were a bit less wary of a random woman walking up to them and starting a conversation. Older, wiser men would have wondered at her motives.

"Hey, fellas," she said, the topmost buttons of her tunic opened long before she was anywhere near.

"Uh, hello," the apparent leader of the little band replied.

"What's that you've got cooking? It smells fantastic."

It was a lie. To call the cast-off meat they were destroying even further with the magical flame edible would be a stretch, even for a Bundabist. And they had the reputation for eating pretty much anything.

"Just whipping up a little something for the fellas," the man in charge of their feast replied as he brushed a glaze on the carcass that actually managed to make it smell even worse.

"Wow, you're a talented cook," she said. "They only serve us morvin biscuits and Boramus jerky on our ship."

"Oh yeah?"

"It's not very pleasant."

"I can imagine."

"But our captain said once we finish up our pickup run, we'll get some shore leave on the next world we stop at. Nice as Drommus is, I'm hoping we won't be here too long. Just gotta find that slave kid we're supposed to pick up, and then we're off to make the drop. And *then*, shore leave."

"Slave kid? Well, shit. You're in luck. I know for a fact Darvin's got a kid on his ship. Sick bastard's been trying to sell him off to anyone who'd take him. But he hasn't had much interest yet. The kid may be young, but most of the fellas prefer girls to boys. At least usually."

"That sounds like it might be our kid. You know what he looks like? Not some amphibian or something like that, is he?"

"Nope, just a violet-skinned kid. Pretty normal-looking, really."

"That might be the right one," Demelza said. "Thanks!"

"Hey, aren't you gonna stay and join us for a bite?"

"I'll try to come back as soon as I can. I want to thank you *personally* for all of your help. But first I've gotta tell our captain. Drommus is kind of a maze, and he's probably searching high and low for this kid."

"Hurry back," the man called after her.

"You know I will," she called back with a huge grin.

The grin fell from her face when she was out of sight. "Captain Demarzik, it looks like we've found our boy. He's aboard the vessel belonging to a pirate name Darvin," Demelza transmitted over the skree Corann had given her. "He's docked in the third landing zone out from the marketplace. Big, beat-up looking ship."

"You found him? So soon?" the captain replied. "Great news. I'm having my men head that way now."

"We will await your arrival," Demelza sent, then tucked away her skree and headed along to her and Hozark's rendezvous point.

While she had been casually carousing with the little band of pirates, Hozark had gone on a much different sort of a fact-finding mission. First, the Wampeh had made a quick loop of the area around Darvin's ship. There were several rowdy groups of pirates congregated at a few of the local establishments, and he wanted to be sure to note which might be part of that ship's crew.

If fighting broke out, as he was growing increasingly sure it would, they stood a far better chance of success knowing where all of Darvin's men might be, both on and off the ship.

Hozark had also brought his shimmer cloak with, and once he had surveyed the patrons of the bars, taverns, and houses of ill repute, he slipped into an alleyway and donned his shimmer.

Gaining access to the cargo hold of the ship in question was child's play, but the main body of the craft was still locked up tight, and the number of pirates right at the door from both the cargo hold and the exterior would make a stealth entry difficult.

They needed a diversion.

Hozark tucked behind a stinking pile of refuse and shed his shimmer cloak, then made his way back out along the pathway to meet up with his Wampeh associate.

"Lalaynia and her people are on the way," Demelza quietly told him when he arrived. "There's a boy on board this ship, and he matches Happizano's description."

Hozark nodded. "The ship is buttoned up tight. Guards at the entrances. No way to pass unnoted. It seems their persona-non-grata status as Outlanders has made them more than a little paranoid. And with good reason, from what I overheard in the pubs."

"Oh?"

"Darvin has quite a few enemies on Drommus. And we are going to use that to our advantage."

To any observing the casual stream of rough-and-tough pirates making their way through the streets, it would seem just like any other day with men and women of action going about their affairs.

But what they didn't notice was that a great many of those pirates were from Lalaynia's crew. And as they passed one another, the plan was relayed with crisp efficiency.

"Tell the others. There's gonna be a fight. Draw in as many of Darvin's men as you can."

And so the message was relayed, passed orally and invisibly. In mere minutes, dozens were ready to act. All they were waiting for was the go sign.

"This is going to be fun," Lalaynia said as she discussed their next moves with the two Wampeh. "Bud's wrapping up at another landing site, but he said he'll try to get here as fast as he can."

"We will have to begin without him. Enough of the crew are off of the ship that this may be our best opportunity to draw out the rest," Hozark said.

"He'll be pissed if he misses all the action."

"I am aware. But the boy takes priority, I am afraid."

Lalaynia nodded her agreement. "So, you two ready?"

"That we are."

"Well, okay then. I'll be seeing you on the other side," she said. "Of the fight, that is. I don't believe in life after death, and even if I did, I have no plans of crossing that bridge just yet."

She shared a single nod with the assassins, then headed off to raise a ruckus the likes of which Drommus hadn't seen in decades. And if she was successful, it would be a fight that would also make her quite a lot of coin.

"Cap'n," her right hand said as she strolled over to her crew.

She looked over the men and women she'd fought with for so long and smiled. This was going to be fun.

"All right, my dearies," she said. "Here we go."

CHAPTER FIFTY-FOUR

"Hey, watch where you're going!"

"Watch out yourself, idiot."

Moments later, fists were flying, along with more than a few spells for good measure.

That was all it took to set things in motion.

Normally, bystanders would have just watched the two men have at it and that would be that. Maybe they'd place wagers on the outcome, but soon enough the local enforcers would step in and quiet things down.

But Lalaynia had greased the right palms with Ghalian coin for this occasion, and a blind eye was turned. At least for a little while.

What began as a simple squabble quickly turned into more of a brawl. And once each man's crewmates saw what was happening and joined it, that brawl turned into a rumble.

And that's about as far as it would have typically gone. But Demelza had riled up the nearby pirates, telling them Darvin's gang was plotting to steal their food.

It was a ridiculous story, but they had fallen for it. And Lalaynia's men, clued in to the story, reinforced the lie. More and more pirates from more crews than hers were joining into the fight, and despite his ship being parked right there, Darvin's men were beginning to lose.

On cue, the doors opened, and more of the Outlander's men flooded out to join in what had quickly escalated into a riot.

The fighting was spreading, and the multiple outcroppings overhanging the flowing lava were becoming jammed with increasingly angry men. This was getting a bit out of hand compared to the original plan. But these were pirates. What was to be expected, really?

"Leave some for me!" Bud called out as he rushed into the fight."

"How'd you get here so fast?" Laylania asked.

"Laskar dropped me and Henni off. He's overhead, looking for a safe place to land."

"Here? Fat chance," she said with a laugh as she cast a stun spell, dropping one of Darvin's men. Paralyzed as he was, he fell over. Right into the lava. "Oops."

"Damn, Laynia."

"It wasn't intentional," she said with a little grin.

The riot had spread into most of the area now, the good pirates heavily engaging the bad ones.

It was a bit odd to consider one faction of pirates *good*, but as they were working on behalf of a Ghalian rescue mission, it seemed that their alignment was on the good side, if only for a bit.

"Hey, where's the girl? You said she was with you."

"She was. But one of your guys gave her a pair of daggers and she took off running. I've been trying to find her."

"Look no further," Lalaynia said with an amazed smile, pointing across the nearby lava flow.

Henni was there, a violet-haired blur of aggression, leaping into the air, her hands flying in a windmill of violence as she literally climbed up a man trying to fight her, stabbing the hell out of him all the way up as if her daggers were a pointy ladder.

The poor man didn't stand a chance. His resistance was futile, and a moment later, he toppled to the ground, a bloody mess.

Henni rolled clear and immediately raced off to have at another one of the Outlander pirates, a thrilled gleam in her eye.

"Interesting friend you have there, Bud," the pirate captain said. "Quite a surprising little thing, I have to admit."

"That's an understatement," Bud said as he watched the diminutive young woman in action, realizing he really didn't know her at all. At least, not like he thought.

For their part, the two deadliest combatants on the battlefield by far had not slain or maimed a single person. In fact, the shimmer-cloaked assassins were doing all they could to avoid so much as bumping into any of the fighting men and women swimming in the sea of chaos.

With great care, they maneuvered to the entrance of Captain Darvin's ship and waited. It didn't take long for the door to open and more men to spill out to join the fight. It was the most pirate thing in the world to do, and they did not disappoint.

Hozark and Demelza, however, were ready, and slipped silently inside the ship. One of the rushing men did brush against Hozark in his hurry, but he was so focused on the danger *outside* that he totally missed the danger *inside*.

The cloaked assassins were making good time through the large ship, clearing it room by room until they might finally find the boy they sought. The first several sections of the ship were fairly easy to move through.

The men who had been clustered there had exited en masse, leaving them room to maneuver. But then things took a turn for the unexpected.

Hozark quickly shed his shimmer cloak. "Do you hear that?"

"Oh no," Demelza said, taking off her shimmer as well.

The din of a massive fight was coming from up ahead. From *inside* the ship.

"They must have breached the cargo bay entrance," Hozark said. "We will have to move quickly."

The two raced along the corridor, trying to make as much headway as they could before they encountered the rioting pirates.

They had removed their shimmers, not because they no longer wished to operate without being seen, but because in close-quarter combat, and against this many people, the likelihood of accidental stabbing or worse was a very real threat.

But if they were visible, their allies would avoid them, and their enemies would follow one of the more predictable attack patterns. And those were easily defeated and countered.

"Hozark!" a young voice cried out.

The boy was no more than twenty meters away, being dragged deeper into the pirate ship by none other than Captain Darvin himself. The assassin could have covered the distance in a flash, if not for the dozens of fighting men and women between them.

He didn't call out to the boy. There was no time, and no need. All Hozark and Demelza did was charge ahead as quickly as they could.

A jolt threw them against the wall, as it did all of the combatants.

"We are aloft," Hozark noted with annoyance.

Demelza grabbed her skree. "We are aboard Darvin's ship," she transmitted before he was out of range of their friends. "The boy is here. We will need a follow craft immediately."

This was quickly becoming a clusterfuck, and it was only getting worse. If Darvin took the ship out of the atmosphere, he had the advantage of numbers.

Magic was simply too dangerous to use in the confined

spaces of a ship in space. One wrong move and you risked killing not only your enemy, but yourself and your own crew as well.

"Coming for ya," Bud transmitted back. "Just hang in there. Laskar, we need an emergency evac. Pick me up *now*!"

"On my way," the copilot said.

It was an open skree, and Hozark and Demelza heard what was going on, as did Lalaynia and her people. Bud was scrambling to track them if he could. Lalaynia's ship was too far to reach and too big to set down and retrieve her in that part of the township.

It looked like it was all up to Bud. Hozark hoped the former pirate was up for it.

When Captain Darvin took the fight to the air, several squabbling factions on the surface saw that as a green light to spread their fighting into the skies as well. A violent snowball effect that was an unintended side effect of the Outlander captain's surprising maneuver.

In no time, multiple ships were aloft, and they were bombarding one another with massive magical fusillades.

Hozark and Demelza powered their way through the fighting men and women on the ship, flinging them aside like they were toddlers, not armed pirates. It was moments like this that the Ghalian prowess was on full display for all to see, and it would only serve to bolster their reputation by those witnesses who survived.

Down on the surface, Henni was still fighting with vigor.

"Henni, come on!" Bud called out.

She didn't seem to hear him.

"Henni! Let's go!"

She looked up from the latest man she had slain. A little splash of blood colored her cheek, but for some reason, Bud thought that it was almost cute. While terrifying at the same time, of course.

"Go on. I'll catch up later," she called back across the lava separating them.

"I can't just leave you here."

"You have to. Now get going. I've got stuff to do."

With that, she turned and raced off to find another opponent to take her aggression out on.

Laskar swung in as low as he could, but Bud still had to scramble to the top of a small structure to reach the open hatch. With a powerful leap, he made his way into the ship and raced to the command center.

"You got 'em still?" he asked.

"Tracking them visually," Laskar replied. "But they're moving fast. I'm afraid once they hit space, they'll jump."

"That's not good."

"I know."

"We've gotta stop them."

"I said I know, Bud. Now, hang on."

The ship raced up while massive bloodshed occurred throughout the streets of Drommus. The ground fight was brutal and fierce, but, gradually, it was beginning to come under control as the township enforcers rolled into the fray before it got even uglier.

But the real ugliness was going to take place in space above.

CHAPTER FIFTY-FIVE

Captain Darvin's battle-scarred pirate ship was actually a rather fast and maneuverable vessel, it turned out, much to the surprise of the pirates observing its quick departure from the ground.

Of course, his own crew were among those watching the ship zoom off into space, and though they kept right on fighting, as one would expect of Outlanders, from that moment on, they battled with a question in the back of their minds. Would their captain come back for them, or were they stuck on Drommus?

Some might have been able to find work aboard other ships, but typically an Outlander crew was an entirely Outlander crew, and they did not mix well with others.

But returning for his men was not something Captain Darvin was worried about at the moment. All he cared about was getting his ship and his cargo to safety, off of Drommus and away from whatever madness was going on down below.

His plan was simple. Hit space and jump away to some quiet spot where he could assess both the number of men left behind on the surface, and the options he had before him. But as he cleared the atmosphere, those plans very quickly became moot.

The ship banked hard, and unlike some better-equipped vessels, its gravity spells didn't completely counter the effect. As a result, the combatants in the corridors were thrown against the bulkhead. Hozark just happened to wind up beside a window.

What he saw shocked him.

"Council ships!" he said, just as the others with a view were noting the same thing.

"What? Here?" Demelza asked, leaning toward the window. "What would the Council be doing at Drommus? It's madness."

"Madness, but apparently our new reality," Hozark replied as he studied the formation of the ships blocking their way. It was one he'd seen before, though not from this unfortunate perspective.

"They're casting a jump-blocking web," he said. "We're stuck here."

The men and women who had been fighting to the death moments before had all come to an unofficial pause as the reality of the situation set in.

"We can't jump?" one man said.

"We're trapped!" a short, sword-wielding woman replied. "The Council of Twenty is attacking Drommus!"

They all realized what that would mean. If the Council actually did attempt to take out the planet's defenses, it would all go up in a massive blast, themselves included. But Hozark didn't think that was what was happening. The blocking spells were the first hint.

"If they wanted to attack, they wouldn't have blocked escape. Less ships to fight is an easier battle," he announced to the surprisingly quiet pirate forces.

"Hang on," a young pirate said, peering out the window. "Not all of those are Council ships. I see some Tslavar mercenaries as well."

This drew a loud chorus of angry slurs against the green-skinned muscle for hire. Of course the pirates had run up against them. It was only expected that raiding, pillaging, thieving types would occasionally clash in the pursuit of a prize.

But this was different. This time, the green bastards had been brought on as hired help to do the Council's dirty work.

"Mercenaries means an invasion," a man said.

"No, it means they're going to try to take out any ship that tries to flee. Blast them out of the sky."

"I am afraid you are both incorrect," Hozark said.

"Oh yeah? What do you know about it?" the man asked, with just a hint of menace to his voice.

Someone was behind all of this, and seeing Wampeh was pretty unusual. Maybe these strangers had something to do with this.

"I know they are not attacking Drommus," Hozark said. "And I know they are not destroying these ships. At least, not yet."

"How can you be so sure?"

"Because, if you would just look out the windows you would see that while you've been arguing amongst yourselves, they have launched boarding craft."

A look of shock was universal on all the pirates' faces as they verified what the Wampeh was saying.

"And if you look carefully," he added, "you will see they are coming right for us."

Suddenly, the fight amongst themselves was backburnered, if not outright extinguished.

"What do we do?"

It was not remotely what Hozark had come here to do, but *all* of their fates were now intertwined, and Happizano's rescue would have to wait. There was no rescuing anyone if they were all captured or dead, after all.

"We form into teams and repel the boarders," Hozark shouted out in his best pirate roar. "This is what we do. Close quarters, no prisoners, and *no magic*. That puts the Council at a disadvantage. They can't cast against us. Not in here. So fight like your lives depended on it. Because they bloody well do!"

The men and women roared in unison and quickly put aside their previous fight to join forces as they geared up for a new one. One against their common enemy.

"Nice speech," Demelza said. "You know, you might have a calling as a pirate, if you ever decide to retire from the order."

Hozark chuckled. "But, of course, no one ever retires from the order."

The boarding ships pursued the fleeing pirate craft as it did its best to prevent them from latching onto its hull. Once that happened, they would breach and be inside in seconds. The longer they could hold them off, the better positioned and prepared the pirate crew could make themselves.

"Look at the markings on the Tslavar ships," Demelza said when she got a good look at them out of the nearby window. "Their markings are obliterated. These Tslavars are not flying under any known colors."

"A secret force, then," Hozark mused. "Suddenly, I find myself wondering if this is not all related to young Happizano after all."

"But would the Council come all the way to Drommus just for a child? It seems so unlike them."

"It is. But the Council activities we have seen of late have been anything but normal."

"Agreed. But another question then springs to mind."

"I believe I know where you are going with this," Hozark said. "If they *are* here for Happizano, how could they have known where he was? Even if he had slipped up and told Darvin who he was, that man wouldn't have a clue as to who his father was, or what his value is to the Council."

"So we are back to the question. How could they have known where he was?" Demelza wondered. "Yes, he stands out somewhat, and perhaps if someone knew he was missing––"

"We will need to figure this out later, Demelza," Hozark said as the roar of a boarding party reached their ears. "We have company." He turned to the pirate group at his side. "They're coming! Swords and blades at the ready. Remember, this is what we do!"

The pirates refrained from their cheers. The time for pep talks was over. It was now time for bloodshed.

A few stun spells shot harmlessly down the corridor but hit no one and fizzled out against the far bulkhead. As soon as their forces were in close proximity, no magic whatsoever could be used.

"Here they come," Hozark said. "Ready, everyone!"

The Tslavar boarding party was prepared for this battle. They all wore practical garments, reinforced against blades instead of magic. And they carried shorter than usual weapons, all the better to fight in these close quarters.

Unusually, though, was the Council goon advancing with them. He wasn't one of the Twenty, but he was definitely a power user. The one who had tested the defenses with those stun spells, no doubt.

They were prepared for the fight in space, or on the ground, it seemed. Not a good sign at all.

Throughout the ship, more and more boarders breached and began their attack. The fighting quickly grew to a fever-pitch as blood flowed freely within Captain Darvin's compromised vessel.

Outside of the ship, the residents of Drommus had come to a similar conclusion as the pirates aboard the ship. Namely, that the Council was up to something, and they all had to fight together to stop them.

Especially as none of them particularly wanted to die in a fiery ball of death if the fail-safe on Drommus triggered, denying the Council of that world, but at the cost of all their lives.

The space battle was fierce, with pirate craft engaging

Tslavar and Council ships alike. And unlike the fighting within Darvin's craft, magic was very much in use outside of the ship.

It was a swarm of confusion and death out there, and in the black of space, where there is no up or down, the conflict seemed even more chaotic. No one was fighting on the same plane. What was left for one ship was down for another, and up for yet another.

It was mayhem. Unorchestrated chaos. And it was only getting worse.

CHAPTER FIFTY-SIX

Hozark and Demelza were fighting in an environment they were amply skilled for, but tended to avoid at all costs.

Wampeh Ghalian were loners. Silent, solitary killers. Melees were not their engagement of choice. There were simply too many variables. Too many things that could go horribly wrong, and not because of any intentional act, but because of the chaos of dozens, hundreds, or more people fighting in close proximity.

It was the type of situation where even the most skilled fighter could fall from an errant blade.

In an open environment, at least they could draw upon their myriad killing spells to create space around themselves and shift the tide of battle. But within the confines of a ship, all of that magic had to be withheld.

Hozark and Demelza both were feeling the frustration of being unable to unleash the force to end this engagement, despite their training. No one observing them work their way through the enemy would have known that both were actively restraining themselves from using that power.

But they had training aplenty, in more techniques of death

and mayhem than those attacking them knew combined, and it was those other forms of combat they were using today.

Hozark had snatched up a sword from a fallen man and was now swinging it with skill as he and Demelza plowed through the boarders. His vespus blade was still safely on his back, where he wished to keep it sheathed until it was absolutely needed.

A glowing blue blade in a Ghalian's hand would be something of note, and he wished to go unnoted. At least, as long as he could.

Demelza was working her way through the Tslavar mercenaries at his side, the two Ghalian instinctively protecting each other's flanks as they battled.

She was putting on an impressive demonstration of sword and dagger play with the fine set that Master Orkut had lent to her for her quest to help his friend. If Visla Jinnik was in need of assistance, despite her significant skills, she would need all of the advantages she could get, and the master swordsmith had just the thing.

"The boy," Hozark said to her as he ran his sword deep into the chest of a particularly stocky Tslavar invader. "This battle will go on for some time. We must retrieve him."

Demelza spun, her blades ringing off the cudgel that had just come flying toward her head. With the sword locking up the attacker's weapon, she was free to slip the dagger in her other hand in between both his armor plating and his ribs.

The Tslavar let out a pained groan, then fell as she expertly twisted the blade, sending its point on its deadly way, piercing his heart. She pulled it free immediately, spinning back to block another attacker. As she did, Hozark liberated the man's neck of his head.

"A persistent lot," she noted.

"Indeed," he replied, watching the continuous flow of mercenaries pushing against the pirate defenders. "And well-armed. But these men and women are handling themselves admirably, and we have work to do. Happizano was taken this way."

Hozark did not need to say anything more. Demelza was immediately behind him as he moved, expertly slicing where others slashed, parrying and dodging where others swung wildly.

The pair did all they could to avoid further engagement, opting for a speedy course rather than the bloody one. Yes, they could drop a sizable amount of Tslavars on the way if they wanted, but the delay could prove far, far too costly.

The path of least resistance saw them rushing through row after row of pirates, the swarthy men ready for action, forming a rear guard to protect their captain and the control center of the ship.

They may have seemed to be standing around with nothing to do, but all of them had their weapons ready and their eyes and ears alert. It was a boarding attack, but they were not the ones carrying it out, and they knew full well that at any moment a section of the hull could part, allowing the enemy to drop down into the midst.

"We need a dozen reinforcements near the galley area," Hozark said as he and Demelza pushed through the ranks. "Don't just stand there. Twelve of you, get moving."

"We're supposed to stay here. Captain's orders."

"Are you fucking kidding me?" Hozark said, slipping into full pirate brogue. Minus the 'arr,' of course. "If this ship falls because you lot ignored the bastards ransacking the deck and killing your friends, all in favor of standing in an empty corridor *in case* something might happen, I'm sure Captain Darvin'll be *very* interested to hear of your decision."

A look of doubt flashed in the men's eyes. Fear of displeasing the captain was deeply ingrained, and they had just been expertly placed between a rock and a hard place. All it required was a little push to help them to the logical decision.

"Oh, fer fuck's sake. Fine. Look. *I'll* go tell him personally, okay? Just hurry yer asses up and get out there. This is on me. If he wants to take it out on anyone, it'll not be you," Hozark said, walking through the last line of defenses before the command center, heading right for the door.

It was all bluff and bluster, but it was working, though it shouldn't have. He wasn't a member of Captain Darvin's crew. He was just one of the other pirates who was suddenly fighting their common enemy. And yet, with a firm, confident, authoritative tone, Hozark knew he could sway just about anyone.

Act as if it's a given that others will do as you say, and quite often they will.

"You heard him. They need our help," one of the men who had been on the fence said, his decision finally made for him.

There were leaders, and there were followers. And once the followers started falling in line, critical mass was quickly achieved.

"Let's go, lads!" another said, rushing off without a further thought, his short sword held at the ready.

More than twelve wound up racing to join the fray, but that actually didn't much matter. Hozark had simply picked a number that would be enough to make an impact, but not so high that it would appear as if he was trying to thin their ranks.

"Come on, you," he said to Demelza as they reached the door to command. "We've gotta go tell the captain where I sent the others and what's going on in 'is ship."

"Right behind you," she said in her best pirate growl.

This was the moment of truth. When they would see if their bluff worked all the way or if they would have to slay the pirates who would ultimately be fighting the Council invaders.

It was something they desperately wanted to avoid. All they

wanted was to retrieve the boy. And the more pirates they could leave standing to continue fighting the Tslavars at their backs, the better.

The guards had seen what had just gone down, and watched their comrades hurry off at the command of this stranger. But the laws of the herd were strong, and they too seemed to fall in line with the group mentality.

Hozark smiled to himself when the men stepped aside and let him pass. Whatever they had to face inside the command center, it would be done in private.

And when he and Demelza were done, they would most definitely be leaving with the visla's son back in their possession.

Without a moment's hesitation, he walked into the chamber with Demelza at his back. She turned immediately, shutting the door behind them and quietly casting muting spells to silence any shouts of warning or alarm that might come from within.

They were going to get Happizano back, and while they would prefer to leave the pirates standing to fight the Council threat, they would do whatever was required. And that might be bloody.

CHAPTER FIFTY-SEVEN

Hozark and Demelza, in the middle of a pirate-versus-Council battle, and clad as pirates as they were, entered the command center without much of a fuss being raised.

In fact, given the chaos of the current battle swirling both outside and inside the ship, their presence was not all that odd at all.

"What the hell's going on out there?" the captain yelled out. "I've been trying to get a godsdamned sitrep for the last five minutes!"

The half dozen of the captain's personal guards tried to look calm as the man railed on, but they knew how he could be when riled up. Fortunately, his line of questioning wasn't directed at them.

Hozark realized he was talking to the newcomers.

"It's a fucking mess, is what's going on," the Wampeh replied with a piratey growl. "Most recent was the group that boarded through the galley. It's been a bloody fight, but it looks like we're holding our own."

The captain smiled, but without any real joy behind it. He'd take whatever good news he could get, but this conflict was far, far from over.

Seated behind Captain Darvin was a young, violet-skinned boy, staring silently at the ground. He looked terrified, and though no magic was being used to hold him there, he seemed glued in place.

"What's with the kid?" Hozark asked. "Seems kinda quiet for being in the middle of all of this."

Darvin grabbed Hap by the scruff of his shirt and hauled him roughly to his feet.

"The little bastard tried to use a stun spell on me. Can you fucking believe that? On my own fucking ship?"

"The balls on that one," Hozark agreed.

"Ha. They haven't even dropped yet. And lucky for me, probably."

"Why's that?"

"Because," the captain said, pulling back Hap's shirt to reveal the slender, golden control collar around his neck, "this little shit actually has some power in him. And he tried to use it against me. Against *me*!"

"Incredible," Hozark said, glancing at Hap.

The boy's bloodshot eyes spoke volumes about his treatment at the hands of the pirates since he'd been captured, and Hozark felt the anger inside himself growing. It was an unusual sensation for him, as he almost never had an emotional reaction to any of the myriad situations he had found himself in over the years.

But this boy had been mistreated. Mistreated and made into a slave. And *that* simply would not do.

"So, what's the plan for the little scamp?" he asked.

"I've been trying to offload him on Drommus, but there were no takers. But when I mentioned he might have some power, one of the crews that fly with some of Visla Ravik's Tslavars when they're not out on Council business said that he's been rounding up any kind of power he can find. I thought maybe this kid might be of interest to him."

"So you contacted him? Is that why these ships are here? A Council double-cross?"

"Nah, I wish it was so simple. I was about to try to reach that Ravik character when one of my old friends let me in on a little secret."

"A secret?"

"Yeah. Ravik isn't the one really in charge. He's just another visla's bitch. A guy named Maktan."

"I've heard the name," Hozark said, flashing a glance at Demelza. "But I heard he was always a pretty benign one. For the Council, that is."

"Well, looks can be deceiving. That bastard's neck-deep in dirty shit across a dozen systems, apparently. Lots of blood on his hands. And the crazy bastard actually tried to catch one of the Ghalian masters. Can you believe that? Fucking madness, that is."

"You're right about that," Hozark agreed. "And this little bastard is going to him next?"

"If he pays. And if we survive."

Another glance and Demelza took over the conversation, shifting to the business of the attack at hand while Hozark walked over as if to get a better look at the young boy.

"What of these invaders, though? We're in command. You have to know how many breaches there were from here," she said as Hozark squatted down close to the captive boy.

He had hidden in his hand a fine, delicate piece of cloth, no larger than a thin ribbon, really. It was golden, however. Woven from Ootaki hair. And as Hozark pretended to examine the child, he casually began wrapping it around his control collar.

Once in place, the Ootaki magic would block out the collar's spells, freeing the wearer, for a time, at least. Fortunately, the collar was a weak one. He was just a kid, after all, and there was no sense wasting valuable magic on him that didn't have to be.

"Shh," Hozark quietly told the boy as his fingers worked.

Just a few feet away, Captain Darvin's attention was tuned to the Wampeh's associate as he surveyed the original breach information his second-in-command had provided him.

"Six breaches that we knew of before losing contact with our people. They must be blocking our skrees somehow."

"Sounds like a Council tactic," Demelza replied. "But only six?"

"That we know of, I said. Fortunately, this ship is a bit unusual in its design, and the Drook chamber is not where it would normally be expected. A convenient little trick for just this sort of occasion. They may have boarded, but we can still fly so long as my Drooks remain safely hidden."

"You have guards with them?"

"Of course I do," he replied, a bit wary of all the questions being thrown his way. "Who exactly did you say you were, again?"

Demelza was about to formulate a clever reply to hopefully salvage their situation, when a burst of youthful impulsiveness stepped in to ruin any such plans.

"Hozark!" Happizano abruptly blurted when the binding spell on his collar was finally blocked by the Ootaki hair.

Captain Darvin and his men all spun to see what had happened. Why the spells had suddenly failed. Why this strange pirate even possessed Ootaki hair in the first place.

"You were supposed to remain silent, young Jinnik," Hozark said with a sigh.

The captain's guards were the toughest, largest, and best armed of the entire crew, and they had just shifted from casual readiness to deadly intent.

Hozark rose, pushing the boy to the corner of the room. "Oh

well. There is nothing for it now," he said, surprising the men by tossing his sword away.

The confusion only lasted a moment, however, as he then drew the glowing blue vespus blade from his back.

The men were all notably uncomfortable at the sight of the weapon, if not knowing exactly who, and what, they were dealing with, being aware that their new opponent was something far different than they'd initially expected. Different, and dangerous.

To their credit, they held their ground, even going so far as to begin a threatening advance.

"You can stop now and focus your attentions on the real enemy aboard this ship," Hozark said. "I only want the boy."

"Get him!" Darvin said, swinging his sword at Demelza, who quickly blocked his attack and drove her sword through his chest.

It was a rather humiliatingly fast demise for the feared captain of a band of rough and deadly Outlanders. But he had just learned a vital lesson. One he took to heart, quite literally, with Demelza's fatal blow.

Never underestimate your opponent just because she's a woman.

A similar lesson applied to believing yourself at an advantage merely because you possessed numerical superiority. But not all were fast on the uptake.

The guards, rather than taking the hint, seemed to have their resolve strengthened at the sight of their fallen captain.

"Very well, then," Hozark said. "If you are truly certain you wish to do this, we may as well begin."

CHAPTER FIFTY-EIGHT

It should have been a straightforward slaughter, over almost as soon as it began, but there was one little problem. Literally little. A young boy, in fact.

"We've gotta get out of here!" he cried out, rushing right past everyone.

"No! Hap, do not––" Hozark called after him.

It was too late.

The boy threw the door open wide, dissipating the carefully laid muting spells Demelza had put in place. Worse yet, the abrupt opening made people on the other side take note. Even worse than that was the fact that there was now a full-fledged battle underway in that corridor.

And it immediately spilled into the command chamber.

The guards, faced with the choice of fighting off Ghalian assassins or Tslavar mercenaries, shifted their focus to the deadly, though far less deadly, invaders. This left a small but very exploitable window for the Wampeh to make their escape.

The room was a kill box of a sort. At least with that many bodies in it. The corridors, on the other hand, were open enough, and branched off at regular intervals, allowing one to move and flow with a battle.

"Happizano, stay by my side," Hozark commanded.

The stubborn child, for once, heeded his call.

With the boy between them, Hozark and Demelza led him out into the fray, deflecting stray attacks and slaying those making intentional ones. The farther they managed to get from the command center, the easier it was becoming to move. It seemed the Council forces had congregated there, hoping for a decisive victory.

Only, the pair of Ghalian assassins spoiled their fun, and were now speeding off through the ship, slaying all who attempted to halt their progress. Demelza and Hozark had room to work now, and they spread out a bit farther to better control the area around them.

Demelza circled to the front, leading the drive ahead, while Hozark engaged a group of pursuing Tslavars. It seemed word had gotten out that the boy had escaped, and the enemy was now on their tail.

"We need to get to one of their boarding craft and commandeer it," Hozark called out to his partner. "It is the only way to break free of this madness."

Demelza nodded once and pushed ahead. She knew precisely where one of those ships had latched onto the hull, and they could be there in under a minute, if fighting stayed light.

Naturally, at that moment, another wave of battling pirates and mercenaries flowed into their path, their fight spilling from corridor to corridor. Demelza wielded her sword and dagger with grace and speed as she attempted to clear an exit route for them, when a flash of gleaming blue whipped at her head from the side.

She barely managed to duck, deflecting the vespus blade at the last instant with her sword.

"You," she said, knowing the attacker's weapon before she even saw the woman wielding it.

Samara smiled her pointy-toothed grin and laid into the woman, a flurry of blows raining down on Demelza like a storm beating upon a ship tossing at sea.

But then, slowly, and much to Samara's surprise, Demelza began to gain her footing. To find a flow. To, incredibly, hold her own against one of the greatest swordswomen the Ghalian had ever known.

She shifted from defense to offense, her sword and dagger moving at blinding speeds as she forced Samara to give up her ground and defend for once. For the vespus-wielding assassin, it was a novel experience, and Samara actually smiled at her when they broke free and began circling one another.

"You've gotten better," Samara said.

"And you've not learned when to leave well enough alone," Demelza replied, then launched into a series of strikes, parries, and false attacks.

She was putting on an impressive display, and though she was still no match for the woman's skills, Demelza could at least delay her long enough for Hozark to join the fray.

And join he would.

Hozark disposed of a trio of Tslavar attackers, then stepped back and let the pirates press ahead in an attempt to reclaim this section of the ship. He turned, already aware of Samara's presence by the faint tug of magic from the necklace she was wearing. A deadly gift he'd given her ages ago. A pendant that contained potent magic, should she ever find herself in need.

Never had he pictured himself being the potential recipient of that magic.

Samara's eyes darted to the boy hiding behind Hozark. He stood firm in front of the youth, protecting him with his body in a way she had never thought she'd see him behave.

"I have to take him, Hozark. Please, just give him to me and walk away."

"You know that will not be happening, Sam."

"Don't be foolish. You are hopelessly outnumbered here. And before you say you are making a good showing against the boarding parties, just know, this is only a small first wave intended to feel out the ship's defenses. The *real* boarding teams are just now arriving."

He actually felt the shift in the pirate ship's pressure as either a large number of small craft, or a small number of large ones, pierced the hull and soft-sealed with it as they sent their forces inside.

She saw the realization in his eyes. "Give him up, Hozark."

"You know that is not happening," he replied, steeling himself for the onslaught. "But tell me, Sam. Why are you tied up in all of this? It is unlike you. He is just a boy. An innocent."

It was the tiniest of flickers, but he saw a flash of remorse in her eyes.

"You know it is the wrong thing to do," he said, pressing the issue.

"Let it go, Hozark. I do not wish to harm you, but I will if I have to," she replied.

"Then I am afraid you will have to," he shot back. "I see your blade is properly powered this time."

"As is yours. But not for long," she replied.

She cocked her head a fraction and smiled. Then she leapt into action just as a wave of newly boarded Council forces flowed into the mix.

Demelza instantly had her hands full, driven back toward where Hozark and Samara had already engaged in their deadly dance.

Samara didn't care about the Tslavars, and several fell by her hand as well as Hozark's if they got in the way of her progress.

The pair of glowing blue blades crackled with energy as they clashed, each of them ready to do their master's bidding, but finding their progress stymied by a weapon of similar abilities.

Demelza took the opportunity the former lovers' battle afforded her and pushed Happizano into a corner, then positioned herself in front of him to best keep him safe.

One after another, her attackers fell, piling up in a bloody stack all around her while Hozark and Samara did the same with any hapless enough to get in the way.

"Your skills have not lost a step," Hozark said as he and Samara broke free, circling one another.

"And yours have grown impressively," she replied. "And that Orkut blade of yours. I must admit, it is most impressive."

Hozark dipped his head in a nod of acknowledgment.

The two had been more than just friends. More than just lovers. They'd come as close as Wampeh Ghalian could ever come to being a bonded pair. And while that simply was not done, the connection between them apparently still remained. And despite the years that had passed, and the fact they were now trying to kill one another, it was, nevertheless, readily apparent to both.

"It is a shame it has to be this way," Hozark said. "You could come back to the order. It is not too late."

Samara sighed. "If only you knew of what you speak. My way is cast in stone. My path is clear. And, dearest, you are standing in that path."

He smiled at her, a sad look in his eye, knowing only one of them would walk away from this engagement today.

Hozark jumped back, nearly bumping into Demelza when a fighting cluster of Council goons and pirates abruptly spilled in from an adjacent chamber. It was of no matter. They'd clear out, and the two assassins would get back to their task at hand.

Or so they thought.

Samara's eyes went wide as she felt the magic in the air. She spun to where the Council forces were arriving from to see a Council caster rushing into the mix. He was obviously not acquainted with the rules of battles aboard ships in space, made painfully apparent by the rather powerful spells he was casting with reckless abandon.

All of the combatants, Tslavar and pirate alike, ceased their fighting, all yelling out at once some variation of, "Stop, you fool!" But their voices were lost, as it was already too late.

His spells had done their work far too well, and the man was about to receive a first-hand lesson on the reasons no one, not even a Council representative, cast combat spells in space.

Samara was already running the other way, making a sprint for the nearest boarding craft in desperate hopes she might be able to make it. As for the rest of them, it was clearly too late.

The spells breached the hull. First opening a small tear, but quickly blasting the craft wide open, the air, debris, and people inside all sucked out into space as the sealed compartments of the ship failed catastrophically from the foolish man's magical barrage.

Hozark and Demelza grabbed Hap between them and held fast. Air was almost gone, there was perhaps a second or two before they would be sucked out into the vacuum. It was just enough time for Hozark to cast a Hail Mary spell the likes of which he'd never attempted.

The trio was flung into space as the pirate ship broke into pieces, but rather than suffocate and freeze, they found themselves encapsulated in a tiny bubble of atmosphere, protected from the icy death around them.

Demelza was astonished. She'd never seen anything like it. Never even heard of anything like it. But, somehow, Hozark had saved them. His eyes were squeezed tight, his grip on his vespus blade turning his knuckles even whiter than they already were.

"This spell. What is it?" she asked, confused.

"A ship's umbilical spell," he replied through gritted teeth.

It was then that Demelza realized why he was straining so as they drifted in space. This was a type of magic that was not meant to exist without a surface to connect. Two, actually. It was supposed to link one ship to another, but, somehow, Hozark had closed off both ends and provided them a safe shelter.

But it would not last long. The sheer amount of power it required to keep the spell active was immense, and Hozark was straining with all of his might to maintain it.

He had already drained his own power dry, as well as the konus on his wrist, and was now pulling the last dregs of his vespus blade's store of magic, the blue glow fading as his magic began to falter.

"Hold on to me tight," Demelza told the boy, hoping to at least provide him a modicum of comfort at the moment of his death.

The air in the bubble suddenly chilled. The vacuum was about to take them. Again the temperature dropped, and this time the air abruptly became a lot thinner and difficult to breathe. It was only a matter of moments before the spell failed altogether.

A hard jolt yanked the trio just as the brutal cold hit them and they found themselves unable to breathe. A second later, they were most unexpectedly lying on the hard deck of Bud's cargo hold.

Bud was strapped to the bulkhead to keep from being sucked out when he opened the sealing spell and cast a retrieval loop to pull them in. As soon as they were safely inside, he sealed the ship and called to Laskar to get them the hell out of there.

The copilot was all too happy to comply and quickly flew them out of the cascading battle and into the darkness of space.

Hozark attempted to sit up, then collapsed, out cold, his vespus now devoid of its customary glow. He had used up every bit of power he possessed and then some, but, miraculously, Demelza and the boy lived.

The question now was, would he?

CHAPTER FIFTY-NINE

The pale man had not stirred an inch since he had been placed on the soft bed, no matter what had gone on around him. For a master Ghalian to slumber through anything in his immediate vicinity, let alone directly following a fierce battle, spoke volumes as to the degree to which he had been drained.

At long last, however, he roused. Not from voices or commotion, but to the most wonderful smell.

Hozark painfully pulled his eyelids apart and peered at the people hovering over him. Demelza was seated on the edge of his bed with a mug in her hand, steam faintly wafting up from its lip.

"Uzabud, sit him up a bit, please," Demelza asked.

"You got it, Mel," he replied, pushing a pillow beneath his friend's back, shoulders, and head until he was propped up a bit.

"Here, drink this," Demelza said, tipping the mug to his lips. "But slowly. It is still hot."

The heat of the fluid, along with the wonderful salinity, fats, and proteins in the broth, all felt amazing sliding down his dry throat. It felt as though he'd been coughing up sand, and the soup seemed like a magical, liquid bandage to heal that hurt.

In reality, he had simply been unconscious for so long that his throat had somewhat dried out in the process.

He tried to sit up farther but found himself unable.

"Lemme help you," Bud said, pushing another pillow into the mix.

"Thank you, Bud," Hozark croaked. "Oh, I do not sound well," he noted with a pained grin.

"Well, you did sleep for three days," Bud replied.

"Three?" the weary killer said. "Well, I take it we survived, then?"

Bud laughed. "Yeah, man. You survived. But only barely. We got to you as fast as we could with all the crazy shit going off around Darvin's ship. I mean, damn. The Council had a serious hard-on for that guy."

"There is a child present, Uzabud," Demelza noted.

"Yeah? And he's seen things that make a little salty language seem like a picnic with rainbows and fluffy clouds," he shot back.

She sighed. "Your point is valid, I suppose."

"Yeah, and besides, a kid's gotta learn the ways of the world. Toughen up. Be prepared to kick names and take ass, fucking people up like nobody's business!" Bud joked.

"I believe you meant kicking ass and taking names," Laskar corrected.

"No I didn't," he replied with a wicked grin.

"We are all accounted for?" the master assassin asked.

"Everyone is safe," Bud replied.

In truth, some were more than merely fine. Some were quite well.

Henni had found herself on the battlefield that day, and it had been a liberating, cathartic experience. All of that pent-up emotion from the things she'd endured over the years had just flowed out of her once she was given free rein—*truly* free rein—to go apeshit crazy.

And that she had.

By the time Bud and the others looped Drommus and made their way quietly back to the surface to retrieve her while the Council fought up above, she had succumbed to the blood-lust and was elbow-deep in battle.

Or, more accurately, in her enemies' torsos.

She was something of a dynamo when it came right down to it, and hardened pirates were now steering clear of the small woman with violet hair and eyes that contained galaxies.

Eventually, she calmed down, but for a long while after, the girl was buzzing around the ship as they flew as far from Drommus as possible. Then the post-battle fatigue hit, and she slept for a day straight.

It wasn't as long as Hozark had been out, but it was impressive in its own right.

"You know, Demelza told us what you did, man," Laskar said. "That was incredible."

"It was not pleasant," Hozark said.

"But it's impossible. To use that type of spell in that way? It's unheard of. It shouldn't be doable."

"Impossible things are often done by those unaware they can't be," Hozark replied with a weak grin.

"Very mystical master of you," Bud said with a chuckle. "But seriously, how did you manage it? Laskar's right, it shouldn't be possible."

Hozark looked at the friends standing around him, then repeated the words immortalized by Master Haiweh centuries before his time.

"We adapt," he said. "We improvise. We overcome."

Happizano walked up to the reclining Wampeh and quietly stood beside him.

"What troubles you, young Jinnik?" he asked.

"You rescued me," the boy said.

"Of course we did."

"But I ran away. I stole one of your ships and ran away, but you still came for me."

"You are our friend," he replied. "There was no way we would not come find you."

He omitted the parts about them being pissed he had stolen that ship, the amount of coin it would take to repair all of the damage it incurred, and the countless dead because of his foolish attempt to flee to a world unsafe for his return. There would be time for that later.

"Captain Demarzik? In the battle, she––"

"She's fine, Hozark. Relax. I can't say the same for those bastards who took Hap, though. Their ship was blown clean in half, as you know first-hand. Holy shit, that was a mess. Once we picked you guys up, we got out of there just in time before the whole damned planet jumped into action."

"The *whole* planet?"

"Well, it sure seemed like it."

"It was a *lot* of ships," Laskar confirmed.

"Yeah, and it was glorious. Once the folks down below realized what was going on up in space, they all joined into the fight. Those poor Council bastards didn't stand a chance. I mean, imagine that. A pirate stronghold, and all of the different factions putting aside their personal issues to come together against a common enemy."

"Fuck the Council," Hozark said with a weak laugh. "Arr."

"Did you just say '*arr*'?" Bud asked with a chuckle.

"It is an inside joke," Demelza said.

Hozark's smile turned serious.

"Samara. She was there, aboard Darvin's ship when that fool caster blew it apart. Is she dead?"

"I can't say for one hundred percent certain, but I'd be willing to bet she got out of there in one piece," Laskar said. "I was watching as the ship tore apart, and a few of the boarding vessels nearest the breach were able to disengage and get clear."

"But the battle——"

"Nah, they were long gone as soon as they broke free. They just jumped away before shit got really crazy. But a bunch of their other ships weren't so lucky, and they took one helluva beating, am I right, Bud?"

"That you are, my friend. That you are."

They had recovered the boy successfully, and without sustaining any losses. At least, not to their own crew, though the pirate captains had suffered more than a few.

And Samara lived yet, it seemed. The revelation brought a little smile to Hozark's lips. Sure, she had been trying to kill him, just as he had been trying to kill her, but he'd expected nothing less. She was a consummate professional, after all. It would have been disrespectful to pull her blows.

Hozark settled deeper into the comfort of his pillows and began the long, slow work of getting in touch with every inch of his recovering body.

"So, where exactly are we?" he asked. "If it has been three days in transit, we have to be heading somewhere relatively far."

"Oh, we are," Demelza replied. "We are heading to meet with Master Corann."

CHAPTER SIXTY

Seated on comfortable chairs on the Wampeh Ghalian master's porch, a trio of pale, unassuming Wampeh sipped on herbal tea while snacking on the delicate pastries spread out on the tray in front of them.

To any of the locals and neighbors, it seemed like just another day for the kindly woman hosting her 'niece' and a guest. She was one of the bright spots in their little community, and she smiled and waved her hellos whenever one would pass by.

Little did they know, the number of people she had killed in her day was greater than the population of their little neighborhood.

The motherly woman watched the steam rise from her cup, contemplating what she had just learned, not only of young Happizano's rescue and those who had taken him, but of the Council members who showed such interest in the boy.

"Samara?" Corann stated, more than asked.

"Yes," Hozark replied.

"Fascinating."

"And not in a good way," Hozark added.

"She actually boarded the pirate's vessel in an attempt to retrieve the boy?"

"In the later waves, yes. The initial attack was to ensure he was actually aboard and determine the nature of the defenders' numbers and location."

"A sound tactic."

"Indeed," Hozark said. "Samara came with a retinue of Tslavar shock troops. It was quite a battle, I must admit."

"Fighting within the tight confines of a ship often is," Corann agreed. "But you prevailed."

Hozark nodded, turning toward his teammate. "Thanks to Demelza's skill and determination, yes. She not only defended herself admirably against Samara and her vespus blade, but she even put her on the defensive for a moment."

Demelza felt her blush reflex fighting to engage, but she tamped it down. Flattery from the leaders of the order was nice, but success was the ultimate prize. And they had been successful in an extremely trying situation.

"You had Samara on her heels?" Corann asked. From her look and tone, Demelza could see she was genuinely impressed.

"Yes, but it was just the flow of the battle."

"Nonsense. Do not downplay your achievement. She is one of the greatest swordswomen to ever come from the order. Some have withstood her onslaught in the past, though not for long. But only a very, very small few have ever put her on the defensive, regardless of the situation."

"It was quite a showing," Hozark agreed.

Corann took a long sip of her tea as she pondered the situation. "Samara is proving to be a most unusual player in this affair, Hozark. Her reappearance after so many years is in itself a shock. But now, to have her tied up in Council affairs? *That* is highly disconcerting."

"And the boy is involved. We now know for a fact, this was

not merely a coincidental conflict with the Council. They were there specifically to retrieve him," Hozark said.

"But the boy says he never told them his identity, which is a surprise, given how the lad talks."

"Indeed, but Captain Darvin appeared to have no idea who the boy was. He was trying to sell him off, but only because he contained some power. Apparently, Visla Ravik is pulling power-user slaves from across the systems, but Darvin had not yet contacted him."

"But if that is the case, what I still do not know is, how did the Council know where he was?" Demelza asked.

"And how is Visla Maktan involved?" Hozark added.

"Maktan? You mean Visla Zinna Maktan of the Council of Twenty is actually involved as we had heard whispers of?" Corann asked. "It seems so highly unlikely."

"I know. He has never seemed to be the aspirational type. He is powerful, no doubt, but that affords him a comfortable existence on the Council of Twenty without any further efforts needed."

Corann looked unimpressed. "He inherited the seat from his father, as he did from his. The man is an unimpressive legacy member living off of what his forebearers accomplished."

"I agree. But Captain Darvin also let us in on a little bit of unusual information, Corann. He said that Visla Ravik was not the man *actually* behind the amassing of power users. He said he heard it from reliable sources that Maktan was the one behind it the whole time."

"It just seems so unlikely. And our spy network still has no whispers of Zinna Maktan being anywhere near these events."

Hozark paused as a neighbor walked by, smiling as warmly as Corann and Demelza were.

"Hello, Barris!" Corann called out as she waved.

A minute later the man was out of earshot and Hozark continued.

"There is more still, Corann. Captain Darvin also relayed something he learned. Something that only a select few outside of the order even know about. He knew about the attempt to capture Master Prombatz."

"He what?" she replied, genuinely surprised.

"And, apparently, that was on Maktan's orders as well. That Aargun was taken instead was simply a terrible mistake. But Maktan appears to have been targeting us."

"He would have to know that would bring the wrath of the Ghalian upon him."

"But the power-hungry often do the unexpected," he replied.

The three sat and sipped their tea a long moment, contemplating the unexpected situation unfolding before them. To have multiple members of the Council of Twenty working in conjunction was one thing. To have one of them directing the others to target a Ghalian master was quite another.

It was a ballsy move. And one that would likely cost Maktan his life.

"What of young Happizano's father?" Hozark asked. "Our priority should be returning the boy to his side."

"In that effort, we have both good news, and bad, I am afraid," Corann replied.

"What do you mean, Corann?"

"We found the boy's father. Where he had gone to perform his duties at the request of his mystery Council summons. But as you have noted, it would appear we now know who used that Validity seal. Only full Council members can, and if it was not Ravik, then Visla Zinna Maktan has to be the one."

"So, you found the man. This is good news, Corann, though I am admittedly concerned as to what the bad may entail."

"The bad news is Visla Jinnik is no longer at that location. He arrived, settled down an uprising, then moved on to another system to do the same thing. Five times he did this, and five times our spies tracked his movements. And then, he vanished."

"Vanished?"

"Yes. He performed as required, using a fair amount of power to put down some of the more difficult groups of insurgents. Then, he abruptly went off-grid, and no one, not even our most deeply embedded spies, know where."

It was a bit of a surprise, to say the least. For someone as powerful as Visla Jinnik to drop from sight, especially with the Ghalian spy network's best agents tracking his movements, it was clear some serious power was in play.

Worse, that meant that Happizano would not be returned to his father, and they had no idea how long it would be before he would be.

"The boy," Hozark said after a moment's thought. "He needs a familiar place to stay. One that he feels safe in. Can he stay here with you, Corann? He seems to have taken a liking to you."

"Alas, I have a contract I must attend to, Hozark. And as for a familiar and safe place, you and your crew have proven that your ship is the most dependable and protected place for him at this time."

"But he will most certainly not approve of this," Hozark said, not liking the idea of becoming a full-time caregiver one bit.

"No, he will not. But he is a child, Hozark. And sometimes the adults must do things in a child's best interest even if they do not wish them to."

"This is not an ideal situation, Corann."

"No, it is not. But for the time being, he stays with you. Our spies will continue searching, and you know as well as I that they will eventually find Visla Jinnik."

"Which could take weeks, if not months."

"As you said, it is not ideal. But, I am afraid, he is your responsibility for the time being. Good luck with that."

Hozark was a Ghalian master, one of the Five, but at that moment, it took all of his self-control to not sulk like an upset teenager. In a week filled with unexpected developments, he was most assuredly *not* thrilled about this one.

Hozark and Demelza walked back into Bud's ship and called a meeting in the galley. Demelza handed out some fresh-baked pastries to the gathered crew, courtesy of Corann, while Hozark prepared some hot, sweetened Boramus milk.

It was mostly for the boy's benefit, the comfort food, but the rest of the crew would enjoy the treat all the same. They'd had a tough go of it of late, and it looked like they were finally getting to slow down, at least for a bit.

Finally, with food and drink in hand, Hozark asked for everyone's attention.

"It would appear that a visla named Maktan is behind the recent events," he began. "The attack on Prombatz, the experimentation and torture of Aargun. The most recent conflict at Drommus. Everything, it seems, leads us back to this one man pulling the strings."

"So, why don't we just take him out?" Laskar asked.

"Because he is well-protected," Hozark replied. "And in addition to that, we do not know how many of the other members of the Council are aligned with him in this power play. He seems to be amassing magic, and we do not know to what end."

"All the more reason to take him out."

"Laskar, please. This must be handled with the utmost care. Rest assured, his time will come, but first, we have other issues to deal with. And we may need Maktan alive, if we are unsuccessful on our own. It will take time, and soon enough we will have a new course of action. But for now, we rest and recover from our efforts."

"What about my dad?" Hap asked. "Does that mean I can go

join him now? You said Corann was having your friends find him."

Hozark sighed. "I am afraid your father has moved from the location we believed him to be at, young Jinnik. You will need to remain with us a little while longer. But rest assured, our people are actively looking for him, and as soon as they find him, we will reunite you both."

Hap, for all of his recent tantrums and acting up, was surprisingly quiet about it. Being rescued from both a bad situation, and then an absolutely terrible one, both times by the same man, had given the youth a bit of a new perspective on things.

He was not thrilled, it was clear, but, for the time being, this unlikely group of men and women were his temporary family, and they would protect him to the best of their abilities.

"So, the kid stays, huh?" Bud asked.

"It would seem that way," Hozark replied.

"Well then, we should get you some coloring pads and a toy box," the former pirate joked.

Hozark, exhausted from their recent battle and nearly draining himself to death protecting the boy, was not amused.

"I am a Ghalian master, Bud. Not a babysitter."

"Hey! I'm not a baby!" Hap blurted angrily, throwing the last of his pastry at the assassin. "Don't you *ever* call me that! Ever!" he shouted, then stormed off to his room.

Henni let out a laugh, then went back to playing with the dagger she'd taken to carrying with her pretty much everywhere.

The master assassin looked around the galley at his gathered crewmates. It was like a dysfunctional family of epic proportions. And he was stuck with them for the time being.

Hozark ran his hand through his hair and sighed. "*This* is going to be a long flight."

EPILOGUE

Far across the galaxy, a lone ship flew unobserved through the inky black of the space between systems.

The chains binding Visla Jinnik were massive, and enchanted at that. The ends of the links held him firmly to the bolts mounted to the ship's walls. In addition to that, he had a thick magical control collar fastened around his neck.

He was a very, very powerful man, and to keep him under control, something more than just the possession of his son was needed. So the collar was employed, its magical binding spells reinforced regularly due to Jinnik's extreme power.

It was to keep him in check, just in case. He supposed he could understand their fear of him. He *was* dangerously powerful even when not forced to work against his will. But what he didn't know was that the boy had been rescued not too long ago.

If the visla caught wind of that little tidbit, he would cease working for them of his own free will at once. Then, he would likely slay everyone around him in an instant for good measure before rushing to his boy's side.

The door opened, and a stocky Tslavar mercenary walked into his cell, dropping a tray of food at his feet.

"Eat. Keep up your strength."

"I've done as you've asked. I've stopped rebellions, even killed your enemies for you. But now you must tell me. Where is my son?"

"We have him tucked away far from here, and that's all you need to know," the man replied. "And you'll continue to do as we say, or your son will suffer for it."

The visla's skin began to crackle with angry magic. In an instant, the control collar shocked him to the ground until he was nearly unconscious.

"Yeah, you might want to remember your place next time, *slave.*"

Visla Jinnik slowly righted himself, then, impressively, managed to shake off the stun spell and rise to his feet. He glared at the man, but he kept his magic in check.

"I will do as you say. But know this: if any harm falls upon my son, I *will* find a way to make you pay."

"Great. Nice threat from the one in chains," the Tslavar chuckled.

Jinnik glowered but resigned himself to his present situation. "So, what now? Another little uprising to put down?"

"Don't you worry about that. We'll be at our destination real soon."

The Tslavar was telling the truth, and just a few hours later the ship exited its jump just outside of orbit of the planet Garvalis. The smelters had been hard at work when they learned of their pending arrival, and very soon, they would be tapping into a visla's power.

There were a lot of weapons that needed charging, and he was going to do it for them. Even if it drained him of every last drop.

PREVIEW: DEATH FROM THE SHADOWS

SPACE ASSASSINS 4

It was an incredibly short period of time, but the tales of slaughter and carnage at the hands of a strange visla, one of whom none had ever even heard of, were spreading slowly through the conquered systems.

Rebellions were quashed with his iron fist, and entire planets fell to the mysterious man with the Council of Twenty's forces behind him.

Thousands had perished at his hands, and those who had been fortunate enough to find themselves spared had been subjugated or forced into slavery. After the hostilities ceased, a small contingent of Council forces would remain, their presence an enduring threat of what would befall the citizenry if they rose up once more.

And then, without word or warning, he would depart, off to the next unfortunate world that had drawn his attention.

Word of the man had reached Visla Tordahl well before the Council force appeared in orbit above his world, and he had taken ample precautions against such an incursion.

For many years the Council of Twenty had coveted his realm, and it seemed the day had finally come where they were going to make an attempt at it. But he was not giving up his world without a fight.

Additional forces had been called in to defend against the mighty new caster, and Visla Tordahl had spent considerable time pouring his power into the konuses and slaaps worn by those newly enlisted men. They were wielding considerable magic, and it would not be an easy conquest for this mysterious visla and his Council troops.

The Council ships, however, remained in orbit, sending in a contingent of Tslavar mercenaries instead. The first wave of attackers to crash upon the shores of Tordahl's defenses would not be the Council's finest, but, rather, paid goons whose lives were of little consequence.

The large sum of coin expended in their slaughter would ultimately be worthwhile if the world fell. And the men of action who so willingly joined the fray were promised sizable pillage in the pursuit of this world. It was enough to drive them headlong into the blistering defense, against their own best interests.

The first wave made it to the ground, but at the cost of nearly all of their ships, and a hefty portion of their men. Nevertheless, the deep-green Tslavar forces emerged from the broken craft with bloodlust in their eyes, charging into the fray with near reckless abandon.

The attacking visla's plan, it seemed, was to force the local reinforcements to expend much of their combined power on the violent pawns thrown onto the playing field. And it was working. Spells were flying thick and heavy between the opposing forces, and many fell on both sides.

Visla Tordahl's stronghold soon fell under attack as well, as the Council craft that had been holding back swooped in and launched a barrage of fierce magic, pounding the defenses, forcing them to not only defend themselves, but to also reveal their key casters' positions in the process.

With that, they were more easily targeted, and the attacks upon them refined. It was a clever ploy, Tordahl had to admit, but he was fully powered and ready. From what he could see of the attackers, it looked as if his men would push back this force.

Yes, there were a large number of mercenaries on the move, and they were pressuring his ground forces fiercely, but the Council had appeared to have only sent a limited contingent of actual Council craft. It was an unusual strategy, and one that would fail, the visla was pleased to note.

Slowly, his forces drove the attackers back.

"Advance. Destroy the attackers, and show no mercy!" Visla Tordahl commanded over his skree.

The troop leaders on the ground received the message and commenced their push, driving the mercenary forces into a hasty retreat. Magic was expended without reserve, and the barrage was brutal in its intensity. There was no way the Tslavar mercenaries could hope to fight against such a display.

A lone ship streaked down to the front lines from above, the magical defensive spells thrown at it dissipating as if they were no more than tissue paper.

"Increase the intensity!" Visla Tordahl commanded his casters, an unsettled feeling growing in his gut.

The ship continued on its path, unharmed and unfettered, until it landed just in front of the retreating forces. The craft's hatch opened, and a tall man wearing a high-collared coat stepped forth and strode onto the battlefield. Tordahl's troops immediately recognized the new arrival as the principal threat facing them and redirected all of their efforts against him.

The man was obviously a visla, and an incredibly powerful one at that. In fact, he was so strong that his magic was actually visibly crackling off his body in waves. At the sight of him, Visla Tordahl felt that sinking feeling in his gut solidify into a solid lump of fear.

He was a powerful man, but *this*? This was something he had never encountered before. For the first time in his life, he was not the strongest caster on the planet. Not by a long shot.

"I am Visla Jinnik," the invader bellowed out, his voice amplified by a projecting spell that carried it all the way to Tordahl's stronghold. "Surrender now and you will be spared. This is your one chance. Do not waste this opportunity."

The newcomer continued walking toward the front lines, the defensive spells parting for him and the attacks still being cast bouncing off his own shielding spells. He stopped, surveying the hundreds of men and women casting against him with all of their might. It seemed they were not giving up so easily.

Visla Jinnik shook his head and sighed.

"So be it."

He raised his hands and uttered the words to a particularly potent spell, the unleashed magic blasting out in a fierce wave. Tordahl recognized the spell immediately and threw up his defenses just in time to protect himself.

His casters and men attempted to do the same, but the vast majority were either not strong enough, not quick enough, or both.

The men closest to the origin of the spell burst into a fine mist. The magic blasted through them like a wave knocking down a child's sandcastle as if it were an afterthought. But the power continued, spreading out as it went, laying waste to those too weak to defend themselves before shifting to a stunning spell.

It was a particularly horrible piece of magic. One that the very few who even knew how to cast it refused to utilize. Only the most violent, and most powerful, would even think to. And only the absolute strongest even could. But this man, this Visla Jinnik, was wielding it with his full power, and to devastating effect.

Visla Tordahl felt the power buffet his defensive spell. As soon as it had passed, he replied in kind, casting the strongest spells he knew in rapid succession, the deadly magic flying true toward the invader.

Jinnik was forced to focus more of his power on defending himself. He actually smiled at that. It was good to see someone standing up for their world. Defending it against the Council no matter the cost. He respected the man for it, even as he returned the attack, his magic flying straight for the visla now that he had revealed his position.

Tordahl desperately cast his strongest defensive spells, throwing up a powerful shield of magic around himself. It held for a moment, allowing him an instant to marvel at the sheer power of the man taking his life. Then his magic failed, and the spells flew true, dropping him to the stone floor of his stronghold parapet, dead.

Word of the visla's fall spread immediately through the forces, and all who still survived surrendered at once. Without the visla supporting them, there was simply no way they had any hope against these attackers.

And this Jinnik, whoever he was, was so powerful, and so brutally deadly, that they knew their choices had been reduced to dropping their weapons or death.

The Tslavar forces surged forward, collecting the dropped arms of the fallen. Most were drained of magic to the point of being little more than paperweights, but they were taken all the same. Then the men and women were separated by perceived value.

Many would be sent back to their homes to work the land—to keep the realm thriving. But a great many would face a different fate. Those were pulled from the others and forced to kneel while one of the Council lackeys secured gleaming golden control collars around their necks, the magical restraints sealing into a seamless band as the captives entered their new life of slavery.

The Ootaki and Drooks who had been in Tordahl's

possession were rounded up and taken to the Council ships, the spoils of the conflict, now a part of the invader's power supply.

And like that, another world fell to this unusual visla and his Council forces. It was a pattern that repeated on many worlds, though not all of them were rebellions in need of quashing. Some were outright conquests, as Tordahl's land had been. An asset grab.

Visla Jinnik was an unknown. A man who had apparently never been a part of the Council of Twenty's machinations in the past. But suddenly, out of the blue, he was now a most powerful tool of the Council, and one to be feared and reckoned with.

Jinnik surveyed the dead and enslaved of yet another world and sighed. He then turned and walked back to his ship to take his leave of this place. People cowered in fear as he passed, wary of the man who had enslaved them all.

Little did they know, he, too, was wearing a thick control collar, hidden underneath his high-collared coat. He was as much a slave as they now were, and with his young son held captive, he had no choice but to do as he was told.

And that meant carrying out these horrible acts, all in the Council's name. But if it meant saving his boy, he would conquer endless worlds if he had to.

"You did quite a number on that one," the Council emmik running the operation said as he locked Jinnik back in his cell.

"Too many dead," Jinnik replied with an exhausted sigh. "When will this end?"

"Sooner than you expected," the emmik replied with a curious chuckle.

The ship lifted off and departed the system, and after that, reports of this Visla Jinnik's actions across the galaxy suddenly fell silent.

The man who had slashed and burned his way across a good many worlds, it seemed, had abruptly vanished. And no one knew why, or where he had gone. But the fear of him remained, and that lingering dread would last a long, long time.

The vendor stalls of Sorlak were something of a marvel for those unfamiliar with the more colorful marketplaces in the Delvian systems. The loose network of inhabited planets encompassed in those realms were chock-full of artisans, craftsmen, and all manner of agriculture.

As a result, the marketplaces on each of the habitable worlds were bustling places of commerce, and shoppers and traders from far and wide frequented them on a regular basis.

Of those worlds, Sorlak was the most civilized. A quiet planet, for the most part, with its distance from the pulsing, yellow sun at the center of the system putting it firmly in the comfortable zone of perfect temperatures year-round. It was not an Eden, but definitely a pleasant place to be.

That was not to say there was no violence or crime, but the Council more or less stayed away, and the outlaw and mercenary types found it more suited their needs to simply shop on those worlds than cause drama. But no world, even the most civilized, was entirely free of that element. Those sorts just tended to stay hidden more.

Naturally, when the pair of deadly Wampeh Ghalian assassins strode through town, they immediately clocked the most unsavory of the lot with an ease that came from years of practice. For one of their profession, ignoring a potential threat, no matter how minor, could prove fatal.

Hozark walked at the front, leading young Happizano, the son of the powerful Visla Jinnik. He had rescued the boy not once, but twice from kidnappers, the first of which had taken the boy to coerce his father into doing the Council of Twenty's dirty work for them, drawing from his great magic stores at their bidding.

The second time the boy had brought upon himself after stealing one of the shuttle craft belonging to Hozark's pilot friend, Uzabud, in an attempt to find his way home on his own. Unfortunately, the youngster not only lacked the requisite skills to manage that sort of a voyage, but he was also unfamiliar with even the most basic of captain's skills.

Like how to identify threats in the void of space. Threats like pirates, for example.

Happizano had been captured by a band of Outlander pirates and taken as a slave, ready to be sold off to Visla Ravik, though that was later revealed to only be a front.

The *true* puppet master behind it all was Visla Maktan. One of the Council of Twenty. And for whatever reason, he was amassing power however he could.

That included young Happizano, and not just for the power his father held, but because the youth appeared to share his father's gift. Ultimately, Hozark and his friends had rescued the boy from the pirates as well as the Council.

And the Council had brought out a deadly asset. Hozark's former lover, Samara, whom he fought aboard the stormed pirate craft before being blasted out into space and damn near dying in the process.

But they had survived, and since then, Hozark had been saddled with the youngster while they sought out his father in order to return his son to his side.

Hap, for all he had been through, seemed in good spirits. It had been a few weeks since he had escaped the kidnappers' clutches, and he had rebounded as only a ten-year-old could. Of course, a bit of additional attention had to be paid to keep his spirits up.

"Young Jinnik," Hozark said, handing the boy some coin. "We have spent much time in transit, and you have handled yourself quite well. Why don't you go purchase yourself a treat?"

"Really?"

"Yes."

"Thanks, Hozark," Hap replied, then trotted off into the sea of potential customers milling about the stalls.

Demelza had been walking behind the pair, her sharp assassin eyes making sure there was no trouble lurking around the corner. But this was Sorlak, and trouble never materialized. Nevertheless, the stout woman was ready for action if need be.

Uzabud and his copilot, Laskar, were off galivanting elsewhere in the marketplace, eating, carousing, and acquiring baubles they had no use for, no doubt, along with the best alcohols they could procure.

Bud had once been a space pirate, after all, and some habits died hard.

Henni, the angry, violet-haired young woman they had rescued several worlds back, was resting up aboard the ship after eating far too many Horakin berries. She would be fine, eventually, but for the moment she did not want to stray too far from a restroom.

Happizano headed straight for the sweets vendors farther along the winding stalls in a rush. He was like a kid in a candy shop, and while these were outdoor vendors and not actual storefronts, the analogy held true.

"And two of those sticky buns," he said, completing his purchase with still a bit of coin to spare for perhaps one more treat before they lifted back off into the utter boredom of space.

It was not the greatest environment for a ten-year-old to pass his days and weeks, but necessity was necessity. He was a target, after all. A third kidnapping simply was not an option.

"Hey!" he blurted as a couple of larger boys bumped into him in passing.

"Watch where you're going," the nearest one said, then headed off with his friend.

Hap felt something was odd about the two, and a moment

later he realized what it was. His pocket was now lighter the few coins that had been there just a moment ago.

"Hey! Come back here!" he shouted.

The older boys took off running, and young Happizano chased after them as fast as his legs would carry him. They weaved around carts, then diverted abruptly into a long alleyway. Hap plunged in headfirst in pursuit, the echoes of his footfalls ringing off the hard walls.

He rounded the next corner to find the larger of the two boys standing there waiting for him.

"I'll take those," the boy said, his hand extended.

"You can buy your own. Oh wait, that was *my* coin you stole," Hap said, holding his bag of sweets tight in his grip.

"Give me the bag."

"No." He turned to leave, but the other boy had stepped behind him and was blocking his way. And he was moving closer.

"He said hand over the bag."

"They're mine," Hap protested.

He didn't even see the first punch coming, nor the second or third. In a quick flurry of blows, the two larger boys had driven him to the ground. The nearest bent down and snatched up the bag of sweets.

"Ya shoulda just given 'em to us," he said, laughing as he walked away, eating poor Hap's sticky buns.

Happizano slowly pushed himself up to his feet and brushed off the dirt. His nose was bleeding, but only slightly, and his cheek had been scraped by one of the boys' fists.

Little did the boy know that Hozark had been standing nearby, invisible beneath his shimmer cloak, watching the whole thing unfold. The youth had shown courage, chasing the larger boys, and he had even stood up to them when the tables turned. But he was not familiar with the ways of the rough back alleys found on every world.

Happizano had been raised in the privileged confines of a powerful visla's estate, and these sort of things were utterly foreign to him. It was a painful lesson he had just allowed to occur, but Hozark knew it had to unfold without his intervention. The boy had to learn, and the best way to do that was firsthand.

The Wampeh assassin silently slipped out of the alleyway as Hap wiped the dirt from his palms and clothing and walked back to meet the others.

"What happened to you?" Demelza asked when she saw the telltale signs of a fight on his face.

"Nothing. Can we go, please?"

Hozark gave Demelza a look. "A good idea. Head back to the ship. I shall follow shortly."

ALSO BY SCOTT BARON

Standalone Novels

Living the Good Death

The Clockwork Chimera Series

Daisy's Run

Pushing Daisy

Daisy's Gambit

Chasing Daisy

Daisy's War

The Dragon Mage Series

Bad Luck Charlie

Space Pirate Charlie

Dragon King Charlie

Magic Man Charlie

Star Fighter Charlie

Portal Thief Charlie

Rebel Mage Charlie

Warp Speed Charlie

Checkmate Charlie

The Space Assassins Series

The Interstellar Slayer

The Vespus Blade

The Ghalian Code

Death From the Shadows

Hozark's Revenge

The Warp Riders Series

Deep Space Boogie

Belly of the Beast

Odd and Unusual Short Stories:

The Best Laid Plans of Mice: An Anthology

Snow White's Walk of Shame

The Tin Foil Hat Club

Lawyers vs. Demons

The Queen of the Nutters

Lost & Found

ABOUT THE AUTHOR

A native Californian, Scott Baron was born in Hollywood, which he claims may be the reason for his rather off-kilter sense of humor.

Before taking up residence in Venice Beach, Scott first spent a few years abroad in Florence, Italy before returning home to Los Angeles and settling into the film and television industry, where he has worked as an on-set medic for many years.

Aside from mending boo-boos and owies, and penning books and screenplays, Scott is also involved in indie film and theater scene both in the U.S. and abroad.

Made in the USA
Middletown, DE
21 August 2021